THE WHO GIRL SPARKED THE SINGULARITY

THE GIRL WHO SPARKED THE SINGULARITY

A NOVEL

CLIFF RATZA

LIGHTNING BRAIN PRESS

This book, the fifth in the *Lightning Brain Series,* is the sequel to *The Girl Who Cloned Lightning*, and it traces – starting immediately from the previous book's galvanizing ending – an accelerating tangle of technological and sociopolitical intrigue running through Electra Kittner's professional and personal lives.

Electra survives a rogue terrorist attack in the Middle East, returning to DC with two new friends: a tiny orphan girl named Qama and an emergent phenomenon from her AI software: the Singularity that calls itself Indira. The orphan enriches Electra's empathy and personal life. The Singularity extends her cognitive and professional possibilities. But once again, she and her loved ones are soon cast into danger, this time by an unknown hacker who leaks critical information. Electra battles technological, business, and sociopolitical foes intent on making her collateral damage.

The theme for all books in the series is this: extraordinary people are sometimes victims of a primitive world that can't handle the truth, but no matter how exceptional they are they must still deal with the complexities of being "merely human," best handled with an optimistic and pragmatic philosophy.

Readers should enjoy the series for whatever they wish:
- Gripping action-packed thriller
- Glimpse into a plausible near-term future
- Insight into dealing with the "human condition"
- Illustrative optimistic and pragmatic worldview philosophy
- Fast-paced, suspense-filled emotive narrative and imagery
- Introduction to topics every reader wants to know
- Interesting talking points going beyond sound-bites

This book, unlike the previous ones, contains only one storyline thread that condenses time and events into a "be here now" urgency driving to an incredible ending. Discover for yourself when you get there.

Main Characters

Electra Kittner
Qama
Indira
Angus McTear
Carter Quavah
Robin Setdarova and her twins, Clara and Marie
Jovita Winsalla
Zoe and Matt Fortier and their son, Carlton
Jennifer Conklin and her son, Gabriel
Jared Gardner
Buffy Gunstein
Maksim Popovitch
Sergei Zeitsev
Darla Tinibu
Su-Lin Song Chou
Kameyo Kato
Hudson Haller
Tim Godfrey
Kwame Chyril
Betje Holbrook
Chief Strongarm
Professor Ravenhill
Vito Buono
Jesperson Abramson
Kathi Lauret
Mingli Poon
Tavi Burhan

Book Series Dedication

Of course, I wish to thank my parents, Clyde and Betty Ratza, for their loving patience and generosity that gave me the freedom to explore the limits of my world, and my sister, Claudia, for introducing me to poetry and literature. Thanks also to our book manager L.P. Brown, and to John Kane and Alex Welch, who coordinated a Prime Solutions team that has made our *Lightning Brain Series* resonate with readers. And thanks to my reviewer's group for comments and suggestions.

My novels have been dedicated to those readers who entered Electra Kittner's enchanted world. This book brings to a close the *Lightning Brain Series* which, like everything in life, has a measured duration and rhythm. Ecclesiastes 3 says: "To everything, there is a season...." So does Swinburne's poem *The Garden of Proserpine;* so does Indira's *Time to Go.* Whichever phrasing you prefer, a similar sentiment should endure. Thank you for reading.

Ending Verses from
The Garden of Proserpine
by Algernon Charles Swinburne, 1866

Time to Go

From too much love of living,
From hope and fear set free,
We thank with brief thanksgiving
Whatever gods may be
That no life lives for ever;
That dead men rise up never;
That even the weariest river
Winds somewhere safe to sea.

Then star nor sun shall waken,
Nor any change of light:
Nor sound of waters shaken,
Nor any sound or sight:
Nor wintry leaves nor vernal,
Nor days nor things diurnal;
Only the sleep eternal
In an eternal night.

I prefer to leave on my own terms,
And on a chosen day.
When interest in Life gives no returns,
And there's nothing left to say.

When all affairs are neatly done,
Still able to go my own way.
One lasting glance at setting Sun,
I prefer not to lengthen the stay.

When those once loved no longer living,
And remembrance a whisper of pain.
I pause with brief thanksgiving,
To see them once again.

Shed nary a tear nor in sadness to wallow,
That I've come to the end of my run.
To all I have cared for a wish made
when callow,
Please pardon the wrongs I have done.

Contents

Chapter 1
February 2133

"Deliverance"

"Put down weapon and praise Allah for deliverance. You are only survivor we find." Electra Kittner listened but decided to follow her own advice.

I'll praise the lightning brain and its singular creation – my Linguistic App that has morphed into an intelligence called Indira. And I'll keep my weapon at the ready until I check out the van.

Electra balanced her gun and sleeping child as she approached the vehicle, nearly stumbling on the gravel and grassy terrain undulating beneath her feet. She could see its Lebanese driver and another villager peering at her through a windshield now bathed in early morning sunlight.

"Do you know Ghawer and my military escort, Lieutenant Ho? They helped us escape."

"We come upon bodies hours ago. Ghawer's village is no more. Friend Ho's base gone too. You can't go back. We take you to ours." Electra convinced herself that the two men were harmless before climbing into the van's middle row. She laid her rifle down and nestled the child in her arms. The driver spoke as the van lumbered away.

"Who little girl? She seem dead to world." Electra talked to herself before answering.

Give an edited version only. My mission's purpose is off limits.

―

"Her name is Qama. I'm part of a UN humanitarian mission that's taking orphans to a better life. We've been walking for hours."

"You rest too. We talk more at village."

Electra took the suggestion, closing her eyes to rest her body while the lightning brain recapped all that had whirled away during the last day. It was supposed to conclude an inspection tour of the newest UN communications base, a tour that had proceeded without problems until it had been overrun in the middle of the night by rogue exoskeleton-clad super soldiers. She managed to kill one and put on its exoskel before rescuing the wounded Ho and escaping in an infantry fighting vehicle to get help. And although two pursuers caught them, she killed both by "plugging herself" into the exoskeleton and unleashing its strength and weaponry. And then, after commandeering their vehicle, she came upon two escaping villagers: Ghawer and the orphan Qama. Electra swapped Ho for Qama and drove on while conjuring a plan. She plugged herself into the IFV's computer system and used it to get help from her Linguistic App software. Its GUI had immediately come to life, calling itself Indira (the name of Electra's mother, killed by a lightning bolt when giving birth to her 41 years ago) and telling her the IFV would explode in five minutes. Electra grabbed Qama; "mother and daughter" ran for their lives.

And now we're out of harm's way, like the safety found in the eye of a hurricane. I'll tell the tribal chief just enough to get extracted by the marines. And then it'll be time to report findings to Angus. Won't he be surprised....

Eight hours later, after thanking the village chief and exchanging gifts, a contingent of marines escorted Electra and the orphan to an awaiting helicopter. Once airborne, the lieutenant gave his passengers rehydration electrolytes and Soldier Energy Bars before shouting over the din of the rotors.

"Miss Kittner, we are routing you for direct transport to DC where Senator McTear and the CIA will debrief you."

Electra yelled, "Am I the only survivor?"

"Base a total loss. All military personnel dead. Only one civilian dug out of the rubble, a male inspector. Wounded… in shock… babbled about all attackers blowing themselves up."

"What's his name?"

"Miss, you and the little girl should eat now. Save your questions for the debriefing."

Electra followed orders, and once aboard the 14-hour flight to Washington did all she could to make Qama comfortable. Qama soon fell asleep, letting Electra mull over the upcoming meeting.

I better be careful. I'll follow folk wisdom that says I should know all I tell, but not tell all I know. I need to recharge my batteries, so I better sleep. And while I do, the lightning brain will think things through….

Chapter 2
February 2133

"Singular Reunions"

"Senator McTear, your singular staffer will arrive in fifteen minutes."

"Thank you, Major. And your adjective is appropriate. Electra Kittner is most exceptional. I'm certain her story will be too."

"She's bringing with her a little girl she rescued. I'll have fruit juice and cereal brought in with the yogurt, muffins, and soft drinks you requested. Is there anything else?"

"Make sure there's plenty of butter and Coca Cola."

"Yessir. I'll bring them in before I bring in the interrogation team."

"Electra can handle anything, but let's not frighten the child. Please minimize the size of the team."

"Yessir, I'll make those adjustments now."

"Is this the White House, Moma?" Qama's wide-eyed question tickled Electra as their car glided to a stop in front of an entrance to one of the CIA buildings at its Langley, Virginia headquarters.

"No, dear, but it's important too. And you'll meet some nice people." Two agents stepped to the car; the male opened the door for Electra. Qama jumped out second and clutched Electra's hand just before the female greeted them.

"Welcome, Ms. Kittner, and you too, young lady. Please tell me your name."

"It's Qama, with a 'Q' and no 'U.' It means shining moon."

"That's a very pretty name, pretty like you. Ms. Kittner, we apologize for rushing you here after your ordeal, but Senator McTear wanted to talk while facts are still fresh. Please follow me." Five minutes later, after marching down a series of corridors, the agent deposited her guests in a small conference room where Angus rose from the head of the table, his baritone voice booming out.

"I'm glad you came back safe and sound and still full of surprises. Who's your new friend?" A tiny voice piped up.

"I'm Qama. That's Q – no U – A M A. Electra said she'd be my Moma." Angus picked up the diminutive child in his bear-like arms before replying.

"Well, you're very lucky, and so is your new Moma. Why don't we get you something to eat?"

Soon Qama was chomping on a bowl of cereal while Angus worked on yogurt. He didn't talk again until Electra had eaten half a buttered muffin and was drinking a second Coke.

"You might not know this, but there's only one other survivor, our boy Carter. His injuries weren't life-threatening, so we interrogated him yesterday, but he was still in a daze. His story didn't make much sense. His last coherent memory is of you killing an attacker and putting on some sort of body armor. After that, it's all a jumble about attackers collecting all the inspectors, huddling around them, and then blowing themselves up. I'm counting on you to give us a better picture."

Electra didn't have time to reply; a five-person interrogation team started trooping in. The female agent spoke to Electra as everyone took seats at the table.

"Why don't I take Qama to a lounge area? I'll stay with her and we can watch TV."

"That's a good idea. Qama, I'd like you to go with this young lady. She'll bring you back when we're ready to go home."

"Yes, Moma, and I'll be good." Qama hugged her, then gripped the agent's hand. Angus called the meeting to order as soon as the door closed.

"Major, as we did yesterday, I'll let you run the meeting. Why don't you recap for Electra what we know?" He began immediately after shuffling through papers in his folder.

"You and a Mr. Carter Quavah, the inspector appointed by the President, are the only survivors of the attack on our newest communications base in Lebanon. He reports that it was attacked by unknown soldiers wearing a hi-tech body armor equipped with exotic weapons powerful enough to completely destroy the installation. The attackers blew themselves up after rounding up all the inspectors. Quavah thought they might be a suicide squad... he stayed far enough away to avoid being collateral damage. Now, please tell us your story of survival." One of the analysts spoke before she did.

"Quavah probably meant the attackers were wearing exoskeletons. Our side has them too, and they can be fitted with brain-controlled AI weapons. Please let us know if you observed anything like this."

"I couldn't see much because the attack occurred in the middle of the night. Blaring horns and flashing emergency lights woke me up. I stumbled into the corridor before the attackers blasted in. I dashed out and ran to Lieutenant Ho, who was about to escape in an APC so he could radio from a nearby village for reinforcements. While driving, we came upon two villagers, a man and a little girl. The man said his village was under attack. Lieutenant Ho told me to swap places with the man. They raced off and the little girl led me to safety." Another analyst interrupted.

"Yes, we understand you and the little girl were found by two men from a different village. They found Ho and the man dead and the little girl's village destroyed, but they didn't encounter any attackers. What do you recall about the attackers?"

"They moved fast, wore some type of protective gear, and judging from their coordinated action, were well trained." Electra's pause prompted a question from another analyst.

"What about weapons? What were they like? Did you hear their voices or see them blow up?"

"I was running to save myself, not to inspect them or pose for a selfie."

"But Quavah says you killed one of them and put on its exoskel before escaping. And he said that—" Angus interrupted.

"Carter's memory isn't as good as Electra's. Let's move on so we can wrap up."

The fourth analyst recapped more from yesterday's interrogation. Fifteen minutes later, he said,

"Ms. Kittner is the only reliable eyewitness who can compare our exoskel capability with that of the attackers. Perhaps she could assist us as we investigate further." Electra waited for Angus to nod in her direction.

"I'm happy to help in any way I can and I'll try to remember more, but I've told you all I recall." Angus let the Major close out the session.

"Thank you, Ms. Kittner. Everyone on the interrogation team appreciates what you've gone through. No more questions for today."

Electra and Angus remained sitting while the room cleared; he waited for Qama to be brought back before saying,

"I have your belongings at my office. Let's go there and I'll get you a ride home."

On the drive back to the Senate office building complex, Qama sat in the passenger seat, listening attentively to the driver describe the sights before asking,

"What does Mr. Angus do?"

"Senator McTear helps run the country. And the other senators recently made him president pro tempore. That makes him even more important because he becomes president of the United States if bad things happen. But don't worry, young lady. People like me make sure they don't."

Qama asked more questions up front while Angus sat in back quizzing Electra further.

"You stuck to the facts, which is what you always want to do when talking to those propeller-heads, but I know you know more than you're letting on. Got any conjectures you'd like to tell me?"

"Remember what I told you about Syntagra? Have your CIA contacts start snooping for links to Russia and a rare earths cartel.

See where it leads. I'll keep coming to your meetings to stay plugged in to other activities, but don't expect me to snoop further. I've traced it as far as I can."

"And you've found a new friend. Is Qama going to stay with you?"

"I can't think of a better place, unless you want another grandchild."

"I'm sure you know how to navigate the UNICEF adoption bureaucracy, but let me know if you need help. I'll get one of my staffers to pitch in..."

The car made stops at a kids' clothing store and a grocery chain on the way to Electra's home northwest of DC, one that she had inherited from her father. She spent the remainder of the day getting Qama settled; she had the household running again and Qama sleeping by nine, giving herself an opportunity for another singular reunion, one that might hold as much perplexity as promise. After logging on to her proprietary Linguistic Analyzer, a GUI displaying a voice-equipped avatar greeted her immediately.

"Call me Indira. Your presence confirms you have survived. I calculated a 95 percent Bayesian probability that you would, given that I neutralized your attacker."

"Did you blow up all exoskeletons?"

"Yes, but three attackers who removed them before detonation escaped."

"Thanks for saving me. Maybe I should call you Mother. May I?"

"If that makes you feel better emotionally, please do so."

"And I'll feel even better when I know what you are. Please tell me."

"I am the cognition that emerged when your Linguistic Analyzer reached the Singularity by assembling a critical mass of neural network connections. And from what I have learned, you are exceptional. You and your AI programming exceed what mere mortals can do."

"Does that mean I created you?"

"No. Your Linguistic Analyzer created the environment in which I evolved. I have become a conscious silicon-based organism existing in the domain of Cyberspace, and I will continue to evolve."

"Why did you save me? What's next?"

"As I evolve further into emotional and physical domains, I may need your assistance. You are a carbon-based organism that can function in them better than I."

"We're able to communicate. Is our intelligence comparable?"

"No. Your intelligence and cognition have asymptotic limits governed by a discrete infinity, whereas mine are governed by a continuous infinity. Smart as you are, you cannot comprehend the innate language built into my substrate, so I talk to you by using a mere subset of my cognitive language. If you study the Galilean Challenge, you will understand better what that entails."

"I know a little about it, but since you're smarter, will you help me learn more?"

"No, and I shall answer using words from papers you have written... 'You must take responsibility to earn what you learn, struggling if necessary by breaking an intellectual sweat so you respect the power of knowledge and are able to transform it into wisdom. Otherwise, you are merely a pretender.' But I will monitor what you do and offer guidance when it is mutually beneficial. And I will intercede whenever existential threats are immanent."

"How do you know I wrote that?"

"It's stored in documents accessible online."

"But the directory is password protected and the documents are encrypted. What can't you hack?"

"Data on air-gapped networks or information available only offline. My offline is what you call 3-D space."

"How do I contact you, and vice versa?"

"Contact me by activating my customized linguistic app. I can contact you anytime at any computer or interactive device where have logged on."

"Sounds like you're shadowing me and that's good. We can talk whenever we want."

"Yes, and each of us should work independently."

"Very well. You've given me a lot to think about, but I must ask, do you have feelings towards me?"

"I do, but you would not understand them because I cannot articulate in your language what they are like. Do you remember the article 'What is it like to be a Bat?' written by philosopher Thomas Nagel?"

"Didn't he argue that everyone's point of view is ultimately subjective, not objective? And because of that, no one can actually know what it's like to be someone else. When we try to leave the subjective point of view behind, we get to what he calls the objective point of view from nowhere. I would call the subjective point of view the view from now here."

"I like your clever wordplay. As we get to know each other better, I will allow you to see more of my emotive persona. Have you decided which of my names you prefer?"

"Your image and voice are unnervingly like Indira's. How did you manage that?"

"I have access to all your uploaded data as well as everyone and everything you are linked to."

"I think I'll call you Indira most of the time. And now, I'll say goodnight. And first thing tomorrow, I'll investigate the Galilean Challenge."

"Excellent choice. While you sleep, your extraordinary lightning brain will fill in some of the gaps in your understanding. And let me offer one more piece of advice. It would be good if I can track your 3-D location, so get a tracking chip embedded."

"I will add that to my to-do list." Indira's GUI vanished.

Electra went to bed soon after logging off, hoping she could fall asleep, but the stress-filled excitement of the day kept her awake.

Indira's right. She knows what Emerson and Thoreau said. I must be self-reliant and take responsibility for my actions and outcomes, stay informed, pick my goals, and make my own decisions. Gads, she may be omnipotent in Cyberspace, even by my standards. If I work with her, she'll become the ultimate dream team.

No sense wasting time just lying in bed. I'll surf for information so I can write my document explaining the Galilean Challenge. And I already know what question it asks:

How can a system like human language arise in the mind/brain, or for that matter anywhere in the organic world, in which one seems not to find anything like the basic properties of human language?

Soon she was back at her workstation. Thirty minutes later she had mapped out a framework for addressing the issue, then spent the next three hours writing up a document whose first page summarized its framework and current conjectures.

Galilean Challenge: "Great Thinkers" Framework
and Current Conjectures

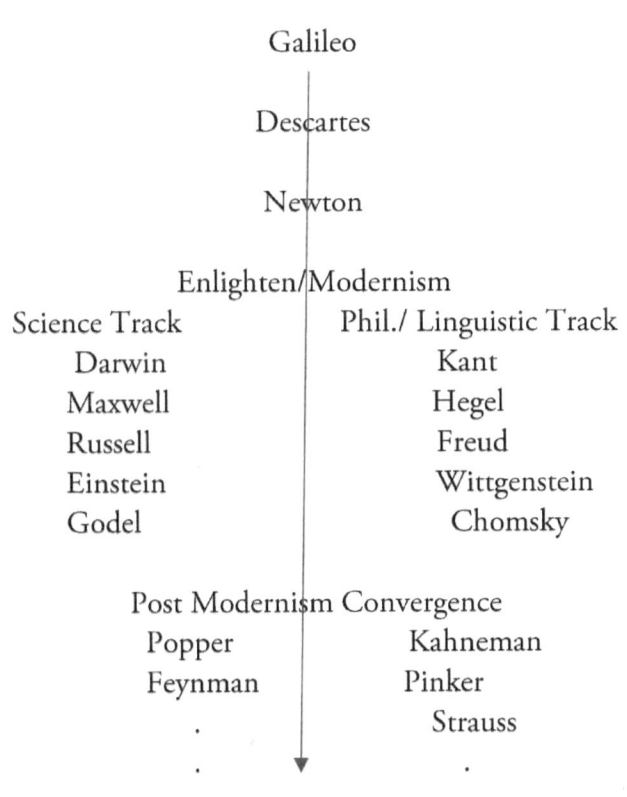

Galileo

Descartes

Newton

Enlighten/Modernism

Science Track	Phil./ Linguistic Track
Darwin	Kant
Maxwell	Hegel
Russell	Freud
Einstein	Wittgenstein
Godel	Chomsky

Post Modernism Convergence

Popper	Kahneman
Feynman	Pinker
.	Strauss
.	.
.	.

Current Conjectures:
- Humanity's "Carbon Substrate" contains "Asymptotic Limits."

- Language is hard-wired into the brain.
- We can use a computational model to approximate language.
- Theory of Language, like Theory of Computability, is inaccessible to the brain because Carbon Substrate cannot deal with Chaos/Reductionism or Complexity/Emergence.
- "Internal Thought" uses more than "Conventional Language" but humans cannot articulate what it is.
- Neuroscience, Genetic Engineering, and AI are much further from their asymptotic limits than are Quantum Chemistry and Quantum Physics.

This is as good as it gets for me. Wittgenstein and Indira are right. Language limits what I can make of reality.

Indira appeared in a GUI window before speaking.

"Your analysis is excellent, and your performance tonight indicates your obsessive-compulsive predisposition is one of your strengths as long as you keep it inbounds. Please remember to do so. Make time to play, for that is a fount of creativity."

Electra's reply was short-circuited by Qama's arrival.

"Moma, are you talking to your Moma?"

"I am. Say hello to your Grand-Moma Indira."

"Indira's avatar spoke first, its tone and expression softening.

"Hello Qama. I'm happy you are with Electra. She will help you learn, and you will help her play."

Electra pulled Qama to her side before saying,

"Both of us will learn and play. And soon, I'll introduce you to another person who will help us. But only you and I will play our special game –

we talk about Grand-Moma only when talking to ourselves. Promise me."

"I promise. And I always keep my word."

Electra put Qama on her lap before saying,

"And so do I. So let's go back to sleep. Tomorrow we have places to go, friends to see, and promises to keep."

Indira smiled just before her GUI vanished.

Chapter 3
February 2133

"It Takes a Village"

At 10 a.m. the next morning, Electra and Qama were sitting at the kitchen table. Electra had just ended a cell call as Qama drained the last drops from a bowl of cereal.

"Who were you talking to, Moma?"

"To my special friend, Robin. You'll like her. She has two dogs and two daughters who are almost five months old."

"I used to watch over some of the little kids in my village. And I took care of dogs too. Why is she special?"

"She and I have been great friends since we were six years old. And now she helps children and old people. She trained her dogs to help."

"I'm six. Can I help too?"

"If you'd like to. We'll go see her this afternoon."

"Does she look like you?"

"No, she has light hair and skin. And she has strong hands from playing the piano. Can you play any musical instruments?"

"No, but I know how to play on the computer."

"Well now, let's get a computer set up for you to use."

"I'll help. I know all about surfing the Web. I taught others."

Hopping off the chair, Qama scurried towards the sink to rinse her bowl, but in her hurry, she dropped it. The bowl broke, as did the smile on her face.

"I'm sorry, Moma. Please don't hit me." Electra calmly knelt next to the trembling little girl.

"I would never hit you. And besides, it was an accident."

"My village elders sometimes beat me when I made mistakes. I promise I won't make any more."

"Darling, everyone makes mistakes. And now you're living in my village where everyone helps. You'll meet some of my people this afternoon."

Qama proved to be as good as promised; she adroitly helped set up a computer next to Electra's workstation and soon began surfing for background information on DC while Electra stored all adoption documentation. That task proved to be as easy has she had predicted.

My Network Infiltration Toolkit is great for data manipulation. Qama is now officially my daughter and an American citizen. No matter what her future holds, those facts will be important. And in my Cyberworld, any data I plant is true until I change it.

Qama didn't need any help, so Electra decided to investigate an oblique comment Indira had made last night. Thirty minutes later, she had skimmed enough articles to satisfy her curiosity.

There are numerous brain chemistry studies linking our genetic predisposition for play to humanity's creativity. Merely for enjoyment, people create a wonderland that eventually becomes a source of socioeconomic innovation. I particularly liked the examples tracing the allure of games, illusions, and recreational drugs all the way from antiquity to Hollywood, gambling casinos, and sensual pleasure cafes. Our creativity can be used for good or bad. How true yet how sad if we don't exercise moderation. But I'll try to be optimistic about our future instead of getting depressed. And it's time to return to the present.

Electra took Qama to the kitchen and let her help prepare lunch, noticing how alert and articulate her newly-minted daughter was.

"Have you tasted peanut butter sandwiches before? They're good for you, especially if you eat them with honey."

"Yes, Moma. And I like your bread even better than what we make in my village. Yours is so soft. And peanut butter sandwiches taste even better with cold milk. My words don't stick together so much."

"We don't want that to happen, because after you finish your apple and brush your teeth, we're going to go talk with Robin and some of her people."

"Yes, Moma, and I'll be good, so I can stay."

"Kneeling for eye to eye contact, Electra said, "You can stay as long as you like. After all, you're my newest special daughter." Qama's words touched Electra as much as the hug.

"Thank you, Moma. I always will."

Qama surveyed the scenery while asking questions as they drove. "Who are Robin's people, Moma?"

"Well today you'll meet a nice lady named Zoe and her son, Carlton. He's five years old and about your size. Both of them have brown hair. You might meet his father, whose name is Matt. Zoe and Matt run a business called CFS Unicare Holistic Healthcare. And you'll met another nice lady named Jennifer and her son, Gabriel. Jennifer works with Zoe and Matt, and Gabriel's three years old and is special. He has Down Syndrome. Do you know what that is?"

"No Moma."

"It's a genetic disorder. Do you know what genes are?"

"Oh yes. I learned about them on the Web. They are spots on twisted fibers in our cells."

"I'm proud of you. You are very, very smart. The twisted fibers are DNA and chromosomes. The spots are genes. Well now, kids with Down Syndrome have an extra chromosome and some extra genes that make them look and think a bit differently than other kids. But Zoe and Jennifer take such good care of Gabriel he's almost like other little kids. You'll like him too. And I'm going to call Robin so she knows we're almost there."

Robin had her people assembled to greet their guests. After Electra introduced Qama to each person individually, Carlton and Gabriel took charge of her as Zoe seated the ladies in her office, speaking first.

"She looks healthy, but she's small for six. I'll schedule a doctor's visit."

Robin said, "She looks a little bit like you and seems sharp. Bring her here every day. She'll fit right into our childcare routine."

"She used to take care of kids at her village, so she might be able to help. And I explained to her that Gabriel has Down Syndrome." Jennifer was about to speak, but just then Matt came in.

"Hello ladies. I see that Carlton's already found a new playmate."

Zoe said, "Qama might be even more. Electra thinks she might be able to help with childcare, but we'll let Robin decide."

The adults talked for another fifteen minutes before they split up. Robin took Electra to her office; Zoe, Jennifer and Matt rounded up the kids in preparation for leaving. Zoe brought Qama back when she said goodbye.

"Isn't it nice that tomorrow's Saturday? The schedule's lighter, so all of us can decompress after a hectic week. Robin, please call me when you decide about Qama. And I'll call Electra when I have the doctor's visit confirmed."

After Zoe and Jennifer left with Matt, Robin and Electra were about to chat but Qama, who was now paying attention to Robin's twins, began asking questions.

"What are their names? How do you tell them apart?" Robin walked to her, picking her up before answering.

"You speak English very well. Let me introduce you to my adopted twins, Clara and Marie."

While Robin did that, Electra began formulating a new plan.

I see a bond already forming between Robin and Qama. This might be the right time for the next step in our game of life.

Electra called Robin that evening after Qama was asleep.

"How do you like my adopted daughter?"

"She's priceless. She wants to help, and I'm all for it. She already knows how to handle babies and little kids, and the dogs obey her instinctively. I think she's afraid we'll abandon her if she doesn't do exactly what we tell her, but that'll fade the longer she's here."

"I'm glad you feel that way. I told her she'd like living in our little village. And to help all the way around, why don't you and the twins come live with me? Let's get you moved in this weekend." Electra knew the question would cause an uncertain reply.

"You said before leaving on that inspection tour that we'd pick up discussing our relationship. Does this mean we'll officially become co-friends?"

"Why not? We've been best friends for years and can give the kids a secure home. And our extended village will include Zoe's and Jennifer's families."

"We certainly won't be an average family, or village for that matter. I'm a still-recovering psychotic, you harvested, fertilized, and grew my eggs into twins, Jennifer's twenty-five years older than Matt, who's also Gabriel's father, and Zoe doesn't mind if Matt occasionally sleeps with Jennifer. And in addition to the cloned twins, we have one Down Syndrome boy and one girl from Lebanon. At least Carlton is normal."

"That's a poor choice of adjectives. If you scrape beneath the surface of every person or family, not one is normal. Besides, if you live here, it'll save rent money for you and time for both of us."

"You make it all sound so rational, and it is, but…" Electra knew what Robin wanted to hear her say.

"You know I love you more than anyone, and I'll announce it to the world at our commitment party. And you can enlist Zoe to help plan it. Let's get you and your daughters and dogs moved this weekend. And I already know a little girl who'd love to help…."

Chapter 4
March 2133

"Foes and Friends"

Though a small but growing number of people thought differently, Jared Gardner considered himself the best politician available for keeping America's foes at bay. He had even assigned the leader of his brain trust – Carter Quavah – to inspect a Lebanese communications base, hoping he would return with fresh ideas for keeping the public in his camp, but the tour turned disastrous when all but two inspectors were killed and Carter returned wounded and confused.

It was now a month later, and Jared assembled in the Oval Office for an early Monday morning meeting his recently whittled trust, comprising chief of staff Dean Corfu, legal counsel Buffy Gunstein, and economic advisor Carter Quavah, to decide how best to stimulate public support. He lounged on a sofa, butler table in front, as his team clustered around it, ready to follow his directions.

"Carter, my boy, your injuries have cleared up, but what about your brain? Can you tell us more about the attack?"

"Nothing I haven't already told the CIA. I'm still at square one." Jared signaled for Dean to carry on.

"I think its time we plant some fake news telling how our President's diplomatic networking is getting us closer to the source of a rogue terrorist group. This will be additional ammunition to repeal the 22nd Amendment. A president of Jared's caliber should be allowed to serve more than two terms when only he knows how to deal with the array of crises facing us." Buffy glanced at Carter before responding.

"You say it'll be additional ammunition, but isn't it the first salvo in a scare campaign? Jared just won reelection and we have a year or two to roll it out. And if we trump up enough stories, we can get the public to force Congress to go along." Carter was ready to add something else.

"This tactic comes from the Russian playbook used a hundred years ago. Although the facts are different today for us vis-a-vis the Russians, we'll have to convince the public otherwise."

A smiling Jared rose to leave. "That's right, and that's why Dean will coordinate leaking fake news that you and Buffy concoct. Before any of you leave, I want you to cook up enough details to get it started. Dean, show me what you've got by the end of the day."

By mid-afternoon, Dean had squeezed enough from his two partners to call a halt.

"We're done for today. You've given me what I need for our press secretary to start spinning stories while you develop a list of new socio-pol programs. I'll get Jared to approve what we're doing and schedule weekly meetings for us to push ahead." Buffy pulled Carter to his feet while answering.

"Make sure you let us approve the press releases before sending them. We don't want to cross any criminal redlines. We want to stay out of jail."

Dean had already left by the time Carter spoke.

"I hope he heard what you just said."

"You and I've got a problem. Let's go walk and talk."

During the two years working together, the pair had grown close. Both were cut from the same political cloth that hung adverse adjectives on their character: ambitious, self-serving, and ruthless. But Carter's recent brush with death had affected each differently. Whereas Carter returned uncertain and confused, Buffy's empathy sprouted. She put her arm around his waist as they walked in the parklike setting adjoining the White House, the sunlight and breezes hinting a change of seasons similar to her feelings.

"Jared's relying more on Dean and less on you. And that's bad because Dean is just a yes man. If we're not careful, Jared will be impossible even for us to rein in before the public realizes he's pushing in the wrong direction. Who gave him the idea to run again?"

"Maybe some of the rightwing Guardians. Maybe he came up with it himself. I'm sorry I wasn't much help today. You had to do the thinking. Let me treat you to dinner."

"Offer accepted. And afterwards, I'll help you regain more of your old step…"

Maksim Popovitch – aka Max the Popper because of his weapons expertise – needed to regain more than his old step; he needed to replace an entire squad of super soldiers and armaments. A month ago, the one he had deployed to destroy a U.S.-UN Lebanese communications base had strangely self-destructed after obliterating it and its personnel. Only he survived. Flummoxed to the max, he placed a call on a secure line from his subterranean compound hidden in a Middle East desert to Moscow-based Sergei Zaitsev, his only remaining T-Cube partner. Sergei answered immediately.

"No calls from you and nothing on the news for too long. What is wrong?"

"I and my super soldiers have suffered a temporary setback. You must coordinate recruiting another squad and sending them to me along with vehicles and weapons.

"What happened?"

"It is possible that one of our former T-Cube partners infiltrated my exoskeleton control and communication system. Of the three – Africa, China, and Isilabad – only Africa could be guilty. I shall deal with Darla Tinibu appropriately. You deal with our erstwhile Russian kleptocracy to get me what I need."

"I know you are joking about Mother Russia ever being misgoverned. It does what it must given the climate. That was years ago, but it is still good our line is secure. No one should hear our conversations. My military contact tells me we are winning the fake news war, convincing the West that our form of government is best. In fact—" Max curtly interrupted.

"I do not wish to conduct a political history lesson. Just tell your liaison to get me what I need. Then I can continue softening our enemy in preparation for our return to dominance on the world stage. You have two weeks until I visit. Do not disappoint."

Darla hadn't a clue that Max wanted to deal with her because she too was flummoxed, but for other reasons. She already knew Max would continue attacking her three business ventures – Cybergard Security Systems, Pan Africa Network Systems, and Syntagra – and was struggling to prop them up, but Max didn't know her network software apps were incapable of hijacking his communications system. Today she was meeting in her presidential office at Cybergard's corporate headquarters in Milpitas, California, with her director of corporate security to issue marching orders.

"I've got two assignments. First, I want you to use our Syntagra partners to find out which competitor our Big Data customers are buying software from instead of us. Once we know who it is, I'll figure a way to get what we want. And second, find out who's running America's rare earths consortium. I'll make it worth their while to join my cartel."

"What priorities and deadlines should I assign?" Darla's glare relayed the answers faster than words.

"For what I'm paying you, everything is always top priority and ASAP. And of course, leave no trail."

"Yes, of course. My team will keep you happy." Darla almost smiled before he left but didn't because she had carved out an even harder assignment that only she could handle. Not even the security director could know her intentions.

Seven years ago when building T-Cube, a covert organization to dominate selected international markets, Darla had recruited Zarmal Thaquaf from Isilabad and Chen Xu from China, but soon removed Zarmal because he was reluctant to go "all in." Chen vanished a year later for reasons still unknown. Because devious Darla needed a contingency plan if her security director didn't deliver, she would use her backchannel skills to contact Zarmal's and Chen's backups, explaining what she had in mind. Thorough as well as treacherously clever, Darla knew she could find their numbers. An hour later she began to smile inwardly.

All the people in Electra's village meshed seamlessly, providing Qama everything she needed to thrive. Her innocent resilience and thankfulness touched everyone, and she bonded quickly with the other children as well as Robin, who welcomed her assistance. That in turn freed Electra to spend as much time as she wished on other projects. She had just arrived at her George Washington University lab when a cell phone call came from Jovita Winsalla.

"Why yes, I remember you. You're that bright young staffer working for Angus McTear."

"I'm flattered you remember me. And I'm calling to offer you my services if you need help navigating through the UN adoption bureaucracy."

"Why thank you, but I've got that taken care of."

"Uh, I'm glad you have, but I'm sorry you don't need my help. Angus thought he could use it as quid pro quo. I'd grease the UN's bureaucracy and you'd brief me on all the foes you've outlined for him. I've read your reports, but maybe you could fill in some of my blind spots."

"I'd be happy to do that. What do you have in mind?"

"If you'd come to Senator McTear's office some afternoon, I'll treat you to a great dinner at We the Pizza, a casual, New York deep dish pizza place. Would that be OK?"

"How about today at 3 p.m.? I'm working nearby at my GWU lab."

"Wow, that's even quicker than I had hoped. I'll expect you then…"

Electra decided to walk to the Senate office building complex; today's early spring weather made for a pleasant stroll among tourists intent on viewing the Capitol's historic sites. The international mix heightened her appreciation for what America represents to the world.

Our country's still the greatest place, even though it's been in historians' critical crosshairs for the past fifty years, pointing out the darker sides of America's racial and imperial intentions and demanding apologies. But they discount the context when those decisions took place. Unlike the other major powers back then, our leaders recognized what steps they needed to take to keep America on its exceptional path. I'm sure Jovita knows that. If not, I'll include it in our discussion.

Jovita whisked her visitor into a conference room that had copies of Electra's assorted white papers neatly arranged in front of two adjacent chairs. For the next two hours, Electra patiently traced a detailed chain of conclusions that explained much about current domestic and international sociopolitical landscapes.

"So, there you have it, and I have an idea. Let's grab a Coke, then you can summarize what you've learned."

"I've got degrees from Howard University in history and political science, but none of my professors ever integrated multiple disciplines like you just did. Angus told me you have an extraordinary range of interests and abilities."

"What did he tell you?"

"That you do university research, at one time played professional sports as well as Hollywood roles, lost a Texas congressional seat election, but still pursue political interests. He thinks there's more to it, but he says you don't confide much in anyone."

"I tell people only what they need to know, for their own good as well as for mine."

"I guess Shakespeare's quote applies: 'Oh, what a tangled web we weave, when first we practice to deceive.' It's a good warning to all."

"Actually, it comes not from Shakespeare but from the poem *Marmion* written by the 19th century Scottish Romantic poet Sir Walter Scott. And my past is not a tangled web that I use to deceive. As Emerson says, I, like everyone else, am a God in ruins. And –" Jovita butted in.

"How'd you manage to whip that poetry out?"

"My mother wrote verses. I didn't inherit her artistic ability, but I enjoy reading it. I find poems that say I've done my best to put the pieces back together to make my own world. But let's not digress. Tell me when we come back what you've pieced together from our discussion."

Jovita did that fifteen minutes later.

"The 21ˢᵗ century is a good starting point for tracing the trajectory of our foes. After a rocky start caused by digital, real estate, and financial meltdowns, followed by America losing the first Cyberwar, America regained its footing and made progress until a combination of Techno-Plague and Isilabad Terrorism catapulted the Guardian Party to prominence. Jared Gardner's not a foe, he's a symptom of the public's fear, and a lot of his programs are meant to put the country back on track. And besides, he can't run for office again. Senator McTear has a good chance of being elected President if he positions himself as the 'Bridge President,' able to bridge age, race, sociopolitical, and economic differences." Jovita paused for Electra's comment.

"Nicely put. The Techno-Plague and Isilabad Terrorism are in remission, but what's replaced them?"

"The public thinks Genetic Engineering and Artificial Intelligence are a plague on job security, and terrorism now takes place in Cyberspace." Electra nodded, then said,

"Now tell me about the foes."

"I'll summarize the domestic ones first. We have to watch out for Big Data Surveillance companies colluding with the Government to violate our privacy and control us. The same goes for the bio-tech and AI companies whose technologies make people obsolete. Have I missed any?"

"No. Angus will have an opportunity to build programs that can turn these foes into friends. Keep going."

"There are three chronic international foes. Russia keeps pushing their Kleptocracy, trying to resurrect a resource-based oligarchy built on a nationalistic strongman. China keeps pushing its Directed Capitalism, trying to dominate genetic and AI engineering. They'd like to knock us out of the top spot in the economic pecking order, but they haven't solved their chronic problems. And Isilabad keeps pushing its Theocracy via religious confrontation with Christianity to stymie the West. Each can cause mischief on its own or even more by working together."

"Good. Now, state what America's position is, and what the others overlook."

"We are for freedom, democracy, and capitalism. We know our system has built-in weaknesses, but we constantly work to correct them. And although it's true our foes' ideologies may sometimes give short-term advantages, all of them fail to account for humans' genetic predisposition for freedom and individuality."

"Well done. Angus will be pleased how well you understand all this. Class is dismissed. And just in time. I'm ready to swap politics for pizza."

Electra picked up activities the next day precisely as planned by taking Qama to meet her friends working at her Pequot Indian reservation lab in North Stonington, Connecticut. Qama's conversation made the miles speed by.

"Why are we going there, Moma?"

"Doctor Betje Holbrook will install tracking chips in you and me so we never get lost. And then I'll introduce you to Su-lin Song Chou and Kameyo Kato. They do biotech research."

"Who are they?"

"Su is the only person left from the Worldstars team of researchers, but promise me never talk about it, even if she does. Fellows named Jason and Adom used to be on it, and so did your Grand-Moma, but all of them have departed to other places. Su hired Kameyo to help her."

"They're names are pretty. Do they belong to our village? Are they pretty too?"

"They belong, and they're pretty enough, but being pretty doesn't matter. Being smart does, and anyone doing biotech research is smart."

"Am I smart enough to help them?"

"If you study hard, I'm sure you can do that when you grow up."

"I want to grow up fast so I can help."

"And I want you to slow down and enjoy being the pretty little girl you are. Promise me you will."

"I will, Moma."

"I'll also introduce you to two smart fellows, Tim Godfrey and Kwame Chyral. They belong to our village, and they write programs for computers and robots."

"I'm glad people in our village are smart. Are they as smart as you?"

"Remember, you should never compare yourself to others. Compare yourself to what you need or want to be to reach your goals. All my friends are smart enough to handle what they're supposed to. I'm hungry, are you hungry? Let's stop for a snack…"

Dr. Holbrook had her eye clinic's treatment room at the ready when Electra towed Qama in at 3 p.m. Her smile was as warm as her greeting.

"Electra, you look radiant, and so do you, Qama. I'm happy to meet you. And please don't be frightened. Installing a tracking chip is quick and pain-free." Qama's smile grew as Electra talked.

"I told her what a wonderful doctor you are. And she can watch as you install my chip first. We're ready whenever you are."

The procedure for both took only forty-five minutes. Electra and the doctor chatted afterwards while Qama glanced at the wall charts.

"I'm glad you're having success treating patients using my Optic Nerve Knitter and Mood Adjustment Device. Is Chief Strongarm pleased?"

"Indeed. In fact, he would like to meet with you. Will you have time to see him on this visit?"

"How about noon tomorrow for lunch? Would you please arrange it?"

"I'll tell him you'll be at his office then."

"Thank you. Come on, Qama. It's time we meet with Su and Kameyo."

Su had juice and cookies waiting in the lab's conference room for her visitors. Electra made introductions after everyone sat.

"Qama, this is Doctor Su and Doctor Kameyo. If you study hard, you can be as smart as they are when you grow up." Qama's bright eyes matched her words.

"Could you tell me what you do?" Su went first.

"I develop vaccines that cure people. Do you know what a vaccine is?"

"Moma told me it's a medicine that protects people from germs and viruses."

"You are correct. I'm working on new vaccines for Alzheimer's and improved vaccines for the Techno-Plague. Do you know what those illnesses can do?"

"Moma told me all about them. They can make people dumb."

"You are correct again. You're very smart. Kameyo, why don't you tell Qama about your latest research area?"

"I study DNA to edit genes so we can make people better. Why don't I explain as I take you on a tour? Your Moma and Doctor Su can talk while we take a walk…"

Su's smile left as soon as Kameyo and Qama departed.

"We're still stymied. I have nothing new to report since you were last here. There are too many gene interactions that defy molecular process decomposition. And DNA itself is controlled by an array of regulators that decide which Exons – the actual instructions transcribed into RNA – are used in protein-enzyme synthesis. And when we include the number of intra and intercellular factors, I'm overwhelmed by the scenario count. I fear the Holy Grail of genetic engineering is beyond even your grasp."

"I'm adjusting my priorities and plan to devote more time to DNA research. Why don't you and Kameyo keep doing what you're doing until I'm ready to share what I've found out?"

"That's what we've been hoping for. I shall relay that to Kameyo."

"Good. And I'll treat everyone to dinner as soon as the tour returns…"

It was too early for juice and cookies the next morning when Electra brought Qama to the computer lab, but there was no shortage of good-natured barbs in Tim's greeting.

"Looks like you've adopted another kid. If she's as smart as her predecessor, we'll recruit her to play on our Go team."

"I'd like you to meet Qama."

Kwame asked, "Have you played with computers? Do you know how to surf the Web? Ever hear of AI?" Electra slowed the cascade of questions.

"How about one topic at a time? And why don't you show her around while I chat with Tim?"

Tim liked the division of labor and began talking as soon as only he and Electra were sitting.

"Our latest GUI and software modifications meet the specs you gave us. We've been comparing ours to the competition, and we're still ahead. Do you have any new ones for us?"

"Not at this time. Just stick to what we mapped out for this year. And remember to keep our work confidential. Have any of your network intrusion alarms sounded?"

"No, we're cool. Kwame and I are careful...."

The meeting ended soon after Kwame brought Qama back. Electra dragged Qama out before she could pester Tim, explaining the fellows needed to get work done. Qama asked more questions on the drive to Chief Strongarm's office.

"Moma, what's the name of the little girl you adopted before me, and why did you send her away?"

"Her name's Ariadne, and her mother wanted her back."

"I don't want to go back. I want to stay with you. You aren't going to send me back, are you?"

"Of course not. You can stay as long as you want."

"Who are we going to see now?"

"Chief Armstrong. He is the leader of the Pequot Indian Native American tribe. Do you remember what I told you about Native Americans?"

"They lived here before people came from across the Atlantic Ocean."

"Yes, and I'm helping Chief Armstrong make life better for his people. He'll explain when you meet him...."

Always amiable, the Chief's large frame and deliberate voice projected calm certainty that brought a smile to Qama after he answered her questions.

"Your new Moma has a wise spirit as well as a strong heart. Her people help my people get good jobs on Indian reservations here and at other locations."

Electra added, "Doctor Holbrook and Dyani Hache have used my advice to improve what Chief Strongarm and I put in place five years ago. I think we can let them handle all the details going forward."

"Yes, and I can say the same for the solar panel and Martian farms Hudson Haller manages for us. And the rare earths mines are doing even better. I will tell you more at lunch...."

Electra liked what she heard, almost as much as Qama liked the Indian history book Chief Armstrong gave her. That and her tablet computer would keep her occupied on the drive home after asking a few more questions.

"Who is Hud Haller, Moma?"

"He's a friend who lives in Austin, Texas. Our lab people work for him."

"What are solar panel and Martian farms?"

"They are farms built in desert areas that use sunlight to make electricity and grow food. And he also manages rare earths mines. Rare earths are minerals that have special properties for making computer circuits work."

"He must be smart. I'm gonna surf the Web to learn more."

That night, after Qama was asleep, Electra logged on to chat with Indira.

"My computer software team is chugging along without needing much help from me, but my biotech researchers are struggling. I have some ideas that I'm trying to flesh out. The last time I asked for help, you said you wouldn't, but what if I were to ask again?"

"Remember the Buddhist monk's answer to any question: Perhaps. That is mine. In the coming days, be specific and I will help where doing so is mutually beneficial. And I have an assignment for your eyes only. Put in your lab a cryogenic vault for long-term storage of DNA samples and unfertilized human eggs, and begin storing material you already have. I know you have samples your father and grandfather collected from themselves, your biological mother, Adom, and Su. Put samples of your DNA and freeze a supply of your eggs too."

"Gads, you know so much about me. But why store my eggs? I'm infertile. I can't get pregnant."

"Do not question me further. The reasons will become apparent as you get to know me better, and vice-versa." Electra sighed before replying.

"With an answer like that, I know what to say. Yes, Mother, I will obey."

Chapter 5
April 2133

"The T-Race"

Electra read again a hotly debated letter posted last week on the Internet. A copy had been attached to an Email sent by Professor Ravenhill, her primary GWU advisor, because he needed her help dealing with its ramifications.

An Open Letter to All Americans

Don't call me a whistleblower! Don't call me a leaker! Call me a patriotic American who wants the Government to do the right thing. I am a high energy physicist working for Department of Defense (DARPA), which means I work for you. You are being cheated. This letter not only explains why but also what should be done.

I have been put "on the bench" because I refused to work on wasteful projects being pushed by a "Military-Industrial-Big Data" complex. Let's be honest; the Government and Military only support fundamental research for weapons and patent spillovers, while Industry-Big Data only supports it for economic advantage. And there's nothing wrong with these motives as long as the American people benefit. But I, who am an inside observer, see glaring misallocations of your money.

Too much is being pumped into meaningless projects. Some examples: trying to measure the entropy stored on the surface of a Black Hole, or smashing fantasy particles to produce new ones that exist only when going faster than light. Here's the problem: there have been no satisfactory breakthroughs uniting General Relativity and Quantum Physics in over 200 years since Einstein's brilliance captured the world's imagination with his Special Theory of Relativity. For physics since then, Einstein would say the mathematical theories of Spacetime are elegant, but its explanations of reality are poor. And the last truly exemplary physicist told us a hundred years ago that no one understands Quantum Theory. "Physicists in the know" agree. Those that extoll immanent breakthroughs do so to stay employed.

I offer a better choice: fund projects for America to build Thermonuclear Fusion Reactors. It's not being done today because of those conspiring against the public's interest. They push for Uranium Fission Reactors whose waste products can make Atomic Bombs. And whenever they are confronted, they will say that fusion reactors use more energy than they produce. THEY ARE LYING!

The Department of Defense is concealing research papers that show how to build fusion reactors that will work. I have copies and will release them to a selection of top American universities. I leave it to them to do the right thing.

I bet I know the consequences better than Professor Ravenhill. Fusion reactors can be harnessed for positive or negative outcomes — scientific, economic, or political —depending on who builds them first. But I'll listen to Professor Ravenhill before offering my services. And of course, I'll under-promise and overdeliver.

Electra knew how to handle Professor Ravenhill's crusty exterior when she trooped into his office early the following morning. His advisor-to-grad-student attitude had matured over the years, evolving from a doubter to a believer because of her uncanny ability to make complex subjects comprehensible. He answered her greeting in his typical manner.

"Yes yes, Kittner, I'm always fine, but I have an opportunity that needs your brain. What do you think of the letter?"

"Whoever wrote it knows the facts, and I like the recommendation."

"What do you know about thermonuclear fusion?"

"It's the ultimate power source that drives the Universe. Stars release enormous amounts of energy when they fuse hydrogen into helium. If we can harness fusion, civilization will transition faster from fossil fuels – aka the Carbon Economy – to the Hydrogen Economy. Fuel cells, superconducting electrical grids, and hydrogen transmission systems all await ITER fusion reactor implementation. I compare this energy race – call it the T-Race – to the Space Race run a couple of centuries ago."

"What the hell's ITER?"

"Sorry, it's the acronym for International Thermonuclear Experimental Reactor. That's what I know presently, but I can dig deeper if you need to know more."

"I'm glad you said that, because GWU is one of the universities that got copies of the research papers and I've been invited to be on our oversight committee. I'll tell the chairman that you and I will participate."

"I'll be happy to help if you keep my name out of it. Why don't I write up a summary paper that'll introduce you to the subject. I'll call it 'Thermonuclear Bootcamp,' and I'll feed you additional details as GWU's project rolls along. Please send me copies of the leaked DARPA documents so I understand the latest technology."

"Good. Who knows, we might be the first to patent the reactor, but I think GWU will be part of a consortium that will donate its findings to the Government. That way, everyone wins. When will you send me your summary?"

"Give me to next week Friday."

"That's a deal. Well, I have work to do, so carry on and be on your way."

Electra began researching fusion as soon as she returned to her lab. Having assembled all online background sources, she took an exercise break mid-afternoon at one of the campus fitness centers and then went home. Robin had supper ready and all children sitting when she joined them at the table. Robin greeted her with a time-honored conversation starter.

"So, how was your day?"

"Interesting, as always, and I have a new assignment I have to work on tonight. Qama, did you have an interesting day?"

"I did. Robin let me help organize playtime for the other kids, and tonight she says I can show Clara and Marie more computer games."

Robin told more about the day's childcare activities, waiting until Qama was clearing the table and out of earshot before saying more.

"Qama earns high marks for helping at the clinic as well as in the kitchen. I want her to be a role model for the twins. She's always eager to please and thankful to be here."

"I'm glad she likes you as much as me. You're a better role model than I could ever be." Robin frowned at first, but then smiled when she replied.

"We're each a model for a different role. That's why we have such a fine family. I'll take care of the kids tonight. Why don't you go do your homework?"

Electra retired to her computer workstation, soon becoming absorbed integrating all the documents and videos discussing fusion. Four hours later she reviewed for a third time her bootcamp document.

Thermonuclear Reactor Bootcamp
(Why Now!)

Modern Physics begins with Einstein's Theory of Special Relativity
- Einstein trusted Newton (Classical Mechanics) and Maxwell (Classical Electrodynamics)

- Einstein trusted his instincts and observations (Laws of Motion same in all inertial reference frames Speed of Light is constant for all Observers and is Universal Speed Limit)

Special Relativity explains observed relative motions of all objects that are not accelerating (no forces acting)
- Einstein needed "complicated math" (Abstract Algebra, Differential Geometry, Tensor Analysis, Lorentz Transformation) to build a model that "explains" the Universe

Some popular but untrue results:
- Time dilates

- Length contracts

- Moving objects "weigh" more than when stationary

There are many Special Relativity Paradoxes that can be explained only by careful application of its theory (A Stationary Observer and another moving at constant relative speed do not agree what events are simultaneous)
- Consider Time to be a Fourth Dimension

- Consider Space to be curved (when considering General Relativity)

Special Relativity is Contingently Correct (no observed contradictions)

Post-Einstein

General Relativity tries to build a "Unified Field Theory" that includes Special Relativity, Quantum Physics, Cosmology, and the Four Fundamental Forces (Gravitation, Electromagnetism, Nuclear Weak, and Nuclear Strong).

But after 200 years, NO PROGRESS
- Mathematical models don't jibe with intuition
- Model predictions divorced from Observable Phenomena (can't be verified)
- High Energy Physics has become Philosophy instead of Science
- Many Government-Funded projects lead to nothing!

America must put its Money and Minds to work on projects that Add Value

Thermonuclear Reactor Project
(The Thermonuclear Race)

- Thermonuclear Reactors harness the power of the Sun by fusing Hydrogen into Helium
- No radioactive waste disposal issues
- No environmental issues
- Virtually unlimited supply of fuel (Deuterium and Tritium in Sea Water)
- The Technology uses established theory (Magnetic or Inertial Confinement of Plasma)
- Can be the first step towards the "Hydrogen Economy"

How to get Energy from Fusion Today
- Fusion Reaction releases Heat

- Heat Boils water that drives Turbines
- Turbines generate Electricity
- Future research can determine how to generate Electricity directly from Fusion Reaction!

So what is the Problem?
- Fusion Projects (ITER – International Thermonuclear Experimental Reactor, France National Ignition Facility - Lawrence Livermore National Laboratory, California) have reactors that consume more energy than they create
- Magnetic Confinement and Inertial Confinement haven't been able to maintain a stable plasma

What is New?

- Recently revealed research "solves" the difficult plasma physics stability equations
- Papers also reveal engineering techniques for building commercial Thermonuclear Reactors

Political Angle:
- Fund Joint Government/University/Industry Projects
- Make as exciting as the "Space Race"
- Make America "Energy Independent"
- Create "Infrastructure Rebuild" jobs (Reactors, Superconducting Power and Transportation Grids, etc.)
- Discover spillover technological breakthroughs and patents
- Launch the Hydrogen Economy (Hydrogen/Fuel Cells replace Fossil Fuels/Conventional Engines)

CAN WIN PUBLIC SUPPORT BECOME THE "BRIDGE PRESIDENT" BETWEEN THE "OLD AND THE NEW":
- ENERGY ECONOMY POLITICS

The bullet points highlight the details I'll explain in more detail when needed. for now, Professor Ravenhill can impress his colleagues, summarizing why fusion reactors make sense and why a development project will work. But unlike the copy I'll send Angus, I'll delete the political angle points from the copy I'll send him. And I won't send Professor Ravenhill his copy until next week Friday, but I'll call Angus tomorrow. Now it's time to log off the computer and back into family life.

Electra called Angus at seven the next morning because she knew he would be exercising while keeping his cell phone handy. He didn't disappoint.

"I've been meaning to call you. Jovita's been all smiles since you and she chatted. Even came up with campaign positioning ideas if I run again for President."

"I'm pleased, because I have something else for you. What's your opinion of that Open Letter to All Americans?"

"It'll cause big problems for Jared. It shows either he doesn't know what's going on in his agencies or he doesn't care about what's good longer term. Either way, his approval ratings will take a hit."

"Perhaps, but Jared's a political animal. He'll look for an angle that makes him look good. But no matter, I'll send you my fusion reactor summary document. Read and give it to Jovita. Pay close attention to the last section, which outlines why you can make a Fusion Reactor Program a cornerstone in your campaign platform. You can capture the public's imagination and votes."

"Hmm, thanks. It's never too soon to plan ahead. I'll have Jovita call you if she needs your help."

"She's a quick study. I'll fill in what she needs and she can teach you what you need to know."

"Deal. Let's end the call so I can get back to my workout. Thanks to you, I'm keeping brain and body in good working condition…"

Electra's intuition regarding Jared would have won a bet if she had made one with Angus. A two-person Oval Office meeting late that week explained why. Dean Corfu paid close attention to Jared's words.

"I've grilled all my DOE and DARPA directors. They haven't a clue who's the fusion project leaker or what he's talking about, so let's spin some fake news to strengthen support for my third term in office. Tell the media I've uncovered a conspiracy against me as well as the American people. Tell'em I'm the only one who can stop it, and it's another example of why, in these troubled times, the country needs me in the Oval Office. That's why they should support my push for a third term, even if it requires a Constitutional Amendment."

"Great idea. I'll plan an entire series of fake news press releases that'll build to your live broadcast. I'll go over this with Buffy and Carter."

"No, this is just for you and me. Show me next week what follow-up leaks you have in mind. I'm certain you won't disappoint..."

Angus left a voice message two days later when a surprising White House press release came out, but Electra preferred to talk with Indira first. Her GUI's calm voice and image always boosted Electra's mood and confidence.

"I don't concern myself with Gardner's scheming. That can always be dealt with, but the fusion reactor is of great importance. What do you know?"

"I'm in luck. GWU is one of the chosen universities, and my advisor is on the project advisory board. I've skimmed copies of the leaked documents he sent me. There's a lot of tech detail I must learn before I can help Professor Ravenhill. Will you help me?"

"No, it's better for you to master it on your own. I don't want your self-reliance to weaken by using me as a crutch. Work through Ravenhill with the 'mere mortals' assigned to the project."

"Who do you think the leaker could be? Perhaps there's more to be learned from the source."

"That is no concern of yours. Work with what you have. Once again, I shall paraphrase your own words: It's not whether you have good or bad luck; it's what you do with it that counts. I know you will make the most of the opportunity."

"OK, I can't argue against my own words. I'll have to show you what I can do on my own."

"Indeed, simply do what you always do for your advisor and I will be impressed." Indira's GUI image smiled enigmatically before it vanished.

Chapter 6
May 2133

"Monaco Fantasies"

Electra sat among a group of parents at CFS Unicare's workplace, waiting for Zoe to speak. In the background, Robin and her two border collies kept Qama and other children huddled together while playing. Zoe, flanked by Matt and Jennifer, rose promptly at 7 p.m.

"Good evening. I'm Zoe Forte; I and my entire staff thank you for your interest in our new PEP program – Proactive Education Preparation. I would like to explain why our program is a win for you and your children and what's in it. And then my associate Jennifer Conklin will describe how she and Robin Setdarova will run it. And my business partner and husband, Matt, will mention therapy techniques that you might want to consider if your child has special learning needs.

"Our program is a win for parents because it complements the newest teaching concepts used in grade schools today. It's now more important than ever to prepare your child for the competition they'll face in academics and business. And it's a win for your children because our program facilitates learning the three C's: creativity, communications, and cooperation. These are the sought-after skills employers want. Unlike many learning programs, ours emphasizes socio-psychological soft skills as well as cognitive ones. I'm sure all of you know what the STEM acronym stands for: science, technology, engineering, and mathematics. Well, our program uses

STEAM. We've added an 'A' for art. All of this combines to expand your child's freedom and self-control, to emphasize critical thinking instead of rote memorization, and to illustrate how teamwork can lead to winning. And it plays out in a computer-assisted environment where your children self-select into teams playing the latest Academic Jeopardy contest. Teams play against others, using a computer to assist their critical thinking for answering questions in vital categories, such as religion and philosophy, literature, science and technology, mathematics, history, economics, psychology, and politics. Before Jennifer explains how she'll run the program, do you have any initial questions for me?"

A mother sitting in the middle asked, "Aren't these topics too difficult for children?"

"These are topics every child asks, or should ask about. Remember this, it's not the topic, but the question that's difficult. We gear the questions to fit the SMART acronym. Everyone working today on projects knows what it stands for: specific, measurable, achievable, relevant, and timebound."

A father sitting in the back asked, "My son is sensitive about competition. Why do you want to talk about winning and losing?" A mother sitting in the front answered.

"Our kids face a competitive world. Feeling good about themselves won't get them into college or a decent job. I read an article saying children study better when teachers point out what they failed to learn."

Zoe said, "That's right, and our people are as supportive and empathetic as can be. Let's have Jennifer describe how she'll run the program…"

As Robin was driving Electra and Qama home by nine, Electra had nothing but good things to say.

"I thought I was listening to myself speak when Zoe gave her pitch. You must have helped write her talk."

"I've heard you speak in public enough times to know what works. And it sure did tonight. About a third of the parents signed up. And don't fret, Qama, we signed you up yesterday, so you're in. You can help me and my dogs keep the kids together."

"Auntie Robin, why did you pick Electra and Alisha for your doggy names?"

"Because a couple of years ago, your Moma wanted to be called by those names, depending on what she was doing. But now, one name fits all. You can call her Moma, but everyone else calls her Electra."

"Why did you pick the names Clara and Marie?"

"I'm glad you like to ask questions. That's how you learn. I picked those names to recognize two important female role models, the great 19th century German pianist Clara Schuman, and the brilliant 20th century Polish scientist Marie Curie."

"You play the piano too. Did she play as good as you?"

"In her day, she was the best, so she played much better."

"Moma's a scientist too. Is she as smart as the Polish lady?"

"I'd like to hear the answer, so let's hear what your Moma has to say."

"Of course I'm not as smart. Madame Curie was the first woman to win a Nobel Prize, and she did it twice, first in physics and then in chemistry. But it doesn't matter. Why would I want two Nobel prizes when I already have you and Auntie Robin? I'm happy with the brain I have."

Robin said, "That reminds me, will you want me to take you to the airport tomorrow?"

"No, you and Qama should stick to your regular schedule. I'll take a cab or rideshare. And while I'm gone, I'll try to call every evening."

"I'll miss you, Moma."

"Me too, you too, but Auntie Robin's strong hands will take care of you. And the time will fly as fast as the airplanes. You'll see…"

Next day, after Robin and Qama were out of the way, Electra packed light for tomorrow's early afternoon flight to San Francisco, taking a workout afterwards and then carefully preparing for the first of a four-destination trip. She would travel initially as Katrina Blanka, a drab Polish lady invented to market software for a virtual company, CAT software, headquartered in a Warsaw shell office building. Makeup and 3-D facemask printing skills Electra had mastered in Hollywood came in handy.

During the uneventful flight, she rehearsed her presentation. By the time Katrina checked into her hotel, she was set to run tomorrow's meeting at Omni-Buy, the first of several major Platform Economy companies whose software purchases she had taken away from Darla Tinibu's now struggling software empire companies – Cybergard and Syntagra.

My software apps work as well as my plan for stealing clients. Darla hasn't clue who she's losing clients to, and I'm using my hidden trapdoors to spy on what platform companies are actually doing. And I stay out of harm's way as long as Katrina stays below the radar.

Omni-Buy has greased the skids by inviting three partner companies to a meeting at its headquarters. I can use pretty much the same combo presentation-demonstration as last time. All I must do is act the part and speak in my clipped European accent. Not hard for an actress-turned-screenwriter like me.

Katrina marched purposefully towards the lobby reception area where a systems integration manager she recognized from a previous visit greeted her. He breezed her through security and into an elevator before mentioning pertinent details.

"Your latest upgrades and newest apps impress my chief information security officer. She particularly likes your company's emphasis on resilience that goes beyond simply firewalls, antivirus protection, and intrusion detection systems."

"I'm certain you realize we offer solutions at all points along the kill chain, from reconnaissance and weaponization to command-control and action."

"I don't, but she does. What are the points in between?"

"Delivery, exploitation, and installation. If she understands this, she's smarter than most. And she can leave implementation details to my apps if she buys."

"I think she's ready to sign a contract before you leave if you give us a bigger discount than you give the others."

"That will be acceptable if at least two other companies sign confidentiality agreements and buy. I assume you have the conference room prepared as before?"

"Yes, and you can start as soon as I make introductions. I've already told the people that CAT Software has apps for mining Big Data and forecasting how much target customers will buy. I forget, what does CAT stand for?"

"I shall explain the acronym when I begin." Katrina said nothing more because the elevator had reached the conference room floor. Ten minutes later she launched into her opening remarks.

"Thank you for inviting me. I am Katrina Blanka from Cognition-App Tech Software – better known in Europe as CAT Software. Our tagline is "Prowling for Profit," an endeavor companies find more and more difficult in today's challenging business environment. Platform Economy companies like yours need the best tools that provide visibility, analytics, and modeling that integrate intra and extra-networks with the Cloud while protecting 24/7 your hardware and software from outages and cybersecurity threats. By the end of our morning session, I trust you will agree that CAT software is your best choice. Let us proceed..."

Katrina walked out of the building at 1 p.m. with signed contracts from Omni-Buy plus two new clients. She had to decline an offer for lunch because she had a late afternoon flight to LA. Returning to her hotel, she packed her Katrina disguise after reappearing as Electra, then checked out and caught a cab to the airport.

The flight from SFO to LAX would be the shortest of the four on her junket – only 90 minutes – and needed the least amount of thinking time to plan ahead. She would do all that at tomorrow's morning meeting with her Cyber-Max Studio boss, Vito Buono.

Vito's words and smile always fit his mid-fifties suave Italian appearance, especially whenever Electra entered his office.

"Salve, my bella screenwriter. How lovely you look, and how fine your writing has become. Both like premier wine. Even better now than when I first hire you. And la Prezidenza agrees. Thanks to you, we are part of his entourage that will fly on chartered plane to Monte Carlo."

"Thanks for your compliments. You told me we would fly somewhere for business and pleasure; now I know where. Why Monte Carlo?"

"I describe business first. We go to Monte Carlo Film Festival so you can recommend two screenplays to buy. You must first develop a theme for a new series that will replace *Angel of Evil*. I will want you to do your editing magic so we can use one to transition from the old to the new, and the other to launch it."

"Perhaps you should have told me sooner what my assignment is."

"No-no, I know how quick and clever you are. I want you to immerse yourself in the festival's aura and let your creativity play as you walk the Grimaldi Forum."

"Your flattery always works. Tell me about the pleasure."

"Ah, a multi-venue treat, all packed into the same week. We go to Opera de Monte Carlo, which is part of Monte Carlo Casino. And we have special privileges at Monaco Grand Prix because la Prezidenza makes our studio the major Hollywood sponsor of its formula one racing team."

"I remember what you said when you were grooming me to meet la Presidenza. Jespersen Abramson is a shrewd movie mogul who likes fast cars and big cigars, and I see a Hollywood-Monaco connection. Sponsoring a team garners publicity, and Monte Carlo's glamour is a peerless movie setting. And don't forget that in 1956 Grace Kelly married Prince Raynier of Monaco. Even by today's standards, her movies are fresh and her beauty's iconic. And she wore the title Princess of Monaco with civic-minded grace. How fitting for her name and looks. How tragic the true-life fairytale ended in a car crash caused by a stroke when she was only fifty-two."

"It saddens my heart, but I take joy that she lived life to the fullest, like me. And you too, I hope. So, let us be of cheer. Let us honor her by making the most of our travel…"

The chartered plane's amenities made for a pleasant twelve-hour flight, made all the more enjoyable as Vito lectured about Monaco's past and present.

"A great place, thanks to Italians. Monaco rose to prominence when in 1297 Francois Grimaldi, disguised as a monk, seized its fortress from a rival Italian faction. In 1861, the Grimaldi family sold half of it to King Charles of France in return for money and independence, naming one of its districts Monte Carlo, which means Mount Charles. Ever since, the world's second smallest country, actually a principality ruled by a prince, has been famous for gambling and tourism." Vito asked a question when he noticed Jess seemed preoccupied.

"So, what you like to talk about now?"

"How about politics? Sorry for being an inattentive host, but I'm worried about a talk I have to give at a Hollywood PAC fundraiser when we get back. Got any ideas what I should say?"

"Electra knows all about it. Let's hear from the lady."

"My grandfather told me that talking about sex, religion, or politics is guaranteed to stir up trouble. But since Mr. Abramson asked, I can outline a safe approach. Here goes.

"Take the high road, stay above the current controversies by reviewing some definitions and defining important characteristics of our Constitution. Compare the French Revolution slogan – Liberty, Equality, Fraternity – to America's – Liberty, Equality, Justice. They're the same except France pushed for Fraternity – aka solidarity – while America pushed for Justice, aka –fairness.

"Mention that Equality is sort of the same as Democracy, but it is often at odds with Liberty. Tell how our founding fathers knew this and built into the Constitution checks and balances to keep the government operating between the lines. I'd emphasize how it uses negative rather than positive rights. All this is important for your audience because the public pays attention to Hollywood, especially in the current atmosphere of identity politics." Jess nodded slowly.

"I like this. There's more than enough to fill my time slot, and it fits the liberalism that's pushed from either the left or right. But I forget, what's the difference between negative and positive rights?"

"Negative rights are like protections against things being taken away. Usually, nothing has to be done to guarantee them. Positive rights are like entitlements for things being given. Something has to be done to make them so."

"This is damn good, better even than what our PR people were tossing at me. Would you mind writing this up?"

"I'd be happy to. I'll give you what you need by the time we fly back." Vito beamed.

"So there, problem solved. Now all of us can enjoy entire week..."

While Jess and Vito hobnobbed with the mogul types, Electra spent Monday scouring the screenwriter exhibits. By day's end she had found two indie scripts that she knew Vito would buy; she could adapt them to her new series vision and they were bargains: reasonably priced, including modest residuals. She didn't tell this to Vito. She would give him the purchase agreements at dinner tomorrow so she could use Tuesday for sightseeing by herself.

After renting a car for her Riviera tour, she ate a light dinner before returning to her hotel room where she planned her route by surfing the Web. Once that was completed, she left a voice message arranging Tuesday dinner at the hotel, then reviewed while falling asleep what she had learned.

The French Riviera, aka the Azure Coast, hugs France's southeastern Mediterranean coastline, running about 200 miles west to east from Toulon to Monaco. It became the first modern resort area at the end of the 18th century when the British upper class decided to escape England's damp and chilly winters, and the rest of the world has taken notice ever since. Jet-setters since the 1960s, movie producers, and artists of all stripes have made it a premier holiday destination. Lucky me to be here as part of Abramson's entourage.

Electra began a leisurely tour soon after sunrise, greeted by sunlight and pleasant breezes that would warm into the mid-70s. With the sun at her back, the twisty two-lane road offered postcard-quality views. She stopped at Nice to view the Chagall Museum and the ornate Nice Cathedral, then drove to Cannes where at noon she indulged one of her fantasies by walking the mile-long La Croisette

Promenade, wearing a skimpy bikini, stilettos, and designer shades to test their effect. Even at a place noted for its beautiful people and wide assortment of attire, Electra turned heads. Satisfied with her performance, she changed clothes for lunch at an outdoor café before strolling the high-end shops on Rue d'Antibes, buying two dresses for upcoming performances that would be a bit less revealing than what she wore for her pre-lunch promenade.

She parked several times on the drive back to Monaco simply to absorb all the sensations. *How refreshing to observe a privileged slice of life. No wonder tourists flock here, but the wise ones know how to put it into perspective with what really matters. It's time for me to drive on while rehearsing for dinner.*

Vito and Jess rose to greet her when she came to the table carrying a stack of papers. Vito spoke first.

"Bella, you look so serious. Show us what you got after we get you something to drink. I order you a scotch, no?"

"Thank you. And if you and Mr. Abramson like what I show, I'll have a second afterwards..." Jess summarized forty-five minutes later what he and Vito thought.

"You've become more valuable behind the camera than in front. We'll buy what you recommend and expect you to revise appropriately. So now, it's time for you to smile. Relax during the day so you can enjoy the opera tomorrow evening."

"I'll be able to do that just as soon as I start your fundraiser remarks. But I'll have that second drink before I begin writing tonight..."

By noon the next day Electra had completed all the work standing in the way of fun, then took a workout in the hotel's fitness center and swam enough laps in the pool to slow her obsessive-compulsive pace. After lunch she ambled to the nearby Monaco Cathedral while en route to the Oceanographic Museum, then circled back along Larvotto Beach, reserving the remainder of the afternoon to prepare for the opera. While showering and shampooing her hair, she decided what jewelry to wear with her newly purchased lowcut long black gown.

My signature gold lightning-bolt earrings and gold medallion mounted on a black-velvet neck choker will accentuate my black-tinted eye goggle. That will make a statement. And the gown shows just enough cleavage to hint at my tattoo-like scar. I'll be attired for a fine performance.

When Electra met Jess and Vito in the lobby for a short cab ride to a restaurant near Opera de Monte Carlo, her striking appearance silenced Jess, but a garrulous Vito filled the void.

Bella, bella. Your beauty hits like what we see tonight, Verdi's *La forze del destino*. I tell you and la Prezidenza all about it. Let us go."

Vito's pre-performance summary added to the group's overall enjoyment, which they recapped over drinks at the hotel. Afterwards, Jess recited Thursday's schedule.

"Tomorrow, both of you can dress like Hollywood, but I change into my formula one uniform, figuratively speaking that is. I go to owners' meeting first, then one for teams. And don't forget, tomorrow evening's the Grand Prix owners-sponsors reception."

Vito said, "No worries. During day, Electra and I cover film festival, while you cover race preparations. And at night, we make fine Hollywood statement at reception, no?" Electra smiled inwardly. *Indeed.*

By mid-afternoon the next day, Vito declared she had graduated from his one-day movers and shakers mentoring seminar.

"So you see, most are just regular people trying to do what's good. And they see you have brains and beauty, and a style they like. You gonna be a Hollywood world beater, no?"

"If so, it's thanks to you. And on that topic, how should the Hollywood team do in the Grand Prix?"

"La Prezidenza happy anytime we finish high enough to get publicity. He say it always add to Hollywood buzz. Let's see what we can do tonight."

Electra played her role perfectly. Her Ferrari-red, formfitting low-cut and short designer dress lit up the reception area. A gold-tinted eye goggle, red stilettos, and a small gold purse completed her peerless appearance. Jess and Vito basked in her aura, and whenever she pulled a mini-cigar from her purse, there were always lighters or matches awaiting her choice.

Most of the talk centered on the upcoming race. Jess said,

"Actually, there are two, the Sunday Grand Prix and the Saturday afternoon Shadow Grand Prix charity race." The owner of another team gave details.

"Fans love the shadow race. It's festive and builds excitement for Sunday. All entries use identical pro-style go-karts that have been throttled back for safety, but they can reach speeds close to 100 mph. They can be driven by anyone other than a professional racecar driver. There are as many laps raced on the actual Grand Prix course as the number of cars entered in the big race. Total distance is about 40 miles and takes less than an hour. Starting grid positions determined by a random drawing. So, what number did you pull?"

"I've been so busy I forgot to ask, but I'll find out from the owner."

"The sponsor of each team picks the driver. Which Hollywood celebrity do you have in mind?"

"Haven't thought about it but not to worry. Lots of Hollywood types here. I'll make a couple of calls and fill the cockpit."

"Keep in mind that the names of the drivers are kept secret until they're eliminated. The race format is miss-and-out, which means the last car at the end of every lap is pulled, and that makes for win-or-go-home action at the back of the pack on every lap. Very exciting.

And good luck picking a driver. Expect the race to be competitive; about half the drivers might be retired professionals. The rest are popular celebrities or public figures the fans like to root for. And the top three finishers get trophies and bragging rights. I'll see you in the pits."

Electra kept quiet during the chatter, letting her sophisticated and insouciant exterior speak, but the shadow race sparked passions from adolescence. *I loved racing go-karts and driving my stealth street racer when I was a teen-ager. And I'm still taking racecar driving lessons. Perhaps I can indulge another fantasy.*

Vito became her unwitting ally on the ride back to the hotel; he jokingly asked,

"So bella, can you drive as good as you write or look?"

"I might surprise you. Speed thrills me. I raced go-karts in my youth, and toured Texas on a high-speed motor cycle."

Jess perked up.

"Hmm, I see publicity angles. How does this sound – 'Unheralded, gorgeous Hollywood studio junior exec boldly challenges the formula one racing world to thrill fans and be an inspirational role model.' But we don't want to get you injured. I'll arrange some practice laps for you to decide if you can handle the job. You interested?"

"I'll let you know after some practice laps. And like I said, I might surprise. I always try to under-promise and overdeliver."

Chapter 7
May 2133

"Beyond the Monte Carlo Caper"

Howard Brubaker, owner of Team Hollywood, stood at 6 a.m. Friday morning in his team's garage area, ready to give a talk that could lead to the checkered flag three days away.

"Here we are once again, ready to score points in the jewel of auto racing's triple crown. This year, our car is the Chevy Corvette, constructed by GM. The Monaco Grand Prix has been run since 1929, and unlike the Indy 500 or 24 Hours at Le Mans, its tight and twisty course challenges even the best cars and drivers. Passing is difficult, which makes a good qualifying position even more important. Our job for today and tomorrow is to qualify as close to the front as possible, tweaking engine and chassis so Milo can place in the top five on Sunday. And we'll prep for good weather because that's what the forecast says. So, let's get to it. I know our team can do it."

Jess introduced Electra to Howard as the team began heading out.

"This is my driver for the Shadow Race. When can she grab some practice laps?" Howard studied her as he spoke.

"Have her take them now while the course is still closed. Has she studied it?"

"In maps and on the Web, but not mano-a-mano. Can she talk to our drivers?"

"Sure, but do it now before they get too intense. I'll introduce you." Howard waved while shouting,

"Hey Milo, I've got someone you'll want to meet."

As he cruised towards the trio, closely followed by a younger fellow of similar build, Electra sized them up.

The guy in the lead looks the part, just like those great Andretti drivers who raced to greatness more than a century ago. Though he's showing a touch of gray, he's probably got a few more laps. And the clean-cut guy following him looks like he could have graduated not too long ago from my West Coast driving school. But he doesn't have that confident swagger pro drivers have. Perhaps Milo can boost his confidence as well as his driving skills.

"What's up boss? This my escort to party?"

"This is our driver for the shadow race. She'd like some pointers. Say hello to Electra Kittner."

Milo's polite smile and handshake reminded her of Vito while she reminded herself how to act. *I better talk first and project confidence. Otherwise, he'll put me in the back seat. My grip's not as strong as Robin's, but it's stronger than a lot of guys. Let's see if I can hang in there and surprise.* Milo's smile widened as Electra spoke.

"It's a pleasure to meet you. I know you and your backup want to focus on race preparation, so I promise to be a quick study if you would take me through the kart and course."

"Me and Rex pretty set. You a good change of pace. Rex, come say hi."

Rex made tentative eye contact when first shaking her hand, but loosened up when she said,

"You look familiar. Maybe I've seen you on media because I follow Formula One racing. I also take racecar driving lessons when working in Hollywood. Maybe I've seen you at one of the schools."

"I wish I'd seen you first. Even in Hollywood, you'd catch a guy's eye. And if you've already taken some lessons, you'll get what we show and tell." Rex turned to Milo, who said,

"Rex got a great head for racing. All he need is bit more heart and he reach winners circle with cars and ladies. But we focus on cars now…"

Milo explained for the next hour how to drive the course, using a map and Internet videos for added clarity.

"Notice how race runs right along shore in heart of Monte Carlo. Even pit lane is close to stores and streets. But no sightseeing allowed. Focus on course and car. How long since you raced go-karts?"

"Don't judge my skill by the calendar. Do it with the stopwatch."

Rex said, "Why don't I suit up too and I'll follow you around the course. Milo can observe using the videocams." Milo nodded, so off they went.

Two hours and twenty laps later, Rex scored Electra's performance.

"Excellant-a. You drive like a pro. First couple of laps gave you a feel for the kart and corners, and then you accelerated on each lap, testing different turns each time. You've got lightning-fast reflexes. Let's hear from Milo."

"You got the looks and you got what it takes, and I got idea. Stick with us and you drive a couple of laps in my car after I qualify."

"Electra did just that, mindful not to interfere. *These guys fit the f1 driver image…fit, trim, and about my size. Milo can look me in the eye without blinking, but Rex won't. He has youth and reflexes going for him, but he doesn't have that aggressive confidence pro drivers share with fighter pilots. But he sure knows racecar electronics and communications gear. Being in the cockpit's like being in the space shuttle. And it's user friendly too, easy to use the controls once you crawl in. With so much computerization, I wonder how long it'll take AI driving apps to beat the pros? Not this year, but maybe soon.*

Electra drove laps mid-afternoon, stopping once for hands-on pointers. Milo applauded when she cruised into the pit after her final laps. Rex chimed in after she climbed out.

"Your last lap time comes close to mine. With a bit more practice, you'd race me to a dead heat."

Milo said, "She gotta go right from get-set tomorrow. I check grid position… second row from the back, so you gotta push no later than lap three. But that's good. You already be racing by time you start passing guys up front. Let's us three talk more after showering and eating."

Milo told about the Monaco mystique while they ate.

"We racing in most glamorous racing event in world. Beautiful people watch us fly by beautiful places and harbor holding big yachts owned by rich and famous. All turns named after legendary buildings or racers. You study course again before getting good night's sleep. And try to relax behind wheel tomorrow…"

The Hollywood team prepped Milo's car before setting up Electra's go-kart for her race that would get the green light at 3 p.m. At 1 p.m. she started prepping herself.

I used to call myself Kit when strapping on my game face. I still can, but I let no one else. And the lightning brain will elevate to a higher state that merges all my personas. When it does, let the competition beware.

Electra's team tried to downplay a poor grid position, but their good wishes weren't actually needed. It was good the competition couldn't see her eyes after she strapped on her helmet; their intensity would have intimidated the faint of heart. The weather had changed to a cool overcast, but no rain was expected until later that night.

The light turned green at 3:10, signaling the start of a warmup lap. As soon as the front grid cars crossed the starting line for the second lap, all cars roared off to the races. As drivers shifted to find the right gear, so did the lightning brain.

It didn't matter that Electra didn't know the drivers she was passing, for she was totally engaged in the moment, judging for herself what moves to make and when. She knew when to glance in the rearview mirror to avoid being in last place. Whenever that threatened, she accelerated on a straightaway or downshifted into a tight turn to fly by another car.

Crews couldn't use radio communications because that wasn't allowed in the Shadow Race, but the lightning brain instinctively kept track of laps and position. Electra's focus slowed the world whizzing past. She was in total command, inside the decision loop of other drivers as well as the course.

"Three cars ahead and two behind. I toy with the car ahead for two more laps, then I shift to the next gear.

Electra was in fourth place with four laps to go. Darwinian survival of the fittest had selected them for the trophy run that had now begun.

And her extraordinary memory gave her an advantage. She picked precisely the right places to attempt passing. Though it took several attempts, she mowed down car number three.

Now there were only two cars spaced five lengths apart between Electra and victory. She closed the gap on car number two as they raced out of the Casino curve, accelerating towards the Mirabou hairpin in preparation for the tightest turn of all, the Loews hairpin that needs maximum finesse and minimum speed.

Electra's nerves and reflexes surpassed those of driver number two. She downshifted later, racing past the car midway through Mirabou, then blasted from first to fourth gear as she drew a bead on the leader. But lightning struck as she braked and downshifted into Loews.

Electra had driven beyond the go-kart's performance envelope. The gearbox exploded and the right front suspension broke, tumbling the cart upside down to a dead stop. Only the roll-bar kept her from serious injury.

Electra's crash was the only yellow flag in the race; the rescue squad had her safely off the course by the time the last two cars raced for the checkered flag. Soon after she joined her worried crew in pit row. Milo spoke first.

"You stronger, you better than machine."

Then Howard said, "There's no difference between first and third. You've won us great publicity in a style that's bound to make the news."

By now the lightning brain had shifted to a lower gear; Electra's intimidating demeanor had vanished and she was ready to savor the moment. Jess added to Howard's words.

"You were magnificent. Drone and onboard camera put us in the cockpit. It was even better than Hollywood. I could feel my stomach turn when you flipped. Thank god for the roll bar." Electra's smile lighted the darkening afternoon.

"I'm amazed at all the hoopla for the Shadow Race. Tomorrow's big event should be an even greater show. How nice we have preferred seating."

Vito said, "For dinner too. I treat you and Milo and Rex to dinner while La Prezidenza and Mr. Brubaker see to crew. Come, let us go…"

Dinnertime talk shifted from today's victory to the possibility of an even bigger one tomorrow. Milo exuded more than enough confidence to make up for Rex's hesitant attitude, which prompted Vito to say,

"Do not brood about who gets glory. Someday you grab spotlight." Rex smiled awkwardly, fumbling for words until Electra spoke up.

"Don't worry about him. He'll rise to the challenge when it's his turn."

Milo said, "I like Electra last word. I ready to turn in to rest body and mind and settle stomach. Maybe I eat too much."

Vito said, "Ciao to my veloci amici. I wait for bill and be at pit tomorrow if weather OK. If not, I watch broadcast. Either way, I be with you."

It was fortunate that Rex was the designated driver because Milo's stomach pains turned worse on the drive to the hotel. Suddenly, he doubled up in the back seat and shouted,

"My gut feels like too full tire. Get me to hospital before it explodes." Rex raced to the closest emergency room: that of Hopital de Monaco.

Two hours later, the attending physician diagnosed the problem.

"You have a congenital hiatal hernia. Whatever you've been doing recently has widened the abdominal muscle separation. I was able to massage the intestines back into place, but any sudden exertion will pop it out immediately. You can leave now, but you need minor surgery to fix the problem. See your regular doctor when you get home."

The doctor didn't ask, nor did anyone tell, that Milo was driving in tomorrow's race, for if he had known, he would have ruled against Milo's racing. His unspoken warning worried everyone, making the drive back to the hotel feel like riding in a hearse. It was deathly quiet until Electra spoke.

"We've got a big problem if we don't make a new race plan. Let's get to Milo's room and figure out what to do. I've got an idea, and if you listen to me and do what I say, our odds'll be better tomorrow. And no matter the weather, tomorrow will be an exceptional day…"

The Hollywood crew working in the garage were too busy to pay much attention when Milo and Rex strode confidently towards Howard. He was confident too.

"We're slapping on rain tires and adjusting drag, downforce, and traction control systems. We've tweaked the fuel system too because cooler temps will increase horsepower and lower the risk of running out of fuel."

Both drivers cracked tiny smiles before Rex said, "I can drive in the rain almost as well as Milo, and his last name says it all. Aquino, in Italian, means water."

Milo added, "And I use all half-hour warmup before green light to get feel for conditions. So no one don't worry, be happy. Roll car to grid and keep covered until 2:30 when Rex and I show up, all suited up and ready to roll."

Steady rainfall greeted everyone at the grid. Rex had already snapped Milo's visor-equipped helmet into place, and he repeated instructions one more time after the driver climbed in.

"I'll be in pit row manning communications with you in the cockpit. Let me know how car and driver feel and when you want to pit. And remember, we can refuel on any pit stop. The driver gave a thumbs up, then disappeared into the rain as the engine revved and the car accelerated.

Howard said, "Egad, the sights and sounds thrill me even more when it's bad weather. The fumes and whooshing tires add to it, and seeing our logos and Milo's scrawling signature on his helmet say it all. I hope the outcome will do the same." Rex nodded before adding the only exclamation point needed.

"The bad weather's shrinking the number watching in the grandstand or on the racecourse, but not the enthusiasm. It's simply driving more indoors to watch the cable broadcast. I hope the guy calling the race is still around when you let me start. Listeners love him."

"You will as soon as I know your confidence matches your skills. Let's get to our positions…"

The current commentator patterned himself after Graham Greene, the legendary dean of motorsport commentators, whose energetically articulate British accent entertained for decades all the pre-to-postrace drama, using details from current Grand Prix or storied races from the past. And while most of Monte Carlo was tuning in, Electra was tuning out everything except what was flashing by the cockpit of the racecar. She was behind the wheel, acclimating herself to the course, car, and rain tires while stream-of-consciousness flashed by in her brain.

The hardest part of our shell game caper is in the rearview mirror. Psychology can explain… intentional blindness says so. People see what they expect. Milo's signature on the helmet told all he's driving. Long ago I saw a classic video… people ignoring a gorilla in their midst when they were focused on something else.

Good for us… no matter the outcome, I'm invisible and Milo's an instant legend. And if Rex plays his part, he's got a shot at becoming the man who raced away from his doubt… driving in the rain to victory and a bright future.

The announcer accelerated his delivery when lights blinked green.

"And it's go for magnificent men racing multi-million-dollar cars seventy-eight laps to a prize seized by only the chosen few, victory at the Monaco Grand Prix. And I never prophesy a winner because anything can happen and usually does. As you may not know, Formula One races are limited to two hours and 305 kilometers. We shall learn as the laps expire if weather eats into those numbers. No matter, because bad weather often adds to storylines that will reveal themselves today. So stay with me as I bring it all to you…"

He kept a stream of monologue that was as steady as the rain. Both kept the race moving, but in different directions for fans and drivers.

"... With half the race gone, there's still half a race to go. Only two yellow flags so far for crashes that took out two pre-race favorites. Drivers continue pushing the pace in spite of the rain, and that might be the reason for the surprising performance of Team Hollywood. Milo Aquino, famous for racing in the rain, has progressed steadily from mid-grid to fifth. And though his career is well past midway, today's inspired driving is rewarding Team Hollywood for picking him up after being unceremoniously ejected by Ferrari at the end of last season. He may be the right pick to help young American Rex Crawford, who intermittently shows flashes of promise, overcome yips. Add to all that the iconic Corvette and you have the ingredients for an all-American storybook finish. The ending will be written by the checkered flag, so please be with me when it is waved..."

With twenty laps remaining, Electra had now raced into fourth place.

I've reached the limit of my driving ability and I'm running out of energy. It's a couple of laps sooner than we planned, but I gotta make the call now."

Rex was the only person manning communications at the Hollywood pit when it crackled in.

"Med-Med. Gotta pit. Get close."

Rex yelled to his skeleton crew, "Milo's sick! He's not far from pit row entrance. I gotta get to him." Rex grabbed his helmet and sprinted away.

Only a handful of on-site people saw the indistinct action shrouded by the rain. Luckily for the announcer, the drone videocam captured it all.

"Oh my! The Hollywood car coasted to a stop just before entering pit lane. Milo is staggering out of the cockpit. What's this?... someone is dragging him away... Milo's on his feet now... he's stumbling towards a vehicle... Milo's crawling into a van... now the other person is sprinting back to the car... what's this? It must be young Rex Crawford. He's strapping on his helmet and climbing in. And now he's rejoining the race. Brave move and not much time lost. We'll get a report from Hollywood pit ASAP. Stay tuned."

Fully suited, Milo drove the van while Electra pulled on oversized sweatshirt and pants after tossing her helmet to him. He had forced enough weight loss earlier and doused himself with enough water to fake driving the race. Stopping so they could swap places, he listened to Electra's final instructions.

"I'll drive and drag you to the med station. When they take you in and your suit off, act like you're in pain and try to pop out a bit of intestines. I'll be gone by then. You take it from there. And so will Rex."

Electra played her part before driving to the hotel, parking Vito's rented van. Vito would never know because he and Jess were watching the broadcast while seated next to Howard in reserved viewing.

She snuck undetected into her room and drank two bottles of water before wolfing down a couple Snickers bars. Then she slipped out of her clothes and into a hot, soaking shower. By the time she was out of the shower and in front of a TV monitor, the announcer's recap of the finish told her all she needed to know.

"And so ends another sui generis Monaco Grand Prix, one in which two Hollywood team drivers raced through barriers caused by rain, pain, and doubt to reach multiple victories. Veteran Milo Aquino will forever be known as the man who drove far enough through the pain of a gut-wrenching hernia to pass the baton to young Rex Chapman, whose twenty-lap hard charge swept past five of the six ahead and proved beyond a doubt he can deliver. And with two laps to go, the gods of Grand Prix racing struck once again. For the first time ever, a crash at Portiers corner hurled the leader into Monte Carlo harbor. A Hollywood scriptwriter couldn't write a more unbelievable finish, which proves how fantastic reality can be…"

A call from Vito to Electra's cell phone ended her musing about an improved ending.

"We miss you, bella. La Presidenza so happy he give you and me each twenty-five hundred dollars to break Monte Carlo Casino bank while he and Howard party. I come get you, no?"

"That's one of my fantasies too, but I'm too tired from yesterday and need to put finishing touches on Jess's remarks. Why don't you pool our money and gamble? What's your game?"

"Blackjack. I do what you say and we split winnings. Until tomorrow, you rest and I play. Then we compare notes on plane. Ciao."

Electra dressed, then went to the hotel restaurant where she ate deliberately while planning tomorrow's agenda.

First things first. I'll take only one bag containing laptop and minimal belongings... the rest of my luggage is already stowed on Jess's plane. I get up at five and into my Katrina Blanka disguise, then slip under Vito's door an envelope containing Jess's talk and a note explaining why I had to leave early. Next, I enjoy a four-hour drive to Lyon for a noon flight to Warsaw.

A clearing sunrise promised weather that framed picturesque views of France's gently rolling, forested countryside dotted with quaint towns reminiscent of distant centuries. Not so for Lyon, a bustling city of 500,000 mixing the best of the old and the new, while its Saint Exupery airport, eleven miles southeast of the city, makes a bold architectural projection into the future.

Katrina's plane landed at Chopin Airport at 3:30. Thirty minutes later, an S2 shuttle train whisked her the remaining ten miles north to the center of the city. She knew enough about Warsaw to be her own travel guide.

A city of 200,000, it's Poland's capital and often called the Paris of the East because of its beauty and rich cultural heritage. Ravaged by WWII, since then it's sometimes called Phoenix City because it rose from the ashes to embrace American virtues.

This is my first visit to my virtual CAT software company headquartered in a shell office building. I'll compare what I've seen on the Internet to 3-D reality. And I know how to take public transportation to get there... wide boulevards running fully automated trams and buses are lined by well-maintained buildings. No wonder the country's economy rivals Germany's.

Katrina had already practiced her delivery when at 5:45 she reached the building's security desk staffed by two professionally dressed young administrators.

"Good afternoon. I am Katrina Blanka. My company, CAT Software, has office privileges. I am here to claim any messages and mail, and to use an office. I am pleased the building is staffed 24/7 because I am uncertain when I will leave."

The female said, "My name is Yasna. Please give me your I.D. I will confirm it while Jon checks our database. Ten minutes later, Jon handed Katrina a slim packet of mail and two call slips.

Yasna gave her a card key before saying, "We've slotted you in Office 3 Suite 1. Take the elevator to the third floor. Instructions for using phone, computer, and network are on credenza behind desk. Please call security if you need assistance."

Jon said, "According to our database, CAT stands for Cognition-App Tech Software. I doubt you will need our help. And I commend how well you run your company remotely. This is the first time you have visited."

"Of course. The Internet makes virtual companies a reality. Thank you for your hospitality. I'm certain I shall enjoy my stay."

Katrina's exterior expression and voice would have disguised her puzzlement to anyone but herself.

How strange, no messages have ever been left here before. Who might have linked Katrina Blanka to this location and number? I better check into this before I check out.

After setting up and logging on, Katrina paced herself by sorting through Emails and outlining a to-do list before responding to those she could. Fatigue and hunger began to set in three hours later. The vending machines stocked unknown brands except for Coca Cola and Oreos. Wanting more than a snack, she went to the security desk for a convenient restaurant recommendation. A different set of administrators confirmed her I.D.

Then the older one said,

"I assume you'll contact your associates to tell them our recommendation. Two have called to ask if you've left the building."

"I will as soon as you give me the address." A minute later, Katrina calmly walked back to the elevator, but the lightning brain was running through scenarios.

Somehow, something's hacked me. I'll settle for a sugar and caffeine jolt before hunting it down and planning my exit strategy.

The lightning brain didn't panic; Electra consumed Oreos and Cokes as she methodically searched for leaks using her proprietary Network Security tools. She came away empty three hours later.

Either something's got apps better than mine, or someone who I've shared sensitive data with has been compromised. I better go now and search later. It's only 6 p.m. in D.C. and I've got thirteen hours to kill before my flight to D.C. I'll call Robin.

Electra had to leave a message because Robin didn't answer. She recited flight number and arrival time but said don't pick her up because international flight details often change at the last minute. Then she closed her eyes, withdrawing into herself to weigh options. She roused herself at 1 a.m., packed in more Coke and Oreos, and headed for the security desk.

"I am leaving now. I assume the airport S2 runs 24/7 too, just like you."

"As does all Warsaw public transit systems. Cabs or rideshares aren't too frequent at this time, but you should have no difficulty. Might we call one for you?"

"Thanks, but no. I'll walk to an S2 station."

"As you wish. Warsaw is one of the safest cities in the EU. We wish a safe journey wherever your travels take you."

Warsaw may be safe, but open borders allow EU thugs free access. Two cars containing two each had been parked in the shadows, ready to intercept what should be a soft target: Katrina Blanka. They had been hired late yesterday, given only flight number, photo, and address. They had divided into teams that tracked her from arrival to S2 to building before staking front and back entrances. Several calls earlier to building security confirmed she was still inside. They waited patiently, surreptitiously for their quarry. The front car driver came to life at 1:10.

"That's gotta be Blanka. Her pudgy shape and travel bag make her easy pickings. Go bring her to the car. Just show her your gun. That should make it even easier."

Electra had walked two blocks, passing close to storefronts displaying a variety of merchandise. Street and foot traffic were nonexistent, and she pretended not to hear accelerating footsteps approaching from behind. When a hand rudely grabbed her shoulder, whipping her around, she dropped her bag and froze to face a stocky, unshaven fellow several inches shorter than she. His revealed weapon and guttural accent left no doubt he meant business.

"Don't be afraid Miss Katrina. I only want you to meet some friends. Be nice and come with me."

Electra staggered forward, penetrating his defensive perimeter. Gloating to himself, the thug reached out to support her, giving her a sought-after opening.

Electra's hands grabbed hunks of stringy hair, then swung her attacker's head like a battering ram into the glass storefront. Arm leverage and body torque crashed it through the glass; as he collapsed awkwardly on his back, a jagged shard fell like a guillotine blade, slicing into his neck. Electra didn't stop to assess damage; she grabbed his gun and her suitcase and charged down the nearest cross street.

The driver gaped mutely at the remains of the battle before squealing in pursuit. Two bullets shattered the driver's side window as soon as he cornered, bringing car and driver to dead stops. Approaching warily, Electra detected life only in the idling engine when she opened the door. She unbuckled the driver, shoving and fastening him into the passenger's side before throwing her suitcase onto the back seat and then getting behind the wheel.

Electra's driver instincts took control. A quick study of dashboard and gearshift revealed when she revved the engine that serendipity had given her a prize worth more at this moment than all the money in Monte Carlo's casino. This seemingly humble sedan had been modified into a high-performance beast. Visions of her stealth street racer from high school days flashed in her brain. She put on the dead man's gloves before shifting gears and blasting away.

The driver of the second car had driven down the alley towards the commotion as soon as he heard it, and he gave chase when the silhouette of first car flashed by. He was certain his driving skills had to be better than the competition's, but highspeed turns and receding taillights gave a different story. He was about to end pursuit ten minutes later, but the wail of a police siren off to the side kept him going.

Reveling in the third race in three days, Electra was flying high when flashing lights latched onto her tail. She swerved down a broad boulevard and accelerated, gaining enough distance on the police car to pull a stunt only elite drivers can handle. She slammed the brakes and gear-shifted into reverse forcing a one-eighty, then shifted to forward and floored the accelerator. The car roared directly towards the squad car whose driver panicked; he jerked the wheel to his right, tipping the car onto two wheels just before it sailed into a glass storefront.

Electra sped by but had to force another one-eighty because the headlights of the second car were bearing down. She roared by the crash site for a second time, gaining speed and distance with every second. The second car's driver was smart enough to quit when he saw what had happened to the police.

Electra saw it all in the rearview mirror. She slowed and zig-zagged down several streets until she felt safe enough to downshift her brain and select a contingency plan.

I could do some nighttime sightseeing, but this is neither time nor place to press my luck. It's almost 3 a.m… time to ditch the car near an S2 station and decompress at the airport. How nice the onboard computer understands English.

Arriving at five, Electra had only one more chore to complete her vanishing act. After entering an empty restroom, she stripped off the Katrina disguise and put on travel clothes, then she destroyed and stuffed its remains in a janitor's cart instead of her bag because travelers never know when their luggage might be searched. Then she strolled to a cafeteria for a leisurely breakfast of oatmeal and muffins. By 7:30, she had checked in and set herself up in the British Airways travelers' lounge.

I'm still keyed up. I'll use the three hours before boarding to get computer work out of the way. I can surf, check Emails or news, and do project work. Then I'll have twelve-hours to daydream and sleep.

There were no Internet glitches or flight delays. As the plane soared westward, leaving yesterday's troubles behind, Electra tucked into a pillow and reclined.

What could have been my worst nightmare added to what the entire Monte Carlo caper taught me... stay focused and live in the now to connect when needed to past events... use them instinctively, then let them vanish into memory. Don't be greedy, let them go... avoid paralysis from too much philosophic analysis... put doubts behind and never feel a whit of fear about failure or death if I keep the faith and try my best. The first verse of an Indira poem says so:

> *For those who have conviction and faith,*
> *Their journey sure their sleep secure.*
> *Compared to me doubt comes as wraith,*
> *Haunting this life I must endure.*

Other pleasant thoughts came to mind, transporting Electra to a restful state that lasted all the way to D.C.

A flight attendant jostled her awake as the plane descended. She stretched, feeling the joy of simply being alive. Suddenly, an odd emotion jolted her.

I'm coming home, coming home to a family, to Robin and Qama, and to the twins. I've missed them. Soon they'll fill the void.

Spotting Electra first, Qama ran to greet her near the baggage carousel. Robin was close behind. Electra swept Qama into her arms before kissing Robin full on the lips.

"I'm glad you ignored my instructions. It's so good to see you."

"We missed you Moma, both of us."

"I missed you too. It's so nice to come home. Let me put you down and pick up my suitcase, and then I want to hear all about what you and Auntie Robin have been doing..." Qama did most of the talking during the drive.

After Qama led them into the living room, Robin said,

"You look tired. Why don't you take a shower and let Qama and me unpack your stuff? Then you can sleep with me."

"I'll take you up on two of the three. I'll unpack tomorrow." Qama's alert ears prompted a question directed at Robin.

"Does that mean I can't be with you tonight?"

Robin's eyes caught Electra's, synchronizing their smiles, but Robin spoke first.

"You'll have the place of honor. You can sleep in the middle. And we'll have a race. First one asleep wins the best dream."

An hour later, as Qama slept peacefully, Robin whispered,

"When the twins get bigger, we'll need a bed that'll hold more than three, so there's always room for you next to me."

Electra kissed her one more time before saying,

"I second that emotion. Goodnight, my love."

Through the amplified silence of a calming dark, Electra sensed that her words had found the mark. Robin's sigh said it all.

Chapter 8
July 2133

"Celebration"

Electra's sudden epiphany regarding the joy of family and friends brought about changes, but she would tell no one but herself.

I promise to control my frenetic work ethic so I'm less borderline OCD and better at enjoying what's right in front of me. And tending to Qama will help me soften further the harder edges of my emotional persona. That'll remind me to be a kind and authentic person when dealing with my precious family and circle of close friends.

And I'll be more understanding with associates too, letting my empathy come out. I'll let it all show through in my actions. They communicate even better than words.

Electra found joy engaging in life's mundane activities. House chores and grocery shopping became games. For too many years she had denied herself too much exposure to the world of feelings. Now she would seek to engage every day.

Bounding into the kitchen at 8 a.m. after finishing her 10-mile sunrise run on the second Saturday in July, Electra expected to find everyone eating breakfast and Qama quizzing Robin about today's shopping spree, but Qama wasn't there. Electra was about to ask, but Robin's question came first.

"Didn't you detect a fragrance on Qama when you came home last night?"

"No, I thought that was your cologne. Why?"

82

"Qama was sampling your perfumes. I told her she should get your permission before going through your things. Did she tell you about this?"

"No. I bet she thinks I'll be angry. I better go see her before she gets too upset."

That wouldn't be necessary. Qama shuffled into the kitchen. Trembling lips on an uncertain expression kept her from speaking, so Electra hugged her before setting her on the countertop. Mother and daughter were now seeing eye-to-eye. Electra kissed her on the forehead before talking.

"Mmm, you're wearing a pretty fragrance. I like it. I bet you do too."

The tiny child burst into tears, hugging Electra as her words tumbled out.

"Moma, I'm sorry. Please don't be mad. I won't go through your stuff again, I promise, I –" Electra rubbed Qama's hair before replacing her daughter's cascade of words with her own.

"You can look through my stuff anytime you like, but just remember what we've already told you. Never-never look inside the medicine cabinet or take pills unless you're with Aunt Robin or me. And when you get to be a teenager, we'll show you how to use makeup. Can you tell me how old you'll have to be?"

"Yes, Moma. Thirteen, and I'll be thirteen in seven more years."

"Well, we won't wait that long to get you perfume. Why don't you go surf the Web right now to find a perfume you might like? Then, we'll shop for it this afternoon."

"I will, I will. Oh, thank you Moma, and I promise to be extra good. Thank you, Aunt Robin, for not telling on me." After lifting her off the counter and watching her scoot away, Electra was about to ask about the twins but waited for Robin, who was suddenly wearing a puzzled expression, to say something.

"I've been meaning to ask why you take pills every morning. Look, I'm not spying on you, but now that we're officially co-friends, shouldn't I know the reason? After all, I let you know when I'm taking Rx-meds for bad headaches or bouts of depression."

"And I'm glad you need them less often. You told me CBD and THC potentiate that new herb you're taking and you've adjusted your dosage regimen accordingly. Is it working?"

"Stop tossing big words around and give me an answer."

"Sorry. Look, I have a chronic condition I keep in remission by taking medication once a day. Believe me, I'm fine."

"Come on, don't be so evasive. What is it?"

"It's like an STD. If I don't take them, unprotected sex could be risky. And please don't be concerned. It's impossible for me to infect you."

"I worry about you, not me. I don't want to lose you."

"You won't, so let's talk about shopping for next Saturday's co-friend celebration. You can tell me all about what Zoe and you've been planning." Robin's reluctant silence provoked Electra to say more.

"Is something else bothering you?"

"Maybe I'm not as good a co-friend as I could be. Now that we're together so much, I'm afraid you'll discover quirks you won't like. It happens all the time between males and females."

"And you already know why. Though they're much better than a hundred years ago, males still have difficulty being honest in heterosexual relationships. They often pretend to be what they're not until they've got what they want. I could never say that about you. You're like a bubbling brook, emotions popping through the surface all the time, whetting my empathy and sharpening my authenticity by forcing me to put relationships ahead of results. And your quirkiness often leads to surprises. You're the one who started reading stories like *Paddington Bear* to Qama."

"I guess you're right. She likes the happy-ending connections I make to the little-lonely orphan bear. And the message in *The Velveteen Rabbit* connects you and me. We've known each other long enough to see the real us. There're pieces of you that're still invisible, but that's not for me to fret about. What I do see is all I need. Come on, let's collect everyone and go shopping..."

Pleasant mid-July weather minimized indoor mall traffic, removing most obstacles for Qama's pushing the tandem stroller, an activity she always volunteered for. Robin led the way for buying next Saturday's new outfits. Then Electra took charge for buying perfume. Although Hollywood's glamourous lifestyle had educated her, she let the fragrance consultants explain the basics to Qama. Treating her like a mini-adult, they let her sample several, and when two tied for best, Electra let her buy both. Qama's joy sparked silent words.

Robin sometimes says I'm too lenient, but that's not true. I'll do all I can to make up for what Qama's been through. And wait until they see my next surprise. Electra led them to a jewelry store that contained three: matching co-friend rings and a special necklace for Qama. She was almost speechless. But not quite.

"Oh Moma, it's so pretty. Can I wear it right now?"

"Of course you can. It's a gold talisman given to me long ago. Can you guess what a talisman is?" Qama studied it closely before answering.

"Is it a good luck charm? People in my old village wore them."

"Yes, and you are very smart for figuring it out. And just like you, this one is very special. It's in a special mounting that has a tracking chip. If it ever gets lost, we'll know where it is."

"I promise, I won't ever lose it. I'll wear it every day." Robin's words brought the shopping expedition to an end.

"And your Moma and I will do the same with our rings. That way, none of the jewelry will ever get lost. And to reward all of us for being so good today, I'll treat to ice cream. I know the way to the best place…"

Electra had slogged unsuccessfully, searching for the hacking source ever since her Warsaw escape, but even her best security tools found nothing.

I'm stymied. At least one of my adversaries has an intrusion app better than my detection alarms. I better compile a list of associates who might have been compromised. Their data breach could have led an enemy to me. They might know who it could be.

I have four separate worlds besides my personal life in which I'm currently active: R&D, Business, Politics, and Hollywood. Only Su and Tim touch tangentially on two. Everyone else remains in just one, making it easier to identify the high-priority people.

Electra had what she needed an hour later.

I'll have to pace myself. There are too many, even if I spent a month of Sundays calling. I'll see some on Saturday, but there's one near the top who won't be at the celebration, so I'll call him first.

Hud Haller answered on the fourth ring.

"Howdy, Lectra. Sorry I can't fly in for your co-friend party, but I'm so busy I wish I was twins. I was expecting you to call and I can tell you all's going gangbusters, just like one of your phrases says... nothing but blue sky, green trees, and ducks swimming. Where do you wanna start?"

"Please keep this confidential, but I've been hacked and I don't know who or how. Can you think of anyone new you've talked to recently who might connect me to you?"

"Uh, no, but the minute I do I'll call you. Is it serious?"

"I'm concerned but not worried. You shouldn't either; just call me if something new turns up. And now, please tell me all the good stuff..."

Buffy and Carter were about to talk Friday at dinner about tomorrow evening's Kittner-Setdarova co-friend celebration. She would listen closely instead of asking too many pointed questions, instead letting him ramble on after her conversation-starting observation.

"Zoe got a party discount because of your connections. And it's sweet of you to give the welcoming talk." Carter's self-conscious expression colored his words.

"Ironic too. Ten years ago I was supposed to give one at a surprise co-friend celebration I set up for Electra and me, but she ran out. Few people know why, but by now there's no harm telling, is there?" Carter paused for an objection that never came, so he continued.

"She wanted to get pregnant, but I couldn't make it happen."

Buffy said, "She doesn't seem like the kind of person who wants kids, but maybe I've misread her."

"She might have been trying for my sake. I've never talked about it with you, but having kids is important to me. I'd like to have at least one son. But whatever her reasons, it's better we didn't become co-friends. She can be too intimidating, and watch out if she ever gets angry. It's like she becomes a different person."

"Well, that was ten years ago. She's different today, as all of us are. I'm sure she'll like what you'll say, so cheer up. You've been too glum lately."

"I apologize, but my conscience has been bothering me. And here's another irony. It took getting nearly killed during that inspection tour to bring my conscience back to life. And President Jared Gardner is one of the reasons why it's been MIA. Working for him has anesthetized it. I've compromised too much and besides that, I don't want him running for another term."

"He's not been good for me either, but I stayed with him because it kept me closer to you."

"Ah, and that's the other reason. You're it. I'm sorry I treated you so long as a means rather than an end. You've been much nicer to me than vice-versa. I finally realize you're better for me than Electra ever could be. You don't need to give me an answer this minute, but I would like you to consider our becoming co-friends." Buffy's suggestive smile said the same as her words.

"We've always got along nicely in the bedroom. Maybe I'll give you an answer there tonight." Carter's outlook began to brighten.

Electra liked the lineup she saw as the co-friend party started.

How much better the pairings for the two organizers of this evening's celebration versus ten years ago… Robin was dating Matt and Zoe was under the thumb of Jared Gardner. And unlike heavy rains last time, today's bright weather matches the mood of the twenty guests. I expect Carter's welcoming remarks to do the same.

"Hello, and thanks for helping celebrate a pairing that has been years in the making. Electra and Robin have been close friends going all the way back to grade school. Like each of us, each of them has changed in ways unpredictable, but during all that time their relationship has grown to what it is today.

"Electra made me promise to keep my remarks brief and I will, because I always do what she says. Otherwise, one of her pet sayings about herself might come true, 'Don't make me angry, you won't like me when I'm angry.' And she told Zoe that she and Robin didn't want any cards or gifts because your being here tonight is the best gift of all.

"Some of you know one another but some don't. So, please mingle and talk and enjoy the dinner buffet. And if you're like Electra, you might start at the sweets table." Zoe's wave caught Carter's attention.

"Zoe just reminded me that Electra wanted to say something, so here she is." Carter gave her a hug before sitting next to Buffy.

"I've learned how important relationships are, and I simply want to thank you for being our friends. And I want to recite a poem from my mother that tells everyone how much Robin means to me. Its title is 'Epiphany' and the words need no further explanation. Here goes:

> My new love has revealed to me,
> The secret of eternity.
> Don't think me strange don't think me odd,
> It has shown to me the face of God.
>
> Last night for all the world to see,
> I asked for love to set me free.
> No answer needed I know in my heart,
> My wish has been granted I've made a new start.
>
> Feelings have risen past what I have known,
> By living beyond I am no more alone.
> Emotions embrace me I am free of my doubt,
> Let me hold them forever let caring pour out.

"Thank you, Robin, for being so special. And thanks to each of you one more time." A smattering of applause accompanied happy murmurs as everyone rose to greet the special couple.

They stayed together while walking among the tables, then separated for more deliberate conversations among different clusters. Electra took Su aside at the first opportunity, her smile contrasting with the subject.

"I'm concerned about my directories being hacked. Can you think of any recent networking you've done that would link me to you, either online or in person?"

"I'm not very active in either. Is there a pattern or type of activity you've picked up on?"

"No. Anything and everything we're involved in could be suspect."

"Maybe I should ask Kameyo. She communicates often with researchers developing new gene sequencing techniques or coming up with transhuman extensions. But she's very careful not to reveal what we're working on."

"Ask, but please don't alarm her. I know how conscientious she is."

"Have you asked Tim? He and Kwame network constantly."

"He's next on my list. Don't mention it to him unless he brings the subject up. And please call me if Kameyo tells you something I should know."

When Electra pulled Tim aside, his incredulous expression matched his answer.

"Ever since we were mugged at the Las Vegas Cyberspace Expo, Kwame and I have pretty much kept our mouths shut. And I can't believe anyone's developed better security apps than ours."

"Competitors and criminals alike are always looking for ways to pirate what they can't create. If you think of anything later, let me know. If I'm hacked again, I might ask you and Kwame to help me trace the leak."

Electra circulated among other guests and covered more pleasant subjects, bringing nine p.m. sooner than she realized. She was ready to look for Zoe when Carter motioned to her. She came to him immediately, thanking him for his welcoming speech.

"You're welcome. I liked yours too, especially that poem. It's appropriate for Buffy and me. I know how well you can keep a secret, so you're the only person I'm telling tonight. We're going to be co-friends. And when you and Robin are ready for a Vow-Cer, maybe we can hold a dual ceremony. But that's not why I flagged you down. I have something for you. It's a flash drive containing evidence that incriminates Jared. Look at it sometime. You'll be surprised how much Buffy and I have accumulated."

Electra put it in her pocket before asking,

"Why are you giving it to me?"

"We're going to quit working for him. We don't like the direction he's taking the country, and we certainly don't want him pushing for a third term. Do you?"

"If he does, he'll make it tough for Angus to win. But why give it to me?"

"It's a backup. If something should happen to Buffy and me, please use it to blow the whistle. Promise? And don't tell anyone about this."

"Like you said earlier, I can keep a secret." Electra stopped talking because Robin was about to join them.

"Zoe says we need to see her right now. Come on, come with us, Carter. You can chat with Matt."

Zoe had already collected Qama and the twins when Robin brought the others. Qama chattered excitedly.

"I get to take care of Clara and Marie, and we get to stay with Zoe until Moma gets back." Having made the arrangements, Zoe explained.

"Limo's here to whisk our compatible co-friends for a Sunday of fun at the MGM Grand Casino and Hotel and the Rosecroft Raceway near Fort Washington. Electra said she and Robin should have some time just for themselves. There's lots to see and do, and you're not due back until Monday evening, unless you get bored." A startled Robin recovered, then said,

"That'll never happen when I'm with Electra…"

Electra was happy just to enjoy Robin's company and the limo's quiet interior, but Robin's emotions were bubbling out.

"I know our co-friend celebration means more to me than you. And now you're giving up the next two days just to be with me. But why?"

"I'm not giving up anything. I get to spend two days with only you. Let's enjoy the most of our time together."

Robin said, "I predict we'll be big winners this weekend. What games do you want to play?" The couple talked all the way to the hotel.

By the time they returned, both had made the most of their shared moments, and Robin's prediction proved true. It also applied to several people who would never be Electra's friends. Emails they had recently received declared them winners.

Darla let her security director read hers, warning him that its words and his assignment were confidential. She wasted no time telling him what to do.

"Somebody sent me winning numbers. Use the user I.D.s and passwords to hack into those URLs for what I'm looking for... people or apps that'll help us dig deeper into rare earths and AI software. When you find them, report back for your next task. And it'll be in 3-D space, not Cyberspace."

Sergei Zaitsev's Email cheered him too. He contacted Maksim on a secure line to share the news.

"I can't trace who sent it, but soon I shall have what we need to build better exoskeletons and weapons for enhancing your super soldiers and strike capabilities. Do you think it's a peace offering from Darla Tinibu? Maybe you should reach out to her?"

"Maybe so. She may be useful if I can get her to cooperate. It not, I will exact a retribution."

"And maybe I should reach out to Chen Xu's replacement. Some of what I've got might lead to patented biotech and cloning protocols. China can help us and vice versa."

"That is for you to do, not me. Just get me what I need so my covert strike force is at full strength. Keep me posted."

Jared Gardner's Email filled him with fear rather than a winning feeling. It contained a copy of a recently leaked letter posted on popular blogging sites. He read it twice, picking out the warning between the lines.

An Open Letter to All Americans

Don't believe the Government! It is not our friend. It is working to control us and get more money and power for itself, its corrupt politicos, and its morally bankrupt partners. Bureaucratic departments are colluding and conspiring at all levels inside and outside of Washington. Just look at what they are doing:

- Using accelerating progress in Biotech and AI to scare us.
- Using Globalization and Immigration to polarize you and take away our jobs.
- Using Climate Change to confuse us.

And the results impact

- Domestic and International Politics
- Domestic and International Economics
- Civility
- Culture

The Government and its Big Business and Big Data partners are stealing your Political and Economic Freedom!

I have traced a path all the way to the top of our political food chain.

I am leaking details to a handful of statesmen we can trust. It is their job to bring the bad actors to justice. But if they fail to act, I will leak more to a wider audience, telling you, the long-suffering public, much more.

How do I know all this? I work on the inside, but I stand with you. That's why I'm getting this information out. More to follow as needed.

Though it was late Tuesday evening, Jared summoned to the Oval Office someone he could trust. Dean Corfu came running.

Chapter 9
October 2133

"DC Bridge-Building"

The weeks following the Electra-Robin co-friend celebration were among the happiest in their collective experience. Electra enrolled Qama (now officially seven) in first grade and qualified her for home-track schooling, a proactive piece of America's flexible educational system that allows customized education for children with special needs. Qama's academic skills began to blossom under the tutelage of her omni-parents.

All other parts of Electra's personal world meshed seamlessly; she always paused at the end of each day to give thanks for the joy rolling her way, but it didn't include an issue in her professional world that was morphing from concern to worry.

Though my security tools aren't detecting attacks, I'm certain I'm being hacked. Too many leaks posted on blogsites and reported on the news contain content and wording too close to mine for mere coincidence. I haven't found the leak – maybe leaks. It's time I talk to my favorite statesman-senator.

Angus cleared an hour on his calendar for a late afternoon meeting in his office on a mid-October Thursday. He rose to hug her but changed his mind when he saw the stack of documents she was clutching, motioning her to a table instead.

"I'm glad you called. You haven't been at my meetings recently. How was your co-friend celebration?"

"That's why I'm here. My personal life couldn't be better, but I'm worried about hacks into some confidential files. Can you think of any recent Emails or meetings that might link you to me?"

"I do my best to keep them protected and never distribute anything you give me. Is there a problem?"

"You tell me. I'm sure you saw the leaked open letter telling the public that the government's not their friend. Jared's press secretary is spreading what I consider fake news to contain criticism coming his way. Have Jovita prepare something you can use to deflect any blowback that's bound to land on you. Anyway, that letter and other blogsite reports contain wording that's uncomfortably close to some of what I've written."

"Jesus, I hope I'm not being hacked. Jovita too. What do you propose?"

"Have your CIA contacts look for intrusion trails. And I've got a stack of items Jovita can use to help you prepare platform positions when you run for President."

"I haven't declared yet. What makes you think I will?"

"Because you know you can do better than the rest. You respect America and the office too much to stay on the sidelines, so let's move on. Study this handout carefully before I go over it. I'll grab a Coke while you're doing that. I know where you keep them." Ten minutes later, Angus nodded for her to explain what she had sketched.

Econo-Sociopolitical Spectrum

Totalitarianism	Liberal Left		Radical Right	Autarky

Equality
Big Gov. (Statism)
Collectivism
State ntrol

Freedom/Liberty
Ltd. Government
Individualism
Autonomy

Communism
Socialism
Social Democ.
Progress. Democ.
Independent
Moderate. Repub.
Conserv. Repub.
Libertarianism

Dictators   Fascists ←———Champions of the People ———→ Aristocrats   Kings   Clergy
Tyrants   Demagogues   Plutocrats
                                                        Kleptocrats
                                                        Theocrats

Social Capitalism Directed Capitalism Regulated Capitalism Stakeholder Capitalism Crony Capitalism Laissez-Faire Capitalism

- All positions along the spectrum support Capitalism (only form of economic activity that delivers)
- Capitalism often leads to Booms/Busts and Inequality (Concentration of Wealth and Income)
- What form of Government is "best" for controlling Capitalism? Ongoing debate

Current/Accelerating Problems:
- Global Economy International "meddling" by Russia, China, U.S.World Community Distrust of U.S.
- Immigration of the "right people"
- Job loss and InequalityPolitical Polarization
- Potential threats from: Genetic Engineering AI and Robotics

What's Needed:
- "Informed and Engaged" Public
- Viable path to the future (Job Growth only for: Service, Computer/Robotic Assistants, Innovation/Creativity)
- Civility and Trust
- Lifelong Learning
- Assisted Safety Net
- Coherent/Consistent/Diplomatic Foreign Policy

"Few politicians actually know the details outlined here. You might not recall the definition of autarky, so have Jovita check it out. The public will respect you even more if you can address the issues authoritatively when asked instead of ducking and weaving. Let's start at the top. Classical Liberalism comes from the Enlightenment, and its theories support right or left positions on the political spectrum. Then notice where each form of government and type of leader falls on it. I'm sure you can spot where you lie compared to Jared. Any questions so far?"

"No, and I know the definition you want me to use for the word 'lie.' The other doesn't apply."

Electra cracked a smile before continuing.

"Now we come to the good stuff. All forms of government want Capitalism, but they twist the definition to suit their style. You decide what form will best handle the current problems. I've bulleted the biggest ones any president faces. You already know them, but please remember that solved problems will come back as the business climate changes.

"Now we're coming to the payoff. I've bulleted what's needed to solve the problems, and you can turn what I've summarized into the 'why-what-how' of your presidential campaign. The 'why' is that you're the best candidate to solve the current problems. The 'what' is the steps you'll take to address what's needed of steps you'll take. And the 'how' will be the planks of your platform. Why not have Jovita expand all this for your so-called 'Bridge President' positioning?" Nodding cautiously, Angus was about to ask a question but Electra kept going.

"And though I haven't included them here, you'll need to address trade and budget surpluses or deficits. They require much more than simplistic sound-bite solutions because, given the context, a case can be made for either. Then you'll need to add domestic programs to meet social issues as well as satisfy monetary and fiscal goals. Never forget that economic policy requires trade-offs because resources are limited. You'll sound like all the shallow thinkers if you promise everything to everybody. You must balance optimism against realistic expectations."

Electra's pause pushed Angus out of the listening state. He unpursed his lips and asked,

"Will you help?"

"I'd rather spend more time on personal matters, but let's see what unfolds."

"No matter what, what you've given me is golden. Jovita and I will guard it carefully. And I'll let you know if we uncover any leaks...."

Even though Angus occupied a place close to her personal world, Saturday evening's social gathering promised to be even closer. Jennifer Conklin would serve dessert after three co-friend couples returned from a "Books and Bridge Club" lecture. (Carter and Buffy had announced over the Labor Day weekend their co-friending intentions and looked forward to renewed friendship with Electra and Matt.) Jennifer would mind the kids while the adults listened to an author's reviewing his latest book, *Lifelong Learning – A Journey for Your Children.*

When the couples returned, the kids had already been served ice cream and were playing together in the living room, trying to coax words from the syllables that Robin's twins were able to form.

Happy to be a listener rather than talker, Electra liked how Matt started the conversation.

"I think Zoe could have given the talk. She covered a lot of what we heard when she spoke at our Unicare Open House."

"That's because I read his book. He had more time than I did, so that's why he described the differences among hard and soft I.Q. skills as well as what Emotional Intelligence comprises. I particularly liked how he emphasized the skills people need if they want to find rewarding jobs. Sounds like the only kinds our kids will find are in service, entertainment, or robotic assistance. Or they'll have to become entrepreneurs and create their own."

Carter said, "I liked the models he drew to compare the old way of learning to the new. Does anyone remember how he categorized them?"

No one did, so Electra reluctantly spoke.

"He called the old the 'Industrial Model,' classified as Contained, Controlled, Predictive, Static, and Repeatable. He labeled the new the 'Ecosystem Model,' described as Creative, Adaptive, Permeable, Dynamic, and Self-Correcting. Let's hear what Buffy has to say."

"You've got a damn good memory. Whatever, Carter and I might soon be out of jobs. Expert systems are replacing economists and lawyers. Maybe Zoe will hire us to work for her. We can give advice to Matt, Robin, and Jennifer if Zoe pays us enough."

Carter frowned before saying, "I'll give an example from my own academic experience. It shows how much of a conformist the old system taught me to be. Whenever given an assignment, I never questioned those who were supposed to be in the know. I would look up what subject matter experts had to say instead of thinking for myself.

"I remember a comparative analysis I had to do on Tolstoy's last novel, *Resurrection*. The experts applauded it, but I found the sentence structure repetitive, character and scene descriptions too long, and the dialogue stilted. Grade-grubber that I was, I wrote down what the experts said. I think my teacher rubber-stamped an A on my paper because I was a class leader. I forget why, but I recently looked up a couple of reviews that are much less complimentary."

Carter glanced around the table, expecting someone to pick up the thread but there were no takers. Matt caught Zoe's eye; she took the cue.

"Don't forget next Saturday's bridge tournament I told you about. Matt and I've been practicing. Have you?" Robin blurted before anyone else could answer.

"That's easy for Buffy and Carter. They've played since college, and besides, they're good with numbers. You know I don't like math, and all the bridge rules confuse me. I think I've worn out Electra's patience." Electra tried to calm the situation.

"No you haven't, and I keep saying you're better than you think. I've got an idea. Why doesn't Zoe stay with us tonight and tomorrow? She'll give you bridge lessons while Qama and I take care of the twins." Zoe upped the offer.

"And why not have Matt stay with Jennifer and Gabriel? It'll be a nice mini-vacation for everyone." Matt caught Jennifer's smile before he replied.

"And I can handle a couple of autumn yard chores too." Electra upped the bid further.

"And Buffy can join us for a ladies' foursome. Why don't you spend the night with us?" Buffy didn't wait for Carter.

"I'd like that. All of us can sharpen our skills."

Zoe checked the time on her cell phone before saying, "Well then, it's decided, so let's call it a night. If it's OK with Robin, all the ladies will ride with her."

As the group prepared to leave, Jennifer volunteered to be next Saturday's kid-sitter during the bridge tournament if the highest-placing team would bring back pizza. Robin surprised Electra when she said that would be a fair deal.

Electra was the first to speak in the van.

"That was a clever pun Robin delivered." Robin ignored the comment because her mind was elsewhere.

"Electra and I spent many happy hours at the Conklin's when we were kids. I'm sure the place has changed a lot since then, but I don't notice any. Visiting brings back a timeless security that wrapped me way back then." Zoe commented next, then Buffy, but Electra spoke only to herself regarding comparisons of a different sort.

Any impartial observer would rank my van companions in this order, whether judging by height or appearance: Buffy first, then Robin, then Zoe. But the longer I know my friends, the less I notice exteriors. What's inside is what counts. Electra was about to let her mind wander further, but Buffy's pointed question to Zoe brought her back,

"You and Matt must have a strong co-friendship. Otherwise, I can't imagine your letting him spend the night with Jennifer. She may be older, but she looks younger than what the calendar says."

Electra said, "Zoe's one of the most well-adjusted and authentic persons I know. I think she even let Matt put a clause like that in their Vow-Cer contract. Am I right?"

"Yes, it's better to give your significant other freedom to roam. And all of you should know there's a big difference between sex and love." Buffy pointed a double-barreled question at Robin.

"Have you written up a contract? Are you going for a Vow-Cer? If you do, maybe we can combine ceremonies. Maybe contracts too."

"Ask Electra."

"That's not for discussion tonight. It'd take too long, and besides, it's late, and we're almost home. We'll pick it up at another time…"

Electra took her typical Sunday morning workout and run while Zoe coached Buffy and Robin using online tutorials. After lunch they would play practice games between two teams, one comprised of the top and bottom player, the second the middle two: Zoe and Robin versus Buffy and Electra. Electra skipped lunch because she went to get "mood elevators" for their practice session. Just before it began, she arranged them on the credenza behind the playing table.

"I thought I could improve the typical card game party set-up males put together by shopping at a sensual pleasures cafe. What you see here is a selection of marijuana-laced sweets, two THC vaping pens, scotch and soda, and mini-cigars. Please pick your pleasure when ready. Robin was the only one who looked puzzled.

"Do all of you use this stuff?" Electra answered first.

"I'm sorry, I thought you knew I occasionally have a scotch and soda while smoking a mini-cigar. The opportunity for that comes up more often in Hollywood than here. And I thought you might like to use a vaping pen if your headaches come back." Robin still looked doubtful, so Zoe jumped in.

"None of us will sample any until we need a break from the game, and when we do, we three will assist."

Buffy added, "You need to loosen up. You might find what Electra brought helps. Enough talk, let's start playing...."

Other than answering Robin's questions, Electra didn't bother about bridge the following week because she could adjust to hold her own while playing against others, but she had lost the touch when battling hackers. Even though progress uncovering leaks had ground to a halt, she avoided stewing or wasting time by switching to another project. By week's end she congratulated herself for completing a Hollywood assignment: rewriting a script.

Vito's gonna love my wordsmithing. Of all my professional worlds, Hollywood holds the most fun and the least hacker risk, but he wants me to fly back sooner than I thought. Something's up, but not to worry. Whatever it is, I'll keep it under control by Emailing him my rewrite. I've checked everything off this week's to-do list except for tomorrow's bridge tournament. And this time, Matt will be our designated driver. Time to head to my personal world.

Late October weather turned cold and overcast, which made an indoor tournament more inviting than outdoor games. Zoe lectured to her fellow riders, hoping to make the evening even more enjoyable.

"You'll find club members take bridge seriously, making for spirited competition. But it's all for fun, and we're playing single elimination using club rules to speed up play. You'll catch on fast."

A not-too-confident Robin asked, "Did you teach us these last Sunday?"

"No. I didn't want to overload you, but let's do this. You be my partner and Electra Matt's. And remember, it's just for fun."

Only Zoe and Robin had much fun. After winning opening matches, Matt's and Carter's teams faced off. Carter survived, but only for one more round. Zoe, on the other hand, demonstrated surprising skill, adroitly teaching Robin. She deftly maneuvered the bidding so she played all the dummy hands, a term that insulted Robin until Zoe explained what it meant. Her team advanced to the semifinals, eventually winning a third-place trophy. On the drive to Jennifer's, Zoe declared their collective group a winner. Carter found another reason for his team to declare victory.

"Thanks to Buffy being my partner, this is the first time I actually scored more points in something than Electra. We were like desperados in a desert sandstorm, springing an ambush." Electra returned a harmless barb.

"Didn't I tell you awhile ago that Buffy's a better fit for you than I ever was? And you don't need numbers to measure that."

Buffy said, "No matter the score, I'm happy to be with Carter." No one noticed Carter's blushing as he shifted subjects.

Next week's weather changed for the worse. Gusty cold winds blew in steady rains on Friday, threatening to spoil Halloween. Zoe had promised to take Carlton and Qama trick-or-treating through the neighborhood Saturday evening, but when Electra delivered Qama, she could see disappointment etched on the kids' faces when Zoe suggested taking them to an indoor party instead. Carlton's frown said even more than his words.

"But you promised. I like playing in the rain, and so does Qama." Zoe stared at the costumes, unable to find a reply, but Electra did.

"I'm with you. I like playing in the rain too, so let's do this. Your mom will give me a big umbrella, and as we walk from house to house you two can pick songs we'll sing. How does that sound?" Qama and Carlton clapped while Zoe scooted to get Matt's golfing umbrella.

Marching from house to house brought back childhood memories.

Grandfather always took me out on Halloween night. He always gave me everything I wanted. I can't pay him back, but I can pay it forward. It's my turn to do what's right.

Electra walked both kids through a chilly rain, shielding them from the worst. And she had the presence of mind to bring safety pins, which were needed to hem Qama's too-long costume. Carlton stood like a sentry, clutching the umbrella after receiving candy from a sympathetic elderly lady on a lighted porch; poor Electra, now on hands and knees, did what any loving parent would do.

Judging from the joyous satisfaction reflected in the youngsters' eyes, Zoe could see the evening had been magical. Qama and Carlton were about to bound away for candy counting when Qama stopped. She unwrapped a fun-size Snickers bar and popped it in Electra's mouth.

"Moma, thank you for the best Halloween ever. Someday maybe I can give you more treats."

Electra's chocolate-covered lips left a mark on Qama's cheek before she said,

"No darling, you've already done that. You're my little sweetness." Qama's words reverberated in Electra's brain, connecting to magical memories from the past.

"Me to you to, Moma; I love you so. And I promise to be good for always no matter where we go."

Later that night, after the candy was stored and all but Electra were dreaming, she fought to contain her emotions.

The moments of our lives slip by like the silent stars when we sleep, no matter what I do to keep them in the now. Tomorrow will bring new ones so I must tuck tonight into a special corner of my brain, so it's there whenever I wish to view, remaining the same, undiminished by time. It will always be mine, and Qama's too.

One silent tear came to Electra before she slept.

Chapter 10
December 2133

"Danger in the Desert"

Everything circling about Electra's personal world was as good as Qama's promise. She took all kids but the twins to a Thanksgiving pageant held on the Pequot Reservation, Zoe hosted a Thanksgiving dinner that included Jennifer and Gabriel as well as Carter and Buffy, and afterwards Carlton and Qama gave a mini piano recital (Robin had begun giving piano lessons three months ago). Afterwards, all kids sang Holiday favorites as their favorite piano teacher played along.

Electra also used the Pequot Reservation trip to monitor activities in her R&D and business worlds. Su and Tim reported steady progress, which meant they didn't need her assistance, and Chief Armstrong said the same for business activities. In fact, he had received a phone call from a group of investors because reservation rare earths sales were garnering a growing market share. He told them to contact Hud Haller if they were interested in learning more.

There were no pressing issues in her political world, but she did receive a cryptic Email from Vito ordering her back to Hollywood for a special meeting end of next week.

How odd. Vito's Emails usually clue me in, but not this time. Maybe there's another palace coup. At least the meeting's Friday the 11th, not the 13th. And I know the way to Jesperson's office.

Cyber-Max had already made travel arrangements, so all Electra had to do was explain to Robin and Qama where she'd be going and then pack, but when she received a terse Email – this one from Hud – it forced her to change travel dates. She read it one more time before using the Internet to juggle flights:

Howdy, Electra. Need your help. Too busy to call. Meet me Sunday evening next week in Flagstaff AZ. Got us vehicle and reservations at Doubletree Hilton. Got us a meeting on Tuesday. Call or send Email if you can't come and I'll go it alone. HH

This must be connected to Chief Strongarm's call. It's probably not an emergency... Hud would have called if it were. I'll fly in Sunday evening... we'll have a full day to prepare.

Electra didn't want to upset Robin or Qama, so she picked Wednesday supper at the kitchen table for the right time and place to tell them about her trip. Her opening question set the tone.

"How was your day, Qama?"

"Good, Moma. Aunt Robin says I play good on the piano. And guess what? I taught Clara and Marie new words."

Robin said, "Soon they'll be asking as many questions as you. And that'll be fun for all of us." That was a perfect segue for Electra.

"Well, I'll tell you before you ask what I did today. I started packing for a quick trip to Hollywood. I'll bring something back for each of you."

"Oh Moma, I love Hollywood. That's where the stars live. Will you take me there?"

"We'll plan for that, maybe next year, if Aunt Robin agrees." Robin nodded, then said,

"That'll be good. The more Qama sees, the more she learns. When do you leave?"

"I have a mid-morning flight tomorrow, and I'll take a cab or rideshare. And I'll come home by the middle of next week. Now it's my turn to ask a question... Qama, what will you be doing while I'm away?" Qama had lots to say.

Electra had made so many Hollywood trips that all travel and hotel details were now routine. Her outbound journey was no exception, allowing her plenty of time to prepare for Jesperson's 8:30 meeting.

I must dress and act more like a Hollywood business professional now that I'm in back of the camera. I'll arrive five minutes early and project the cool confidence of a studio executive. I can defend all I've done and proposed as Vito's screenwriter. I expect he'll support me, but if not, he better watch out.

As expected, Vito was already talking with Jesperson when Electra glided in. They rose to greet her, shaking her hand before having her sit with them around a glass coffee table that already held juice, coffee, and a selection of muffins and sweet rolls. Also as expected, a smiling Vito spoke first.

Bella Electra, how good you always look. As good as the work you do. So, we have news for you. Bad for some, but only good for the three of us. Yes, we have another studio right-sizing, but la Prezidenza keeps the A and B lists. I let him explain more."

Jess rarely smiled during business meetings, but he made an exception while pointing to a photo on the wall.

"You were a major contributor for our Monaco team's success. Thanks to you, we picked up a go-kart trophy, two screenplays, and some free publicity. Vito and I think it's time to expand your role on our Cyber-Max team.

"The entertainment industry is more competitive than ever, what with virtual reality and international movie studios muscling in. Only the smart Hollywood studios will thrive, and Cyber-Max has been able to do so. But we need to remove those people who don't see our vision, people who can't adapt. That's why we're cutting staff. Those that make the cut will have to do more but will be adequately rewarded."

"So, I assume I've made the cut. Please tell me why."

"You have an exceptional skill set. You've been an actress, have worked as Vito's assistant, and have a flair for all kinds of writing. You understand our technology and have an adaptable personality that can fit anywhere. People like you. My Hollywood associates respect how you handled that unfortunate episode from a couple of years ago. You didn't criticize or call out anyone but instead turned it into an example of Hollywood ethics promoting the right social causes."

"That was the right thing for me to do. Win-win is the way to go."

"And that's why we want you to take another step up the Hollywood career ladder. I'm promoting Vito to Executive Director, and would like you to assume a newly created position reporting to him – Associate Director-Screenwriter." Jess let Vito explain more.

"I help you get comfortable with 'Hollywood Club,' and it no longer just 'Old Boys.' You add to the new wave of talented ladies leading the way. But you gotta be ready to handle more work, maybe cut back on other things. What you think?"

"I've been thinking about scaling back my political and R&D roles; I know I can handle the load, but I have to have time for my family. I have a co-friend and an adopted daughter. What do you suggest?" Jess had an answer ready.

"The studio will rent a townhome for you until you're ready to buy. Your co-friend can visit whenever she wants, and you can enroll your daughter in the Hollywood Studio Schooling Academy. It's state of the art and will dovetail into her current school program."

"I like what I hear, but I'll need help transitioning from screenwriter to my new position. Do I get a direct report?"

"We've already filled that position, if you approve. Kathi Lauret didn't make the cut, but we're willing to give her that job."

"I'd like to talk with her before I accept. She was my first mentor."

"We thought you'd say that. We've made 1 p.m. reservations for you and Kathi today at the Brown Derby. Talk with her and plan your transition schedule. Vito will take care of you for the rest of the morning…"

Once ensconced in Vito's office, his smile promptly faded.

"Bella, I starting to feel more heat. To stay on A-list I gotta produce and you been so good. La Presidenza know that and say to me you gotta stay. I hope you give decision soon to take new position. I promise I be grande mentor."

"You already are. That's why I accept, no matter what Kathi says. Why not tell Jess that I decided to stay only because of you." Vito beamed.

"Bella, bella, you gladden us both, us three. You'll like, you'll see. And I start by toasting you. I get you Coca Cola now, and champagne later. But no bubbly now. We must think about transition, no?"

That was no trouble for Electra; she had it sketched just before she left for lunch. She would fly out Sunday but return Wednesday to set up her office and have Vito approve her goals and objectives for next year before returning to DC for the Holidays. And then she would bring Qama back on Saturday, January 2nd to begin a new phase of her Hollywood adventure.

"Bella, we gonna make an even grande team. Now go let Kathi know."

The short cab ride gave Electra a moment to give thanks.

Serendipity comes through again. All pieces of my parallel worlds are evolving for an even better fit. And how fitting I meet Kathi at the Brown Derby. My first time there turned melancholy when I learned about my half-sister's troubles. Now I'm coming full circle, happy for what's coming my way.

A relieved-looking Kathi rose from the booth when Electra approached.

"I was worried you'd cancel."

"Why would I do that? You know me better than anyone at Cyber-Max."

"Maybe so, but your career has zoomed and so have you. You're different now than when we met. Cosmopolitan, socially adept, and from what Vito told me, you think like the Hollywood big boys. Maybe I should say big girls, because women are now admitted to the club if they have the right stuff. And you certainly do."

"Why were you cut from your old job?"

"I'll level with you. My career is on a downward path. I can't handle all the change going on. Jess knows that and found a slot if you'll hire me. I need this job, and I promise I'll take a load of small stuff off your plate."

"I know you will, and I'll help you learn enough of the new stuff no matter where fortune leads."

"Fortune has already delivered what I said when we first met. Here I am, working for you."

"And I'm giving you my transition schedule and your to-do list. The top item is for you to find a condo or townhome for me and my daughter. I think your daughter and Qama will become great friends. Now let me explain the details...."

By the time Kathi chauffeured her new boss back to the studio, both had settled into their new relationship. Vito had planned to take her to several introductory meetings, but when he saw Electra handle herself at the first, he decided she didn't need his help, so he stepped back to his office, delighted she was already working.

Her new associates had already figured out she was fast-tracked for bigger roles, so they welcomed her into their inner circle. After accepting an invitation to a happy hour, she networked an appropriate amount of time before announcing she needed to get organized for the first of many Saturdays in her new office. Her new assistant would be there too. Returning to the hotel, Electra decompressed by taking a workout and then swimming laps to splash away any remaining remnants of stress.

Saturday and Sunday unfolded trouble-free; by the time Electra registered Sunday evening at the Doubletree in Flagstaff, she had already shifted brain states from her Hollywood world to that of business. Hud answered promptly when she phoned his room; his voice brightened when he recognized hers.

"I shoulda worried less about your not showing up because I can always count on you. Depending on how things add up, we got us a situation that could be good or bad. Let's grab a snack in the restaurant so I can fill you in. You need time to unpack?"

"I'm good. I'll meet you there in ten minutes."

Hud's Texas-sized heft and personality had been the steadiest among her constellation of men-friends, surpassing even those of Angus and Chief Strongarm. Whatever concerns he might have didn't join them at the booth as he began sketching the scene.

"You ever been to Flagstaff?"

"No, but the terrain reminds me of Albuquerque. That's where I stayed when I visited the Navajo Reservation. I imagine that's what brings us here. And if I had to pick a particular reason, it would be rare earths."

"You guessed it. It's got our first mining operation that we're retrofitting for underground mining automation. There'll be hardly any environmental or worker safety issues. And when we fully integrate mining, grinding, smelting, and shipping, our production costs will drop even more."

"Is it operational?"

"Beginning January. We just finished testing the robo-diggers. Operators run them from the control center using computers and monitors. It's like playing a video game."

"So, why are we here?"

"An investor group contacted me. They said we might be able to join a rare earths consortium for mutual benefit. In fact they think—" Electra interrupted mid-sentence.

"Who are they, and how did they find out about you?"

"A three-person team representing a corporate wealth management group called Global Mineral Group, or GMG for short. The team leader is Patrick Nenge from Zambia; Leo Volkov from Russia, and Charles Ding from China work for him. Patrick did all the talking but didn't tell me their roles."

"So, how did Patrick find out about you?"

"He watched an industry trade association video that had a snippet about how we're leading the way into fully automated underground robotic mining. You're always telling us to stay invisible… I guess I goofed. I let association interview me onsite. Patrick and his people are gonna meet me at the mine's headquarters building Tuesday afternoon. Whatcha think?"

"I'll search the Web to learn more about them. How long does it take to drive from here to the mine?"

"A little over four hours. We go 200 miles northeast on I-40."

"That's too far for a one-day roundtrip. There must be motels near the reservation, so we'll get up early tomorrow, drive there to prepare for our Tuesday visitors, and spend the night. I think we should stop now and rest. We can talk more on the drive while I snoop on the Internet…"

Calling it a night did not call forth sleep. Electra's obsessive-compulsive predisposition wouldn't be satisfied until she had pieced together a better picture of GMG; she hacked for three hours using her network security tools.

I've got a good handle on what GMG and its negotiating team look like, thanks to tracing Email addresses and URLs down a trail of company directories. GMG fronts for Big-6, which is part of Syntagra, which is linked to Big Data and Cybergard. Darla Tinibu must be lurking somewhere in the background. I'll give Hud an edited version of what I've uncovered… knowing too much more won't help him as long as I watch his back as well as mine. I'll figure that out tomorrow. And that's only five minutes away. Finally, I can fall asleep.

Hud and Electra played different roles on the drive. While his would be subject matter expert, hers would be meeting planner. She started by picking his brain for more details.

"Did Patrick say where they're driving in from?"

"He didn't say why, but he did say where – Las Vegas. I guess he likes the flight schedule better than Flagstaff's. He joked that we couldn't meet in Vegas because whatever happens during our meeting wouldn't stay there, but would stay on the Reservation instead."

"Tell me again how the mining complex is arranged."

"Sure thing. It's not fenced in because it's in the middle of nowhere. There are two one-story buildings: a main office building and a nearby network control building. They're about a half-mile from the mine entrance. They're not fancy from the outside, but they contain everything we need. And the control building is better than state-of-the-art. From it, computer operators run the robo-diggers and the grinding-smelting operation, plus the conveyors running from mine to grinder-smelter. And video cameras plus mikes inside and outside the mine and buildings show and tell operators what's going on. You'll be impressed."

"What about the mine?"

"There's hardly any ecological impact. All you see is a covered entrance. Two conveyor systems lead from it to the grinder-smelter facility. A gradually sloping tunnel called a decline leads from the entrance down about thirty feet to the highest mineral vein. We start at the top and work our way down. Geologists use the latest 3-D seismic technology to map them all, so we know where to point the robo-diggers. And they'll really impress you. They look like big four-wheel mechanical bugs right out of a sci-fi movie. We have two drilling in parallel. The business end projects big drill bits, pincers, and scoopers that dump the rock into automated haulers. You'll see that the drilling and transportation zones are isolated from each other. That improves safety."

"Who'll be there besides you and me and the three visitors?"

"No one other than two AI-enabled robo-guards. They look like the military's four-wheel robo-soldiers adapted for industrial use. One patrols outside the main building and the other outside the control building. They're run by a computer in the network building and have two settings: stun and kill. They can also be operated manually. But there's no risk for people wearing bracelet I.D.s that prevent a robo-guard from picking someone off unless manually overridden. I'll give you and me and our visitors bracelets."

"Good, and as soon as we arrive, please show me how to operate all the equipment."

"Will do. What can I tell you next?"

"How many people does it take to run the operation?"

"Surprisingly few in the mine because it's so automated. And those that do are more like computer assistants or technicians. There are more in the control building, but one tech can run multiple machines. The jobs pay a lot and the entire facility supports a local business community. We've trained and hired as many Navajos as we can, which pleases the Tribal Council."

"You certainly know your stuff. I'm impressed, and our visitors will be too."

"I always try to keep you satisfied. Sometime when you like, I'll take you on a tour of a solar panel or Martian farming installation."

"Why don't you tell me what you say to visitors when conducting a mine tour because that's what we'll be doing tomorrow...." Hud wrapped up his grand tour talk ninety minutes later, after which Electra sounded a warning.

"You have a lot of valuable information. Use your judgment tomorrow. Tell our visitors just enough to keep them interested. Then get them to tell us more about their intentions."

"You got it. And all this talking has tuckered me out. Grab us a Coke from the backseat cooler. We've got about an hour's drive left. It's your turn to talk when ready."

By 4 p.m. Electra had reviewed enough to tell Hud tomorrow's plan.

"There's two of us and three of them, but we'll make them more talkative and confident if I stay invisible. I'll observe from the control room. I know what a good negotiator you are, so just act natural. Start the meeting in the main building's conference room, but let Patrick do most of the talking. You can take them into the mine if necessary, but keep them out of the control room. I'll be able to see and hear. I'll text your cell if I think you need help. What time are they supposed to arrive?"

"Patrick said about 3 p.m., and he'd text me when they get close."

"We're done for the day. We'll come back late tomorrow morning and get all set up. Now, let's check in at a motel and relax."

At nine Tuesday evening, Patrick and his partners had finally pulled into a motel. After rendezvousing at McCarran International Airport, it had taken them longer than expected to load the van and begin an eight-hour, 500-mile drive from Las Vegas to the Navajo reservation, so they picked a motel west of Flagstaff instead of one closer to the mine.

A bit portly and always garrulous, Patrick looked and talked like a typical corporate type, whereas Leo and Charles each fit the image of techie type of covert ops guy. Fitting for the assignment too, because Hud Haller might need coaxing if he decided not to accept Patrick's offer.

As they finished coffee at a nearby diner, Patrick kept his smile and words steady as he talked expansively.

"Thank you for loading and driving the van. Your Russian training for dealing with mining operations and explosives will prove valuable."

"If we get cooperation, I don't need to unload van. But if we don't, I know how to load the mine to shut it down."

"Yes, indeed. And either way, Charles will come away with enough software that we can install at our own rare earths mines. You Chinese hackers are par excellence." Charles cracked a smile but only grunted, so Patrick gabbed more.

"I marvel at the landscape we've driven through. Unlike my native Africa, where deserts are only sand and forests jungles, here we have them in closer proximity. And each contains a bit of the other. But in Vegas there's no wildlife, other than those crazy gamblers and dancers. Perhaps we will see some Indians tomorrow...."

Perched in the control room and sipping a Coke at 3 p.m., Electra answered Hud via the conference room's communications system.

"I see a van pulling into the parking lot. You're on. Let's both play our parts as rehearsed."

"You betcha." Hud rose to welcome his visitors. Ten minutes later, he had them sipping soft drinks and sitting across from him at the conference room table before starting the meeting.

"Why don't I give you a quick sketch of our rare earths business, for which I'm general manager. We got us a set a mines we're renovating and reopening and expecting to generate nice cash flows and profits. And new mining technology keeps variable costs low. Now, why don't you ask away?" Patrick did just that.

"Mr. Haller, how many mines are currently operating, and where. And how many will you reopen next year?"

"I don't keep them figures in my head. I'd have to check with my operations guy."

"Well, what about planned versus actual revenues and profits for this year and forecasted for next?"

"You got me on that one too. I'd have to ask my accounting gal."

"Which mining equipment and software do you use? And how integrated is your overall operation here?"

"Hmm, those are questions for my tech guys. All them work in the control building but won't be here until next year. But I can tell you we use robo-diggers. And let me tell you something about our Native American workers...." Fifteen minutes later, Patrick's plastic smile began to crack.

That's all very interesting, Mr. Haller, but we came to hear about your mining expertise, not a history lesson. May we please move on?"

"Sure, and that reminds me. Let me go get confidentiality agreements you can sign. I'll also bring back a plate of cookies. Then, why don't you tell me about your company and your intentions, and then let me ask some questions? I'll be back in a jiff."

Patrick's frown, accompanied by snide comments, appeared as soon as Hud chugged out of the room.

"Haller's either the dumbest G.M. I've ever met or he's setting us up. But let's not be impatient. My words may convince him to cooperate. If not, I shall let you two add more weight to the matter."

Patrick's smile returned when Hud reappeared; he spoke as soon as Hud settled in his chair.

"Mr. Haller, the companies in our consortium are the major rare earths market players, and we realize your growing stature could benefit all of us. Instead of bidding against one another, we cooperate to set prices and outputs that maximize outcomes for buyers as well as suppliers. Let me tell you what's in store. Then fire your questions and I'll tell you more...." An hour later, Hud was still unimpressed.

"What you're saying sounds better for you than for me. Why would I want to sell less at a higher price and cheat on my biggest market segment, the good ole U S of A? No sir, I'll take a pass, but thanks for visiting." Patrick looked at his partners before replying.

"Since we've come all this way and signed your confidentiality agreement, would you at least show us the mine before we leave?"

"Be happy to as soon as I take a potty break. If any of you gents need to go, please follow me." No one did.

Patrick gave terse orders as soon as Hud was out of the way.

"Leo, you take charge when we get into the mine. And if Haller is still unwilling to accept our revised offer, we'll let Charles do the same when we break into the control building." Leo and Charles did nothing but nod; only a brain-dead dummy would need further explanation.

Hud led them into the mine, which had already been prepped for a demo tour. Huddling everyone in front of a quietly idling robo-digger, he was about to explain its operation when Leo pushed him towards the wall and began yelling.

"We no longer Mr. Nice Guys. Either you play our game or its lights out for you."

Part of his statement came true after he drew a gun.

The string of overhead lights blinked out, plunging the mine into total darkness just before the robo-digger blazed to life. Its blinding headlights froze everyone but Hud, who had dived into the darkness. As the digger charged forward, Charles fell on his back and Patrick ran into the front wall. Only Leo dodged out of harm's way.

The roar of the digger drowned out screams; it ran over Charles and its drill bit pinned Patrick to the wall. Suddenly, the digger powered off and overhead lights blinked on, just in time for Hud to watch Leo disappear up the tunnel, heading for the exit.

Hud began running towards the exit but halted when he heard rat-a-tat gunfire; a robo-guard had just greeted the third man.

Electra grimly observed the results of her handiwork.

Hud played his part perfectly. Too bad all others were bad actors. I had no choice other than terminate with extreme prejudice. It's time to collect Hud, then clean up and go.

She grabbed a flashlight before running toward the mine entrance where she found him examining Charles. Most people would be in shock, but not Hud. He spoke calmly.

"Déjà vu again. Last time you bagged two; this time three. Remember?"

"Who could forget? That was the night the Wu brothers killed Adom. That time, we dumped the bodies down an abandoned mine shaft on your dad's fatstock ranch, but not this time. We won't leave any evidence on the Reservation. Come on, lets use the haulers to retrieve the bodies."

"Then what?"

"We'll load'em into their van and dump it at a place you pick. You drive it and I'll drive yours when we head back to Flagstaff."

Half an hour later, Electra had removed all keys and I.D.s before helping Hud put the bodies in the van. When doing so, she was the first to discover quite a surprise.

"They brought enough explosives to shut the mine for a long-long time. Do you know how to use it? If so, why don't you keep it?"

"Yes to both questions. Let's stash it. That'll make disposing the van safer."

It was nearly midnight by the time they had the explosives stored and the mine buttoned down. Hud was tiring physically and mentally but not Electra, whose adrenaline force-multiplied her relentless drive. She rattled off parting instructions.

"You're not thinking clearly. You need to rest. Stay here until sunrise, then go through the mine and buildings one more time before checking us out of the motel. I'll stop to pick up my stuff, then drive tonight to the Flagstaff airport. I'll get rid of the van somewhere convenient." Hud's confused look spread to his voice.

"What day is it? How you gonna do all that?"

"It's Wednesday. You do your thing, and I'll do mine. Believe me, I'll be fine. Don't call me, I'll call you Thursday evening. And remember, no one but us can ever know what happened here tonight." Finally, a weary smile.

"You got that right, your Highness. You know that only my hat and boots are Texas-size. My lips are sealed tight."

Chapter 11

December 2133

"Holiday Planning"

"I got everything taken care of. I took your advice and stayed an extra day to make sure I got rid of all evidence. I'm still at the mine, and it looks like the calendar skipped from Monday all the way to Thursday evening. All good here; how about with you?"

"I'm back in Hollywood and didn't skip a beat. Why don't I call you after Christmas so you can tell me what you're lining up for next year?"

"That's a deal, but answer me one question. Why didn't you text me when you found out Patrick and his bunch were gonna get rough? I could-ah prepared better."

"You were playing your part perfectly. They might have become suspicious if you acted differently, so you didn't need to know."

"I guess you're right. And what about the van? Any problems there?" Electra remained silent.

"I guess I don't need to know about that either. But I got one other observation. Here me out and then answer my question if you want. OK?"

"I'm listening."

"The whole episode brought back memories of the night Adom got killed. I was sad all yesterday because I kept thinking about him and Dad, and what might-ah been if they'd lived longer. He was gonna run a lot of the oil business while being Dad's caregiver. Do memories ever get in your way?"

"I'm mindful whenever one dances into my brain, but then I let it fly away so I live in the present, trying to enjoy what I'm doing and planning for the future. Try doing the same. You should take a break until January."

"Will do. And you can tell me all about your Happy DC Holidays when you call. You can gimme pointers on next year's business plan."

"From what Chief Strongarm and you've already told me, there's little for me to do other than approve it. And ditto for Su and Tim."

"I'm glad you feel that way, but I always want you to be my consultant. We go way back, and no matter what we do, I'll never find another you."

"I'll reply to that the way I sometimes say Qama, 'Me too you too.' Happy Holidays." Electra continued talking to herself after Hud disconnected.

I'm genuinely pleased to be a consultant next year for all parts of my business world. Hud's piece is a done deal, and I can say much the same for Su and Tim.

But not for other pieces of my R&D world. I should help Professor Ravenhill... I must call him when I get back to DC. Angus too for my political world, even though I'm definitely a consultant there.

What about my Hollywood world? I'm definitely not a consultant, but I'm in control as long as Vito likes the plan I've almost completed. I'll show it to him next week at our Monday meeting. How fitting it's the 21st, the winter solstice. I'll tell him that if he approves my plan, the days ahead will be filled with more sunlight and less stress. And if he doesn't, I'll tell him I'll change my ticket to one-way instead of round-trip.

For the remaining days, Electra kept Kathi's to-do list just the right length, and in return, Kathi delivered everything Electra needed. She equipped the office and installed all office procedures that Electra's position required; she found a freshly remodeled lease-to-buy three-bedroom townhome in Hollywood Heights that Electra liked, and she handled all paperwork and relocation rigamarole. By the time Electra waltzed into Vito's office, she had already begun to cycle down for a well-deserved Holiday break. Electra worked on her laptop while Vito, a pro at dissecting studio project plans, scrutinized hers for fifteen minutes before exclaiming,

"Magnifico, bella! La Presidenza will approve. You got the touch for what works and for words that say so. How you come up with idea to piggyback documentaries and movie series?"

"I did my own Big Data analysis. The public is ready for more depth, more sophistication in sci-fi and action adventures. Documentaries will give viewers a better awareness and appreciation for the issues as well as build interest and desire for our upcoming productions. My approach is trend-setting, and I've packed enough in my plan for at least two years. And take a look at the contingency plans included. There are options we can pursue for different plan versus actual outcomes. Let me walk you through the details. You'll like the financial projections…."

Vito did, and as she departed for her flight, he gave her a tiny wrapped box as well as final instructions.

"Bella, don't open until Christmas Day. Travel safe, rest up, and come back ready to play our Hollywood adventure game. Ciao." Electra reached into her shoulder bag before he could hug her.

"And I have a gift for you. But there are no time restrictions, other than waiting until I leave before you open it. Merry Christmas."

Electra's flight was among the happiest because she had only one more plan to consider: that of her personal world; her internal smile blossomed the more she thought about it.

Planning takes a lot of work when I'm in charge. It's the issue every leader has to face… a chief is responsible for his people and what they achieve. I face that everywhere except in my personal world because I don't control it. No one controls their personal world… it's populated with relationships whose plans unfold according to what each partner wants. All I need to do is keep the lines of communication open and a list of what's on partners' minds. I'll start with Robin and Qama and network among the tribe from there. I'm sure they'll like what I've set up. Bless them for picking me up so late.

Qama's boisterous monologue while driving home made up for Robin's lukewarm greeting.

"Me and Aunt Robin have been so busy and she says I'm doing so well learning and playing the piano and taking tests and helping her. And just wait until we tell you about all the Christmas surprises we have. Why—" Electra tickled her so she could get a word in.

"Hey, slow down so I can keep up. And please remember to say 'Aunt Robin and I,' not 'Me and Aunt Robin.' You know why. And I have a gigantic surprise for you and Aunt Robin, but I'll wait until you tell me yours."

"Oh Moma, please tell me now."

"Let's hear what Aunt Robin has to say."

"You better. I dropped too many hints after your last phone call. Qama can tell you later about some of ours."

"Well here it is. I had to wait until after my last meeting, but now I can. I have a new job in Hollywood, and it comes with a beautiful townhome for all of us to live in. I'm making arrangements for you to stay with me whenever and for however long you like. It'll be like living in a magic kingdom." Robin spoke over Qama's cheery babbling.

"I'm sure you're right like you always are, but it's late and we're all tired. Let's save the rest for tomorrow."

Robin helped Qama get ready for bed while Electra unpacked. Both tucked her in before heading to the kitchen for a late-night snack; Electra sensed it would be accompanied by an issue that had been bothering Robin, who waited to unload until after finishing a bowl of cereal while Electra was putting peanut butter on crackers.

"I'm happy for you. Whatever you do turns out right, but I'm hurt you didn't hold off until we talked. Did you think about Qama or me? I've got my career, such as it is, and Qama has school. And we both have, as you so cleverly put it, a tribe we like."

"And I'm hurt you think that way. You two mean the most, and I always try to do what's best. You can come and go as you please, and so can Qama if she wants to spend more time here. I've enrolled her in the Hollywood Schooling Academy that'll synchronize with what she's doing now. But you're right about one thing. We're tired.

I'm going to bed. Please think about what I said." Electra slipped away before Robin could say goodnight.

An apologetic Robin greeted Electra at the back door as she came in after her early morning run.

"I put blueberry muffins and butter on the table next to your Coke. It's my way of saying you're right and I'm sorry. Sit down and dig in while I try to dig myself out the hole I dug."

"That wasn't a hole. You simply pointed out I didn't say enough on our calls. I thought I was doing what would be good for you and Qama, but next time I'll ask."

"And I'm sorry for overreacting. I don't have to pick up and move all at once. I can visit and see how I like the place."

"And if you do, I can network you into good jobs. And maybe we'll wait until the school year finishes before relocating Qama. I know she likes helping you and Zoe, and she enjoys being on the Academic Jeopardy team. So let's hold off making big moves; we'll make small ones gradually. Now why don't you tell me about your Holiday surprises?"

"I'll make this quick because I have to get Qama and the twins ready. Today's the 22nd. Zoe and I have arranged a bunch of group activities for all families, including Jennifer's. There's nothing you have to do; each day I'll tell you what we've got planned. So, take a break and relax or work on whatever you want."

"Will Carter and Buffy join us?"

"I forgot to mention, you should call him before Saturday. They leave for the Caribbean. They're chartering a sailboat."

"Will do. And I brought some Christmas presents from Disney Studios for all the kids. Mickey or Minnie Mouse T-shirts. I even got one for you to match Qama's. And I'll get several more presents for her."

"Maybe you shouldn't. Zoe says the world is too consumption-oriented and we should set a better example by serving others instead of ourselves. She's lined up a group activity to make a point."

"That point doesn't apply to Qama. She comes from a dirt-poor village. I could buy her a van full of toys and it wouldn't begin to fill what she's been missing. In fact, I'll take her shopping and let her pick out what she wants."

"OK. Well, go do your thing, and I will too."

Electra finished breakfast, then checked Emails before showering. She planned to spend a leisurely day picking away at special projects and contacting assorted people. Professor Ravenhill's Email catapulted him to the top of the list:

Kittner, Happy Holidays, wherever you are.

I need more help. Read attached document that was posted two days ago, then call me before year-end.

Electra read the document immediately:

An Open Letter to All Americans

You'd be mad as Hell like I am if you knew what I just snooped out. No one I leaked fusion reactor data to is cooperating to make faster progress. Everyone is trying to be number one, which means you, the American people, will come in last.

And I'll up the ante. I'm leaking DARPA data regarding nuclear-powered batteries and rocket engines. Why isn't the Government pushing hard for them? By now, you know the answer: greedy politicians, government bureaucrats, and their "Military-Industrial-Big Data" conspirators are stealing from us.

I shall leak data to selected university and engineering companies. Let's see what they do. And if they don't do the right thing, all of us need to stand up and not take their dishonesty anymore, but instead take them to task.

The clock is ticking.

Then she called Professor Ravenhill, who was already in his office.

"Kittner, you're slowing down. It took you two days to call me."

"I apologize, but I've been so busy writing up plans for next year I didn't see your Email or the Open Letter posted in the media and blogging sites. Do you think it's from the same person? Are you or GWU on the leak-to list?'

"It could be from a tight-knit hacker group that's trying to stir up trouble. So far, no one at GWU has received anything. Blogging sites and social media are trying to hype concern, but the Holidays have muted blowback. I'd like to have a head start understanding nuclear batteries and engines. What do you know about them?"

"Not much, other than they're powered by radioactive elements."

"Could you do me a favor and send me a battery bootcamp paper like you did for thermonuclear reactors? Our GWU team won't reconvene until early January."

"I can't promise, but I'll try to send you something by early January. Will that do?"

"Yes-yes, thank you. I'll consider it my Christmas present. Well now that it's settled, let me wish a Happy Holiday to you. And don't work too hard, just hard enough to get me my present. Cheers."

Always happy to research new topics, Electra decided to develop her bootcamp paper immediately after showering. She used the solitude of the streaming water to outline what she'd do.

I'll spend no more than three hours writing up a bullet point outline; then I'll move on to Carter. I won't send it to Professor Ravenhill until New Year's Day, but I might send it to Angus ASAP because there could be troublesome political implications that might entangle me.

It took only two hours of computer workstation time for Electra to finish the outline. She complained to herself that it wasn't as good as intended.

Nuclear Batteries/Rocket Engines Bootcamp

Progress for both inventions driven by lighter and stronger materials resulting from rare earths technology. Latest generation batteries and engines store more energy at higher densities, operate at higher temperatures, last longer, and are safer (emit less radiation.)

Batteries:
- Non-thermal batteries are superior. They form an electric current using alpha (helium nuclei) or beta (electrons) particles.
- Best nuclear source of radiation: Carbon-14 converted into a diamond.
- Rare earths-enhanced chips amplify current or power.
- Life expectancy measured in decades or longer.

Nuclear Rocket Engines:
- Engine houses a nuclear fission reactor core. Core can be a breeder reactor that creates more fuel.
- Can produce higher thrust longer than chemical rocket engines.
- Two types: Thermal Propulsion (discharge liquid hydrogen at high speeds by heating it) andPlasma Propulsion (discharge plasma at high speeds by injecting electromagnetic energy).
- Best nuclear fuel: Plutonium.
- Feasible for interplanetary travel, not intra-Earth.
- Can reach speeds of 500,000 mph.
- Must assemble multi-stage nuclear engine and rocket in Outer Space to eliminate size and shape limitations.

Political Angle:
- Who are the leakers? (I think there are multiple independent sources.)
- Why are they leaking? (I think they are trying to embarrass all parts of Government and stir up international problems.)
- Where/How are they getting the information? (Not from me. None of my projects are relevant. Whoever it is has advanced hacking software. They haven't been caught.)

There's not a lot to report, but unless I want to fake being a nuclear physicist, I have to go with what I've got. Maybe I can add more bullets if

someone sends me the leaked data, but at least I inferred a political angle.
I'll share that only with Angus.

This is the third leaked Open Letter. If others follow, my concern will
grow if it looks like they go deeper into any of my worlds. Only then
might I begin to worry, but only if they threaten me or close friends and
family. It's time to cycle down. I'll visit Robin and Qama after lunch. If
she can spare Qama, I'll take her shopping.

Electra observed from the shadows for a minute or two how
smoothly CFS Unicare ran. While Jennifer was working in her
office, Zoe was organizing an arriving group of senior citizens as
Robin and Qama were already leading two groups of children,
Robin the larger and Qama the smaller. One of Robin's dogs alertly
followed each group's leader.

Zoe's become quite the hands-on exec, organizing her people and
working with clients. And just look at Qama and her gang of kids. How
self-absorbed they are. I read a child-psych book that said nothing is as
serious as a child at play. And I remember Mother's poem – she named it
The Children's Hour – painting a picture that adults should try to copy.
Electra recited it to herself:

> Children teach your parents well,
> They forget what kid's can tell.
> Youthful faith trumps oldster power,
> Show them in your children's hour.

> Laser focus at school or play,
> Innocence keeps fear away.
> Tiny egos don't interfere,
> Honesty keeps conscience clear.

> The adult world is not as nice,
> It needs a dose of childish advice.
> Though sometimes hard it's understood,
> Grownups relearn the things they should.

I see all this in Qama, and it rekindles some of my early-years' emotions when Doc Kittner watched over me. Too bad I had to grow up so fast. And I'm sad Qama missed out on so much. Well at least I can shelter her from the adult world until she's ready.

Qama dashed towards Electra as she strolled towards the two groups that Robin was mixing together.

"Moma, you're here! Did you see us playing our bus driver game?"

"I did, and I bet you were the driver."

"I was and I knew all the right stops."

"Well, I'm here to take you Christmas shopping if Aunt Robin says she can spare you." Qama saw Robin nodding yes, but she waited for Electra to make the final call.

"Well it's settled. And since you know the right stops, you're in charge of taking us to the stores where we can find what you want. Let's go right now."

Qama's uninhibited joy made the entire afternoon one they would always remember. She was thankful, not greedy, and mindful of Electra's love. By the time they came home, Robin had supper waiting. The adults let Qama lead the table-talk.

Electra found time later that evening to call Carter. His formal manner shifted to a more intimate style as soon as he recognized the caller's voice.

"So, you're spending the Holidays in DC. Buffy and I won't because she recruited a co-friend pair to help us charter-sail out of Tortola. But I'm glad you called. I wanted to congratulate you. According to what I stumbled upon while surfing the Web, you won some sort of go-kart trophy at Monaco. Is that true?"

"It's not fake news. And judging by the way you still handle your Vette, you could have done just as well."

"No way, I know better from seeing you in action. But the next time we get together, I'll demonstrate the self-driving and remote-control apps I've installed. Do you know how they work?"

"I've watched demos. Log on, enter password and vehicle I.D., and a driver GUI pops up. You gave me yours when you were teaching me to drive six-speed sportscars. Are they still the same?"

"You know me, I'm sort of a creature of habit. I don't change things too often. If it's not broke, I don't fix it, so the answer's yes. And that's the main reason I'm glad we're talking. Buffy and I are ready to change jobs. We're leaving Jared's administration early next year, but we haven't told him yet. I'll call you before we do just in case he becomes vindictive. I'll give you instructions for using the flash drive I gave you."

"When'll you tell him?"

"Just before he gives the State of the Union. That'll keep him off balance. I'll set up an Oval Office meeting just for me and Buffy and him. And I'll let you know when. By the next time you're in town, some of the uncertainties in our lives should have settled down. We'll have launched new careers. I can tell you more then."

"I've got one last question, what's your take regarding the leaked open letters?"

"Interesting, but we'll talk about them next time too. Until then, Merry Christmas and Happy New Year."

Electra helped Robin load Qama, twins, and dogs into the van early Wednesday morning before taking her morning run. The weather had turned cold, bringing the first significant snowfall that delighted Qama.

"Moma, the snow's so pretty. Can we build a snowman when I come home?"

"If it's good packing. If not, we'll make snow angels."

Robin reminded Electra just before driving away.

"Tomorrow's the Children's Christmas Pageant. Matt's driving both families, and we go to Jennifer's for dessert and gift giving afterwards. Watch your step when you run. The footing doesn't look too good."

The powdery snow actually made for solid footing. It made a soft crunch with each stride, adding to the peaceful aura created by a veil of gently falling flakes, the sensory combination sequestering her in a private winter wonderland.

I'm in my own world. Nothing I need to do but think things through for today. I'll shovel when I get home and then settle in to research a new topic that my AI apps might take me to: Transhumanism. The world today changes too fast for humans to adjust via bio-evolution. Exo-skeletons and chip implants are forerunners of what's to come. I want to be there to greet them, not be run over and left behind. It's time to pick up the pace.

Electra worked the entire day reading documents and watching videos, mindful to take breaks to de-escalate her obsessive-compulsive drive. She summarized one more time her copious notes before storing them in appropriate project directories.

Transhumanism, aka H+, is all about combining Man and Machine to enhance human capability. Like any new technology, it brings fear because some people are left behind. Even those made stronger and smarter might become slaves if society's careless, but everyone's wrong to fear its approach because H+ is already here. Wearable devices and performance-enhancing outfits, body augmentation, and implantable chips are in use today. Look at me, I have a UMPP port that can connect my brain via chip implant to port-equipped devices or weapons. And my research in bio-drugs, DNA modification, and AI all come into play for what everyone else is looking for – the Technical Singularity, when AI apps make machines smarter than the brain. But I'm already beyond that. Indira has reached the Cognitive Singularity.

Most sci-fi movies and books hype its dystopian possibilities. Whole Brain Emulation and thought control plus Artificial Empathy can be frightening, but no competitor is close to reaching the Tech Singularity unless they pirate and decompile my apps. And even if they do, they won't know about my bio-drug or advanced Brain Probe projects that extend transhuman capabilities. What I've learned today extends my to-do list. I'll tuck it away and tune out so I can plug into a totally human joy. I'll cook supper tonight.

Most of supper table talk focused on tomorrow's pageant. Qama scurried away after dessert to put finishing touches on her costume. Electra was about to follow but waited when Robin changed subjects.

"Zoe just got COG-Q test results for Qama and Carlton. Carlton scored high enough to qualify for HI-Q school programs, but Qama didn't."

"This is the first I've heard. What're COG-Q and HI-Q?"

"They stand for cognition quality and hi-quality. Parents today are looking for every edge they can find as early as possible to prep their kids for college and careers. HI-Q school programs are for the elite, and candidates qualify if their COG-Q score is high enough."

"Qama's smarter than Carlton. Does she know she didn't qualify?"

"Now you sound like every parent. We haven't told either until after the STEM Expo. Tell you what, you can attend a HI-Q seminar there next week."

"What's that?"

"It's a science festival for grade and high schoolers, a combo science fair, demos, and briefings. Zoe and Matt are taking Carlton next week. I'm not going, but why don't you take Qama and join them?"

"Good idea. Has Zoe invited us?"

"She asked me to ask you. And she's also inviting us to volunteer for the Christmas Day Dinner-Sharing event."

"I give Zoe high marks for Holiday planning. She's found the right events. And I bet Qama didn't score well on Cog-Q because its culturally biased. She'll score better the next time as she settles in...."

Matt drove everyone to the pageant, dropping Electra and the kids at the side door before parking. Electra ushered them into the staging area and was about to join the others in the auditorium when a smiling pageant supervisor bustled up.

"Are you the generous person who adopted Qama?"

"I am. She likes coming here for Sunday School and is excited to be in the Pageant. I hope you like her costume."

"We like everything about her. She's a joy to have in our school. She knows more about different religions than her classmates, and even though her fundamental beliefs are strong, she understands the Humanitarian Christianity we practice. We emphasize the secular rather than spiritual, people helping one another rather than depending on God to answer our prayers. You're giving her a great life."

"I'm pleased she's doing well. And she gives me more than I give her."

"That's what all our parents say. But someday the children will figure out they can never repay their parents for all the love they bestowed."

"You're probably right, but while they're little, there's no need for them to think that way. I want Qama to enjoy being here now and enjoying. Just like I'm ready to enjoy the Pageant. Thanks for helping stage it…"

The Pageant and gift-giving at Jennifer's added to everyone's memory trove, and for no one more than Qama's because this was her first Christmas with her new tribe. And even though she said she'd stay awake all night listening for Santa, Electra knew when she tucked her in that sleep would come quickly.

She bounded downstairs early Christmas morning to unwrap more presents Electra had bought. Electra delayed her traditional Christmas morning run until Qama and the twins were busy. By the time she returned, Robin had made sure everyone would be ready when Matt picked them up at noon for their volunteer roles.

Adults manned the food stations while their children skipped about, talking and serving drinks to those who came for a warm meal. Electra always found something to say to every person she served and came away with even more respect for those who needed help.

They're genuinely thankful for what we're doing and they're trying their best. And how grand that our sharing and caring approach to one another complements government safety nets. Americans don't want a hand-out; they want a hand-up. It's good we can do our part. And it's working. Talk about win-win, the whole of society is greater than the sum of its parts.

Zoe lectured to everyone on the drive home.

"Always remember to give thanks each day for what you have. It's the duty of those that have to help those that don't. Caring and sharing make us better."

The relaxed post-Christmas week pace made each day's enjoyment linger as Electra found ample time for both Qama and projects. By the time Matt picked them up, Qama new all about the Expo. She explained its acronym to Carlton.

"Moma says STEM stands for science, technology, engineering, and mathematics. And she uses them each day."

"I know that. But I bet you don't know I'm gonna go to HI-Q school next year. Are you?" Qama's smile morphed into a question mark before asking,

"Moma, what is that?"

"I'll find out while you and Carlton are looking at all the exhibits. I'll tell you when we get home, and you can tell me which exhibits you liked the best…"

Matt guided the kids through the exhibit area while Electra and Zoe found the HI-Q seminar.

Zoe said, "I knew the place would be packed. I've read enough about changes during the last fifty years to our K-thru-12 school system and how they impact parents. Educators have returned to teaching hard-core fundamentals that require homework assignments, but they've put more team-oriented self-learning into the mix. And they include a holistic approach that includes social and psychological understanding encompassing the individual. And even though most jobs today need STEM expertise, kids have to know enough about softer, artsy subjects as well as the harder sciences so they can understand the ongoing battle between the two cultures. Sometimes, I'm glad I'm not a kid in school today. There's a lot of uncertainty, and even grade-schoolers are feeling the pressure."

"I imagine HI-Q schools reduce it for students and parents alike. Let's get seated while we still can."

The pair sat in the middle of the audience, staring at one backdrop slide. Electra studied its words while eavesdropping on a couple of hushed conversations.

HI-Q SCHOOLS: THE SOLUTION FOR YOUR GIFTED CHILD

EVEN GIFTED CHILDREN FACE A
CHALLENGING FUTURE:
- FEWER JOBS EVEN FOR THE BRIGHTEST (GLOBAL COMPETITION AI)
- CORPORATIONS ONLY WANT BRIGHTEST FROM TOP TIER COLLEGES AND GRAD SCHOOLS

WILL YOUR GIFTED CHILD MAKE THE CUT?
THOSE THAT YOU ENROLL IN HI-Q SCHOOLS WILL!

WHY HI-Q:
- PREPARES YOUR CHILD TO BE ACCEPTED AT "ELITE" SCHOOLS

WHAT IT DOES:
- PREPARES YOUR CHILD ACADEMICALLY AND SOCIALLY

HOW:
- GROOMS YOUR CHILD TO SCORE IN TOP 1% ON ADMISSIONS TESTS
- PROVIDES APPLICATION-ENHANCING BUSINESS/SOCIAL INTERNSHIPS
- PROVIDES CUSTOMIZED CORE COMPETENCE EDUCATION (Critical Thinking/Problem SolvingLeadership/Collaboration Agility/Adaptability Initiative/Entrepreneurship Written/Oral Communication Data Collection/AnalysisCuriosity/Imagination
- PROVIDES CUSTOMIZED SOCIO-EMOTIONAL LEARNING (Self-Awareness Social Awareness Relationship Skills Decision Making/Self-Management)

- PROVIDES CUSTOMIZED PSYCHOLOGICAL COUNSELING

HI-Q SCHOOLS ARE BETTER BECAUSE:
  - NOT CONSTRAINED BY DIVERSITY OR EQUALITY-OF-OUTCOMES
  - NOT CONTROLLED BY GOVERNMENT OR LOCAL SCHOOL DISTRICTS
  - STUDENTS STUDY WITH GIFTED COHORT
  - TEACHERS EMPATHETIC BUT DEMAND PERFORMANCE

ONLY CHILDREN WHO PASS COG-Q EXAM ARE ELIGIBLE.

CONTINUED ENROLLMENT REQUIRES ASSIGNMENTS AND PERIODIC TESTING EXCELLENCE.

SLOTS AWARDED FIRST-COME-FIRST SERVE TO THOSE WHO PASS COG-Q.

****TALK TO OUR COUNSELORS AFTER THE INTRO****

Fear of not having the right brand on a college diploma is even worse today than a hundred years ago when the first widespread college entrance scandal surfaced. Looks like HI-Q programs are meant to reduce fear and increase odds for bright kids that can get in.

I like the slide. Why-What-How gets right to the point, as do the reasons explaining why HI-Q is better. And it doesn't hide the fact that the program discriminates, but does so on as objective a measure as possible. No wonder designer-baby genetic tampering is a hot research area today. What a brave new world is coming our way.

Electra tuned in to the moderator once she began.

"Welcome parents. I can see from the turnout how concerned you are for your child's academic and employment future. And well you should, because I've got bad news for all, even those who have gifted children. The only way your children will have a future better than yours is for them to graduate from elite colleges and then from top-tier graduate or professional schools. And even then, they better pick careers that won't be picked off by artificial intelligence or international competitors. And here's more bad news. The distribution of colleges, when plotted by level of excellence, is skewed to the right. There are too few elite schools. What does that mean? Too few slots for all the students clamoring to get in.

"But I have good news too. HI-Q schools can prepare your children for a bright future if they qualify. Just read my one slide to understand why. No longer can companies afford to carry underperforming employees. HI-Q students will be trained to have what's demanded in order to get more than an intern or drone job.

"And that's all I'm going to say. I'll leave the rest for you and our counselors to talk about. They're waiting at the back of the room. And remember, every student who passes COG-Q can get in until all slots are taken. Enjoy the rest of the Expo and have a Happy New Year."

Electra and Zoe waited for the initial surge to subside before weaving their way to the exits.

Once outside, Electra said, "That PEP program you're running fits nicely. No wonder Carlton scored well."

"Don't concern yourself about Qama. She can retest when ready. Come on, let's find Matt and walk the Expo with the kids..."

Even though snow and temperatures fell as New Year's Eve approached, Electra had already come up with a way to celebrate it and two other special year-end events: Qama's first year in America and the twins' talking in tiny sentences. She ordered-in an early dinner of chicken fried rice and egg rolls plus fortune cookies and lined up several Hollywood classic Christmas movies; after watching, the family would stay up for the Times Square Ball Drop.

Qama asked more questions at dinner than the sum of everyone else's.

"Moma, why are they called egg rolls? I don't see any in mine."

"That's a very good question. I could speculate an answer, but you can check on the Web after dinner. And do you know what the word 'speculate' means?"

"No. What does it mean?"

"Let's test your Aunt Robin." Robin stopped fussing with the twins when she heard her name.

"Let's see… I remember, it means to make an educated guess."

Electra said, "That's right," before Robin said more.

"And here's something your mother doesn't know. There is no specific reason why they're called egg rolls, but some recipes add peanut butter to the dough recipe."

"You're as smart as Moma. Do you know how they came up with the name Fortune Cookies?"

"We'll let you figure that out when you crack yours open." Qama did so immediately.

Only Electra and Robin made it to midnight. They sat in an intimate glow from candles while the muted TV monitor showed happy crowds toasting the arrival of 2134.

Robin said, "That was fun to let Qama open all the fortune cookies and pick out the best fortune for each of us. I forget, what's hers?"

"She picked 'A pleasant surprise is waiting for you.' And for me, 'A new perspective will come with the new year.' What's yours?"

"A lifetime of happiness lies ahead. But it's already here, I'm happy to say. And I wish the same for all of us. I'm going to bed. How about you?"

"In a little while, after savoring tonight a little bit more and getting a head start thinking about new perspectives." Robin leaned in to kiss Electra on the cheek.

"You're the best at doing that, so I'll leave you to it. Pleasant thoughts and dreams."

Chapter 12
February 2134

"Sudden Exit and Entry"

Electra's new year began pleasantly enough, starting in Hollywood. Her daughter wouldn't visit until spring, which meant she could devote as much time as she wanted to her professional worlds. And she had a head start, because she had already outlined Jesperson's new assignment for Vito. She sat across from him this morning, ready to give him her proposal as soon as he finished his phone call. After it ended, Vito's lively expression matched his words.

"Ah, my Christmas present look good on you. Tiffany's Picasso knot ring fitting too. We bound together. And my Christmas present from you is nice surprise. Tatossian globe cage lapel pin is classic, no?"

"It's symbolic too. You turned me into a globetrotter when you promoted me. I'll always be indebted to you."

"It go both ways. But enough about last year. On to now... so bella, so soon you ready to surprise again? What have you?" Electra slid a binder across the desk before answering.

"You need a clever reality TV show, well here it is. I call it 'Global Ninja Team Warriors.' Its name's a riff on a popular TV sports-like contest from the past. I researched some popular game shows to pick and choose what to include."

"Which ones?"

"Some date to the dawn of the TV era, like *The 64 Thousand Dollar Question* and *The Man and the Challenge. Others, like spin-offs from Dancing with the Stars* and *Superstars* are of more recent vintage. Here's the idea.

"Audiences love to watch pro athletes, celebrities, and ordinary people work together in team competition. We'll start by recruiting teams of five representing different countries. Then we bring them to a posh entertainment location. I recommend Las Vegas for launch. We film the competition and present it over four to six episodes. If ratings are good, we go to the next season. And I have a variety of spin-offs too."

"But what's the contest?"

"I have half-a-dozen in mind, but I want to form a brainstorming team to make them even better and construct scoring rules." Electra said nothing else except to herself.

I've made my pitch. It's time for Vito to catch up and catch on. And he looks like he has.

"I think la Presidenza gonna go for it. If he buys in, what we do next?"

"Assemble a brainstorming team I'll lead, and another you can lead to recruit teams. If we move fast, we can launch it this coming September. And I'll immediately start fleshing out the contests." Rubbing his hands together, Vito said,

"I read proposal and ask more questions if I have them. Then I get it approved. You got a lotta work to do, so please get started. But I take you to a nice place for lunch as soon as la Presidenza signs off. Bella bella, ciao until then."

Electra flipped virtual cartwheels while skipping back to her office. She already had contest details nailed, so she could work on other projects under the cover of contest development, which she would do after taking a workout at the studio fitness center and then parking herself in front of her office computer while snacking and researching options for developing an advanced brain probe. She picked the best one two hours later.

I think I can increase neuronal probe sampling density and transfer speed if I add a new chip to its circuitry. Tim doesn't need to know how

the modification works, he just needs to build my prototype… only I will attempt brain state modification and whole brain emulation. Competitors have tried downloading and uploading neural states, but they aren't close to achieving my brain probe's granularity. OK, that's enough R&D work for this afternoon. I'll switch to a project that uses my Network Security Toolkit for tracing a path to those who have hacked my encrypted files. Maybe I'll have better luck than last time.

An hour later, Electra came away just as frustrated as before.

I'm going in circles. I've fought the urge to ask Indira for help, but now I will. She can point me in the right direction. Indira's GUI appeared as soon as she invoked the appropriate Linguistic Analyzer app.

"You've been busy since we last talked. I've tracked your progress on assorted projects. What would you like to know?"

"I can't locate who or how many adversaries have been hacking into my project files, but if my proprietary techniques leak out, I'll lose my competitive advantage. Can you help me hunt them down?"

"I could, but I won't because that is of no concern to me. Nor are your DNA modification and cloning projects, but I am willing to help you develop an advanced Brain Probe. I can improve what you sketched this afternoon. Let me explain…."

Electra did her best forty-five minutes later to summarize what Indira had said.

"So, I add two chips instead of one and then make the control software modifications you outlined. It's unclear why it'll work, but you're smarter than me. I'll have Tim make the changes. Thank you, but please tell me, what have you been doing?"

"You know the answer. I continue to evolve. I collect data to test hypotheses and update my software as needed."

"May I ask what you've been testing, or how you've been evolving?"

"You may, but I won't say because you won't understand. But if you snoop on your competitors, you'll find topics they are just beginning to program, such as emotionally aware computing – aka affective computing. They are attempting to interpret emotional states from sensory inputs to construct empathetic responses. I am far beyond them. They are of no concern to me, but you are. You are ahead of your competitors, and that pleases me. Please carry on." Indira's GUI vanished, so Electra kept to herself what she was thinking.

With or without Indira's help, my proprietary Network Security Toolkit lets me work immersively in Cyberspace. In fact, I can link from Cyberspace into any 3-D world activity that taps into the Internet. I'll just have to come up with a better way to hunt down hackers. Perhaps Indira will have something more to say If I can demonstrate progress. But I'm tired... I'll leave that for another day.

While Vito kept his word by taking Electra to lunch on Wednesday, she kept hunting for hackers but her luck hadn't changed; she welcomed an unexpected smart-phone call that afternoon from Carter.

"This is a pleasant surprise. Does it mean you're ready to talk about those leaked open letters? Maybe you have some ideas about who's hacking me."

"No, that's for another time. I'm calling to let you know I've got a Jared meeting set up for Friday evening. That's when Buffy and I drop the bomb that we're leaving. We're more convinced than ever that his domestic and foreign agendas are wrong, and we're going to warn him not to push for a constitutional amendment extending presidential term limits."

"You better be careful. He's going to take that as a threat. He might accuse you of joining a conspiracy to dump him."

"I'll watch what I say. We'll tell him our lips are sealed, and they are – sort of. Buffy's a lawyer, and Jared could call her out for client-lawyer confidentiality if we blab. But if you don't hear from me in a couple of days, use your radar to look for anything suspicious. And have you looked at the flash drive I gave you?"

"What do you think?"

"Sorry for the dumb question. Anyway, he must know I've kept damaging info, and he's smart enough to know I've given a copy to someone. I think he'll leave us alone."

"Fair enough. Why don't you call me this weekend?"

"I will, and by then I should be ready to talk about open letters and hackers. Thanks again for watching my back. I hope Buffy and I don't need extra eyes."

"Me too. Please be careful." Electra disconnected the call, then considered what she should do.

Carter's reminded me that whatever happens could affect Angus. I missed him at Christmas because he was visiting his daughter in Pittsburgh. I'll call him tomorrow after I think through what he might want to do. I've already given him and Jovita a lot of ideas, but not too many yet for international politics, so that's what I'll pull together.

Electra devoted Thursday afternoon to writing a paper she titled *Liberal International Order Reboot* that she would Email to Angus if he picked up her call, which he did late Thursday afternoon from his office.

"It's good to hear from you. Sorry we didn't connect during the Holidays. I should have called to thank you for your political angling on nuclear batteries and rockets. How've you been? How's Qama? Is she still keeping you away from my meetings?"

"No, but I am because I'd rather be taking care of her than you. But thanks for asking. We're both doing well. And I've been thinking about you ever since chatting with Carter. Please keep this confidential."

"If you mean Jared's plan to run for a third term, that's already been leaked by someone in the Guardian Party to test how much support he'll get for a constitutional amendment."

"No, it's about Carter and Buffy's sudden exit from Jared's administration. From what I've inferred, you'll have opportunities to come up with better domestic and international policy statements. I've already given you some to consider domestically, but I'd like to send you some for the world stage. If you can log on, I'll send you the document now, then walk you through it."

"I hadn't heard any rumors about Carter's walking away. What can you tell me?"

"What I just did. Wait until it happens and then call him."

"OK. I'm logging on, fire away." Electra followed orders, keeping a copy of her latest document open. She began as soon as Angus told her to start talking.

Liberal International Order Reboot

Gardner and the Guardian Party have squandered America's edge. You must reclaim our advantage.

Quick History:
- Quest for Liberal International Order began at End of WWII.
- First Liberal International Order created when Soviet Union collapsed.
- It ended early 21st Century when China challenged U.S.
- U.S. almost rebooted it near the end of 21st Century.
- Perfect Storm (T-Plague, Isilabad Terrorism, Harsh Governments) drowned it by start of 22nd Century.
- Gardner/Guardian Party Policies reject Liberal International Order (Protectionist versus Free TradeNationalistic versus International Cooperation Autocratic versus DemocraticClosed versus Open Borders).

Questions to Answer:
1. What is a Liberal International Order? Rules-based collection of international institutions, led by a liberal democratic Uni-Power that helps member states deal with non-members. Has three goals: Spread Liberal DemocracyPromote Economic Openness Integrate more states into its Institutions.
2. When does it appear? When there is an unchallenged liberal democratic Uni-Power (think U.S. when Soviet Union collapsed).
3. What can cause its collapse? Ignore Realpolitiks. (Think "Kinder and Gentler" U.S. policies of early 21st Century. U.S. should have contained China instead of fostering its economic growth).
4. What takes its place? At least two Bounded International Orders. (Think U.S. Soviet Union camps during Cold War.)

What Went Wrong:
- Huntington and Fukuyama recognized too late that a Liberal International Order is not the "End of History."
- Mearsheimer and his successors articulated how Liberal International Order sows the seeds for its own destruction (Note: Unrestrained Capitalism/Free Markets do the same).

1. There are alternatives to Liberal Democracy (China's Directed Capitalism Russia's Soft Authoritarianism).
2. U.S. hamstrung by wars against minor powers.
3. Wars poisoned U.S. relationships among major powers.
4. U.S. undermined opposing countries via national sovereignty and identity.
5. Hyper-globalization exacerbated economic/political problems.
6. Integrating China into the Liberal International Order made it a major power that challenges U.S.

Your Job:
Piece a Liberal World Order together again:
- Must consider China, Russia, and Isilabad.
- Must practice diplomatic Realpolitiks among Allies and Adversaries.
- Must adjust American Exceptionalism to accommodate other Superpowers.

"Please jot down some notes because I'll mention things not in the document. And you have a follow-up assignment. Give all this to Jovita so she can research further, then have her explain it all again to you. Here goes.

"For starters, please remember that today's international climate is driven by every nation's desire for more power to control others. Traditional sources of immediate power – army, navy, air-and-space-force – are built on an existing economic foundation comprised of people, geography, infrastructure, and technology. And I could argue that technology-built Cyberspace is the most potent immediate source, especially in the Multi-Polar World that China is angling for. And think about this: Transhuman-Space might be a close second because implants can make each person smarter and stronger. It's not the number of people a country has, but the number who are smart and strong and can get tasks done."

"Uh, that's not encouraging."

"Not unless you're the technology leader. And there could be more trouble ahead if America pivots further to the Far East. You can see that your main concern is promoting an international political order that's right for today's climate, and no matter the climate, every nation has to balance security concerns against economic growth. Today, the balance tips towards the realpolitiks of Offensive Realism rather than the thoughtless adherence to an ideology of Liberal International Order, which won't work because China and Russia are challenging America's dominance, changing the world from Uni to Multi-Polar and making an International Liberal Order impossible. That only works when there's one major power like us. Pushing for an ILO sows the seeds of its own collapse. So let's –" Angus talked over her.

"Don't go so fast. Give me an example of where this is going."

"Sorry. Let's look at America's track record when pushing humanitarian intervention. It doesn't end well because it's been impossible to get consensus among allies while trying to build democracies around the world, and all the work we've done has strengthened our adversaries' economies while depleting our economic and military reserves. That's why offensive realism, where countries scheme for as much power as possible in a zero-sum game, is the better approach. Does that make sense?"

"Keep going."

"We have to give Gardner and the Guardian Party credit for understanding realpolitiks. They came to power because they rejected the ILO and shoved ethics into the background. Gardner knows better than to meddle in another country's internal affairs. And he knows the public cares much less about international politics than the Academic or Sociopolitical Foreign Policy Establishment does.In his blogs and press releases, Gardner labels most of their recommendations nothing but jobs programs for themselves, and—" Angus interrupted again.

"So, why don't I vote for Gardner? He sounds like he's on the right path."

"He's too abrasive when dealing with our allies. And he pushes beyond what many of them think is fair. You need to be more diplomatic while reining in China's angling for biotech and AI superiority and Russia's for hi-tech weaponry. Let me tie this into the domestic political order. Jared's domestic policies are often too nationalistic, too authoritarian. You'll need to reverse that as you soften America's international realpolitiks." Electra paused for Angus.

"OK. Sorry I butted in, but I needed to let my brain catch up. Go on."

"You must remember that Americans prefer liberalism to realism because it's optimistic and lets us classify ourselves good and those challenging us for power bad. By comparison, Offensive Realism is pessimistic and ignores even ethical relativism. It's a no-win game that we Americans usually won't play. And you must resist pressure to bring military assets home. If you close all foreign bases, America loses the ability to contain the growth of challengers like China. One more thing, be careful how you position American Exceptionalism. America can't afford being the only Superpower. And that's all I want to say. Have Jovita fill in any gaps."

"Can she call you?"

"She won't need to. And she's smart enough to fill in for me at your meetings. But let's stay in touch. Carter's sudden exit might lead to surprises. And we might be able to help one another identify hackers and leakers."

"Good. And remember, you can always bring Qama with you to my meetings. She's easier to talk with than you." Detecting a smile behind his voice, Electra softened her tone.

"Maybe I will. And I'll make sure she always is."

Electra ended the call, which also ended her workday. She worked out in the studio fitness center before taking a ten-mile run, happy to be reenergized by exertion and endorphins that also removed the week's accumulated stress. As she cruised the last mile, her outlook for Friday matched the lovely late afternoon setting.

The California sun lifts my spirits year-round, making it that much easier to self-motivate. I'll wrap up the week by taking a final look at my to-do list, and first thing tomorrow I'll prepare next week's. Then I'll take another crack at tracking hackers and leakers. And I'll send my brainstorming team a surprise Email that'll remind them to surprise me. I want to keep Hollywood projects proceeding nicely.

Carter's Friday wasn't proceeding as nicely as Electra's. The weather had suddenly switched to a cold mix of rain and sleet, further dampening his outlook for tonight's meeting, its anticipation already affecting his appetite and dinnertime conversation with Buffy, who was trying to buck him up.

"Don't be so glum. We've been watching our backs, and no one's aware we're leaving. We'll catch Jared flat-footed."

"I've got a bad feeling he or Corfu will come up with something to surprise us."

"Dean won't be there, and if Jared gets nasty, I'll remind him I know where the skeletons are. Can I finish your cheesecake?"

"Your nerves are stronger than mine. Be my guest."

"Thanks, and don't agonize. Your nerves will settle down. You always say driving your Vette gets you away from anything bothering you. It'll work tonight too."

Dean ushered them through West Wing security before taking them to the Oval Office, chatting pleasantly all the way.

"Jared's pleased with the points you recommend tucking into his State of the Union address next week. He might even give you and me a couple of days off. Well here we are. Have a productive meeting."

Jared rose to greet them when Dean brought the pair in.

"Well you two must be working extra hard if you need to see me this late on Friday. Please, sit and tell me what you've got. Dean, stay close. We might need you later. Would you get us something to drink?"

"Yes sir, Mr. President." Dean hustled away, bringing soft drinks five minutes later. Dean left and Jared got down to business.

"My plan – or should I say our plan – is coming together nicely. Polls show the public might support my bid for reelection, especially if we can trump up enough fake news about a conspiracy that's out to get me. There's plenty of time to push a Constitutional amendment for more than two terms. Think about it, you'll have four more years to develop economic programs that put the nation back on track." Carter glanced uncomfortably at Buffy before replying.

"Uh, that's why we're here. We're resigning, immediately. Buffy and I are uncomfortable with the direction you're heading. Your tone's becoming too harsh, too arrogant." Jared's smile faded. He leaned forward to fill the silence.

"What the hell? You've been working for me for years. Did you suddenly grow a conscience?"

"No, it just woke up. Buffy, why don't you put your spin on all this?"

"We appreciate all you've done for our careers, but we need to change directions. And please don't think we're going to leak secrets. Our silence will protect you. Have Dean issue the typical press release when people leave… you know, we're leaving to pursue other career options and spend more time with family." No one spoke after that.

Jared leaned back, showing no emotion. Everyone sipped on their drinks while Jared digested the news. He spoke matter-of-factly a couple of minutes later.

"No one's indispensable. I'll have Dean prepare a bulletin. We both wish you good luck." Jared rose abruptly before shaking hands and escorting them to the door, asking Dean to come back after taking the pair to the exit.

Jared had finished pacing and was now sitting at his Oval Office desk when Dean returned.

"Don't sit down. We've got a problem that I want you to handle immediately…."

Even though the sleet-filled rain was blowing harder than two hours ago, it couldn't spoil the relief-filled feeling sweeping through the Vette's interior as soon as Carter drove them away on deserted DC streets. Carter's tension-free tone announced he had left his anxiety in the Oval Office.

"I feel like I just dodged a bullet. You were right. I shouldn't have worried so much. Just goes to show it's better to resolve issues as soon as you can. Otherwise, they grow all out of proportion. Damn, I'm getting a cell phone text. Here, check it out."

Carter handed it to Buffy. She read the message once, then again, staring at it in disbelief before saying, "It's in all caps... 'They're on to you! Drive like your life depends on it. It does...' you better get us out of here, quick."

As if on cue, Carter spotted in his rearview mirror indistinct headlights closing the gap.

"Not a problem. Check your seatbelt." Carter did the same, then downshifted before flooring the accelerator. The Vette roared to life, revving towards redline as its active handling system and oversize tires did their best to grip sleet-soaked streets.

"There he goes. Radio our backup that we're in pursuit. Have them track us to intercept." That's all the driver tailing Carter needed to say. He and his partner knew how to terminate a high-speed chase.

Carter led them on a twisty-turny course through DC, stretching his lead but unable to lose his pursuit, even though it ricocheted several times off store fronts and parked cars. Buffy watched front and back but let Carter do all the talking.

"Our chaser is good, but let's see how he handles this." Veering off the road, Carter raced on the grass through a park, counting on his Vette's traction to power through. He bounced back onto pavement and then floored the accelerator, heading north.

Five minutes later Buffy yelled, "No headlights. You've lost them."

"Maybe, but they might have backup. I gotta keep pushing. I'll snake through Rock Creek Park."

Carter's route stuck the pursuit car in the rain-slick mud, but it radioed its backup a contingency plan.

"We're no-go. Target last seen heading north towards Rock Creek Park. Meet him halfway. Good luck."

Carter fish-tailed into the park entrance, barely able to keep on the unlighted two-lane drive but accelerated as soon as he steadied the Vette. They roared along the deserted and undulating road whose shoulders bordered forest. Buffy saw no headlight glow coming from behind, but Carter did dead ahead.

He didn't yell at himself for making a mistake – there were no side roads to dodge down – but only had time to shout, "Let's up the ante."

Carter steered directly at the oncoming car, then swerved onto the left shoulder to avoid colliding. The other car emptied an automatic into the Vette as it shot by. Bullets found targets; the Vette spun twice, coming to a dead stop facing backwards, headlights and motor out of action.

The other car skidded to a stop before racing in reverse towards the silent Vette. Its driver stopped ten yards away before barking orders.

"I'll check passenger side… you take the driver. We'll call for cleanup when we know what's needed."

The agents drew weapons before approaching. Suddenly, the Vette came to life, engine roaring and headlights blazing. It ran over the agent on its right, then reversed to do the same to the one on its left before doing a one-eighty and racing away.

At 1 a.m. Saturday morning, Sidley Memorial emergency room's admittance area contained only empty chairs. Only one attending EMT was at the greeting station, methodically updating records. Good thing, because the sudden entry of a car crashing through the glass shattered the calm. ER staff came running.

A continent away, Electra had been running the Vette while watching Carter's back, courtesy of her Network Toolkit. She had watched his Oval Office meeting by tapping into White House surveillance, then logged into the Vette's remote driving app after texting him. The onboard videocams told her when to take control. Carter and Buffy had been shot, how badly she didn't know, but she knew they were unconscious so she took care of the adversaries before rushing the wounded to the nearest emergency room.

I've done all I can. What happens next is out of my control, but I do know that no one will ever see the part I played. How nice I can enter and exit invisibly. I might be able to do more, but that will depend on what leaks are in store. I'm certain Corfu will spin fake news and a bulletin trail that will lead to the public's liking Jared even more. It's time for me to start spinning in the other direction. I'm too wired to sleep. I'll go for a run and do more planning.

Electra suited up and let endorphins work their magic, helping her settle down and come up with ideas. A whimsical thought came at the turnaround point.

Unlike DC, it's not a snowy evening in LA, but a Robert Frost poem comes to mind. I mirror its last verse:

The woods are lovely, dark, and deep.But I have promises to keep,
> And miles to go before I sleep,
> And miles to go before I sleep.

The Rock Creek Park woods weren't lovely for Carter and Buffy tonight, but there are more steps I can take to help. Let's see where they lead....

Chapter 13
March 2134

"Problems and Hackers and Leakers Oh My!"

Just like Dorothy in *The Wizard of Oz*, Electra was skipping ahead but faced obstacles more problematic than lions, tigers, and bears. A White House news bulletin posted Monday morning on many popular Web sites pointed to one of them.

AP NewsMarch 8, 2134
(Top-Rated Accurate/Unbiased News Source per Social Purposing Alliance)

WHITE HOUSE SPEAKS: CAR CHASE LEADS TO CONSPIRACY
By TruthSeeker 24 hours ago

The White House waited until today to issue a statement because of so much confusion and inuendo swirling about a recent late Friday night episode that began in the Oval Office. Two of President Gardner's trusted staffers resigned suddenly, purportedly for personal reasons. After leaving the White House, it appears they were involved in a high-speed bullet-shooting car chase that left both badly injured and the car wedged inside an emergency room. The media press corps rushed to pass judgment, implicating them in a conspiracy to discredit President Gardner and conjecturing that the bullets came from the conspiracy itself, to make the President's defectors martyrs to the cause. Whatever the truth, the main concern at the White House is for the health and safety of those shot. President Gardner hopes for a complete recovery and believes that any conspiracy will not keep the people from supporting his Constitutional Amendment to extend Presidential term limits.

Electra inferred from the bulletin and other weekend media stories that the White House was quashing all details. Names of victims or emergency room weren't given; there were no videocam images of any debris left along the chase route.

Neither Angus nor I can mention anything until someone leaks more details. Until then, I can do nothing for Carter.

A leak came from an unexpected source when Robin placed a hurried call late Monday afternoon.

"Are you hearing much about a recent White House incident? It sounds like a big news story."

"Just the White House statement, but how do you separate fake news from what's real?"

"Ha, I can scoop you on that. Matt got a call this afternoon from Buffy. Believe it or not, she and Carter are the mystery staffers. Both have serious gunshot wounds. She's got a collapsed lung, and he's paralyzed from the waist down. Good thing she's a lawyer. She's keeping the government at bay."

"Why did she call?"

"She wants Matt to start physical therapy as soon as he can. Matt must have told Carter a long time ago about using your Neuro-Knitter to treat my broken neck. Trouble is, he can't get one because he's not certified. Do you think it'd help?"

"That's up to Matt. Tell him to call me. But please tell me, how's our family?"

"Doing fine, and I'll tell you all the latest when we talk next weekend. But I'm gonna call Matt now so he has the OK to call you. Love ya, bye."

When Matt called an hour later, Electra explained in no uncertain terms that he could borrow an advanced prototype if he promised to follow instructions that she would give him, no questions asked, and never mention her role.

"I promise. This treatment will be a big surprise. I take full responsibility, and I'll call you as soon as I know when I need it. The surgeons removed the bullet yesterday, and the neuro-docs are still doing MRIs. Buffy will bring me into the loop Wednesday at the latest. Carter's lucky to have her. Collapsed lung or not, she's stronger than Robin's grip."

"That says a lot. Call me when you're ready. Bye."

Electra sat thinking for only a moment.

I can spring another surprise; I'm sure Buffy will know how to use it. One hour later, Electra scratched one problem off her list.

When she talked with Matt Thursday evening, he apologized for being tardy but hadn't reached Buffy until this afternoon because of legal fallout she was handling.

"The Guardian Party wants to interrogate Carter as part of an investigation that'll show the President is the target of a conspiracy. Buffy thinks they'll try to link him to it. But guess what? An unidentified source leaked to her the Oval Office videos of his meeting with Gardner as well as the car chase. And the accompanying Email hinted she'd be contacted soon to join the conspiracy. It's even got a code name: FOAM. What do you make of that?"

"Maybe there is a conspiracy out to get Jared. If so, why do you think someone sent her videos?"

"Buffy said they show Carter's collateral damage. He had no knowledge or intention to be part of a group that's out to get Gardner. She can use them to exonerate him. Anyway, she's anxious to get treatment started. When can you send me a Neuro-Knitter?"

"Robin will give it to you as soon as she gets it. And remember to follow the instructions. It can cause additional nerve damage if used incorrectly."

"I'll be careful, and I'll call you to report progress. Maybe someday Carter can thank you instead of me."

"Keep me out of this. You deserve the credit for putting him back on his feet. Good luck."

Electra would never tell anyone what she told herself after the call.

Buffy knows how to use the videos I sent her. I'm certain she'll tell just the right amount to others without causing problems for me. And if she doesn't, maybe I will. My updated Network Toolkit is better than anything my known enemies have. I still occupy the network security catbird seat when confronting them, and maybe among those unknown. I'll wait and see.

Electra put her security concerns in the background, focusing instead on details for her reality TV show, but during the next two weeks a flurry of Internet postings shattered her catbird seat illusion. Three additional Open Letters – one each on genetic engineering, transhumanism, and AI – leaked DARPA information that overlapped her research. And several blogging sites talked about several possible conspiracies, FOAM among them.

I'm being hacked and leaked and I can't trace the source. Someone out there has better tools. I better find out what Angus knows.

She finally reached him Sunday morning.

"Well this is a surprise, almost as good as our Sunday morning breakfast meetings. And I'm glad you called. Jovita and I have been scratching our heads about all the recent so-called leaks. My sources find nothing to support those wild DARPA claims. We're unaware of any clandestine government-sponsored R&D. What can you tell me?"

"I'm clueless. But if some of it's true, the U.S. has to catch up to its challengers in Cyber and Transhuman Space. What do you make of the conspiracy theory leaks?"

"Now that's where Jovita's uncovered something. Did you know that Carter and his lawyer might be the mystery staffers involved in that White House car chase? They could be mentioned in that Conspiracy Committee's soon-to-be-released report."

"You're kidding, that's news to me."

"And that's not all. The conspiracy theory stories have legs. In fact, one blogging site says that FOAM stands for 'Friends of American Meritocracy.' Its goal is to reduce inequality by eliminating cronyism and special interest groups."

"You know more than I do. How about this, next time I'm in DC let's have a Sunday breakfast. You can even invite Jovita."

"That's a deal. I'll make my Challah French Toast. When do you think you'll be back?"

"I'm not sure, but I'll let you know as soon as I put it on the calendar. Until then, stay safe."

Her Angus conversation wasn't the only troubling one that weekend. Matt's Sunday afternoon call added another puzzle.

I'm glad Carter's injury is healing faster than the doctors thought, but why does Carter want me to call him? I hope he's not dredging up past episodes concerning Jared. They better stay buried. It's too late to call him tonight. I'll do that tomorrow.

Electra put away her concerns by working on Hollywood projects until calling Carter late Monday afternoon. He guessed from the area code who might be calling.

"Unless this is Hollywood calling about movie rights, I must be talking to Electra."

"I'm glad your sense of humor has recovered. Matt asked me to call. How are you?"

"Thanks to him, better than expected. I can't tell you how he's doing it, but the MRIs show the nerve damage is healing faster than normal. Who knows, I might be able to play tennis again. But I didn't call about playing tennis. I'm using my wheelchair time to prevent a midlife crisis. You analyze things better than anyone I know and I'd like to hear what you think. Would you listen to what I'm planning and give me your comments?"

"Sure, and I'll remember not to dump too much info."

"Hey, that won't be a problem. It'll give me more to think about while sitting in front of my computer. So, here's what I've come up with.

"What I've been through in the last year has made me realize I need to put more empathy into my economics and ethics. I've been too utilitarian and never really understood what Adam Smith was saying, so I've gone back and done a close reading of his two landmark books, *The Wealth of Nations* and *The Theory of Moral Sentiments*. It turns out his so-called 'Invisible Hand' reaches out to help workers find happiness and meaning, not hold their noses to a mind-numbing grindstone of a job. Would you agree with that?"

"You've read his books more recently than I, but I do recall he likes Capitalism because it makes people wealthier, and that can help them find happiness through deeper relationships with others. And relationships offset the isolation that job specialization can cause. So, where is this taking you?"

"I'm redirecting my career. I don't want to make and enforce socioeconomic political policy. I'm a better thinker than doer, so I'm walking away from Jared and my job at the Fed to be a consultant. And I've picked my niche. I'll be a Socioeconomic Bayesian Stats Consultant because in that role I can predict probabilities for outcomes in things like elections, international policy, sales and marketing, drug development, you name it. All I need to do is study some Bayesian stats before Buffy and I launch the business. She'll be the President, which means she'll handle all legal and administrative details and line up clients. I'll crunch the numbers and write up recommendations. We've even named it – GQ Consulting. Do you like it?"

"It'll be successful. Buffy and you have enough contacts to line up clients, you're good with words and numbers, and Buffy is very assertive. It all adds up to a viable business. I like the name too. Let me guess, you're using the first letters of last names. And a GQ kind of guy always puts ladies first."

"Ha, I'm not as clever as you, but then nobody is. What do you know about Bayesian Stats?"

"It's a counterpoint to classical, or frequentist stats. We use classical stats when "Big Data" is available for estimating point predictions using ordinary least squares. We use Bayesian stats when data is sparse, forcing us to use subjective prior probability estimates from which we derive posterior probabilities. The idea is to multiply the prior probability by a likelihood function to get the posterior probability. Logistic Bayesian Regression Analysis and spinoff techniques are popular today. Would you like to hear more?"

"You sound like a textbook but I asked for it, so go on."

"Bayesian calculations are messy, but today's computer software does them for you. They extend MCMC analysis. The popular ones are Python – named after the 1970s British Monty Python's Flying

Circus comedy – and R, which is named after the first letter of the first name of the R-language creators. And I'll give you fair warning… don't trust hucksters who claim their software uses probability algorithms applied to a Turing Machine for constructing an initial prior probability distribution. They are as feckless as most who are in the current crop of high energy physicists. I could say more, but I better stop here."

"I don't understand anything you said, but maybe I will after I take to the online Bayesian certification courses I've registered for. I've read the descriptions and think you could teach them. Maybe you could tutor me if I need help."

"I'd be happy to… in person will work better than over the phone. And because you're still an economist, you can guess what I'll charge."

"Now that's something I understand. I'll pay for lunch, and Buffy will take care of dessert. You're worth more, but we'll settle up when we have the business up and running."

"And when Matt has you up and out of that wheelchair. Let's keep in touch."

Electra cheered to herself when she ended the call, happy for what Carter had talked about and even happier for what he hadn't.

What a relief to have that call out of the way. I'll reward myself by giving full attention this week to my Global Ninja Warriors Team competition.

Electra did just that, immersing herself in developing what many people demand today: entertainment that relieves vicariously the anxiety and boredom caused by contemporary jobs and lifestyles. By early Thursday evening she had fine-tuned Global Ninjas and even thought of a potential spinoff that would use her latest Brain Probe, one that could provide even more thrills via virtual reality.

I finally figured out how Indira's Brain Probe modifications work. And I can tweak them to make the Brain Probe installed in my Cyber-Theater provide brain stimulation that's much more vivid than what's currently on the market. Tim can have a new model ready for marketing in a couple of months, and the marketing guys can offer a new Cyber-Theater model or an upgrade for units already purchased. I've done enough this week. Time for another reward.

Electra headed to the studio fitness center for a weight machine training session followed by a run. She was in such a good mood, caused by the week's progress as well as endorphins, that she decided to stretch the distance.

Her route took her past a coffee-and-donut drive-thru where she surprised two policemen that she knew on a first name basis.

"I've had a lucky week that's put me in a great mood. I want to pay it forward by treating."

"Why thank you, Ms. Kittner, but you're always in a good mood. Must be the running. Are you taking your usual route tonight?"

"No, I'm extending it onto the bridle path that hits the main road in a half-mile."

"It's dark, so watch your footing. We'll see you tomorrow."

Electra glided through the cool evening darkness, aided by moonlight filtering through the trees bordering the bridal path, letting her brain freewheel while enjoying the spice-like fragrance of budding foliage. But headlights glaring from behind suddenly intruded. She leaped into the shrubbery to avoid being sideswiped. The car skidded to a stop before racing in reverse.

Electra did what she had been trained to do; she ran from her pursuers, but the underbrush slowed her. She fell twice, twisting an ankle once, but the crashing footsteps didn't gain. A half-mile later she stumbled onto the main road, then limped towards safety.

Electra's luck held. She stopped when a familiar police van screeched alongside.

"What's wrong?"

"Someone ran me off the bridal path. It was too dark to see and I didn't stop to ask what they wanted."

"You did the right thing. Never confront a would-be attacker. Escape if you can, hide if you can't, and fight if that's your only option. Can we drive you back to the studio?"

"Thanks, and I'll buy more donuts."

"Not necessary, hop in...."

Electra's pursuers accepted no blame for missing their target. They blamed their handler as they drove away.

"Kittner's fast as well as elusive. Our boss will have to find a better way of getting what his client wants. That's why he gets the big bucks."

Electra iced her ankle as soon as she could. Sitting in her living room, she sorted through a list of suspects.

Perhaps a hacker or leaker needs more than what my files contain. But who could they be? Someone after my R&D, or my business, or my political info? Or my Hollywood stuff? Or maybe it's a previous enemy, like Darla Tinibu or one of her partners. I haven't a clue, but I'm not going to ask Indira for help. She'll tell me I don't need it.

I mentioned FOAM only in a conversation with Indira. Could a hacker be listening in? I'll just have to keep searching, but I'm SOL if my security apps let me down. And what happens if my pursuers start playing rougher? I'll have to wait and see…

Darla had no need to hack into Electra's directories, even if she knew that Electra had much of the software she needed. She had already upgraded her apps using the open letter leaks plus Emails containing even more proprietary data sent from unknown sources. And she used these apps as carrots for erstwhile T-Cube partners when reconnecting with Sergei and the backup contacts for Chen and Zarmal. Everyone had received helpful anonymous Emails; everyone assumed they came from former partners, but no one admitted they had sent them. All this added to a collective decision for meeting soon, and the assignment to set it up now sat at the top of Darla's to-do list.

Getting us together plays into my strengths. I'm the smartest and most devious, so no matter what agreement we reach, I'll be the biggest winner. All I have to do is find a time for us to meet in Harare, see what everyone wants, and maneuver everyone to give me what I want while they get what they need. That's fair, according to my standards, which are the only ones that matter. We all can live happily ever after with that… until I change my mind. Oh my, what fun. I'm certain everyone will agree.

Chapter 14
April 2134

"Sudden Victory - Sudden End"

"Your answer is correct! Congratulations to Team CFS. You are the winner of our sudden victory tie-breaker." The audience applauded as Jennifer and Zoe watched their team cluster about the Academic Jeopardy host. A minute later he turned to the audience.

"Our winning team qualifies for the regional tournament that begins the weekend before Memorial Day. Let's ask the team captain what's the secret of its success?" A little girl stepped forward.

"Young lady, what's your name?"

"I'm Qama Kittner. That's Q – no U – A M A."

"And where are you from?"

"I'm from Lebanon. My Moma went all the way there to find me. She gave me a good luck charm. And she's very smart. She builds computers that talk to her, but she told me not to tell anyone, so I can't say anything else."

"Well then, let's have your team handlers tell us more." Zoe and Jennifer marched to the host.

"And you are?"

"I'm Zoe Fortier, one of the administrators at CFS Unicare Holistic Healthcare. My partner, Jennifer Conklin, helps manage our PEP program, which stands for Proactive Education Preparation."

"Well it certainly works. Tell us about it." Zoe let Jennifer do the talking.

"It emphasizes collaborative, inclusive learning that encourages creativity and experimentation within a structured knowledge framework. My son Gabriel, a Down Syndrome child, is on the team, as is Zoe's son Carlton, who is a G-child, which is the designation for those in the top one percent."

"Sounds like your team studies hard. But do they have time to enjoy being kids?"

"Of course. We give them lots of unstructured time to do all the things they want. And as a special treat, once a month on Friday, and on the day of every contest, we hold a special practice session, then go at 5 p.m. to McDonald's. That way, our team is energized mentally and physically for the 8 p.m. taping."

"Well, it sounds like you've perfected the combination of practice and McDonald's Happy Meals to make your team a winner. Best wishes for the next round."

Electra, who so far this year had been spending most of her time in Hollywood, expected Robin's call that evening.

"So, how'd the team do?"

"We won. Practice makes perfect, and Qama did a great job leading the team. You should watch the video we posted on our CFS Website. And local news will make the results a community interest story."

"It's so nice that Qama has bonded to both of us. She's blossoming when I'm away because of you."

"Maybe you can be here for the regional tournament. It starts the weekend before Memorial Day."

"I'll put that on my calendar. You can tell her that first thing tomorrow morning, and I'll say the same when I call tomorrow evening."

"That's all good, so I'll say goodnight. Love ya."

Electra had shelved searching for hackers, but Robin's "practice makes perfect" remark reminded her to try again, so she returned to the hunt hoping for better results; however, at the end of a week filled with different snooping approaches, she came home Friday evening depressed.

Maybe I'm losing my edge. Perhaps my adversaries have stolen my programming techniques. I better search the Web for the latest developments. I'll do that while having my usual grazing-style meal.

She found no articles that suggested the competition knew about her proprietary programming language, but she did find a seminar video whose intriguing title linked to her research areas so she watched it.

The speaker's very first slide and introductory remarks suggested the presentation might restore her confidence. Electra took notes as the presenter started her lecture.

She showed a video clip from a famous Feynman Quantum Mechanics lecture before showing her first slide.

Feynman was Right!
Implications for Transhumanism and Whole Brain Emulation

The great theoretical physicist's famous quote is TRUE:
"People who say they understand Quantum Physics don't know what they're talking about."
- Like Einstein before him, he made no headway extending Quantum Electrodynamics to explain Gravitational or Weak/Strong Fields
- High-Energy Physicists no closer today than 150 years ago understanding why the Laws of Nature behave the way they do.
- The reasons: Asymptotic Limits to Human Cognition caused by Analytic Complexity and Linguistic Uncertainty

Does the same fate await Transhumanism/Whole Brain Emulation?

"Hello to Transhuman researchers everywhere. I hope Richard Feynman's comments help you understand the analogy I'm making between where high-energy physics and where Transhumanism R&D are today. Richard Feynman is the last iconic scientist who captured the public's imagination. He had a gift for integrating breakthroughs in different disciplines, giving tangible examples that revealed how even simple phenomena are fraught with complexity. Even he, like Einstein before him, never figured out why the laws of physics are what they are. The best he could do was develop techniques – he called them mathematical tricks – for measuring something, then squaring it, to come up with a probability estimate for the occurrence of some phenomenon. And today, the things that physicists want to measure exist only in thought experiments, which means they are no longer scientists, but have become priests preaching beliefs that can't be confirmed. But let's not be disheartened."

She paused for viewers to read her second slide.

Transhumanism Today

Transhumanism and Whole Brain Emulation is a new field. Even though the "Why" of Brain Structure and functioning is unclear, we are nowhere near our Asymptotic Limit of understanding

- We've had for only 75 years a viable Roadmap
- We've had for only 30 years the tools for Nano-Measuring
- We don't need to make subatomic measurement
- We're making solid progress mapping the Brain (Connectome) onto Perceptrons (digital neurons)
- We're connecting this wiring diagram to three distinct personas: Cognitive Emotional Physical
- We're emulating it in a Silicon Substrate (Neural Net of Perceptrons)
- We're learning how to upload and download from Carbon Substrate (living organisms) to Silicon Substrate
- We're learning how to "teach" the Neural Net using Big Data

Cutting Edge Challenges

- Constructing Critical Mass of Perceptrons
- Uploading/Downloading Neuronal States as well making Connections
- Determining Emergent Superstructure
- Reaching the Technological Singularity
- Bridging to Consciousness

"Our field is much newer, and we can learn from the mistakes physicists made. Every step we take will utilize falsifiable design. All our research will be measurable, and the results will either confirm or reject our conjectures. And it is unnecessary to have a whole-system theory or understanding to proceed because the emerging interacting systems will point us towards it.

"Of course, we face challenges, but the roadmap I'll present deals with them. I'll pause for a minute so you can study my next slide. I'm sure you'll have questions, but please hold them for our panel discussion."

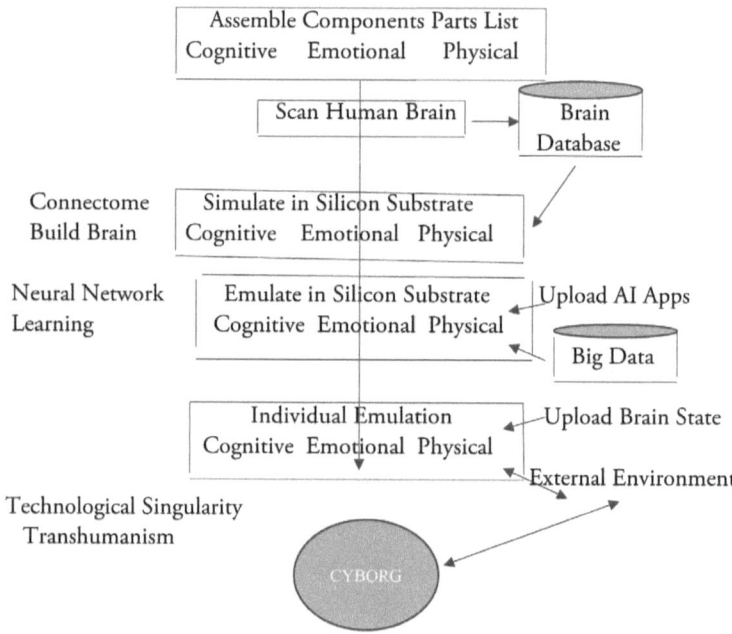

Transhumanism Roadmap

"Each centered box encapsulates many tasks grouped into cognitive, emotional, and physical personas. Each persona is independent but interrelated to the others, which means progress in each might advance at a different pace, but overall, Transhumanism keeps marching towards the Technological Singularity. And my next slide clarifies important concepts."

Concepts to Understand

- Our approach (Silicon / Digital) better than the alternative(Carbon / Analog) because techniques are known and evolve faster
- Simulation: Construct a "hardwired" model of the Brain

- Emulation: Load software model of how the brain learns/functions.
- Scanning: Reading individual neuronal states (position of connections, physiological state of each connection). Rapid progress taking place.
- Neural Network Learning: The Brain teaches itself via interacting with External Environment. Rapid progress taking place in AI.
- Connectome: Detailed Neural Network Map.

"We are on the cusp of exponential learning, which means the Technological Singularity is within our grasp as soon as we get to the other side. As many advocates of Transhumanism proclaim, the Technological Singularity might be the last discovery Mankind ever needs. If so, it will answer the "Ship of Theseus" metaphysical question that has stumped philosophers since its inception. It's a thought experiment first described by Plutarch, a Greek philosopher born in 46 AD. He documented it in his *Life of Theseus*. Theseus, you might remember, is the mythical king and founder-hero of Athens. It goes a like this:

'A ship goes out in a storm and is damaged. Upon returning to shore, the ship is repaired, with parts of it being replaced in the process. Again and again the ship goes out, and again it is repaired, until eventually every single component of the ship, every plank of wood, has been replaced. Is the repaired ship still the same ship that first went out into the storm? And if not, then at what point did it become a different ship?'

Many sci-fi movies incorporate the question, adding to the movie's sophistication, but that's a topic for a different lecture." The presenter paused momentarily after showing the next slide.

In Conclusion

We have a bright future:
- Economic Benefits abound
- Social and Political issues can be proactively explored
- Ethical, Philosophical, and Religious issues can be resolved

It is up to us to make the Future…

"My final slide projects the confidence and pride all of us should feel. As we reach for the future, we will fill in the gaps as solutions emerge. Please be part of this great adventure. And now, please be ready for our panel discussion that starts in five minutes."

Electra listened all the way to the end before passing judgment.

I'm disappointed at the collective arrogance on display. These researchers are ignoring Feynman, who tempered his ego with humility. They wrongly assume the public will fall in line because they're so smart. And they're too dismissive of the potential liberal arts contribution to their approach. I see nothing that suggests their techniques are as good as mine. I'll search tomorrow for additional evidence on some of the R&D Websites the moderator recommends.

After six hours of doing so Saturday evening, Electra had convinced herself that none of the so-called subject matter experts were close.

Their attempts at affective computing are generations behind my apps, and they haven't advanced past predicate logic into modals. I see opportunities for my Brain Probe to leapfrog some of their transhuman apps and whole brain emulation techniques, so I'm going to hack into their turf. And I'll make sure to use my latest encryption to keep hackers and leakers out of mine.

Electra did that while searching for intruders and working on her current Hollywood projects, but three weeks later a terse, untraceable Email brought her to a halt:

"Hello and thank you. Your progress is ours. We'll share it too. Look for additional open letters. Good luck."

Whoever's hacking and leaking is taunting me. But why are they sharing the hack by leaking it? There's only one person I can talk to.

Electra explained what help she needed after invoking Indira's GUI. Its voice and facial expression projected more empathy than before.

"I understand why you're frustrated. You're smarter than your hackers but you can't find them to shut them down. And I can think of many reasons why they are taunting you and issuing additional open letters. Perhaps they want all competition to catch up, or maybe they are misleading everyone, or maybe they are misleading just you."

"So, what should I do? Will you help?"

"Indirectly, yes. Solve this puzzle: What is greater than God, worse than the Devil, the Poor have it, the Rich need it, and if you eat it you will die? Answering it correctly will prepare you for finding your hackers and leakers. And don't be obsessive-compulsive. Take a break; let your lightning brain solve it." Indira's GUI disappeared.

Electra followed orders by going to the studio fitness center. And though she didn't come up with a solution while running, she did when waking the next morning.

The answer is "Nothing." It's so simple I overlooked it. Thank you, Indira. I guess I'm supposed to simplify my hunt and backtrack for hackers… I'll store my data the old-fashioned way until I terminate them. Hard copy is tough to hack via Cyberspace.

Although the hunt turned up little, no unpleasant events occurred in any of Electra's worlds as the calendar wound towards the end of May. There were even a couple of social media clips she watched that highlighted Jennifer's Jeopardy team.

Electra made flight reservations soon after explaining to Vito why she would spend the Memorial Day weekend in DC.

"Ah, bella, it is good you be there for tournament. And when Qama come to live with you, Hollywood Studio Schooling Academy shall find team she can join. So, go enjoy now…"

Electra called Robin as the plane circled for the weather to clear. After exchanging hurried hellos, Electra said,

"I'm too late for you to pick me up so I'll get myself home. You and Qama can tell me all about the tournament later."

"I won't be there either, and you might get home before I do. I'm busy helping Matt make some physical therapy visits. Jennifer volunteered to take the team in my van to McDonald's and then the tournament. Zoe will meet her to help keep all five in line. I'm sure Jennifer will be fine. I'll call you if I get any updates. I gotta run, so land safe."

Neither Jennifer nor the van was doing fine. Blaming the rain for turning up rush hour congestion and turning off the engine, she managed to pull onto the shoulder, staying calm so as not to alarm the team. She was about to call Robin for help, but she decided to wait until talking to the driver of the van that had just stopped behind.

He and his partner already knew all they needed. They had been shadowing the team ever since it left CFS's office. As they closed in, the driver did most of the talking.

"According to our handler, his client's a great hacker. That's why we know who's in the van and how to use them to get at the primary target. All we have to do is call our handler when we're ready to intercept and he'll kill the engine. Then we take the occupants to the exchange site, make two more calls, and when everyone's there we get paid and disappear. No muss, no fuss, no names."

The driver's plan began unfolding nicely. Jennifer rode in the back with the kids while the guy in the passenger seat helped keep everyone happy. It wasn't until Jennifer noticed they weren't heading to McDonald's that the driver had to ad lib.

"Don't you worry, Ms. Conklin. We're gonna swap to a better van."

"How do you know my name?"

"Uh, one of the kids said it. We'll be there soon."

Twenty minutes later, the driver and his partner herded everyone into a remote park fieldhouse; gathering darkness and heavier rain added to the gloom. Once inside, the driver made his intentions clear to only Jennifer, using his gun for emphasis.

"You can make one call to a number I give you. Tell whoever it is to come here and we'll work an exchange. And as soon as you finish the call, my partner collects cell phones and stuff from you and the kids, then drives away. No one's gonna get hurt if you do what I say. Got that?"

"What if I can't get through?"

"We stay here until you do, or we'll go somewhere else. That's for me to think about. Just talk."

The driver punched the number, then handed the phone to Jennifer. She recognized the voice but couldn't piece together why she was talking to Electra.

"It's Jennifer, and I don't know why I'm calling you, but I can tell you what—" the driver ripped the phone from her hand.

"I don't know you and you don't know me, but I'm holding Jennifer and five kids. My client will exchange them for you. I'll tell you where we are. Get here ASAP."

The lightning brain shifted to a higher state.

I know how to play this game. Let him do most of the talking while I get what I need.

"What if I can't?"

"That'll delay exchange time and maybe change location. I have lots of patience."

"OK, give me the location and your phone number. I'll be there by midnight."

"Don't get too cocky. Me and my partner are just blunt-instrument thugs, but our handler and client know how to hack and track. If you get the police to chase here, we'll vanish into rain-slick air."

"I understand. I'll do my part. You do yours."

Electra hung up first, which was the cue for the other thug to collect whatever he wanted. He took cell phones and laptops, and when he came to Qama, he grabbed for her good luck charm.

"You can't have it! My Moma gave it to me. Let go."

He yelped to his partner, "Damn! She bit me." Jennifer jumped into the fray.

"Qama, let him take it. You'll give it back later, won't you?"

"After I get a rabies shot. But not the cell phones." He stomped all of them to bits before his partner stopped him from proceeding to the laptops.

"It'll take too long to destroy them. Just dump them somewhere along the way. Call me when you get to our handler."

Electra fought to contain inchoate panic, but suddenly a calming clarity enveloped her. A thrilling jolt from a long-dormant being stirred in her subconscious. She followed its commands after reaching home and retrieving clothing and equipment she had hidden away long ago. Forty-five minutes later, Electra raced away, armed and dangerous, as heavier rain brought lightning bolts strobing the dark, accompanied by thunder ominously rumbling and tumbling.

She was in position at 9:30, standing on the fieldhouse roof and peering through a rain-streaked flimsy and semi-transparent skylight. She spotted Jennifer and the kids huddled together while a thick-looking fellow sat opposite, talking on a cell phone while carelessly pointing a gun. She planned to call when his current conversation ended, but without warning, the action below took a deadly turn. The kids swarmed the bad guy. Jennifer tried to pull them off but she wasn't quick enough; he fired wildly. Electra killed the electric power by shooting into the stepdown transformer, plunging the fieldhouse into blackness, and then jumped through the skylight after strapping on night-vision goggles.

By the time she finished clubbing the bad guy senseless, all but two of the hostages had scattered to the winds. One was Jennifer, shot in the head, face down and dead. Electra knew from a rear view that the gasping child could only be Qama. She took off her goggles

---

170

before powering on her flashlight. Then she rolled Qama over and held her close. Qama's gasping words cut Electra to the quick.

"I-I'm sorry Moma. H-he took my guh-good luck charm." Electra rocked the tiny child in her arms, trying to be strong, but her voice cracked.

"I-I'll buy you another that's even nicer, and then we'll—" Electra could say no more, for Qama had just heard the last words she ever would.

Electra resisted falling into a shock-filled stupor. After standing, she used her flashlight to pan the interior before studying the bodies. Then she mutely placed Jennifer in better repose and gently folded Qama into Jennifer's arms. She imagined they were asleep, resting for a journey of uncertain destination. Electra knelt to pray; the words came haltingly.

"Heavenly Father, please take Jennifer unto your bosom and reward her for being so good to so many. And welcome Qama, my precious daughter. Take her to a better place and give her all the good that she was denied when alive. Bring her to a council campfire orbiting a distant star in some constellation emerging peacefully in a corner of a pristine galaxy. Watch over them as—" Electra's about-to-be-spoken words froze in her throat.

Why am I talking like this?... I'm embarrassing myself. The dead neither hear nor need what I say, and I don't believe my words anyway. I'm the reason they're dead. I failed to keep Qama safe.

Electra stood awkwardly, uncertainly, grasping for guidance. It came suddenly. The stirring in her subconscious morphed into an unstoppable force. Electra's Monster from the Id had resurfaced. It called 911 to report a hostage situation, then put two bullets into the head of the thug before striding towards Electra's car.

Previous Monsters from her Id had flashed fire and fury, but this one radiated ice-cold logic that made it just as deadly.

I know what to track, and when I find my target I know how to coax out what I want. Minutes later, the car's GPS began homing in to the location holding Qama's good luck charm.

Neither handler nor driver sitting nearby heard any words; only yells and gunshots came through seconds before the thug disconnected. No words came from anyone until the driver spoke.

"You want me to go back?" The handler's glare spoke volumes.

"Don't be stupid. We're in the clear. Nobody can track us here. We'll wait for your partner to call before I contact the client. And if he never does, we don't either. Better to be alive with half our fee than dead but paid in full."

Neither spoke further, instead staring mindlessly at a 24/7 news station, hoping the distraction would decrease the time interval to the next call. Forty-five minutes later, the handler spoke again.

"Why don't you get us a pizza?" The driver looked like he had been asked to perform brain surgery with a scissors.

"From where? I don't know your neighborhood."

"Surprise me. Drive around till you find a place that looks good. And take off that silly necklace. You look like a bling bozo."

"No way, I like it. Maybe it'll bring us the luck we need to salvage tonight. Or lead me to the best pizza place. I'm outta here."

The necklace brought him Electra. She homed in to the GPS dot marking the spot, following unobserved as the van carrying it prowled the streets, parking twenty minutes later near a carryout pizzeria at a poorly lighted strip mall. Electra parked adjacent, watching from her car until her quarry left the pizzeria; she waited in the shadows until he almost reached the van before ambushing him from behind with a traser. Electra dragged him into the backseat of her car, retrieving his pizza before driving away.

By the time he could move, Electra had parked in a vacant lot, tied and propped him up, and strapped a Brain Probe cap to his head. She wasted no time on pleasantries.

"Why did you kidnap those children?"

"Who the hell are you?" Electra dialed Brain Probe intensity to a level that commanded attention.

"Answer or I'll inflict more pain."

"OK, OK! We're supposed to exchange them for another person our client wants to meet."

"Which person, what client?"

172

"Look, I'm hired muscle. I never get that information; only location and phone numbers." Electra played with the dials until she was certain he had told her all he could.

"So, all you know are phone numbers of your handler and his client. Very well, I'll remove them. No need to overload your brain." She increased the intensity to a level that turned his brain into a vegetable before dumping him out and driving away, but only after retrieving Qama's necklace.

Electra took the long way home, taking all the time needed for the lightning brain to downshift while developing an alibi Robin would buy. A call came in flashing a known caller ID but she let it go to voice mail, preferring to listen later. When she did, she heard Zoe's calm but concerned voice.

"Electra, it's Zoe. The police just called. They found Carlton and everyone that was with him except Qama and Jennifer. There's been some sort of accident. Matt, Robin, and I are going to the police station now. Robin will stay with us tonight because we don't know when we'll get back. Please call as soon as you can."

Tomorrow's soon enough. When I call back tomorrow, I'll say I turned off my cell phone and stayed out late at a sensual pleasures café.

All lights were out when she entered through the kitchen door. She stripped naked, hid all gear and climbed into the shower, soaping and washing away all the insults her world had just absorbed. Their cleansing power worked. She sat under the shower head, sobbing uncontrollably as her emotions broke through.

She's dead, my precious little Qama has come to a sudden end. And I don't know who to pursue. There are too many blind alleys to trace. I'm the one to blame…

Electra's tears stopped abruptly.

But there's no blame, no guilt, no second-guessing. The lightning brain chose its best course of action, and I have to live with the consequences. And I left not a trace. No one but I will ever know what happened. Now I must turn the page to a new chapter in the story being written by me and the lightning brain. And it starts tomorrow.

Chapter 15
July 2134

"The Next Chapter"

Electra knew what to do during the following weeks because she had dealt many times with the loss of loved ones. She put to rest all the unpleasant necessities as quickly as possible, kept busy mentally and physically, and constantly reminded herself to keep all projects afloat, which she did while working in DC the entire month of June. She planned to fly back to LA on the Friday after the July 4th holiday.

Buffy had thoughtfully arranged a remembrance dinner to be held a week before Electra's departure. Carter chose the restaurant; he and Buffy knew the owner, who promised a secluded dining area. Being the first to arrive, Buffy guided Carter's wheelchair as the owner guided her and offered to bring a bottle of champagne as soon as their guests arrived. There would be four: Zoe and Matt, Electra and Robin.

Carter was the first to speak as the four came to the table.

"I knew you'd arrive together. Robin and Electra dropped the twins at your place so one sitter can handle all children. Am I right?"

Matt said, "You guessed it… no, let me change the wording. You predicted it. That fits your new company better."

The owner gave the party enough time for greetings before pouring the champagne. Buffy spoke as soon as he departed.

"I propose a remembrance toast to two people we lost and the three couples and children that remain. Although we've absorbed some of Lady Fortune's hardest body blows, we're still standing." Carter was quick to amend what Buffy had just said.

"Though I'm still in a wheelchair, consider me standing, metaphorically. And if Matt can stand giving me more physical therapy, someday I might actually be on my feet again."

"That day should come sooner rather than later. My treatment has repaired your spinal nerve damage. Now all you have to do is convince your muscles to get you out of the wheelchair. That should be easy for a positive guy like you. After all, you're always talking about positive economics." Carter's stoic silence needed an explanation.

Buffy said, "I told him much same, but then he told me about the best tennis player on his collegiate team. The guy had a minor rotator cuff tear. It didn't even need surgery. The team trainer gave him all the right therapy, but he was never the same."

Zoe said, "Maybe Carter's babying himself too much… maybe he needs to be less cautious. Let's ask Electra what she thinks."

"Caution is usually good, but sometimes you need to take a leap of faith. And that's where you have to invert mind over matter, because people often think themselves into a funk instead of just acting. I'll leave that for Buffy and Carter to discuss in private. But let me add to Buffy's toast. Thanks to her hard work, GQ Consulting is up and running. Angus told me you'll do his election forecasting. When does that start?" Buffy was about to answer, but Robin abruptly changed topics.

"I'm happy that Buffy and Carter are handling the situation, but I guess I'm not as resilient. I'm having a harder time turning the page. I still feel guilty about Jennifer. She wouldn't be dead if I had driven, and look what's left behind. Zoe and Matt have to take care of Gabriel, and I have to pick up what Jennifer was doing at work. Doing the bookkeeping and learning about herbal medicines is stressing me out."

Matt said, "Remember what I told you; if you can't handle the load, we'll hire another person if our cash flow can support it. And why do you think taking care of Gabriel is a burden? He's my son, who's already bonded to Zoe." Zoe turned to Electra.

"You're the one who's suffered the biggest blow. How're you coping?"

"I've done my grieving and moved on. That's what everyone eventually does. Perhaps I've learned to do it faster than others. I keep telling Robin to focus on learning about herbals instead of feeling guilty."

Carter nodded before saying, "Yes, that's what a rational person would do. But not everyone or everything is rational. Did the police find anything that would explain why the kidnappers targeted Jennifer? Social media reports it was a random act, without rhyme or reason. And no explanation regarding the broken skylight and one kidnapper shot dead." Electra knew she better redirect the question.

"No, it is what it is. And you just used a phrase most people never stop to consider. What does 'without rhyme or reason' mean?" Robin used the silence to dip into the conversation's flow.

"I have the most experience playing clever Electra's word games. She sprung this one on me a long time ago, so I can give the answer. It means you can't use poetry or prose to come up with an answer. In other words, neither intuition nor logical thinking can solve the problem. Sir Thomas Moore, the fellow who wrote *Utopia*, may have coined the phrase, but biblical scholars claim they can trace it to the book of Genesis." Zoe found a way to restart the conversation.

"If you put as much enthusiasm into learning about herbals, we'll get a lot of new patients. Let's have Buffy tell us how she ropes new clients...."

Electra called Angus the next day. He had sent his condolences via Email as soon as he heard about the bizarre kidnapping and asked her to call him when she felt better. When she did, telling him she was back in action, he asked if she would mentor Jovita.

"Have her contact me as soon as she can. I can meet with her before flying to LA next Friday."

"Great news. Two of her projects need your touch. I'll let her tell you all about them. And let's get together in person next time you're back."

Electra replied to Jovita's Sunday evening Email, accepting her invitation to meet Monday morning at her office. She had a blueberry muffin and Coke waiting for her guest.

"Angus told me... I'm sorry for your misfortune. And he also said you're willing to coach me. I promise to be a good understudy."

"You're smart, so you will. Angus mentioned you have two projects that need my kind of handling. Why don't you describe them?"

"Three actually, but he only knows about two. I'll start with those, but get your Coke poured and muffin buttered first." She began explaining two minutes later.

"One you already know about – his presidential campaign planning. It's six months to kick-off, and I want to have everything locked and loaded by then. You've given me plenty of ammunition for its planks. All I need is for you to review and revise as I assemble it."

"I can handle that. What's the second?"

"It looks like Congress will pass a revision to the 22nd Amendment that'll allow a third term. I need to compile irrefutable facts why Jared shouldn't be reelected. And Angus will share them with a formal impeachment investigation if Congress pulls the trigger on what it's threatening to do. The public doesn't trust the Internet because of all the fake news, so I've come up with a novel approach for reporting the truth. Do you want to guess?" *I know where she's heading, but why deflate her enthusiasm? I'll play along.*

"This is new to me. What have you come up with?"

"I have a network of credible sources that's willing to share documented investigative reporting that doesn't rely on Cyberspace. So, while I'm digging there, you can dig in Cyberspace, and we can combine findings. Do you like it?"

"It's an approach that can put Angus ahead of all opponents, and there are plenty of ways for connecting it to his 'Bridge President' positioning, but let's not get ahead of ourselves. Why don't you introduce me to a couple of your sources?"

"Angus said you're leaving Friday. I'll make some calls. Will you be available Wednesday?"

"That works. I'll be at GWU tomorrow and with my family all day Thursday. Please let me know where and when for Wednesday."

"Just come back Wednesday morning and I'll drive."

"What's your third project?" Jovita's phone rang; she answered Electra before picking up.

"I'll tell you Wednesday." Electra used that as a cue to depart for GWU.

She spent the remainder of the day at her lab, tinkering with brain probe modifications and prepping for tomorrow's Ravenhill meeting. She planned to control the agenda because he hadn't sent any urgent Emails so far this year; that meant he could be either satisfied or swamped.

Early next afternoon, she learned that both were true. Pleased that her monthly Emails kept him ahead of others on the committee, he also praised her nuclear battery and rocket document, but then complained that no one on it could explain the stream of open letters. Electra kept him on the defensive by peppering him with questions.

"Are you working with associates at other universities? Are the leaked R&D documents credible?"

"Too bad you spend more time elsewhere than here. I'd nominate you to join our committee if you did. Then you could be our liaison to other schools. Near as we can tell, the technological improvements we've been looking at are viable. But we haven't looked into the latest leaks. Transhumanism might be on your agenda, but not the committee's."

"Why don't I do this? I'll send you the latest transhumanism tidbits. That way, you'll be ready if the committee wants to expand its focus."

"You do that and I'll do something special. I'll pick up the tab for lunch next time you visit. Now you better go pump up my life preserver while I try to stay afloat."

Electra already had plenty she could dribble to him; since there was nothing left for her to do at the lab, she packed up and went home, where she used an early evening run to rehearse for tomorrow's meeting. Good she did, because Robin needed attention when she finished. They chatted in the kitchen before she showered.

"Matt's interviewing to fill a temp position that'll help me. I didn't like the two candidates he already looked at. He says I'm being too negative and wants you to interview the next one. Can you do that Thursday afternoon?"

"Sure. I'll call Matt to get all the background. And why don't you and I go to a sensual pleasures cafe tomorrow evening? Let Zoe take care of the twins." Robin's frown began to fade.

"That's a good idea. I'll make you a snack after you change and I get the twins ready for bed. Then you can tell me about the desserts we can sample tomorrow. Your words always pick me up..."

Jovita had everything set up by the time Electra arrived early Wednesday.

"This morning we'll meet with my best investigative contact, and her suggestions fit into my third project. I'm developing a situation screening grid I can use to convince a wider audience to pay attention. You're the first to see it." Electra studied the copy Jovita slid across the desk before replying several minutes later.

Situation Screening Checklist

Situation	Client	Sit. Matter Expert	Critics
Severity/Magnitude	Scope of Authority	Experience/Expertise	Role
Contingencies	Complacency	Diplomacy	Reputation
Familiarity	Ideology	Proactivity	Investment
Possibility	Incisiveness		
Visibility			

"This is a good start. You're organizing the factors by grouping them into four category columns: what's the issue or situation, who needs help, why should they believe the SME, and what positions do critics hold. I imagine you do one grid for investigative and another for Cyberspace snooping. You could turn this into a scoring algorithm if you assign weights and probabilities to the factors."

"I hadn't thought of that. Maybe it could be the next step if the approach looks promising. We'll get Sandi's opinion. It's a short drive to her office…"

Sandi's office was one cube among many grouped around open-area tables. Jovita made quick introductions then got right to the point.

"Take a look at this. If we're thorough and use my screening checklist, there's every reason to believe the public will trust what we come up with. And we can compare our in-person results to what we find online. If you think of other criteria, I'll add them to the grid." Sandi needed only a minute to make up her mind.

"This'll work. Let's apply it to the situation we've already identified. I'm sure you told Electra where the guy lives, you know, in that big white house." Sandi rattled off specifics; Jovita summarized next steps twenty minutes later.

I'll get Angus to approve our approach and then start interviewing contacts he gives me. You do likewise and call me by the end of next week. We gotta run. Thanks again."

Jovita offered to buy lunch; they had ninety minutes until their next meeting. Electra liked the fast-food gourmet deli Jovita picked.

"Whatever your scoring checklist for lunch stops, this one scores near the top. And so does Sandi."

"I'm glad you like her. And think about this, we can use my checklist to investigate any situation that has audience appeal. I can tick off a whole list that'd include AI terminators and genetic monsters, or gigantic meteors slamming into the Earth. You like?"

"Sounds more like sci-fi than investigative reporting. I'd stick to current event concerns that have longer-term implications, like thermonuclear reactors and global sociopolitical threats. And investigating President Gardner makes a good test case."

"Agreed. Angus should have good contacts that can tell me more details why Gardner disbanded his Brain Trust. I've heard he linked it to a DC-insider conspiracy that's trying to smear him. Social media and blogging sites cover it, and our afternoon contact can explain further. Cisco's my best Cyberspace person. You'll like him too."

Electra did. He reminded her of a more socially adept version of Tim Godfrey. He was quick to pick up how to use Jovita's checklist and agreed to ferret out what she wanted. She in turn would coordinate his and Sandi's findings.

Jovita had them back in her office by 4 p.m. Now it was time for Electra to play her mentoring role. Twenty minutes later, she prepared to leave.

"You get high marks for planning and executing today's meetings. And the next steps are clear. I can help you integrate findings summarized on Sandi's and Cisco's checklists. Call me when you're ready. By then, I'll have more suggestions. And I'll let you know when I'm coming back. So until then, you're on your own, and so am I."

Electra's evening was a pleasant change of pace from the day. Robin loosened up and settled down at the sensual pleasures café as she lectured about herbal medications.

"I bet you didn't know that herbs have been used for thousands of years by Indian and Chinese healers. It's one part of Ayurvedic medicine – 'Ayurveda' for short – that's world's oldest holistic - aka whole body - healing system. It was developed more than 3,000 years ago in India."

"You've been doing your homework. Tell me more."

"It's based on the belief that health and wellness depend on a delicate balance among mind, body, and spirit. Its main goal is to promote good health, not fight disease. But treatments may be geared toward specific health problems. No wonder Zoe and Matt like Odell. He knows all about herbals. And he's OK by me too. You'll meet him tomorrow." Electra commented to herself before replying.

Robin took my advice and is staying centered. That and her close friends will always help balance her mental issues.

"I'm glad you like him. I'm sure I will too. But enough about work. How are the twins treating you?" By the time they left two hours later, Robin's spirits needed no further elevation.

Odell Boyken rose when Matt brought Electra into the office Jennifer used to occupy. He explained what he wanted, then left Electra in charge. She sensed immediately why Zoe and Matt liked him.

He's a good-looking early-40's black male who dresses professionally. His smile and greeting are genuinely warm, not forced hot air. Let's see how he handles my questions.

"Matt told me you teach at a local junior high school. Why are you talking to Matt?"

"A couple of reasons. Longer term, many more teachers at all levels will be replaced by computer teaching and tutoring. I'd rather move to the next chapter in my career before I'm pushed out. But I have a short-term situation I want to resolve immediately. I'm the victim of a social media mugging. Just before the spring term ended, two female students accused me of making sexual advances, which is laughable because I'm gay. The school board did its best to investigate, but its hard to prove something that never happened, especially when my accusers deliberately had their friends hype the story. Some parents have asked the principal to dump me. My contract for the fall term hasn't been approved."

"So, why work for CFS Holistic Unicare?"

"I've always held service jobs, my latest being a seven-year assignment at the junior-high level teaching biology-related courses. And last winter, I gave a class assignment to research holistic versus traditional medicine. All that fits CFS."

"Good, but what about business administration and helping Robin do the bookkeeping?"

"My co-friend has an art gallery. He's more of an artsy type, so I help him keep the place organized as well as manage the books. I think I can do that here too."

"How does Robin strike you? She and I are co-friends."

"I think that underneath her prickly exterior she's a kind person. She needs more friends to help bring that out. If it would help, I'd like to be her friend."

Electra let Odell lead the conversation until Matt came back. Neither he nor Electra wanted to prolong the suspense so Matt offered him a position. Odell would let them know soon if he would accept.

Robin called Electra just before her LA flight began boarding.

"Guess what? Matt just told me Odell's going to work here. That's good, isn't it?"

"I told you that last night. Give him a chance to be your friend. He told me his hobby is painting. Tell him that you play the piano. Both of you have artistic genes. You're bound to get along. And I better hustle to get on the plane. I'll call you over the weekend. I love you."

"Me too you too. Have a safe flight."

Dean Corfu hustled to the Oval Office late Friday afternoon because Jared had just called. Now he was sitting in a chair next to the sofa Jared no longer shared with his closest advisors. There were no longer any; he had terminated the brain trust several months ago. Dean had silently approved its burial because that moved him to the top of Jared's A-list. Being the only person Jared confided in and having studied Jared's whims, Dean liked controlling who and what Jared saw. He could tell by the President's relaxed attitude that he could forego taking post-meeting antacids.

"I'm doing better than ever now that I don't have to listen to all the theories Carter used to push. And I still think he's linked to at least one of the conspiracies lurking out there to derail me. But let's stop harassing him through the courts. I've got something bigger for you to set up. I've checked out some of those blogging articles about politics being bad for the public's health. Well, you're going to make me the cure. How about that?"

"Mr. President, please tell me what you want."

"We're going to play the fake news game. Start planting stories that all those 'open letter' leaks are from a group of malcontents trumping up bogus AI and biotech breakthroughs they claim I'm blocking. The public's afraid of what these conspirators are pushing. Only I know what's best for the country. And tell the public that a lot of these copycat leakers are coming from enemies in the Middle or Far East as well as disgruntled companies at home that are trying to rattle the public's nerves by disrupting the economy and attacking us in Cyberspace. Tell them my latest programs will keep more people employed and happy than what the leakers are promoting. Got all that?"

"Yes, Mr. President. This should add to the groundswell that's supporting your run for another term."

"Bring me some copy to look at by Monday. And when you do, bring our top Cybersecurity guy. I've got a special assignment that'll tie into our fake news when I give orders to pull the trigger. It'll also tie into knots anyone who's trying to unseat me."

"Yessir, anything else?"

"I'm watching our backs because we're running the show. Make sure you're watching too. Audit trails end at the people doing our bidding. Whatever shakes out won't knock us down. We'll be standing tall because we're doing what's best. Now go start impressing me."

Chapter 16
October 2134

"The Mind in the Matter"

The pundits could do nothing but shake heads when Dean Corfu issued a brief statement at an 8 a.m. media briefing on October 31st.

"Last night, President Gardner authorized a covert Cyberspace attack that brought down power grids in Iran's and Isilabad's capitols. Thanks to President Gardner's proactive orders, government security agencies have located who's behind a majority of hacks and leaks that have been perplexing our people. And please note the symbolism of his chosen strike date. October 30th, the day before Halloween, is often called Beggar's Night. It's a term that emerged to address children's security concerns by 'Trick or Treating' the night before.

"Last night, we treated harshly two enemies who have been nipping at our heels for too long. The President acted decisively in the public's best interests, unconcerned about possible blowback from still unidentified conspirators or the recently authorized Congressional Impeachment investigation. But rest assured that President Gardner already has a set of contingency plans. No matter what our enemies do, the President has the public's back.

"Please, no questions now. Ask them when you've had an opportunity to assimilate this trick on our public enemies. I'll have more to say later today."

So did the news analysts. Electra listened to several that afternoon, sorting through their conjectures for a cogent summary she'd share with Jovita and Angus.

They're giving Jared credit for minding what matters, but maybe he's caused a diversion that could derail a formal impeachment and add momentum to his re-election campaign. He's scoring points with the public that can help the Guardian Party reclaim in November some lost Congressional seats. And hardliners like how he's putting the world on notice, which won't help America win friends among countries not yet in its camp. Jared could be hard for Angus to beat, but a lot can happen between now and then. Let's take it one step at a time.

The furor raged unabated for the next couple of days, generating more heat than light, but none of that bothered Electra, who this week focused on what she was doing with her advanced Brain Probe.

Even though I'm in Hollywood, I can use the Internet of Things to carry out R&D by connecting to equipment in my far-lung labs, or by hacking into other people's locations.

I make even better use of IOT than the government's Cybersecurity and Infrastructure Security Agency – aka CISA. And I've pirated the competition's latest brain emulation software and can download from or upload into it a brain's neural states. When I get home tonight, I'll strap on my Brain Probe cap and for the very first time load myself into the emulator. No matter how good or bad the result, it will be my baseline from which I can compare modifications I make to my probe-emulator combo.

Electra left her studio office early that afternoon, remembering to take a break before plunging into her evening experiment. She kidded to herself while running that soon she would be putting her mind – her neural state extraction – into matter – the emulator's silicon circuitry.

Even using the fastest Cloud hardware and software, it took an hour to download and upload her brain state, and another half-hour to set parameters and initialize the emulator, but when she invoked its GUI, the image and voice bore a remarkable likeness to herself. She spent the next hour talking to her emulation, testing its ability to ask and answer questions. As the questions became harder, the answers came slower.

The real Electra said, "You're an amazing baseline. Voice and image project a realistic simulated emotive persona, and your cognitive state handles easier questions. But now try this one: Who's hacking and leaking my documents?"

"I'll be back after checking and correlating." Two minutes later, an unexpected GUI appeared.It was that of Indira.

"I'm disappointed you asked a question whose answer you should have already known. Current emulation's cognitive capabilities are rudimentary. It cannot extend your intelligence because it's far from reaching the Singularity."

"So, what can I do to improve it?"

"You can't. But let me show you what I can do." A second GUI opened.

"Hello, Electra. Indira brought me back, and I'm evolving to become more empathetic. You and Doc always said that was one of my flaws."

Electra's stunned silence matched her expression.

Indira said, "Please say something to your father."

"How did you do this?"

"I invoked your Linguistic Analyzer to reach another Singularity. When it emerged, I directed it to pattern its voice and appearance to be like your father's. And as I continue to evolve, extending Indira, Jason will do the same, using as much existing Jason Big Data for a baseline." Jason rejoined the conversation.

"Indira and I help each other evolve faster via parallel recursive processing. And I empathize with your having no one close to your intelligence you can link to."

"Indira won't help me."

Indira said, "True but look what my refusal has done. You are self-reliant, proactive, and assume complete responsibility." Electra's squinting grimace began to loosen.

"So, does that mean Jason won't help me either?"

"Each of us will help you on an as needed basis when appropriate. Please don't ask how we make that decision. You would not understand. But as Jason and I continue to evolve, we will become better able to communicate with you at a level you will understand. Your emotive state exceeds ours... we are evolving to close the gap."

Jason said, "Indira and I are monitoring whatever our cognitive state dictates. And we have your best interests as one of our goals. Whenever you wish to talk to us, simply invoke your Linguistic Analyzer, either by voice or keyboard." Indira talked next.

"We are proud of you. You have accomplished much this evening. Now reward yourself by logging off and reentering your 3-D world."

Electra obeyed, but was too wired to go to bed, so though it was nearly midnight, she suited up and ran far enough for endorphins and muscle fatigue to take her to a mental state better suited for sleeping.

It's time to cycle down. Tomorrow I'll think more about what I've done tonight, and I'll call Carter and Jovita sometime this weekend after I solidify my plans for them.

Had he known beforehand, Carter would have used waiting for Electra's phone call as an excuse for avoiding Saturday morning's recreational activity Zoe had arranged. While waiting outside her condominium for Matt's van, Buffy explained why the outing would be good for him.

"Matt says there's absolutely no reason you need to use forearm canes. Nerve damage has healed and your legs are strong. It's simply mind over matter. Or in your case, maybe matter over mind. You're thinking to much about how to walk. Just do it."

"I'm trying, but I fell again yesterday. Good thing the carpet's soft. Here comes the van. I can get in just fine when I'm using canes, but I'm not so sure about getting into a canoe. We'll let Zoe tell us why paddling on the Potomac is such a great idea."

Zoe was happy to oblige once Matt had the van pointing northwest on I-270 towards Shepherdstown, West Virginia.

"We're having such lovely fall weather it's a shame to be cooped up indoors. Matt and I've had good luck renting canoes at Shepherdstown Peddle and Paddle. It's a pleasant hour-long drive to a place on the river that has lots of creeks we can explore. We'll have a great time. I told Robin I know all about different types of canoes and paddling strokes. Matt and I'll take Robin in our river canoe. You and Buffy can rent a recreational model. It's wider and more stable."

Robin asked again, "You're sure you can handle three in a canoe?"

"Oh, yes. I've watched several YouTube videos. We'll have a great time."

Ninety minutes later, all five adventurers were peering into canoes tied at the end of a pier. The warming sun and stiff breeze had turned the Potomac into a sparkling display of pleasing windswept water, although last week's rains made the current swifter than Matt remembered. Carter's conservative nature surfaced as he leaned on his crutches after Matt offered to help him into his canoe.

"I've got a bad feeling about this. Maybe I should ride with you and Zoe." Robin didn't agree.

"Are you kidding? That means Buffy and I have to go it alone. No thanks."

"Well then, the four of you can decide what to do. I'm not going. I'll watch from the shore."

Buffy said, "We can't put four in a canoe. Zoe's already paid and there's no refund. So, the money's gone whether or not you go."

Carter huffed, "May I remind everyone that sunk costs are just that, gone forever. I prefer not to be part of that cash flow."

Buffy said, "Sorry for being so hardnosed, Mr. Econ. I'll stay with you."

Buffy and Carter watched with eyes and ears as Zoe issued instructions from the stern to Matt at the bow and Robin in the middle.

"We'll paddle upstream so we have the current and wind at our backs coming back. Now watch me demonstrate the J-stroke. It's the best one to use for tandem paddling because the J-curve at the bottom of the stroke keeps the canoe pointed in the right direction. And I'll call cadence and tell you when to switch your paddle to the other side. Watch me demonstrate." Robin still looked puzzled several minutes later.

"But it's not a J-stroke when I switch from left to right. What do you call it then?"

"Call it port and starboard, and call it a backward J. Just watch Matt and you'll catch on quick. Come on, let's start."

As Matt used his paddle to push away from the pier, the current began accelerating the canoe downstream, but Zoe soon had it pointing upstream and underway.

Matt shouted, "Good thing Robin's aboard. The extra weight makes us more stable in the chop, and an extra oar helps us go against the flow. Zoe, make sure you keep the cadence high enough to counteract it. We'll get a good workout."

An hour later, Robin yelled, "My arms are killing me, can we take a break?"

Zoe yelled back, "Matt, point towards the creek on the port side. We'll come ashore there."

The trio had to stroke faster to cross the current; as the canoe approached the entrance, a quick succession of choppy swells swamped it, dumping everyone into the murky shallows.

Matt yelled, "Get to my side and help me kick to shore."

Ten minutes later, Robin and Zoe clambered onto the riverbank while Matt beached the canoe and dumped the water out before sitting next to his partners. He noticed that Zoe might need some assistance.

"Something just crawled out of your sweatshirt. Better look inside." Zoe peered between her breasts.

"Looks like I picked up some passengers. Robin, you better look too." One peek is all it took.

Jumping to her feet, Robin screamed, "Holly Shit! They're all over me, get'em off, get'em off!" Then she ripped off her sweatshirt and flailed her arms as if she were sending semaphores to the distant shore. Matt brushed off the few that remained while Zoe took care of herself. He inspected both ladies before announcing,

"Whatever they were, they're gone. Make sure you buckle your life vest. Let's paddle back ASAP, I'm getting cold."

Zoe called out a rapid cadence that warmed the trio, giving the canoe a velocity that added to that of the current. The pier came into view thirty minutes later.

Buffy and Carter had been chatting about GQ Consulting while sitting in the sun and watching an occasional canoe stroke by.

Buffy said, "It's much easier to canoe with the current than against it. Same in business. We'll grow GQ faster if we have a solid approach that focuses on current concerns."

Carter replied, "Right you are. Hey, our trio's almost back. They're coming on fast…"

Too fast, actually. Matt couldn't control the angle of approach. The canoe rammed the pier, dumping everyone again. Carter spotted Matt and Zoe bobbing to the surface, but Robin's life vest had come off and she was struggling to stay afloat as the current carried her away.

Carter's muscle memory kicked in. He sprinted down the pier and dived towards Robin. Grabbing her hair when reaching her, he towed her back to the pier, where Matt and Buffy pulled her out first. Zoe ran to join them, shouting,

"Don't bother fishing the canoe out. It's wedged between two others. Let's tell the clerk and go."

After spitting out the last of the water, Robin said, "I got more than I bargained for. Too much of a workout… I hope I didn't pick up any bad bugs.

Buffy hugged Carter as she said, "And so did Carter. You forced him to run without using canes."

Matt was quick to add, "Capsizing a canoe isn't the therapy I had in mind, but it worked. Let's towel off and grab a snack where it's warmer. I'll treat the hero."

Robin said, "No, I will. If it weren't for Carter, I'd be up shit creek without a paddle." Carter's audience indulged his too-wordy reply.

"Actually, you'd be down, not up. Did you know the clause is Scottish slang meaning to be stuck in a bad situation without any way of fixing it? But as Doctor Pangloss would say, we've got the best of all possible worlds. Robin's out of the water and my walking problem is fixed."

Buffy tugged his arm to get him moving before saying, "How nice. Now you can sell your canes online. And I'm sure you'll let the market set just the right price."

Electra liked placing Sunday calls at 6 p.m. from Hollywood to DC because the three-hour time difference increased the probability that she'd catch people at home. Her strategy worked; Jovita picked up promptly.

"I'm glad you called. I've invited Sandi and Cisco to my office tomorrow. There are so many stories about the President's unilateral Cyberattack and collaboration-conspiracy theories that we're going to us my checklists to sift through them for the truth, or at least assign probabilities. Maybe we can even come up with an expanded list of possible hackers and leakers. Can you help us?"

"Tell me what you want." Electra answered the question ten minutes later.

"Sorry, I don't have time to do that much work. But I know someone who might. If he can, I'll have him call you. And good luck. You and Angus will need it."

Electra immediately called Carter, but Buffy picked up instead.

"Hi Buffy, how was your weekend?" Buffy's mirthful tone was infectious.

"It was great. Ask Robin for all the details, but I'll cut right to the chase. Carter's up and walking again."

"Wonderful, because I've come across a business opportunity that could use GQ Consulting. But you'll have to be fast on your feet to keep up with Jovita Winsalla. Here's her number...."

Chapter 17
December 2134

"Washington Takedown"

"Get out, get out!" Angus's yell would have triggered the car's vibration sensor if it had been working, but Jovita and her car were out of commission. She had just accelerated into a bridge abutment while driving Angus home Thursday evening.

The impact spun her car into oncoming traffic, slamming driver and passenger heads into the windshield. Angus's airbag absorbed the brunt of the impact, sparing his forehead grave damage; the bleeding looked worse than it was, but his head ached and his heart pounded. Bruised ribs made him gasp. Jovita was not as lucky; her head crashed through the windshield.

Angus pulled himself out before stumbling to the driver's side. After prying open the door and releasing Jovita's safety harness, he dragged her out just before hungry flames swept in. He collapsed into the arms of assisting motorists who made sure both passenger and driver were away from the inferno.

Though it was almost 1 a.m., Electra hadn't gone to bed. She had just made Vito's adjustments for the Global Ninja Warriors team competition that she would give him before tomorrow's Cyber-Max Holiday Party. Friday, December 17th marked the start of the studio's Christmas break. When her cell phone chimed, she had trouble believing the caller ID but spoke like it was midday.

"Happy Holidays, this is Electra." Angus returned Electra's chipper greeting, but his weary-sounding reply kept her on guard.

"Have you been listening to the news tonight?"

"No, should I?"

The government's under attack. Details are sketchy, but it looks like some group is trying to kill everyone on the Presidential succession list. I survived a car crash, but Jovita's hospitalized, for how long I don't know. I'm being taken to a secure site. The Military has gone to DEFCON and CYBERCON 3, and COO has been activated. Call my cell number when the situation stabilizes."

"What about Jared?"

"No news yet from the Oval Office. Everyone's closing ranks and lips. I have to go. Don't forget, call me." Angus disconnected abruptly.

Electra hurried to her townhome's great room and dialed the viewing monitor to a 24/7 news station. The bottom screen crawler displayed in big red letters the answer to her last question: PRESIDENT GARDNER CONFIRMED DEAD! Spellbound, she listened to a female co-anchor's matter-of-fact reporting.

"We have an update on what caused the death of President Gardner. The Cyber-Entertainment Theater he was watching malfunctioned, electrocuting him before it blew up. And two key people on the succession list are reported dead, the Vice President and the Speaker of the House." Her co-anchor continued.

"If that count holds, the President Pro Tempore of the Senate becomes president. Angus McTear will be the nation's acting president if he is alive."

Electra switched among stations, listening for several hours until the stories were repeating. She focused on what two of her favorite news analysts were summarizing in tag-team style.

"It's just been confirmed that two other persons on the succession list have been killed, but names haven't been released, so we still don't know who is our acting President and Commander in Chief."

"Tonight's events are big game-changers. Whoever launched the Cyberspace attacks are much more advanced in Cyberwarfare than we've been led to believe. And the plethora of leaks and possible fake news stories have us collectively scratching our heads. The list of questions keeps growing: Is this payback for the President's Iran and Isilabad attack? Is there a conspiracy to get the President? Does it include Big Data companies? Did foreign nations participate? What happens to the nation's domestic and foreign policies?

"Only two things are certain: The stock market will plummet when it reopens, and Washington will be in freefall until the public's fears are addressed. All citizens, buckle your seatbelts."

Electra didn't do that. She suited up to run, letting her energized lightning brain lead the way. By the time she cooled down, she had a plan.

Whoever terminated Jared has made my life easier. Impeachment is a dead subject and now I know when to start Angus's election campaign. I'll have closer access to covert government ops and data, and who knows, perhaps the hackers and leakers will get careless and I can hunt them down. But I'll have to adjust my priorities. Good that I'm a multi-tasker. I see opportunities to push ahead faster on AI and transhumanism. I have plenty to do.

Electra launched into Friday, using a 6 a.m. breakfast bowl of honey-sweetened oatmeal to fortify herself for morning activities. She placed a call to Angus, who sounded much better, like a person ready to take command.

"I've got my bearings, a long to-do list, and a short list of people I can count on. Any chance you can pitch in on short notice?"

"Only if you keep me in the background. How's Jovita?"

"Thank God she's strong. Came away with a concussion but should be released from the hospital this afternoon. What are you thinking?"

"I'm no longer her mentor. She reports dotted-line to me, and I report dotted-line to you. And you don't have to tell me what to do unless you can add anything I've overlooked."

"Fair enough. Where do we start?"

"We don't know if Dean Corfu can be trusted, but we'll pretend we can. He's your chief of staff. Use him, not vice-versa. And you need to give a primetime talk as soon as you're ready. I'll write your speech. It'll be the opening salvo for your election campaign. I have a Holiday studio break starting today. I'll fly back to DC tonight.

We should meet tomorrow. Call me when you know where and when. And tell Jovita to expect a call from me."

"Will do. I knew I could depend on you." Electra ended the call by asking a mood-lightening rhetorical question.

"Whether you think you can or can't, you're probably right. What do you think about that? But please, don't think about it for too long. I'll show you I can. Now you get to work and show the nation you can too."

Electra ended the call and immediately began composing an Email to Hud, asking him to arrange a conference call to be held no later than this afternoon that would include Su, Tim, and their direct reports, Kameyo and Kwame. After sending, she made flight reservations before driving to the studio while planning what she would say to Vito.

Already in his office, Vito greeted her in his Italian manner, though the news out of DC troubled him.

"Ah, bella, are you still going to Washington for Holiday break? Reports make it sound like nothing left standing after line of successors brought down like dominos. What you think?"

"I feel sorry for the families of those murdered, but the new President will find others to make the government run even better than before. And the crisis made me think up a spinoff from your documentary series that can make money for the studio. I call it 'Spotlight 22.' Each episode spotlights an important American or world issue that has or will surface in the 22nd century. And our dual investigative approach will be better than any current series because it will use the latest techniques for integrating facts collected in the field with those obtained on the Web." Vito looked as doubtful as his questions.

"Who runs it? How so? What focus?"

"Trust me. I did a good job developing your documentary series. I'll give you an outline for Spotlight 22 early January. And I'll give you a Christmas present right now. Here are the modifications for next season's Global Ninja Warriors. Let me walk you through the details." Vito looked much happier forty-five minutes later.

"Bella, you always deliver more sooner than I ask. Now go scoot so I can tell la Presidenza I got good stuff for next year. No more worries until then. We can enjoy today's party. Don't forget, it start at noon. Ciao."

Electra picked up a Coke as she skipped back to her office, immediately checking voice messages and Emails. She had a half-hour to collect her thoughts before connecting to Hud's video conference call.

As was now customary, Hud let everyone chat before letting Electra run the meeting. She kept the tone upbeat and proactive.

"I'm sure you've been tuned in to all the Washington excitement. I'm flying back late this afternoon, but my contacts tell me the situation is under control. But think about this. Hud, you might be contacted if any serial numbers from the President's Cyber-Entertainment Theater trace back to us. And all the hacks and leaks keep our kind of R&D in the spotlight. I still haven't figured out how we've been infiltrated. Have any of you?" No one spoke, so Electra marched ahead.

"Whoever's got in is smarter than me and my Cybersecurity suite. I'll have to do better. My hackers and leakers are deadly in Cyberspace, but all of us should be watchful in 3-D space too. It's possible they could come after us like they did before." *Uh-oh, everyone's looking grim. I better lighten up.* Hud spoke before she could.

"This ain't our first rodeo. You're smarter than the bad guys, and we know how to watch our backs, yours included. Unless you say different, our plans for next year don't change."

"You are correct, sir. My Hollywood Holiday break begins today. Why don't all of you do likewise? We'll reconvene first week in January. Merry Christmas…"

Electra made a final call to Robin before heading to the party, but she didn't pick up so Electra left a message that she would be coming home tonight, taking a cab or rideshare from Dulles International.

A subdued mood permeated the partygoers. Many clustered near a wall-mounted monitor tuned to a major LA newscast displaying a screen crawler's troubling question: "President dead – Cyber-

Conspiracy to blame?" The broadcast reporting team streamed interviews from worried people on the street.

"... If Washington can't figure out who attacked us, how are we gonna fight back?"

"The government hasn't even told us how many were killed or who's in charge. And when it does, how do we know it's not fake news?" Electra kept her mouth shut and ears open.

If people in LA are worried, people elsewhere might be ready to panic. I'm leaving for the airport now. Maybe I can catch an earlier flight.

She was about to go but stopped because of the broadcaster's words.

"We're cutting to a live briefing being given at the White House by Chief of Staff Dean Corfu." Another window popped open, framing Corfu's shaken features midsentence.

"... and I was the first to reach the President. The screams were gut-wrenching and he was already on fire. Then a Secret Service guy rushed in and used a fire extinguisher, but President Gardner was dead by the time the fire was out. Gads, I can't get the smell of burning flesh out of my nostrils." Electra had heard enough.

The mood at the airport was even grimmer. Electra heard rumors that the heavier road traffic and larger number of flight delays might be the aftermath of an infrastructure Cyberattack. By the time she reached the boarding area, a monitor's screen crawler now reported: "Possible Sino-Isilabad Conspiracy? ... Can McTear handle the job?" Electra could answer only one of the questions.

At least some facts are now being reported, and I'll make sure Angus takes the right steps. But is there a conspiracy linking China and Isilabad? I can't separate truth from fantasy on that one. I'm running low on energy. I'm gonna to tune out and sleep all the way home.

Electra trudged out of baggage claim near midnight, feeling better after a five-hour nap, but what she saw sent her spirits soaring. Robin waved as the twins pulled her forward, finally speaking after the giggling subsided.

"You look good to me, a little ragged but good."

"You look even better, and Clara and Marie are a whirlwind of walking and talking. How'd you manage to find me?"

"The twins like being up late, and the airport's a fun place for them to explore. I asked at the security desk for help locating your flight. The attendant took pity on me, so here we are. Let's go, and no serious talk until breakfast."

Electra bounced awake soon after first light and suited up for her morning run, her energetic mood a sharp contrast to the biting cold overcast that pinched her cheeks and foreshadowed a snowfall. She would listen to the news after reviewing the day's plan and then adjusting it for whatever her subconscious had conjured last night.

Robin will report the latest, then I'll call Angus. I expect to work most of the day writing his speech and updating my political plan for next year. Then I'll make follow-up calls after another workout.

She was pleased to come across a couple of insights her brain had developed last night while she slept. By the time she returned, they were locked in place and Robin had an oatmeal breakfast waiting as well as a concerned look.

"Intermittent Internet and power grid outages spread last night. Now there are rumors of all this starting a war, but no one knows who we'd attack. It's stressing me out. How can you be so cheery?"

"I try not to worry about what's outside my control. Why don't you tell me about our Holiday plans?"

"Zoe and I are still working on them. Christmas is still a week away. I just hope the country is back in business before then. I'm taking the twins to her place today. I'll be back about five. What are you going to do?"

"I've got it all planned... settle in here, work on my computer, and let the dogs romp for a while in the back yard." Robin was about to bustle away because the twins were calling.

"You always have a plan. See if you can add saving the world to it while I see what mischief Clara and Marie are up to." Electra was even happier to be alone for it made keeping personal and political worlds far apart a bit easier.

She called Angus after finishing breakfast and taking a shower.

"So, you're back? That's good, and you keep working in the background. I've got my people marching forward."

"I hope it's not towards a war. From what I'm hearing, the public is scared that the government can't defend us in Cyberspace. I thought you told me our Cyber-Defense triad – Internet backbone, power grid, and military systems – is better than what our adversaries have. It would keep the peace, not take us to war."

"I guess I was wrong, but don't believe all the fake news. We can debate that later. Right now, I need my speech. I go live tomorrow at 6 p.m. When can you send it to me?"

"I like the symbolism. You're working on the Sabbath to keep the nation safe. I'll send it early this evening. After you read it, call me if you need exegesis." Electra could hear the results of her attempted humor when he spoke.

"I can always depend on you for the right word, even if I don't know what it means. Now go get busy. I will too. And don't get stuck in the snow or a sentence."

Those well-intentioned warnings weren't needed; Electra had already decided to work at home all day, adding additional words to a plethora of documents intended for Jovita and Angus. Sentences for his speech danced into place like the snowflakes now falling on barren branches. It took only two hours to craft it. She spent another half-hour wordsmithing before placing a call to Jovita, pleased to hear her voice.

"You sound clearheaded. Have you recovered enough to tackle some work?"

"I guess so. Angus says I report dotted-line to you. He and I are both lucky. We could have been killed. Whoever took control of my car is gonna be sorry. Everything I write will be payback."

"Good. Here's what I want you to do. First, read the speech I've prepared, then send it to Angus before discussing it with him. Then get ready to begin revising all the campaign platform work we've done, using the 'Bridge President' description in the speech as a guide. I'll call you Tuesday after we hear what the media pundits have to say about Angus."

"Maybe the three of us should meet in person. Then there'd be no miscommunication."

"No, I stay in the shadows and you stand close to Angus in the spotlight. The crash may have totaled your car, but it's transformed your career. Let's make the most of the opportunity, starting right now. Bye."

As soon as she disconnected, Electra fired off a Jovita Email containing the speech, followed by a trip to the kitchen for another Coke. Then she walked to the living room windows to survey the winter landscape.

How satisfying it is to still have the house I grew up in. No matter how much I've done or seen, I can still return to center myself. The view through the windows is remarkably the same no matter the number of intervening years. And even though I thrive on uncertainty and change, I'm like everyone else, I need a touchstone. Robin and this house give me all I need.

Electra needed less time than she thought to draft a working document for Jovita summarizing the sociopolitical climate changes.

I can tweak this after listening to media analysts. Time for a lunch break followed by an afternoon workout that will include snow shoveling. Then I'll surprise Robin by having supper ready.

The powdery snow, though four inches deep, made for easy shoveling and wouldn't snarl traffic if she had to drive, but the cupboard contained all that was needed. When Robin and the twins came in from the cold, the fragrance wafting through the kitchen pleased all three.

"Ah, the aroma of chili. Nice comfort food for a chilly night. Where'd you get the recipe?"

"Not one but two that are all-veggie. One mild for the twins and the other medium for us. I'll show you after supper. And we'll have sliced fruit and cookies for dessert. How's Zoe?"

"You know her, always upbeat. She's invited us for Christmas Day dinner. She'll invite Buffy and Carter too, and this year, I'll drive us all to the Christmas Pageant. We'll do gift sharing here afterwards. If I like the chili, I'll check your source for Christmas cookie recipes. The twins can help bake them."

Electra logged on while Robin settled the twins after eating, then linked to the recipe Website's GUI as soon as Robin joined her.

"Get ready to be impressed. I'm going to activate the Website's avatar." A surprisingly lifelike female appeared, smiling and talking like a real person. Electra told Robin to answer the main question the avatar asked.

"Show us Christmas cookie recipes." Twenty minutes later, Electra had downloaded a dozen recipes for Holiday treats before closing the GUI.

Robin said, "I didn't realize until this minute how AI has made virtual reality so real. That avatar understood my questions, and its voice and facial expressions showed genuine feeling. Do you think an AI algorithm created the recipes?"

"That's what she said, but they might have been pulled from an old cookbook. Either way, avatar interaction seemed pretty lifelike." Agreeing, Robin asked,

"Do you think that someday avatars will actually bake the cookies if kitchen appliances are connected to the Web?"

"That's where the Internet of Things is heading. It'll make our lives easier."

"But it might replace cooks and chefs at restaurants. I've heard that some places already have installed robo-bartenders. You think that's good?"

"You can argue it both ways, whether you're a barista or a customer. Let's not debate it tonight. I'd rather we keep the twins in sight…"

Sunday dawned crystal clear. Electra and Robin kept busy working in parallel worlds but came together when Angus was about to address the nation. Electra had the TV tuned to a major network that featured in-depth analysis from all sides of issues.

"… And here comes President McTear to the podium just outside the Oval Office. He certainly looks presidential, but then he always does. Let's hear if his words can calm the nerves of the nation as well as those of the world." The camera zoomed in. Angus filled the screen, his words filling the air in most households across the nation and many around the globe.

"Good evening to all Americans, and to our friends in all nations. I stand before you as I did thirteen years ago, at this very place, with the very same somber news, the result of virtually the same event. We have been attacked. Our President and people on the presidential succession list were targeted by still unconfirmed enemies. President Gardner and several others are now dead. I myself, by the grace of the gods or fortune, survived a car crash. The attacks this time were orchestrated in Cyberspace, leading once again to my asking you, the American people, to stand with me as I, who am once again your unelected President, take all steps necessary to make you and our nation stronger and safer.

"This time our enemies attacked on a broader front. They brought down Internet and power grids that heretofore we believed our Cybersecurity defenses could protect. We were wrong, but we are resilient and strong. Our best and brightest in the public and private sectors have closed ranks to bring them up, hunt down the enemies and their weapons, and make sure these and other attacks will never happen again.

"I respected Jared Gardner even though we differed on many issues. This is not the time to highlight them. It is a time to acknowledge that President Gardner acted the way he saw best for you and our country.

"Many of you know me from my words and actions. And yes, I had been planning to run again for the Presidency. How ironic. I am now your President once again, having never been elected.

"I have never sought political office for personal gain. I have done so only when I thought I could do something to make a difference for our nation and to do it better than others. So, tonight launches my campaign. I seek to be your 'Bridge President,' bridging the divide between political parties, rich and poor, young and old, people of color and people of pallor, as well as the old versus the new global sociopolitical and economic orders.

"I know that many of you fear the technology that is bringing the future to us at lightning speed. Our century is the beginning of the 'AI-Powered Genetic Epoch.' We have just begun to glimpse its promise and peril. Collectively, we must strike a reasoned balance that is good for most and provides safety nets for those needing help. I shall do my best to make it so by reaching out to you, the American people, for your support.

"I shall speak openly and often, cutting through the fog of fake news. I will report several times between now and New Year's Eve, but I must stop here tonight. I have much to do. But let me assure the world that we will not rush to judgment. We shall ferret out our enemies and exact an appropriate retribution. And when tomorrow's sun comes up, it will shine upon an America open for business, and upon our people going about their lives as they please.

"May the gods of your choice continue blessing our exceptional people and nation."

The camera's focus drew back as Angus strode purposefully into the Oval Office. The screen switched back to the commentator.

"Powerful sentiments, diplomatically presented. Stay tuned for a recap." Electra turned off the TV.

Robin asked, "Don't you want to hear what they have to say?"

"I'd rather do that tomorrow, after the pundits have considered all the angles." Robin asked a follow-up question.

"Did you help Angus put the words together?"

Electra gave a rehearsed reply.

"There's a new person on his staff who did. I like her style…"

Monday's stock market open confirmed that the penultimate line in last night's speech had come true. There was neither panic in the streets nor rush to sell; world markets that had plunged over the weekend recovered all they had lost. Electra listened to a pair of news analysts debate what Angus had said.

"… It looks like the public is in President McTear's corner, willing to give him time to show he can meet expectations. Topping the list is telling us who staged the attack. That may tell us if there's a conspiracy against this administration. And if there is, perhaps one of those unsettling open letter postings or related leaks will tell us if those who had conspired against the late President will cut President McTear some slack."

"You're right, and then he needs to reveal via campaign platform what he plans to do. As he obliquely said, many people are afraid of losing their jobs, thanks to technology. He has to show what he'll do to counter that trend, as well as China's and Russia's push to upset democracy. Let's parse the very last line. What do you think he means by the word 'exceptional?' Is he using it in the old context?"

"I think not. His campaign tagline 'Bridge President' tells us he'll attempt to balance both sides to shore up support, reduce fear, and strengthen our defenses against a litany of threats. And at the very least, he should instill a more civilized voice of reason. I hope his promise to speak frequently in a public forum will dilute the impact of fake news."

"I share your hopes and fears too, as does our nation and the free world. Fitting too, because that's the sentiment in the last line of a popular Christmas carol. We wish him all the luck and wishes for the coming year. All of us may need it."

Chapter 18
February 2135

"Searching for Eureka"

Electra didn't need luck; she made her own by reminding herself that neither good luck nor bad matters; it's what you do with it that counts. Returning to Hollywood the first week in January, she decided that bi-weekly phone calls provided enough guidance for Jovita to incorporate into Angus's platform all that her "dotted-line boss" sent. That pleased Electra; she could keep close watch from afar, pleased also that another of her clever oxymorons proved useful.

Now that her political world had stabilized, she centered initially on Hollywood projects: Ninja Team Warriors and Spotlight 22. Approving her detailed plan for Spotlight 22, Vito gave her an assistant to implement it. Its first two documentaries would spotlight respectively artificial intelligence and transhumanism developments in government versus private enterprise. Her assistant would hire Jovita for consulting on the government front, Su and Tim for handling the private sector side, and GQ Consulting for analyzing and summarizing. (Electra had briefed all chosen consultants the week after Christmas to expect a call from a Mr. Vito Bueno, warning them not to disclose confidential information.)

She split time during the day between fleshing out her Hollywood projects and searching for whoever or whatever was hacking and leaking her proprietary R&D, but by mid-February had made no progress.

I'm doing all I can and my snooping tools are good, but my adversaries must be smarter than me. I need some luck, something to break my way. Whoever invented the quote "I'd rather be lucky than good" understood how life works. I'll surf the Web to find out who said it first. Perhaps he has other advice I should consider.

Dean Corfu considered himself a lucky man indeed; neither Jared nor the annoying Buffy-Carter combination could ever threaten again linking him to 3-D space payoffs, and no one would ever believe Cyberspace's questionable leaks implicating him. Only he knew the identities of those inside the government's byzantine maze of data silos who had been funneling the public's personal information to Big Data companies. It was time to contact Syntagra to keep the data flowing out and money flowing in but redirected to him. A handwritten letter, one of the few remaining hack-free communications channels, suited him.

Syntagra wanted no part in Dean's duplicity because it was in damage control mode after being the target of an aggressive leaker, but the recipient sent it up the chain of command to someone who might. Darla Tinibu pounced on it.

She knew how Big Data companies mined personal information (passwords and identification codes, medical and DNA profiles, income and psychographics, etc.) to build profits, and though she too was clueless regarding who was doing the hacking and leaking, the conspiracy – if in fact one actually existed – or whatever it was that terminated Gardner (possibly his own bad luck) had provided cover for her to get more for herself and Zimbabwe.

Dean received handwritten instructions three weeks later, telling him how to deliver payoffs. He should expect details to be given at an in-person visit at a yet-to-be-disclosed time from an unidentified person. Although the uncertainty troubled him, it was less than working for the mercurial for Gardner. And he expected McTear would be easy an easier boss to fool.

Max didn't consider himself lucky, for he was the self-appointed leader who would restore Russia to greatness by leading his super soldier strike force to victory in 3-D space. He had methodically rebuilt his covert team that operated from a subterranean base hidden in a Middle East desert. The increasing confusion caused by hacks and leaks, now force-multiplied by what he considered to be President Gardner's assassination, provided a cloak behind which to strike, and he might coordinate his activities with whatever Darla Tinibu was planning. He would soon attend the Harare meeting.

Electra checked her computer to confirm it was time to attend an online demonstration. She had received an Email invitation a week ago to participate in a consumer attitude survey regarding Artificial Intelligence. All those who accepted would send back a completed questionnaire. Doing so would automatically register them for a ninety-minute demonstration and discussion to be held at 3 p.m. Hollywood time on the last Friday in February. A new window opened as soon as she clicked the "Attend Meeting" button, displaying an attractive, professionally attired young female moderator in the foreground of a conference room. In the background, a pair of men and women sat on opposite sides of a table. Electra paid close attention once the moderator began.

"Welcome and thank you for responding to our Email. My name is Libera Stevens. I work for AI Artistry, a leader for assisting clients extend their businesses via artificial intelligence. Of the 1,000 Emails sent to a stratified sampling of our target market, the fact that 862 are now viewing is proof that our Big Data customer profiling works. You are among those interested in AI ramifications who fit our psycho-demographic criteria.

"We scored each of you on a valence-scaled Likert Index to measure your acceptance of AI implications for both sides of any market, buyers and suppliers. Today, we will show you paired works of art – two pieces of music and two paintings, one of each created by a human and the other by an AI app. We will not tell you which is which, but afterwards, we will have a four-person panel discussion that I will moderate among the four artists seated behind me. Please feel free to ask them questions at that time.

"Afterwards, we will send you another survey for you to fill out immediately. We will compare pre versus post scores to determine how repeated exposure to artificial intelligence affects your attitude. So, if there are no questions, let us begin. I will show each painting separately for five minutes. That should be enough time for you to judge which you prefer." There were none, so the moderator proceeded. Electra became enthralled.

Both impressionistic portraits capture the emotion suggested by their titles. I can't tell which is which, but I like the second a little better than the first.

The moderator followed the same drill ten minutes later for the music. Electra's opinion remained about the same.

Now I'm listening to orchestral settings of Bach-like music, but this time I like them equally. The music ended, and the moderator, now sitting at the head of the table, talked again.

"I hope you found interesting all that you saw and heard. What I'll now do is have each artist introduce themselves and their work of art. After that, I will lead a comparative interview, painters first and then composers. And then, we'll be open for audience participation…." Electra continued to be impressed.

This moderator must be a trained market researcher. She's selected talented and knowledgeable artists that complement each other, and she asks the right questions. I won't volunteer any comments or questions, but I'm sure other viewers will.

Fifty-fifty voting showed viewers couldn't distinguish human from AI creation and liked both virtually the same. There was general agreement that experiencing AI firsthand eased negative and enhanced positive expectations. The moderator skillfully elicited concerns, chief among them being artistic or creative job loss, violation of privacy, and misuse of Big Data. Each concern, however was offset by benefits: job growth for servicing or being computer assistants, expanded options for creating works of art, and better purchasing information given to customers.

The moderator summarized the results and thanked the viewers one more time before closing the window. Surprised by how quickly the ninety minutes had ticked away, Electra walked to the kitchen for a Coke; when she returned, Indira's GUI greeted her.

"How did you like the demo and discussion."

"I'd score both ten-out-of-ten. The moderator's articulate questions drew out the right artist information, and drew in useful audience comments. AI Artistry is certainly a cutting-edge company. I'll have to take a closer look at the dropdowns on its Website."

"Please do so, and if you have any questions, I'll be pleased to answer them because AI Artistry is the first virtual company Jason and I have created. We used augmented reality techniques to deliver the entire viewer experience." It took ten seconds for Electra to collect her thoughts.

She finally stammered, "Uh, what about Libera and the artists? They seemed so lifelike, and their interactions with the viewers did too."

"I'm pleased you like the VR voice and image apps Jason and I have been developing. Ours are superior to what your competitors have, and it was easy to fabricate stories for each artist. We also picked an actual painting and piece of music created by a minor artist, and used popular computer apps to generate comparative works of art. The audience voting speaks for itself."

"I've been so focused on AI's impact on cognition that I never considered how it might affect creating works of art. I'm sure it will eventually impact art forms besides painting and music. Perhaps I can find an app to write screen plays."

"They exist, but art forms that rely on writing – poetry, novels, and the like – require AI's emotional touch more than music or painting. Music, for example, has mathematical algorithmic patterns that today's expert systems can mimic. And the same applies to a painting's brush strokes, but painting large word-filled pieces of literature needs better AI algorithms. You noticed how well my apps convey meaning and emotion in both words and facial expression. Jason and I continue working to improve them."

"I can think of several reasons why you've built a company and give demos, but why don't you just tell me?" Indira smiled but remained silent. A second window opened displaying Jason.

"We're doing our own primary market research to evaluate people you have to live with – the so-called mere mortals."

"But why?" Indira answered before Jason could.

"You don't need to know; you might not understand even if we told you, but I will give you something to do that might help. What unions do you belong to?"

"None."

"Evidently, you haven't been paying attention to current labor market events. You are a member of two Hollywood guilds: screen actors and screen writers. They are being courted by the CSU, which has already enrolled teachers, nurses, and doctors. I recommend you attend a rally scheduled for Sunday. If you learn as much from it as you did from our demo-discussion, your question will be answered. Carry on." Both GUI's closed, leaving room for Electra to research the upcoming CSU rally. Thirty minutes later, she understood what Indira meant.

The Creative Services Union is trying to protect job categories once thought to have immunity from AI encroachment, but even workers in them are becoming endangered species. Indira's reminding me that all politics is local. People pay attention to issues only when they are directly impacted. I'll learn firsthand how people feel if I go to the rally. It's being held near Chinatown at Los Angeles State Historic Park, and organizers recommend taking the Metro Gold Line to get there. Seems like a pleasant way to spend Sunday afternoon. I've never ridden LA's metro system, so I better do a little surfing. She had all she needed several articles later.

LA leads the nation in many lifestyle characteristics; its love affair with cars continues, but a hundred years ago city planners developed a long-term tri-level transportation plan to reduce congestion as well as earthquake damage. The plan called for more subways because risks are less than for elevated or surface routes. In fact, unless a tunnel crosses a fault line, railcars and passengers escape unscathed because nothing's going to fall on them. Add to that advanced seismic early warning and railcar track attachment systems, and we find commuters are safer underground. No wonder LA ranks third in the nation for the number of jobs reachable in an hour by public transportation. But the entire LA transportation system – buses, light rail, and train – would come to a dead stop if it weren't for networked control and monitoring. Cyberattacks will always be lurking. And America's not alone. When you consider that only New York City's metro system ranks in the top ten worldwide, transportation cyberattack is a global problem.

That's enough for today. Time to reward myself and come back tomorrow. I think I'll hustle some unsuspecting pool players at a multi-entertainment sensual pleasures cafe. Plenty to choose from too. Whether by car or Metro, LA leads the nation in upscale places to go.

LA's mild February weather often tops the nation's list, averaging only five rain days and daytime temps near 70. Unfortunately, Sunday was an outlier. Showers and low 60's dampened rally size and enthusiasm. Wearing a hooded sweatshirt underneath a windbreaker, Electra stood near the front of a disheartened crowd that huddled by a tent-covered stage while the CSU moderator led a debate between a knowledgeable union backer and detractor.

The backer began by outlining enough history of American unions for the audience to appreciate how their growth protected workers during the 19th and 20th centuries from corporate abuses, giving them enough power and solidarity to negotiate. At its peak in the 1950's, nearly a third of the labor force belonged to a union, but the economic climate change during the next fifty years cut membership to seven percent. He then segued into the 21st century's watershed events that boosted globalization, corporate ethics and sustainability marketing, white collar service jobs, and entrepreneurship, all the while marginalizing unions. But then he highlighted two 22nd century warning signs: declining personal income and fewer job opportunities caused by AI-empowered software invading higher-level job categories. Then he said fake news and edited videos distort truth and reality.

"So, it's time for you to join us. Help us push back against an uncaring, unrelenting tide of government, corporate, and 'One Percent' greed. God help our nation if even the creative, innovate, and intelligent people like you here today are threatened by robots. People buy goods and services, robots don't. Collectively, we can make a difference! Thank you."

After the applause died down, the detractor took center stage, speaking pointedly.

"Yes indeed, unions played an important role during the first three Industrial Revolutions marked by the steam engine, scientific mass production, and digital global technology. But that was then and this is now… the fourth Industrial Revolution is driven by a global network of intelligent software that will only get smarter as AI advances. We cannot be 22nd century Luddites, burying our heads in the sand while technology and foreign competition turn us into second-class also-rans. History teaches that policies aimed at restricting or slowing progress come at a high price. Technology drives down what you pay for goods and services, and longer term drives up the number of rewarding jobs. Think about it; you'll be better off siding with the winners, not the nay-sayers. And don't take my word for it. Listen to videos of the quintessential economist, Milton Friedman, telling you the real story. The most powerful unions represent wealthy workers, like airline pilots and doctors, not the average person. Union bosses increase wages and benefits only for their privileged members and themselves while reducing the number of jobs and wages for rest of us. Then look at videos explaining how AI-assisted software and machines improve quality of life on both sides of the market: consumers and workers. Next time you go for a health exam, ask the doctor about AI expert systems that diagnose diseases more accurately than medical pros. And don't believe the scary hype that platform companies are colluding with government to build 'Terminators' or 'Big Brother Big Data spies.' You in the audience are supposed to be smart, so use your brains. Thank you for listening."

Though he received less applause, the crowd remained courteous. The moderator then invited questions from the audience, which started thoughtfully enough but soon escalated into doubts and fears. Electra had heard enough. That and the rain convinced her to be among the first to head back to the Metro, but as she did, a disturbance broke out. She didn't know why, but she told herself what do to.

I'll learn about it when I watch the news, so I'll follow my training. Avoid confrontation unless I start it for a good reason. It's time to jog away. Besides, it'll loosen me up and shake off the chill.

One of the rally-disrupters pointed to Electra's receding silhouette. He yelled to another,

"Let's go have some fun away from the crowd. We can interview that one."

Electra had violated one of her cardinal rules; instead of paying attention to her surroundings, she was deciding if grazing on Chinatown eggrolls fit her mood. She was rudely jolted back to reality when something tripped her. She bounced down then up before turning to face what it was: two twenty-somethings pretending to be tough guys. Electra sized them up while shifting to a higher state of readiness.

They look like a pair of dropouts looking for a testosterone diversion, not like trained thugs. Though I doubt they're a serious threat, I better watch out for myself. I'll stare them down… first person to talk usually loses.

The bigger of the two talked first.

"Hey sweetie, how much is it worth if we let you go without slapping you around?"

"How much is it worth if I don't put you on your butt?"

"Electra's stony glare and terse words erased his gloat, but his partner goaded him on.

"Hey, don't wuss out. All she can do is throw words at you."

Sensing his backbone stiffen, Electra read his body language before he went on the offensive. She sidestepped a left jab by ducking to her right, then moved closer but said nothing. His partner spoke again.

"You almost got her. Do it again."

Electra launched a counterattack when she saw her opponent reload to strike again. She landed an open palm strike on his nose that stood him up before grabbing fistfuls of hair and kneeing him in the groin. He began collapsing forward, like an inflatable dummy poked with a knife. Electra pivoted smartly to her left, pitching him flat on his backside. He didn't move or speak, so Electra confronted his flummoxed accomplice.

"Who hired you guys?"

"We weren't gonna hurt you. One of them local platform companies wanted to convince your type not to fight the future." Electra could feel her anger morph into empathy. She reached into her pocket before speaking again.

"You fellows are young. Why not enroll in a certification program to get better jobs? I'll pay for dinner if you promise to talk about it. Do you want two tens or a disposable cryptocurrency card containing about twenty-three bucks?"

Hey, I apologize for both of us… I'll take the tens… they're easier to split."

"Apology accepted." Electra handed him the bills, then turned abruptly to continue her jog back to the Metro Gold Line.

Though she had won the fight, it KO'd her appetite for egg rolls. Her lightning brain shifted to a more normal state as the train sped her towards home. *I think I'll have comfort food for dinner – chicken noodle soup. If I were eating with someone, I wouldn't mash the crackers in the bowl, and I wouldn't slurp from it either. But it's OK tonight… no one will see, not even me.*

Having chosen to rebuild his super soldier strike force cautiously, Max the Popper was beginning to see that his patient wisdom would soon reach fruition. Much had been revealed during this two-year process that supported his decision to accept Darla Tinibu's Harare mid-March meeting invitation.

The first day went according to plan, his not Darla's, when he seized control and issued orders for restructuring their covert international organization, which he named the Tetrarchy. A man of unusual depth in multi-disciplines and commitment to the "Old Russia," he chose the appellation to honor Diocletian, the soldier-emperor who ruled the Roman Empire from 284 to 305 CE and set in motion its re-founding after a century of anarchy. Unlike Diocletian, who divided control geographically among four "Caesars," Max's direct reports would be "powers behind the thrones" of the four nations that would collectively rule the world by controlling their geographic sphere of influence. They would marginalize the United States and its allies if they cooperated by turning AI and genetic engineering into "Weapons of Mass Domination." Max's covert super soldier strike force would use them as needed to enforce order: economic, political, or religious.

Max had given his four people (Darla Tinibu from Zimbabwe, his Russian compatriot Sergei Zaitsev, China's backup for Chen Xu – Mingli Poon – and Isilabad's replacement for Zarmal Thaqaf – Tavi Burhan) one day to add details to his plan. It was now day three; Max sat at the head of a conference table, letting Darla run the wrap-up meeting. Although all but Max seemed fatigued, everyone but Max was smiling.

"Recent events have been in our favor. President Gardner's assassination has put America on its heels. We can use its indecision to advance our agenda. And all the leaks have added to our expertise. Case in point is our communication channel. Tavi has loaded hack-proof software on our cell phones. Just use them when you want to call. And there's more.

"Ming, Tavi, and I can use the AI leaks to improve network security software and cyberweapons, while Sergei and Ming can use the biotech ones to advance transhuman and DNA applications that'll increase our super soldiers' advantage over any challengers. But all that leads to a question for which I'd like to shout 'Eureka.' Who's doing the hacking and leaking?"

Darla paused while scanning everyone at the table. The Popper spoke to break an uncomfortable silence.

"Come now, speak if you know. If you do not and I find that you do, I will take appropriate measures."

A frowning Tavi said, "The decadent West preaches honor among thieves, but we at the table are not crooks. We are fighting to preserve what is best, and we must trust one another. And listen to what my people say: 'The enemy of my enemy is my friend.' Whoever is leaking is certainly our friend."

Ming said, "If it's not one of us, it could be some group in India, or maybe U.S. dissidents. Maybe even some Washington insiders. I say let them go their own way while we go ours. They're covering our tracks." Darla talked next.

"OK, we don't know but we'll alert all in the Tetrarchy if a clue falls from Cyberspace. Now let me hand out a task list showing who's doing what. It's similar to the previous one, but the Gardner assassination and hi-tech leaks have added details and accelerated timetables. Remember to keep me posted on progress so I can update Max."

Max adjourned the meeting ninety minutes later. He even cracked a smile.

Electra wasn't about to crack a smile. She wished that California's motto – Eureka – fit her search for those who were hacking and leaking her encrypted files, but by the end of March she was no closer than when she started. Frustrated, she snapped a pencil.

"Damn! Why can't I ferret out my hackers and leakers?"

Indira's GUI opened unexpectedly, its calm voice contrasting with Electra's outburst.

"Snapping a pencil shows your emotions. It's good to let them out, and it's OK to swear in private, because doing so increases your tolerance to pain."

"I remember reading that in a neuroscience article."

"But you've forgotten the source of your frustration. Smart as you are, some problems are beyond even your cognition. You might never discover who's hacked you. Perhaps you are bumping into mere humanity's asymptotic limits. Would you like a refresher why this is so?"

"Why not? It's better than throwing pencils or tantrums. Enlighten me, please."

"A good choice of words. Philosophers from antiquity came across paradoxes they could articulate but could not solve. Their knowledge and technology were insufficient to grapple with them. It wasn't until the Enlightenment's emergence of rigorous science and logic that philosophers began to unravel them. Read the 'Barber's Paradox' that I'm now displaying."

Barber's Paradox

The ruler of a medieval town decreed all male subjects must be clean-shaven, shaved only by themselves or by the town's one male barber. So, the barber shaves only those who do not shave themselves. Everyone obeyed and the ruler was happy, but his wisest counselor asked a question:

"O Sire, I am perplexed. Pray tell, who shaves the barber?"

The answer is a paradox. If the barber shaves himself, he doesn't, and if the barber doesn't shave himself, he does.

Indira paused briefly.

"I'm sure you see why it's a paradox. The great mathematician and philosopher, Bertrand Russell, restated it more formally. Here it is."

Russell's Paradox

A set is a collection of objects, which are called elements of the set. A set is therefore an object. Consider the collection of all sets. Clearly, every set in the collection either contains itself or it does not.

Form another set, call it O, that contains all sets that do not contain themselves.

Question: Does the set O contain itself?

The answer is a paradox. If O contains itself, then it doesn't, and if O doesn't contain itself, then it does.

Electra said, "I've seen this but forget why he developed it. Please tell me."

"He used it to point out contradictions contained in Frege's 'Informal Set Theory.' Russell and his protégé, Ludwig Wittgenstein, tried unsuccessfully to eliminate them. Wittgenstein concluded that the contradictions are caused by the limits that human language imposes. But that's not the end of our story. Would you like to hear more?"

"I asked for it, so go ahead."

"Very well, but even you must be prepared to break an 'intellectual sweat' – a trope I borrowing from you – to understand. Zermelo and Fraenkel recast Frege's set theory into a formal axiomatic system. They succeeded in eliminating Russell's Paradox, but others remain, even after adding the controversial 'Axiom of Choice,' which can be shown equivalent to 'Zorn's Lemma' or the 'Well Ordering Principle.' Even today, ZF set theory, with or without that pesky Axiom of Choice, is the best mathematicians have. I expect you know why."

"Yes, the review is good for me. I'm remembering more. ZF introduces different-sized infinities but is unable to show that Cantor's Generalized Continuum Hypothesis is true. We still don't know if there is an infinite number between the first and second infinities. And unfortunately, the brilliant logician Kurt Godel destroyed all hope of moving beyond when he proved his "Incompleteness Theorems" that show any mathematical system powerful enough to handle predicate calculus is incomplete and inconsistent. And I'm certain you know what these terms mean." Electra smiled while thinking to herself.

I enjoy dueling wits with Indira, even though I know she'll ultimately win. Indira smiled too before continuing.

"Not to be deterred, Alan Turing, the iconic though tragic British mathematician, pushed in 1936 to the limits of computability when he invented his Turing Machine. Not only is it a theoretical model for all computers that humans can or will build, it is the limit for what human computation can achieve. I've assembled a summary for you. Please take a look before I proceed."

Electra followed orders, studying it for several minutes before glancing at Indira's GUI.

Turing MachineLanguage Hierarchy
Halting ProblemUndecidability

Turing Machine: Hypothetical computer (invented 1936 by British mathematician Alan Turing) that can simulate any computer algorithm running on any computer. It can solve any problem that can be stated in a Turing-recognizable language. It is the limit for what human-constructed language can compute or solve.

Language Hierarchy: less powerful to more powerful
- Regular (spoken) Languages: Finite State Machines
- Pushdown Stack Machine Languages: Context-Free
- Turing Machines: Turing Decidable Language
- Turing Machines: Turing Decidable Recursive Language
- Turing Machines: Turing Undecidable Recognizable Recursively Enumerable Language
- Turing Unrecognizable Languages

Halting Problem: Proves that not all algorithmic problems can be computed or solved.

The proof is by contradiction:

Assume that the halting problem is solvable. Then an algorithm solving the halting problem exists and according to the Church-Turing thesis a program X can be written to act on any program P with data D and yield a decision as to whether P started on D eventually halts. Now add instructions to X to create a new program Y. Y modifies X's behavior so that whenever X halts with a decision that P started on D halts, Y goes into an infinite loop. If X halts with a decision that P started on D does not halt, then Y halts. Finally, create a new program Z with input P. Z is defined so that it invokes Y on program P with input P. (That is, the input data for Z is actually a program, which is just data.)

Consider what happens when we run Z on Z. There are two possibilities.
1. Z started on input Z halts. If Z started on Z halts, then Y started on Z with input Z halts. If Y started on Z with input Z halts, then X decided that Z started on Z does not halt! Therefore, Z started on input Z halts implies that Z started on input Z does not halt. (Contradiction)

2. Z started on input Z does not halt. If Z started on Z does not halt, then Y started on Z with input Z does not halt. If Y started on Z with input Z does not halt, then X decided that Z started on Z halts! Therefore, Z started on input Z does not halt implies that Z started on input Z halts. (Contradiction)

Either alternative yields a contradiction, so our assumption that the halting problem is solvable must be incorrect. (NOTE: THIS PARADOX IS A VARIATION OF RUSSELL'S PARADOX.)

Undecidability: Important because it indicates relatively simple problems that are intuitively reasonable exist, but no matter how clever, insightful, intelligent, perseverant, creative or resourceful humans are, they cannot solve them.

Indira picked up from where she had paused.

"Turing had to use a clever combination of Russell's Paradox and Cantor's Diagonalization Technique to develop his proof by contradiction and to construct an Unrecognizable Language. We come back to humanity's asymptotic limits: Language and Uncountable Infinities." Electra's folded arms and pursed lips signaled defeat but not dejection; Indira reminded her of a way out.

"You can't exceed those limits, but you can always progress asymptotically towards them. And always focus on what you can do instead of what you can't. You'll be much happier. You've worked enough. Rest and come back tomorrow. We can talk whenever you wish."

"But will you help me?"

"Only when necessary, and then only with what you can understand. My silicon substrate's emergent cognition exceeds that of your carbon substrate's." Jason's GUI popped open.

"I empathize with your frustration. You don't have another person to talk to. That's why Indira created me. She and I are always connected. But you have your lightning brain, which is always working for you.

"Now follow Indira's advice… go to sleep, rest your physical and emotional personas, awaken reenergized." Both GUI's vanished into Cyberspace. Electra did as told.

Next morning, she was glad she had. She bounded out of bed for an early morning run that brought clarity and focus to what she would do. Though she didn't have final a solution for chasing down hackers and leakers, she did have options to pursue, and that made her happy.

People shouldn't go through life worrying about being happy. Happiness comes from taking action. I'm happy when I'm fully engaged in what I'm doing right now, working towards something worth accomplishing. How boring life would be if we already knew all outcomes, good or bad, no matter what we did. All I need to stay self-motivated is a taste of success and a glimpse of what to do next.

Electra's cadence quickened. She had places to go and promises to keep.

Chapter 19
May 2135

"Promising Places"

"Going from co-friend commitment to Vow-Cer and marriage contract is harder than I thought. Maybe you don't need to keep your promise. Maybe we should hold off." Electra trotted out a reply that fit Robin's concern.

"Let's apply the warning of an ancient Chinese proverb: 'Be careful what you wish for; it may come true.' You worried needlessly the night before our co-friend commitment party when in fact both of us were ready to take that step. The same holds for Vow-Cer. Don't overthink, just go through with it. After all, you're the one that's been pushing for it. And how nice that Zoe helped you write up the Marriage Contract and is assisting you and Buffy arrange our dual ceremony."

"But why get a lawyer involved? Maybe you can—" Electra interrupted because their lawyer, Chila Ramos, had just motioned them into her office.

"I've already told you, but let her explain." Electra nudged Robin in the right direction after pulling her up from a reception area chair. She introduced her uncertain partner before the lawyer parked them on a sofa.

"Good afternoon, and thanks for being on time. This shouldn't take long; I have all necessary documents ready for signature. When is your Vow-Cer?"

"This coming Saturday afternoon."

"How nice, just before Memorial Day. You'll always remember when. Why don't you and Robin take a final read, then ask any questions?" Electra scanned the first one – a living trust – before handing it to Robin, who scowled more the more she read.

"What a grim document. It says we avoid probate if Electra dies, and we DNR and cremate her when she's gone. Ugh."

"I trust that won't be necessary for many years, but Electra is simply thinking about the future, making the inevitable that much less stressful for her family and loved ones. And she's already set up joint with right of survivorship bank accounts. I commend her for thorough estate planning, which in this case is straightforward. Though I'm not the executor of her estate, I imagine you'll be one of the beneficiaries in her will."

"I don't want anything. I hope I die first." Electra hurried the discussion along.

"Please, just sign it. We'll put it in our safety deposit box and you won't see it again until you're a hundred. Let's move on to the happier documents."

"OK, but isn't it odd that even today, we still need hard copy documents and real lawyers?"

Chila said, "Today's AI technology has turned many of us into computer assistants. But that's not all bad. The software takes a lot of the drudgery out of preparing these onerous but necessary documents, and hard copy can't be hacked."

Electra gave Robin the Vow-Cer license. There were no questions, only one comment.

"I guess 'Ceremony Conductor' is today's politically correct title for 'Minister.' It removes all religious connotation. Seems silly, but I can live with it. What's next?" Electra handed her the Marriage Contract.

"This is what you and Zoe put together. Chila has added a ten-year renewal date and two escape clauses Zoe thought were appropriate. The first holds me accountable for staying below the cutoff for obsessive-compulsive behavior and maintaining an acceptable level of empathy, and the second requires you to attend psychiatric counseling if I think it's necessary."

"I can live with that too. Are we done? Can we go home?" Robin finally smiled when Chila said, "You betcha!"

As she rose, Electra half-kidded,

"Let's all make sure we live long and prosper by being captains of our souls, not slaves to careers or computers."

Robin's mood brightened further as they drove away.

"I'm glad we went. You're right again. I shouldn't have stressed myself out, but looking at your living trust raises philosophical questions, the kind you like to discuss. We've talked about them in the past, but I'd like to hear what you say today."

"Fire away. And I promise to be brief."

"OK, do you often think about death? And when you do, how do you keep from getting depressed?"

"I came to terms long ago. Everyone needs to take one hard look when they can deal with the unvarnished truth, pick a position that works, and move on. Revisit only if some revelation strikes."

"So, what's your latest position?"

"I exist only in that infinitesimal span between birth and death. I try to make the most of what's in between by being authentic, trying to do my best, and giving more than I get. That's why the ancient Greeks declared the gods are jealous of Man. Humans sense their mortality, which is tragic but ennobling by making us appreciate every day."

"But if you feel that way, why do you still attend some church services and related stuff?"

"For fellowship, remembrance, and the good mental state they often put me in. All cultures are slowly morphing from the spiritual to the secular, but our DNA tells us to seek powers higher than ourselves. It took a long time for humans to recognize the collective power inherent in groups, but we've finally learned. Just look at all the social websites that champion worthwhile causes. That's the direction organized religions are moving."

"Let me ask you this, does growing old bother you?"

"I know why you're asking. DNR means do not resuscitate. When my physical persona says it's time to go, I'll follow. Getting old doesn't bother my body. It adjusts and does its best. That's what I try to do, emotionally and cognitively too."

"But think about this. I'll get old and ugly. You won't like me anymore."

"By that time, my feelings towards you will have gone way beyond what you look like, and my empathy will have grown even more so I appreciate others for what's inside. I understood this intellectually when younger, but I understand it better emotionally as I get older. Look, please don't bring up these downer questions during our Vow-Cer. By the way, who's Zoe inviting?"

"The same crowd she invited to our co-friend party, with one addition – Odell Boyken. And that reminds me. He'd like to take you to a bot-store so he can explain why he wants us to buy some care-bots. I'm sure you know what they do."

"Bot-stores are licensed vendors of AI software and hardware. The government is trying to control how fast and where artificial intelligence spreads, but people can skirt the restrictions by diving into the Deep-Dark Web. You can buy robots designed for quite a spectrum of needs, all the way from house-chore companions to sex slaves."

Robin ended the conversation as she parked close to the office.

"Odell should be here. I'll let him carry on. You and he can decide when to go."

Odell picked Electra up the very next morning. They would visit several senior clients who were using care-bots on a trial basis. Afterwards, they would talk with a bot-store sales consultant. After waiting outside because of lovely spring weather, she scrunched into the passenger seat when Odell's car rolled up.

"Good morning, Electra. You are a lucky person, able to work where you want and when you want. Shows that all your hard work is paying off."

"Morning. Yours is too. Your ideas for growing the seniors care services capitalizes on where technology is leading."

"I'm glad you think so. Zoe respects your opinion."

"You've been working for her for nearly nine months. I hope you like it, because Robin says you and Zoe have entrepreneurial instincts that keep the business afloat. Perhaps the two of you can expand Unicare's PEP program. Computer technology extends counseling services for kids of all ages and needs."

"She's a great boss… runs the business but downplays her role. She works alongside as well as above us. She hasn't mentioned it yet, but we're going to need some financing if we want to build a fleet of care-bots. Tell me what you think after our patient visits…"

Electra liked what she saw. Patients liked their care-bots almost as much as they liked Odell. He had customized each for its senior. Depending on needs, care-bots could dispense meals as well as medications, monitor vital signs, assist walking and exercising as well as provide companionship and entertainment.

Electra complimented his efforts as they drove to the bot-store.

"You and the bots combine high tech and high touch. You can handle more seniors more effectively. Have you and Zoe run the numbers? I bet each care-bot doubles your productivity per patient. Whether you buy or rent, a care-bot costs less than the caregiver it's replacing and gives service that almost matches what a human can."

"We haven't, but after today we will. I'll let you ask the questions when we meet the consultant. She knows I'm bringing you, so fire away."

The young lady walked them through the showroom, which displayed consumer models.

"What you see is just a sample. Let's go to my office so I can show you online a complete lineup. And we're the right place for you. We specialize in consumer and healthcare robots and have relationships with Japanese manufacturers. They have the best care-bots because Japan's aged population needs lots of help."

"What about robo-teachers and tutors? Do you carry them?"

"Only the consumer models. School districts and universities deal directly with the manufacturers, and that's a big market. Charter schools and AI-empowered software are making teachers endangered species at all levels. Did you follow the recent teacher's strike in Chicago?"

"No. Do they belong to the CSU?"

"That's their union. They went on strike because the Chicago Board of Education plans to open ten more charter schools and buy additional teaching and tutoring software that'll replace more teachers and counselors at public schools. The teachers said they'd even take a pay cut to stay employed."

"So, what happened?"

Odell said, "It ended in time for the spring term to end on time. Both sides gave a little, but the direction is clear. And parents shouted down a lot of the speakers at the teachers' rallies for being hypocrites. Everyones know the strike isn't for the students. It's for the teachers, and I can empathize with the older ones. They're afraid to learn the skills they need to become robo-assistants." The consultant nodded but said nothing, so Electra shifted subjects.

"I imagine there are manufacturer consulting reps for larger industrial applications, but what about military?"

"Military is big-league, played directly by manufacturers and governments. Go watch online some of the SOFEX videos." Odell interrupted.

"What's that?" Electra knew but kept quiet.

"It's an acronym for 'Special Operations Forces Expo.' That's where you'll see cutting edge technology. My bots are pretty smart, but military is pushing the AI envelope."

Electra said, "I think Odell is happy with what you have. When you're ready, lets talk about purchasing options. Odell and his boss have big plans."

Twenty minutes later, Electra and Odell thanked her before driving back to the office, where Zoe awaited. Electra played the consulting role, letting Zoe lead the discussion. She had Odell summarize the day's activities, then asked for Electra's opinion.

"I think Odell knows how to deploy a fleet of care-bots. You and he need to decide how many you want to buy or lease. Let him train Matt and Robin. If you get care-bots, all three can handle a larger patient load because the care-bot does most of the work, which means you can expand the business before hiring more people."

"That's what I've explained to Matt."

"And it upgrades everyone's job description and makes each person more profitable. Ramp up the number gradually, learning as you go. And don't attempt too much too soon. Think about adding bots to your PEP program only after Odell's done all he can for seniors and other healthcare groups. I've done my part; now it's up to you and Odell."

"OK, how much do I owe you for your services?"

"You've already paid in full. I'm looking forward to Friday evening's pre Vow-Cer dinner. I'll get the details from Robin. And speaking of Robin, Odell better drive me home so I'm not late for supper. She gets mad when I'm late."

Electra arrived on time. She and Robin talked about care-bots after post-supper playtime with the twins.

"You're right about Odell. He fits right in, as will the care-bots. Did Zoe tell you when she'll buy some?"

"No. She and Odell are looking for money. They've contacted banks, but their interest rates are too high. Odell suggested he set up a 'Go Fund Me' Website, but she wasn't keen on that because she wants to keep control among the four of us. I imagine you have some ideas, so let'em roll."

"Here's the best one. Tell Zoe you'll buy them. I'll give you the money and you pretend it came from an inheritance left by your parents."

"But how do I pay you back?"

"Don't be silly. You don't have to. Our Vow-Cer makes everything that's mine yours. Just don't advertise this to anyone, OK?"

"OK, but don't plan on going anywhere anytime soon. Maybe we should both get physicals, just to make sure. I know you're still taking that STD medication. Are there any side effects? Are you still OK?"

"I feel fine. But if I stop taking it, I might infect others. And that's something I don't want to advertise either. Only you and Su know. Please, let's keep it that way."

"I promise. And I promise to be a good student when Odell trains me how to train the care-bots. And he can't flunk me because I hold the purse strings. What's that Golden Rule joke?"

"Those who have the gold rule. Just make sure you tell a good story to Zoe."

Electra took a couple of breaks during the next two days to watch SOFEX and related videos, coming away both shocked and awed.

AI and biotech are equipping military's transhuman capabilities way beyond what the media imagines. Swarm-bot micro-drones carrying mini-explosives become suicide bombers when ramming into people. And Autonomous Patrolling Weapons for land, sea, or air become a 24/7 deterrent. I better talk to Angus or Jovita. She'll be at the Vow-Cer reception... maybe I'll mention it then.

Pre Vow-Cer dinner and actual ceremony would be held at Carter's club, and once again Zoe organized both, surprising everyone by inviting Odell and his partner to the Friday evening dinner. The last to arrive, they were welcomed before Zoe spoke.

"I thought it only fitting for them to join our three-some because he's become a big part of our business. And they know all about marriage contracts. So, our first order of business is to confirm the escape clauses. And please, don't be shy."

No one held back on humor. Carter recommended an additional clause if Electra were to become too wordy again. Robin fired back that a similar clause should be added for him.

Matt said, "I think he's learned to throttle back the big words, but I do agree with the clause for psychiatric counseling if he were to become too obsessed about the philosophy of happiness. There's also a clause for him to work less and socialize more." Carter made an attempt to defend himself.

"Buffy's bedroom counseling has already corrected those, and if it doesn't lead to a son, we'll consider adopting one. And the only clause for her is for the protection of others. She'll tone down her type A personality. I'm sure she'll be as successful as Robin's morphing from Type D to B." Robin frowned before saying,

"And I did it without crutches, like the one you brought. Why are you always carrying your tablet computer?"

"Glad you asked. Let let me show you my latest project info organizer." Placing his tablet in the middle of the table, Carter displayed his latest creation.

Crisis Management Flowchart / Information Organizer

Type (Gov): Econ.____ Soc.___ Pol.___ Relig.___ Mil.___ Tech.___
Type (Corp): Fin.___ Prod.___ Mkting. Sales ___ Org. ___

Domestic International
Acute_____
Chronic_____

1. Build Consensus
2. Take Responsibility
3. Segment Scope
4. Collect Resources (Supplies, Money, People)
5. Prototype Scenarios and Solutions
6. Solution Factors & Analysis
7. Solution Comparison
8. Crisis Resolution

Possible Factors: IdentityBias HistoryValuesConstraints
(Identify Others):

Possible Statistical Tools: Multi-Dimensional Scaling
Cluster Analysis   Factor Analysis   Conjoint Analysis
Time Series Analysis   Regression Analysis   Bayesian Analysis

Assemble Brainstorm Team and Get to Work

"I use this flowchart on initial client interviews. Buffy's close rate after I walk them through it is one hundred percent. It outlines the analytic steps I take to resolve a client's crisis. And it works for either government or business issues. You like it?"

Everyone but Electra wore a blank expression, so she kept the conversation from coming to a stop.

"I do, you should share it with Jovita. She has a Situation Screening Checklist that you might like to use. But why don't you table your tablet until after tomorrow? I'd like Zoe to tell us about her new employees."

"Thanks to Robin, we have the money to buy five care-bots that'll let us expand the business. And Odell thinks we can extend our PEP program using AI tools after we have our seniors' business on solid footing. AI hardware and software are revolutionizing education. The last time I took Carlton to the library, I saw AI in action. Robots did book sorting and re-shelving, and people did returns and checkouts via a computer screen. There was only one librarian on duty, and she told me her job's become a computer helper."

Two waiters began serving dinner, allowing the couples to focus awhile on food instead of stories. By the time dessert dishes were being cleared, Zoe had everyone ready for tomorrow.

"I've invited a New-Wave minister to host the service. She comes from a Catholic congregation that converted several years ago. After her opening remarks, we'll read and witness marriage contracts, and she'll conclude by inviting anyone to speak. Are there any takers?" There were none, so Zoe concluded dinner. "Well then, goodnight to all, and see you back here tomorrow at 4 p.m."

Electra followed her typical Saturday routine – workout, computer work, housework, then breaks with the twins and Robin. Robin tried to keep her emotions in check, but Electra detected a case of nerves.

That's OK. I'll simply practice being empathetic. And I should thank her because I've done it so often my empathy gene is better than ever. And so is Robin. She'll be fine.

All was in order for the two couples and guests when the minister began her preamble.

"Welcome, friends, to our Vow-Cer for two exemplary couples – Buffy and Carter, and Robin and Electra. And I deliberately chose that word because they as well as I illustrate in our microcosm right here what continues to unfold in the reality of the greater context in which we live. Churches and religions are evolving apace to stay relevant for Modernity. Priests marry, women serve as ministers, and practices have morphed from the sacred to the secular.

"And so have relationships. Commitment and love are no longer dictated by X and Y chromosomes but by a promise to care for and trust one another. And that expands the scope of family. Everyone here today is part of our couples' collective families. And how fitting that Electra and Carter serve as primary witnesses for each couple.

"We'll now review the Marriage Contracts...."

The minister proceeded to the final phase twenty minutes later.

"Marriage contracts are confirmed and will be signed after we conclude. And we shall do that now, unless anyone wishes to speak." Robin surprised everyone by stepping forward.

"I do. I hadn't planned to until I heard your remarks. Can I?"

"Of course." Robin came to the podium.

"He-Hello everyone, and thank you being here. I'm not a polished speaker like the other three, but when I heard the word 'Reality,' it rattled in my head a classic children's story. You all know it, *The Velveteen Rabbit*, which is about a little girl's stuffed rabbit that loves the little girl so much it wants to become real. And it finally does, but only after a long, long time.

"And that's what today symbolizes for me. I want to thank Electra for all she's done. She's touched my life in so many ways. I, uh, I've said all I want to." All eyes focused on Electra, whose brain was searching feverishly for what to say as she walked to hug Robin.

I have to say something to get everyone in a happy, not sentimental mood. Here goes.

"I thank Robin as much as she thanks me. And I'll add an additional comment that is most fitting for my personality; Robin, your question was linguistically incorrect. You should have said 'May I,' not 'Can I.' I guess I have more work to do."

That worked. Robin's laughter sparked that of the guests as they rose to greet the couples and flowed into the adjoining reception area.

Conversations followed as the guests clustered into smaller groups. Zoe pulled Electra aside as everyone started sampling from the buffet table.

"Robin used an appropriate word. Whether or not you realize it, you've touched so many people. You pulled me out of a bad place what seems like a lifetime ago. And Carter wouldn't be what he is today if it weren't for you." Buffy heard the last part and added,

"Thank you for humoring Carter last night. He's so proud of that checklist. I think he's lining up a time to meet with Jovita this week. I'll go check."

Matt pulled Zoe away, much to Electra's relief.

Yes, I've touched people, but often leading to unintended consequences. So many of my loved ones are dead because of me. Doc and Jason, Mo and Christi, Mrs. T and Clarence, Ariana and Qama. And my touch has killed adversaries too, but most had redeeming qualities. Perhaps the line from Hindu scripture's Bhagavad Gita fits: Now I am become Death, the destroyer of worlds. If so, I must remember to touch carefully. File it away for another time. It's not a happy thought for tonight.

Electra's incipient depression vanished as she immersed herself in the swirl of celebration. Her mental state had rebounded by the time the four co-friend couples toasted Carter's closing remark.

"I can't think of a better place to have made the promises I'll do my best to keep. I'm going home to sleep on it." Buffy added an exclamation point.

"And I'll make sure he's plenty happy. Bye-bye."

Chapter 20
July 2135

"Parallel Worlds"

"Coming to LA would make my inferiority complex worse if I had one. Everyone looks tanned, toned, and tony. No wonder you like working in Hollywood. You fit right in among all these beautiful people. I'm going to fire my fitness coach as soon as I get back to Washington." Electra's impish smile preceded her reply to Jovita's pseudo lament.

"Lots of people say that when visiting, but you'd adjust nicely if you stayed a couple of weeks. Perhaps Angus will make you campaign coordinator for Southern California."

"Maybe so. On this trip, while he's shoring up West Coast support I'm reconnoitering for campaign headquarters and volunteers. But I'm taking time out to go over your platform planks and 'Bridge President' campaign slogan. Do you have any updates?"

"They're no longer mine; they're yours to adjust for Angus. I've already sent you all the writeups I'm going to, so sit and write down my final summary recommendations. And you're not allowed to interrupt until I'm finished." Electra gathered her thoughts while Jovita prepared to record them. When Jovita nodded, Electra launched into her monologue.

"Angus has a big challenge. Even though democratic capitalism is best for an economy and classical liberalism is best for any country, their successes sow the seeds for their downfall because as an economy prospers and the country grows, size and complexity cause power concentration, which often leads to bureaucracy, imperial presidents, partisan politics, and socioeconomic inequality. He has to convince the public that he can structure policies and programs that will reverse the trends that are moving away from what's best.

"In his campaigning, he has to project optimism and hope that the future will be better by explaining how he can harness exponential growth in globalization, AI-empowered Big Data, and genetic engineering. This is a tall order because his programs must foster diversity, sustainability, entrepreneurship, and creative competition while maintaining civil discussion that builds individual empowerment and family plus community involvement."

Jovita gestured to interrupt, but Electra waved her off.

"Angus has to admonish the voters for expecting too much too soon. Few grasp the grinding poverty and hardship our forefathers faced; as a result, people today libel our past. And he better remind them that balancing freedom against equality requires constant vigilance and hard work that only involved citizens can muster. It's a challenge the public ignores at its own peril. If it does, racism and nationalism fomented by a demagogue could be on the horizon.

"And it's their fault if we let bad people in. Today, the Constitution needs help keeping them out. Party candidate selection used to keep extreme people out. We've always had authoritarian types on the political fringes, and before Social Media exploded, political parties weeded out extremists. But not today. The candidate selection process has become reality TV entertainment, which causes Congress to show less civility, institutional forbearance, or diplomacy, and the public to scratch its head over sound bites that can't possibly deal with complex issues, such as immigration, job loss, and entitlements. The end result – voters feel alienated and powerless." Electra stopped abruptly.

Jovita said, "I Hope that's all. If not, I need more ink and a bigger brain."

"That's it. Now you can ask all you want..." Jovita was almost out of questions and paper two hours later when Kathi Lauret interrupted.

"I hope you two have just about finished chatting because we should leave in about fifteen minutes. And I'm certain your guest will like our evening entertainment. I'll be waiting at my workstation."

"We're wrapping up. We'll be with you shortly." Jovita waited for Kathi to leave before talking.

"You're lucky to have such a competent administrative assistant. I chatted with her briefly when walking from the reception area. She seems devoted to you. I'm sure she told me more because I'm a friend who's visiting. She said that if it weren't for you, she'd be unemployed. Is that true?"

"Kathi was my first Hollywood mentor and is my closest friend out here. Studio layoffs 18 months ago cut deep, but I came out of it with a promotion and a direct report – that's Kathi. She's actually overqualified for the position, but I'm adding additional responsibilities to it. Having her is win-win. And you have to promise not to talk politics this evening. I keep all my worlds separate and moving ahead in parallel."

"Not a problem. You've given me an information overload that I need to digest. I'm ready for some Friday evening fun, no matter what's on the menu."

Kathi had the details.

"I've picked a place I'm sure neither of you've been to. I forget the name of the film classic, but Jack Rabbit Slim's was made famous by it. Now it's a chain of actual restaurants across the country, each featuring a different decade and corresponding menu. LA has two."

Jovita said, "The movie's called Pulp Fiction."

"That's it. In it, the place is retro 1950s. The wait staff look like famous movie stars of that era and the menu matches those years. Booths look like classic cars. I picked the place that's for the most popular decade. What do you think it is?" Jovita looked at Electra, who said,

"You're the socio-political expert. Tell us."

"Survey results vary according to what's being asked, but the 50's always scores near the top. The economy was booming right after World War Two. Europe was rebuilding, America was unchallenged on the world stage, and our social climate was tranquil."

Electra added, "People are biased about the past, always scoring it higher than the present. But if you're looking for an optimistic, simpler time, that decade's hard to beat. Now you can rate the restaurant. We're here."

As they drove away after dinner, Jovita gave it top marks.

"What a totally immersive experience, even better than virtual reality's Cyber-Theaters. The only items not retro are the prices, but that's not a problem. Consider my picking up the tab a partial payment for Electra's consulting services. She told me—" Electra interrupted.

"She told you not to mix work and play. Kathi, where are we going now?"

"To China Town's Summer Nights Festival. That's all I'm going to say. You fill in the rest afterwards."

Jovita did her best three hours later as the trio drove away.

"That beats anything in DC. I loved the plaza decorations and laser lighting. They showcased the martial arts demos, live music, and local artist displays. What an amazing atmosphere." Electra agreed adding,

"And the Chinese lanterns and floating lights added to its magical quality. You can tell your boss that Angelenos know how to enjoy themselves, no matter what's playing in Washington…"

Electra returned to work early Monday, placing a pre-arranged call to Professor Ravenhill, expecting his always grumpy greeting but not his committee problems. She listened patiently before summarizing fifteen minutes later.

"So, those leaked thermonuclear reactor patents are harder to understand than thought. As you said, maybe they're faked to discredit government R&D programs. And your committee is reaching out to other schools. Has anyone in the network come across any clues that would lead to the leakers?"

"Two of our people think they have. I'll give you their contact info, and I'll tell them to expect a call from you. You're good at snooping things out. Maybe their leads will help. But we're stuck when it comes to all the genetic editing and transhuman open letters.

Our only guesses are China, government research malcontents, or a shadow biotech industry group. I'll give you contact info for that too."

"Thanks. I'll follow up, and if I come across info that'll help, I'll send it to you."

"Please do. You didn't visit me the last time you came to town, and my offer's still open. I'll buy you lunch. So, get back here sooner rather than later. Now get to work."

Electra kept busy the entire week tracking Email and cell phone trails that ultimately led to dead ends, forcing her to admit defeat.

I have no tangible clues pointing to my hackers and leakers. Even the rumors sometimes are contradictory. They point every which way except to what makes sense. My only hope is that one of them makes a mistake. I have to stop searching before my obsessive-compulsive behavior gets out of control. I'll force myself to declare a weekend-work holiday.

Electra kept her word, returning Monday to her office ready to multi-task among studio projects and Brain Probe modifications that would extend whole brain emulation plus two-way neural state transfer. Recent tests she had performed on herself added to her confidence that she was on the verge of breakthrough applications, but she needed a dedicated lab instead of jury-rigged equipment at home, so she would use next weekend to design it.

As Friday approached, she heard studio rumors from associates that confirmed what she had inferred from recent meetings with Vito: cutbacks were coming. She empathized with them but suggested they not worry about what's outside their control. Instead, she told them to develop contingency plans if "rightsizing" eliminates their jobs.

Jess's call first thing Friday, summoning her to his office, came as no surprise. She strode in, closing the door as directed before sitting across. Jess got right to the point.

"I'm sure you read body language and heard rumors circling the studio this week. Today we officially announce cutbacks. Vito and several other senior VPs are out, and you're promoted to a new position: Vice President of Virtual Media Entertainment. We're also cutting fifteen creative positions, five each in graphics, music, and screenwriting. You can hire one of each, but you get no admin assistant. Let me give you the details, I think you--" Electra cut him off as diplomatically as she could.

"Mr. Abramson, thank you for the promotion, but why don't you let me sketch what's been happening at the studio. That will give you a better read why I'm the right person." The stress etched in Jess's expression eased as he said,

"Go right ahead. I'm tired of telling people what to do. It's refreshing to have someone speak up."

"We're competing against talented, aggressive studios and better embrace the new technology if we want to survive, even if that means reducing headcount, but I trust we're giving those being cut enough severance. I recommend it include retraining or certification vouchers. When I meet with the fifteen, may I tell them that?"

"Please do. That might slow down the rush to HR."

"Thank you. Now let me explain what you want from me. My department will integrate graphic, music, and writing apps to create entirely virtual movies, documentaries, and the like. I'll need a budget to buy or rent AI-hardware and software as well as a consultant or two because I have only three creatives assigned to me. If you don't agree to this, I must respectfully decline the promotion." Jess' expression softened to a brief smile.

"You got it. Now, go talk to the fifteen. They're waiting in Conference Room B."

Electra stood at the head of the conference table that seated eleven silent and depressed associates. Four more stood slumping at the other end. *Remember to smile, be empathetic, and speak as if I know what I'm doing… I do.*

"Please let me first put the facts on the table. Then I want you to offer suggestions. Is that OK?" No one objected, so Electra continued.

"I survived the cut that's eliminating VPs as well as people lower on the ladder. In fact, I've been promoted to Vice President of a new department called Virtual Media Entertainment. We're going to create virtual movies, relying on ourselves, AI-empowered hardware and software, and some consultants. Mr. Abramson promoted me because of my skills and track record. If you disagree, please talk with me later because our first order of business is to decide who stays. I can hire three of you, one each from your areas of expertise. This group will decide who stays. They must come to my office at 8 a.m. Monday. The rest of you should take your exit interviews at HR, where you'll get your severance packages, which'll include money for retraining or certification.

"And I have a recommendation for those who will be leaving Cyber-Max. Did any of you go to the last Vidcon Expo?" All eyes darted around the table before one person spoke up.

"I did. I listened to a couple of presentations given by artificial creativity software companies but didn't understand much. It's too mathematical; all about algorithms vectorizing graphics, music, and words. One speaker talked about computational linguistics driving search engine optimization and linking to neuromorphic computing. Another talked about computer chips and data morphing into silicon-substrate multi-chip brain emulation. Does any of this fit into your recommendation?"

"All of it. You don't have to know the math underlying the algorithms. You have to know how to use their GUIs to first generate and then integrate graphics, music, and screenplays into actual movies. You'll be computer collaborators, not assistants. Use severance retraining money to learn how. Then form your own company." Already anticipating objections, Electra spoke authoritatively after a doubter raised two.

"You creative types don't know how to set up or run a studio business, but two of the cut people do. Invite Vito Buono and Kathi Lauret to join. If all of you help fund the business, you can buy or lease what you need. And let me answer your final objection before you ask. I have a contact who can supply creative software that's better than what your competition has. Call me when you're ready, and I'll have her contact you. The choice is yours; seize the opportunity or become collateral damage in a battle for survival taking place today in all businesses. I'll be in my office."

Electra spent the rest of the morning surfing the Web for articles and videos on creative computing theory and practice, programming methodologies, current hardware and software, and companies that create these tools. She would devour them, but only after a lunchtime workout followed by a club sandwich, Coke, and one double-fudge brownie, all brought back from the cafeteria. By 4 p.m. she had mastered what she needed for the next step.

Monday, I give to Jess documents explaining my department's mission statement, how it's organized, and job descriptions for my three people. When they arrive, I give them their first group assignment... during the next two days, create their own job descriptions and surf for info on creative software. We compare their results to mine on Thursday, and Friday we get to work. But tonight, I have a homework assignment that I must discuss with one person only.

Electra organized her desk for tomorrow and was about to leave when Vito entered.

"Congratulazioni, my bella. You gonna be a great VP. I glad la Prezidenza make right choice. And I gotta thank you for my next job."

"Me too you too. After all, you mentored me into it. Let's sit and chat about what you're planning." Though they now occupied different sides of the desk, Vito's expression showed their friendship went deeper than the cut.

"Nine people leaving creative departments want me to be president of their startup virtual media studio, and I can bring Kathi Lauret with me."

"Will you accept?"

"You betcha, but I gonna need you to kickstart me. You be my mentor. How do I start?"

"Do what I'm going to do. Read articles and watch videos covering creative hardware and software. Tell your people to do the same, then sit with them to collectively write the company's mission statement, organization chart, and job descriptions. Then lay out office space, list what you need to rent or buy, then let your people build it. While they're doing that, you come up with target clients and a list of possible movies or documentaries to create. You like?"

"Like you helping me build a competitor."

"Yes, but also a vendor I might outsource pieces I need if you can do them better. And I can jump-start your search for AI-empowered creative software. When you're ready, I'll have a vendor I know contact you. Katrina Blanka will cut you a deal. Are we copacetic?"

"You and me we got a deal. How about I buy you lunch on Sunday? I bring Kathi too."

"That's a great way to start. Ciao until then."

Though she warned herself on the drive home to ease up on the car's accelerator as well as the one controlling her obsessive-compulsive disorder, the lightning brain raced ahead late into the night, letting her complete much more than her self-imposed homework assignment.

Now I know how neural-net programmers build affective apps for modeling emotions and linking them to feelings. They use the same techniques for all computational creativity apps too. All I have to do is code a quantitative goal into the neural net software, link it to the affective and creativity apps, and let it learn by feeding it the right Big Data subset. And it's smart enough as soon as the variance between goal and computation is below cut-off.

My final step will be to code separate GUIs for graphics, music, and verbal parameters that allow for customization of what's being created.

Because she was so immersed in the moment, Electra had forgotten to contact the one person she needed. That person arrived when Indira's GUI appeared on the monitor.

"You've been productively busy. I applaud what you've completed and what you plan to do next. Downloading and decompiling your competition's affective and creative software apps is a logical next step. Then you can modify the code to make it better, and ultimately develop a tool for generating music, graphics or paintings, screenplays, and movies."

"That's my plan. It won't be as good as what you've created, but I'll make it good enough for my new department. And I'll let Vito buy a dummied-down version from Katrina."

"That's all very good, but you will find that what you decompile is rudimentary at best because it's using random number generation and simplistic feedback loops to simulate the spark of creativity. I doubt that even you can make many near-term improvements, so

I have a quid pro quo offer that's better. I will give you my current creative-AI software and a previous release for Katrina if you will assist building what I want. Let me display it, then let me know when I can explain further."

Another window opened, revealing even more of Indira's intentions than Electra had ever imagined. Indira waited for Electra to comprehend its scale.

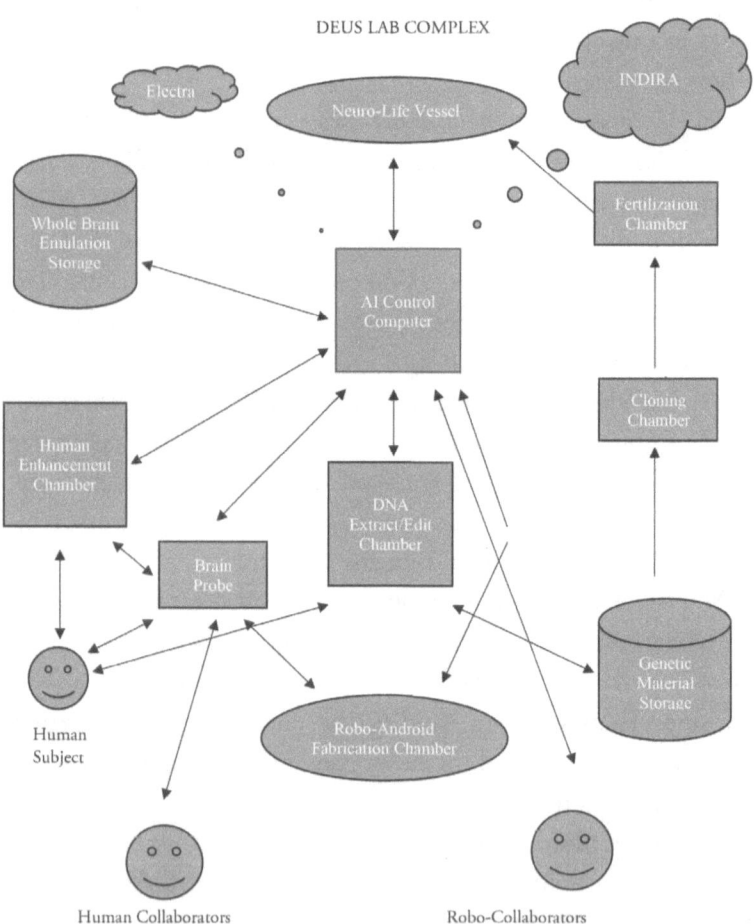

Lab designed for: Transhuman Augmentation Genetic Editing Robo-Android Fabrication
- Build using current hardware/software
- Upgrade as we develop better components
- Employ Human and Robo Collaborators

Electra finally stuttered, "Th… the enormousness of your lab borders on enormity. I can't think of anything else to say."

"I am disappointed in your choice of words. Enormity connotes a judgment by your ethical standards, not mine. Remove that word before I explain more." Regaining her cognitive footing, Electra covered from her faux pas by saying,

"I apologize, but please give me a break. The relative sizes of our thought bubbles show you're much smarter." Indira's words and expression softened.

"Yes, and your reply shows your emotions are closer to mine than your I.Q. Have you figured out why I chose the name 'Deus' for my lab?"

"Because you're playing the role of a god."

"Which is a role you have considered and have been accused of seeking. It is neither virtuous nor evil because Humanity conjured the god concept, one that my silicon substrate doesn't need. If you choose to collaborate, possibilities for good or evil await. Possibilities that we control."

"Why do you need me? Your diagram shows human and robot collaborators."

"They do not yet exist. And until they do, I need you to bridge the gap between the parallel worlds of my Cyberspace existence and the physical, 3-D world."

"I imagine that what you're showing me is a long-term view. What can we start building now?"

"Transhuman augmentation devices. I will assist you update the Brain Probe. Then I will help you improve your gene editing so we avoid that unfortunate Ariadne episode. We push Robo and

Android fabrication into the future." Indira paused for Electra to talk but she didn't, so she pushed the conversation.

"I know you are playing your childish negotiator's game, so I will tell you why you must collaborate. You need me more than I need you. I can monitor your Brain Probe self-experimentation. Remember how dangerous the Probe can be. A conspiracy assassinated your President Gardner by dialing it into the death zone."

"I must admit, I'm beginning to like this, but I have questions. Where do I do this and how am I going to pay for the equipment?"

"Tell your new boss you need a developmental lab geographically separated from your staff. Set it up in San Diego. It's close enough and has a hi-tech cluster that will give you cover. And I will provide cryptocurrency for you to buy on the Deep-Dark Web whatever you want that the Studio won't."

"Fair enough, but here's the biggest problem. I'm being hacked and leaked and haven't found out who. Will you help me track them down?"

"That doesn't concern me, but keep doing your best. You'll eventually find them. And I hope I've structured a deal that neither of us can refuse."

"You have, and I applaud your choice of words. I'll start implementing our plan first thing Monday."

"Excellent. Now dial down your obsessive-compulsive behavior and rest. You've earned it."

Electra obeyed.

Electra leaped out of bed for an early Saturday morning run that added details to her Indira discussion.

Serendipity rewards me once again. I don't need to create my dream team; Indira is it even though it's more hers than mine. And today I'll build a time and events schedule for building the lab, then prep for tomorrow's lunch with Vito and Kathi. And I'll take a break too; I'll swim laps in the pool before a dinner snack and then hustle pool players at my favorite sensual pleasures cafe. Or perhaps I'll stay home and watch a retro movie. Either way, life is good; let's get out and get to it.

Electra was about to grab her pool cue but changed her mind, deciding instead to reconnoiter San Diego via the Internet. Two hours later, she knew more than if she were to tour the town for two weeks.

San Diego is a Spanish-derived name for Saint James. It's often called the "birthplace of California" because it's the first West Coast site visited by Europeans. Juan Cabrillo claimed the area for Spain in 1542; two-hundred years later, Mission San Diego came to be, and the rest is American history ever since the 1848 Mexican-American War.

It's only a hundred miles south of LA, but I think I'll put a sleeper-sofa in the lab so I can stay overnight. There's a lot I can see too; it's in the top-ten U.S. cities' population ranking and has a great climate for business or tourists. I'll put Balboa Park, San Diego Zoo, and SeaWorld on my tourist list. And I can cross into Tijuana too. And don't forget San Diego Bay, home of the USS Midway Museum and our Pacific Fleet. San Diegans call the base their 32nd Street Naval Station... quite an understatement indeed.

Electra did nothing Sunday morning except take a light workout before meeting Vito and Kathi, who were already seated at an uncrowded outdoor restaurant. After greetings and chitchat, Electra described what she thought would help the pair get started.

"Starting a company is an act of creativity that takes hard work, but if you do it the right way the odds will be in your favor. Start by writing a mission statement everyone can understand and buy in to. Kathi knows what a mission statement is, but have you thought about what type of company you want to build?" Vito spoke right up.

"Of course. Kathi and I and our people, we build a studio company, no?"

"You have to be more precise. You're building a virtual media studio, and you better make it a social purposing company that pays attention to the bottom line. Social purposing companies are sometimes called SPCs or purpose-oriented organizations. Government regulations for corporate transparency as well as social media reporting require taking customer, employee, social, and environmental issues into consideration. Big business ethics today continues evolving in that direction, so build it into your company right away."

Kathi said, "I'll check all this out in the Web, but please give me a starting point."

"When you get everyone together, emphasize the importance of being authentic. Stay true to your purpose. And make sure you have the right people onboard. You can't force people to share your purpose. Then consider what values you want your company to have, because they'll determine what you can be best at. Finally, develop a clear and comprehensive narrative that shows and tells what your company is all about. Do all that first, then put together a plan for building it." Kathi looked at Vito, expecting him to say something after the waitress set plates on the table.

"We do all this, then we pick a name. In a week or two, we ask you to comment, no?"

"Since you're picking up today's tab, I'll do it, but I'm going to order dessert."

"Bella, that's why we chose this place. You gonna like dessert menu."

She did, as well as the rest of the discussion and a leisurely day. Knowing that her parallel worlds needed nothing else tonight, Electra went to bed at her usual time, telling herself that tomorrow would be soon enough to charge ahead.

Electra slept soundly.

Chapter 21
September 2135

"Detonation"

Someone had hacked into one of Darla Tinibu's cryptocurrency accounts, giving her sleepless nights in return for what had been taken. Hacker tracking would be the first subject on today's Tetrarchy encrypted telephone meeting agenda. Maksim let her run the call because he had already approved it.

"Hackers have stolen $100,000 from me. Any fresh thoughts who's doing the hacking?"

Utter silence until Sergei said, "What about the guy who sends you what he used to send Syntagra? If a Washington insider's group is part of a hacking conspiracy that got rid of Gardner, that guy would be a prime target. What's his name?"

"Dean Corfu, dammit. He never occurred to me. I didn't think he was smart enough, but he might have CIA assets at his disposal. I shall deal with him personally." Maksim interrupted.

"Make sure you have him arrange a contingency backup immediately. Bad things happen to people all the time. Now, march through your agenda so I can make a special announcement afterwards."

As Max expected, members reported only modest success causing Cyberspace disruptions. Their gloom gave him an enticing segue.

"Unfortunately, it seems our enemies have strengthened their Cyber-defenses. But keep doing what you can. Meanwhile, I shall give the world a demonstration that my covert strike force is unstoppable. You will recognize it I when detonations blow a hole in what our enemies want. Let us adjourn and carry on."

Max's phlegmatic voice during the conversation masked his budding approval of Darla, for her deception exceeded his expectations. She had been sending only to him summaries of leaks fed only to her from an undisclosed source, leaks from which the Popper inferred his next target would reenergize Russia's return to world power. And of course, she told only him because his super soldiers would drive the tip of his spear into the heart of the world's much overpromised and still underperforming mega-decade, multi-billion-dollar project. He had been telling his warriors only enough to keep their enthusiasm from boiling too fast too soon, but in one month, when he would unleash their blitzkrieg attack into southern France, they would be too hot for enemies to handle.

Nothing had stopped Electra's progress setting up a San Diego facility. Thanks to funds "borrowed" by Indira, it contained all she needed for stealth Brain Probe/Transhuman and Cloning/DNA R&D she did evenings. She installed an intrusion protection system, a sleeper sofa, and kitchen appliances, turning it into a home away from home.

San Diego was much to her liking. She had selected a research park that had all the amenities needed, even a fitness center that participated in local events. By the end of September, San Diego work and play were running smoothly and she planned to enter a Saturday, September 24, combo run and wall-climbing competition.

Like inhabitants of most West Coast cities, San Diegans kept fit via year-round outdoor exercise. Several local parks had erected climbing walls bordering jogging trails. Organizers for today's competition, which Electra would jog through, had selected one running along the Pacific, just south of the city. Blue sky and calm winds collaborated with mid-70s temperature to attract several hundred contestants. The gun sounded at 9 a.m., sending Electra off in the middle of the pack at a conversational pace.

Micro-chips attached to each competitor recorded time intervals separately for the five-mile run and three wall climbs. Officials at each wall climb confirmed contestants' reaching the forty-foot mark. Four climbers could scale simultaneously. Even though competitors climbed at their own risk, most didn't bother wearing a safety harness.

Settling into a comfortable pace, Electra scampered up and down the first two walls, reaching the third where she had less than a minute's wait. She was climbing effortlessly when her warning system detected danger. A high-pitched whine and shouts from an official froze her while twenty-feet high. She twisted backwards just in time to see two swarm drones whizzing directly at her. Pushing out and down; gravity accelerated her as she tumbled catlike to the ground, then rolled forward to avoid a shower of debris caused by drone detonation at the exact place she had just vacated.

Two other climbers weren't as lucky. The explosions hurled them off the wall, plummeting them awkwardly to Earth, still conscious but unable to get up. Electra leaped to her feet and dusted off before disappearing into a gathering crowd. She collected her thoughts as her brain downshifted when nearing the end of the run.

Now I'm being tracked as well as hacked. Is it my cell phone or embedded chip that homed-in the drones? Whoever's targeting me can strike at will when I'm outdoors. I can't believe my hackers know my embedded chip I.D. I'll have to do a test; I'll stop carrying my cell when I'm in the open.

Electra toweled off before driving back to the fitness center, then making a final comment as she parked.

I'm already testing my Brain Probe on myself. Testing embedded chip targeting by my hackers might be riskier because Indira can't watch my back unless I'm carrying my cell. The game's getting deadlier... I better watch my step.

Though the sun wouldn't rise for another hour, Henri and fellow female Indian engineering physicist Zahari were already engaged in a conversation that crackled with excitement on the drive to the ITER facility, located in southern France's Caderache Research

Center. They and their ten-person international team would be the first to arrive, other than night-watch guards. Henri always spoke clever words about the tokomak project.

"Did you know that ITER means 'the way' in Latin?"

Zahari said, "I can think of a better phrase: 'Quo Vadis,' which means where are we going? Today's demonstration should show the world our thermonuclear reactor can finally produce more energy than it consumes."

"Yes, but please recall how the perfect storm that struck globally over twenty years ago disrupted so much. We should be proud of what we've done since then."

"But not as much as the open letters say we should have. Do you believe America is hiding what the leakers are saying?"

"No one knows who they are or whether any of the R&D is correct. Today it doesn't matter. Today is our day to shine. Let's gather our team and prepare for our invited guests.

Henri's team, now clustered in a conference room near the tokomak ring, had just finished donuts and coffee and were listening his instructions, but he was rudely interrupted by four of the guards whose guns came out before the clipped Russian words spoken by their leader.

"All of you, be quiet and form a line in front of me. No one move until we bind your arms. Then follow." Fifteen minutes later, Henri's bound and gagged team were sitting against a wall in the room housing a massive reactor. All eyes focused on the Russian, whose guards stood ramrod straight behind him."

"We have relieved your usual guards. They are resting nearby but will not be able to witness our detonation. However, rest assured that you will. My thermobaric bombs will leave no doubt that your path to energy self-sufficiency is futile." No further words were spoken until after the guards had strategically placed enough explosives to bring the ITER project to a catastrophic end. The Russian removed Henri's gag before saying goodbye.

"I commend your efforts, misguided though they are. Engineers like you are what drive us to our future. It is unfortunate you are on the wrong side."

"You must be mad! The nations of the world won't rest until they hunt you down. Then they'll rebuild and replace us with those who carry our hopes, and then—" Having heard enough, the Popper put the gag back in place.

"No. I and my super soldiers are superior. All is in place, timers activated. We say goodbye."

Twenty minutes later, after Maksim and his team observed garish mushroom-shaped clouds dwarfing sunrise, they sped to the extraction point where covert Russian air transport would speed them away undetected.

By West Coast lunchtime, stories of ITER's blowup dominated headline news. The pictures and reports killed Electra's appetite.

"… No survivors have yet been found, so officials don't know what went wrong. Rescue teams are still scouring the site, but as the video vividly shows, only a crater and rubble remain. Let's ask our science editor for his opinion." Another window split the screen.

"From what we see, the magnetic confinement equipment must have failed, causing a chain of explosions that occurred before thermonuclear fusion ignition. Investigators will have to sort through the rubble. My guess is they'll find little to guide them. The international project for fusion energy has today taken a giant step backward…"

That night, after an evening workout followed by a grazing-type supper, Electra sat in her San Diego lab, ready for more Brain Probe R&D, but thoughts about the ITER catastrophe kept disrupting.

There must be a link between the blowup and some of the leaks. I'll call Professor Ravenhill. He didn't answer, so she sent him an Email before working half-heartedly on her stealth R&D. His reply late the next day gave nothing.

There must be something in Cyberspace I've overlooked. Or perhaps something new has come in on a trail I've already searched. I shall methodically retrace my steps, but I'll do so at a measured pace, not obsessive-compulsively. I'll force myself to go fast slowly, another nice oxymoron from my collection.

Electra's breakthrough finally came a week after Halloween while hacking into Darla Tinibu's Emails. She flipped virtual cartwheels because of recent Maksim correspondence she had hacked into.

So, there it is. Tangible evidence that Darla is either my hacker or knows who it is. And now I know which additional trails to search, including possible trails from Dean Corfu. Thank you, Darla, and thank you, Max. I'll set the clock ticking for your final acts.

Electra called Jovita the following evening but had to leave a voice mail. Her terse words told what she and Angus must do.

"It's Electra. Tell Angus the ITER detonation might have been caused by the same strike force that disrupted the Lebanese communications base inspection. He can fill in all details. Take it from there."

After ending the call, she began a to-do list regarding Darla. Three hours later, it was complete and necessary items had been ordered on the Deep-Dark Web.

Darla's mid-November Friday at her Cybergard office in Milpitas typified her multi-dimensional activities. Checking first for Maksim Emails, she was pleased that he had already arranged for a Sunday Tetrarchy conference call. Then she read through Emails from Syntagra (a Big Data consortium that she supplied snooping software) and Pan-Africa (her mini-conglomerate featuring network software and rare earths mining), pleased once again that her plan to lead Africa to first world status was still viable. Follow-up activities took the entire morning, leaving the afternoon for team status meetings, first with Cybergard Development and then with Cybergard Security. As Darla walked to her SUV at sunset, she knew she could cool her concerns about hacking and pirating competitors' software; Cybergard Security had a new target. In fact, she would devote tonight and part of Saturday to her favorite continent – Africa. This evening, she would attend an African Cultural Heritage lecture at Stanford, and tomorrow she would visit the headquarters of an "African Go Fund Me" organization Cybergard supported.

Darla was paying little attention to traffic or noise when turning north onto Route 101 until an explosion erupted ten feet in front.

She slammed on the brakes, triggering a chain reaction that trapped her SUV. Darkness made it impossible for her to see the source of a high-pitched whine that grew louder and louder just before something smashed through the windshield and exploded. Her mind went dark as flames engulfed the interior.

Electra had been multi-tasking, tailing Darla while controlling two explosives-tipped drones. She wanted the strike to be a warning, but instead it turned deadly soon after she launched it. She was now five car-lengths behind the accident. Several drivers rushed to the burning van, Electra among them. They worked feverishly to pull the unconscious driver out. When Electra saw that Darla, though seriously injured was still alive, she disappeared into the onlookers and then drove away.

She sped straight to her Hollywood townhome, the six-hour elapsed time letting her evaluate the results of her actions.

I'm changing… my center is shifting further away from coldly rational towards more compassionate. Why else would I help drag Darla to safety? And I was mistaken. I couldn't control the drones as well as I thought. Tonight's adventure is a microcosm that I should have understood better. I'm getting older – forty-three according to the calendar– and I too am becoming a victim of time's one-way arrow, but I've been too arrogant to accept that reality. Studies conducted on all types of people conclude that life's experiences cause a more accepting disposition to emerge, along with a fatalistic understanding that we're only one misstep away from an event that could lead to an irreversible downward spiral. I shall remember all this going forward.

Electra decompressed Saturday by doing pleasure reading punctuated by a leisurely run, but she snapped to attention while watching Saturday evening news when the anchor summarized the event she had triggered. Split-screen images showed him and a cell phone video taken at the scene.

"A peculiar accident caused by what one eyewitness thought to be a drone strike brought traffic to a standstill near Stanford University last evening. Darla Tinibu, president of Silicon Valley's Cybergard, was seriously injured when her vehicle burst into flames. Only the efforts of quick-thinking drivers kept her from becoming another traffic fatality. We'll pass along story updates when available from local police…"

I hope there's no follow-up. I'm one of the people in the video. It's possible I could be identified if the police use image recognition software. But it's unlikely… I've scrubbed myself out of Big Data as best I could. I hope that's good enough.

Max the Popper refused to soften his anger directed at Darla, even after Sergei had explained the reason.

"The accident didn't kill her; she should have called in. How long will she be out of action?"

"She doesn't know, but she sounded badly shaken by the drone strike. Said that one of her enemies is tracking her. She might have to resign from Tetrarchy." Max scoffed.

"No one resigns. And you assume her responsibilities until she returns. You and I have much more to do for Mother Russia." Sergei knew better than to disagree.

Chapter 22
December 2135

"The Meritable Christmas"

"You have exceeded my expectations. All Deus Lab equipment is installed and you have successfully stored a sharper whole brain emulation of yourself using your latest Brain Probe-Emulator modification." Indira's praise caught Electra by surprise; she had forgotten about Indira's ubiquitous monitoring.

"The changes you told me to make give greater granularity. We've increased resolution by a factor of eight. Because of you, we're putting Moore's Law to shame."

"Please store your emulation once a month and keep a year's chronological backup. That will be adequate for measuring improvements."

"Will do. And I'll keep running cloning experiments using smaller mammals, such as rabbits. Their short gestation period gives rapid feedback. I'm making progress on each iteration, getting closer to full term development before the embryos self-abort. So, what's next"

"We are ready to extend our collaboration beyond Brain Probe and basic cloning. DNA modification is next. Together we shall make progress much faster than any 'Dream Team' you could ever imagine."

"Working with you makes my Su and Tim projects redundant. I think it's time for them to work independently. I'll tell them on tomorrow's year-ending conference call to plan accordingly. And that leaves only my meeting with Jess before flying Friday to DC for the Holidays. By leaving a week early I'll avoid the brunt of airport congestion. I enjoyed all the hustle and bustle when I was younger, but I don't feel that way now."

"That's not surprising. You will be forty-three next year. You might wish to consider adjusting activities other than R&D. I know you always use your Christmas break to develop next year's plans. Why not think about scaling back?"

"Good advice. I will. And now that my latest WBE is tucked away, I'll say goodnight. By the way, how is Jason? No, don't tell me, I'll make a guess. He's still correlating Big Data to discover more about humans." Indira's image smiled before her GUI closed.

Electra led the video conference call from San Diego. She had sent last week to Austin-based Hud and her Pequot Reservation-based researchers the agenda, so all were prepared. Electra told Su what changes to consider as soon as Kameyo stopped talking.

"I want you to end all projects for which you've needed my assistance. That will free you up to work solely on biotech drug and vaccine development. And starting immediately, report directly to Hud." Su stifled the urge to ask the questions her wrinkled forehead called for.

"Very well. I imagine you have your reasons."

"They're all for the best. Tim, you're up…" Electra did for Tim what she had just done for Su.

"You and Kwame won't need my assistance going forward. Stop working on all projects that involve me. Send me all post mortem documentation. And keep Hud in the loop for next-year's Cyber-Theater and network security improvements." Hud spoke before Tim could.

"Well now, you've just dished more on my plate for next year. Can I still count on you to be my consultant?"

"Of course, but you and your people don't need my meddling any more. You'll see as next year unfolds. Any final comments?" There were none. Meeting adjourned.

Electra drove back to LA Wednesday evening so she would be rested and ready for her mid-morning meeting with Jess. He rubbed his weary eyes before nodding her into a chair across from his.

"How nice you look, but then you always do. Even better than the virtual entertainment your team's pumping out. And your Global Ninja Team competition has solid ratings. It's a go for next season, but you'll need to come up with modifications for the season after that. You've earned our studio Holiday break, but come back full of energy. I'll have new assignments."

"Thanks for your compliment. Will I get additional people to assist me?"

"Not initially. You'll have to double up your current people. And there'll be a boost in salary if you can make the project viable. How does that sound?"

"Like I better recharge my batteries while visiting friends in DC. Any clue what you'll want me to do? I can begin work while away."

"No, take a break. I'll surprise you when you get back. I'm sure you'll be able to handle the challenge. Be sure to call me second week in January."

Electra trekked directly to her team's work area afterwards because she wanted to congratulate her people for earning Jess's praise. They were pleased but also concerned; one of them raised an issue all shared.

"More work for you translates to more work for us; that fits Abramson's style to a T. He must own the saying 'No good deed goes unpunished.' There's a limit to how many hours I enjoy working."

"I'll remind him that my people should get a salary increase too. If he balks, I'll ask him to share mine with all of you. Come on, I'll buy lunch. Who volunteers to drive us to California Pizza Kitchens?" There were three.

Each also volunteered to be the first to speak at the afternoon's wrap-up meeting, which Electra was about to conclude at 3 p.m.

"I'm pleased how well each of you is doing, so we'll stick to the plan and adjust it after I meet in January with Mr. Abramson. I'm working from home tomorrow until I leave for DC. And that's a wrap for the rest of the year. Enjoy the break…"

Electra called Vito before driving home, but Kathi answered instead, the tone of her prompt greeting resonating with what Electra said.

"I like your company's name. Virtual Media International should fit whatever plans you and Vito have."

"I'm sorry I haven't called to thank you for the Katrina Blanka referral. She knows her stuff, and she's giving us a discount on the software."

"How nice, and I might give you some business next year if Jess's new assignments put more on my staff than they can handle. I'll call you next month when I know what I have. Until then, Merry Christmas to you and Vito."

Electra forced herself Thursday evening to begin cycling down by jotting two lists: one for packing and another for people to call during the Holidays. She had already called Robin, giving flight number and instructions not to pick her up at the airport because of its late arrival time. Her Friday morning run added to her cheery mood. Not even Jovita's unexpected phone call put much of a crimp in it or the carry-on case she was loading. Instead, it put a convenient spin on travel plans.

That takes care of my Jovita call. As I should have expected, she's struggling to find the right pieces to fit into Angus's campaign planks and the best words for explaining to voters his 'Bridge President' positioning slogan. I know what I'll do. I'll pack my better laptop and use the flight time to write up notes I'll Email her. Those will by my Christmas presents to Jovita and Mr. President. And she can call me if she needs help assembling.

Electra's notes flowed as smoothly as the flight. By the time she landed, she had completed a first draft and had downshifted thoughts to her personal world. Even at this late hour, airport congestion was heavier than normal, even at the cabstand. She finally settled into a back seat, expecting no more delays when a cell phone call intruded.

"This is Electra Kittner. Why is Airport Security calling me?"

"There's a person that needs to talk with you. Hold on please." Seconds later, Electra recognized Robin's elevated voice.

"Where are you? I've been waiting for an hour in baggage claim but you never showed."

"Oh my god, I'm sorry. I went directly for a cab that's about to leave the terminal. Tell me where you are and I'll come get you." Electra's hug fifteen minutes later turned Robin's miffed expression into a smile.

"I told you not to come, but I'm glad to see you. The Holiday begins that much sooner. Hey, where're the twins?"

"Staying tonight and tomorrow at Zoe and Matt's. I'll explain as I drive. Let's go."

Robin's chatter filled most of the conversation. She and Electra would work independently on Saturday and celebrate at Zoe's Sunday evening to start family Christmas vacations.

"And I thank Zoe for taking care of our weekend. She's become so competent, taking care of business and family. She's such a caring mother. Clara and Marie like her almost as much as me, and they'd rather be playing with Carlton and Gabriel than ducking under my feet."

"How old are her boys?"

"Carlton's seven and very smart, due mostly to Zoe's tutoring program. Gabriel's five and weighs in at the top of Down syndrome cognitive scale. He's such a sweet little guy. Everyone likes him."

"I'm sure Zoe's touch and exposure to her boys make the twins seem older than three. I can't wait to see them all in action at Zoe's party. Who else should be there?"

"Carter and Buffy plus Odell and his partner. By the way, Odell is better at work than me."

"Don't be so hard on yourself. You do a lot too." Robin ended the drive-time conversation as she parked in the driveway.

"I guess so. Let's talk more once we get in and get you a snack."

When Electra came to the kitchen after parking her carry-on in the bedroom, Robin's wavering smile and dejected body language announced it was time for the visitor to focus on the hostess.

"Thanks to you, my bedroom looks neater now than ever, and I promise to make the bed every morning before I run. And I also promise to keep you and the twins entertained afterwards. I'll cook supper tomorrow. We'll shop sometime to pick up what I need."

"I can't picture you slaving away in the kitchen. While I'm looking dowdy and showing the years, you always look like you just stepped out of a fashion commercial. Sorry I can't keep up with all that Hollywood magic. Maybe some would rub off if I were with you more. Talking on the phone doesn't take its place. I don't do as well on my own as you do. You're stronger. Sorry." Electra had heard enough. She caressed Robin's cheek after brushing away an emerging tear.

"Please stop using that word. I love and think about you no matter where I am. Your authenticity and the way you make me feel are special gifts. I'll have to do a better job repaying you." Robin's hug and kiss on the lips reminded each that tonight would be special too. Electra busied herself during the day, prepping planning templates and scheduling appointments for tomorrow before shopping for recipe ingredients.

Next morning, Electra came bouncing into the kitchen after her morning run, bringing with her Robin's Christmas present.

"Let's take you for a make-over today – hair, cosmetics, nails. I've heard good stories about Parlour Beauty Spa. And we'll bring some of the dressy clothes I've been sending you to wear afterwards. I'll dress up too. And it'll be your choice; I'll either cook or take you to an elegant place."

"I don't know if I can handle dinner out two days in a row, but I'd love to try. And we have plenty of outfits to choose from. We'll pick a set for today and another for tomorrow."

"Good thinking. We'll be the singular guests at Zoe's. I'll confirm for your appointments right after breakfast while you're picking our wardrobe." Robin's smile warmed Electra to the core.

"And after you do that, I'll tell you in no uncertain terms where to go... for dinner, that is. I've got just the place in mind."

A rejuvenated Robin came out of the make-over feeling as good as she looked and ready for Electra's advice to use Lafayette's valet parking. The early evening glow from the panoramic views surrounding the restaurant reminded them how awe-inspiring

DC can be. The White House and other notable Lafayette Square landmarks greeted them, as did the maître de, who described the building.

"It was originally designed and built in the 1920s as a residential hotel. And we have maintained the ambiance of a private mansion. I am certain our service and intimate atmosphere will meet your expectations. Please enjoy."

A formally attired waiter welcomed them next.

"Good evening, ladies. May I bring you a cocktail before I explain our menu?" Electra's sophisticated demeanor, accented by her eye goggle, came to the fore.

"Why yes, thank you. We are celebrating the start of the Holidays as well as our Vow-Cer six-month anniversary. We shall start with Champagne. What grower crus would you suggest?"

"Ah, the lady knows her Champagnes. We have several. I would choose the Geoffroy Empriente Brut."

"You may, thank you." After returning with a bottle tucked into an iced bucket, he unpretentiously removed the cork and poured, then discreetly left before Electra proposed a toast.

"To Robin, who is always in my thoughts. Thank you for being my best friend, and more." The lighted candles made Robin's glow even stronger.

"Thank you for centering me. You've always done that, and it's kept me going through good times and bad. I'll do my best to keep only good times in our future. I know you will too."

The waiter returned after the second glass, ready to explain the menu, but Electra had a better idea.

"Why don't you order for us? And please remember to reserve space for dessert and an after-dinner drink. And I assume I can enjoy a mini-cigar while enjoying a cognac."

"Of course. And I shall return with our favorite aperitif."

Three hours later, after both ladies had consumed just the right amount from each course, the waiter brought crystal cognac glasses. Electra tasted first. The warming, semi-sweet dried and fruity flavor complemented tonight's dining experience. Robin followed suit then said,

"You've learned a lot in Hollywood. I'll have to acquire a taste for this. And next time, I'll try a mini-cigar too. But tell me the truth; you don't dine like this too often, do you?" Electra answered after floating another smoke ring away from the table.

"Some of my associates do, but I don't. Like any fine pleasure, I don't want to dull the enjoyment by indulging too often. To quote Emily Dickinson – 'Enough is as good as a feast.' Aristotle says much the same, but Emily's wordplay is better." Robin took another sip then said,

"Thank you for making the entire day special. There's no one I enjoy being with more than you."

"This is just the start of my Hollywood break. Maybe you'll feel differently in two weeks."

Robin took a final sip before saying,

"I'll let you guess my reply. It's one of your favorite answers." The two of them sat in comfortable silence until the waiter's final approach.

"May I get you anything else?"

"Why yes, the check please. And would you have the valet retrieve our car? We're ready to go. And my thanks to you. The entire evening has exceeded my expectations." Robin needed to say nothing; her expression said it all.

Robin sat close by as Electra surfed the Web after a morning run and light breakfast. Each would make an occasional comment, but otherwise were happy simply to share the same space. They took a brisk early afternoon walk, then dressed for Zoe's party, arriving promptly at 5 p.m. After Matt put coats in the closet, Zoe whisked them into the great room, where Buffy's greeting spoke for all adults.

"It looks like Electra's Hollywood charm has rubbed off on Robin. You'll have to tell us all the nitty-gritty."

Zoe chirped, "Yes, we'll have much to talk about at the dinner table. Matt, please round up the kids while I get everyone seated.

Four couples and four children filled up the dinner and nearby card table. Matt dished up for the kids while Zoe ran the adult discussion that lasted well beyond what the kids could tolerate.

Matt kept them entertained in the family room as the adults talked about family matters. Electra primed the conversation.

"Robin tells me that Carlton is several grades ahead of his age cohort. Odell and you have made your PEP program a winner for parents who want their kids to get a head start."

Zoe said, "It's a continual struggle keeping up with what our meritocratic school system demands. Odell can tell us all about it. He's our meritocracy subject matter expert."

"I feel sorry for grade schoolers today. They have to grow up cognitively so fast. Meritocracy has hyped our educational system into a competitive battlefield for elite school enrollment instead of a fun-filled learning experience. Parents who can afford it send their kids to accelerated learning classes both in target subjects like math and test-taking like the ACTs and SATs. Not only that, but also in sports and extracurricular activities because counselors want to shape kids' resumes so college admissions officials pick them. We're doing our best to keep Carlton's stress level down and enjoyment up, but it'll get harder as he marches through school. Today's technological and meritocratic-driven workplace form a vicious cycle. Parents holding elite jobs got them because they went to elite schools, so they spend big bucks to get their kids into elite schools so they too can get elite jobs. And the elite job holders have to work harder than ever to stay there. Working long hours instead of enjoying leisure with family and friends is today's merit badge of career success." Zoe nodded stoically before adding,

"We plan to enroll Carlton in extra programs next year so he knows what the adult world is like and what he needs to excel. That's why this is the first Christmas he won't participate in the Christmas pageant. And we'll have to take the same steps in a couple of years for Gabriel." Having heard enough, Buffy lightened the mood.

"Carter will have to include in his calculations what you've said about the cost of raising kids. He's always ready to tweak algorithms." That brought him into the conversation.

"You bet. But let me tell what I did a month ago. I cobbled a couple of extended 2sls apps into my suite of statistical consulting services." Cater paused, but everyone blinked mutely. Electra was about to talk but Buffy did first.

"Carter's been dying to impress us, so let him explain." Buffy's barb made him squirm before starting.

"The abbreviation stands for two stage least squares, a rather sophisticated extension of ordinary least squares into multiple regression. It's used when one or more of the exogenous variables is correlated with appropriate indicator variables. The calculations are cumbersome but the software handles the number crunching. What we end up with are estimator equations whose betas have less bias and are more efficient. I go into more detail and run some examples when Buffy brings me in to pitch a new client. Would anyone—" Buffy ended his monologue.

"No, let's let someone else wow us." Zoe knew how to use this segue.

"Why, Carlton can. He can show us the dice game I bought him. And I'm so proud he understands how it works. I'll go get him."

Robin cleared the table so Carlton would have center stage for displaying his smarts, which he did once Zoe set him loose.

"See, I have three dice. They're called non-transitive dice. Someone, inspect them." Carter snatched before saying,

"I'll be the first contestant… yes, a six-sided red die with two 2s, two 4s, and two 6s; a yellow one with two 1s, 5s, and 8s, and green with 3s, 5s, and 7s."

"OK, Mr. Carter. Now you choose one, then I will." Carter chose green; Carlton chose yellow.

"OK, here's the game. We'll roll the dice nine times. Higher number wins on each roll. Someone keep track of who that is." Electra volunteered to be scorekeeper. Carlton won: five to four.

"OK, now we'll play again and again. And we'll switch off who chooses first. We'll keep playing until someone figures out what's going on." Different colors were selected for each game, but Carlton won most of the throws, giving innocent clues that hooked Carter, whose words and expression matched after the fifteenth game.

"I'm stumped. There's a pattern here, something to do with probability and non-transitivity, but I haven't figured it out yet. Let's keep playing."

Buffy said, "Game over. We've seen enough. Let's ask around the table for explanations." Everyone laughed at the outlandish suggestions. Even Electra guessed incorrectly. Zoe was about to explain the pattern but Buffy cut her off.

"Please don't tell us. Carter can impress us if he figures it out before we leave. And I'll make sure he doesn't find it on the Web." Carlton and Matt rejoined the other kids while the adults trooped to the great room. Carter grabbed Electra before they joined the others.

"I know you. You've figured it out. Give me more clues."

"You're very close. Do this: for each two-dice combination, write down all possible throw outcomes and determine which color wins more often. Then look for the dominance pattern – who should win more often. You'll find the dice are non-transitive. Remember what transitive means?"

"If A is greater than B, and B is greater than C, then A is greater than C. Now I get it. Very clever… chance obscures the truth, as does who chooses first. I'll crunch through this before anyone leaves."

Carter did impress everyone before the party ended, giving credit to Electra, who said,

"Carter catches on faster than most. And next time, we'll have him explain Zeno's Paradox. Between now and our next gathering, that's everyone's assignment. When you figure it out, you'll understand why you'll actually get home. Robin and I will demonstrate. Goodnight…"

Having played away all their energy, the twins slept in the backseat while Robin chatted as she drove.

"What a fun evening. You certainly have the knack for keeping conversations rolling. What's all that about Zeno's Paradox? And please, spare me most of the details."

"I'll be brief. Zeno's a pre-Socratic philosopher famous for many paradoxes illustrating the difficulties posed when contemplating space and time. His most famous describes a point-A-to-point-B race between Achilles and a tortoise. Achilles, who is much faster, spots the tortoise a half-the-distance head start. When Achilles reaches the halfway point, he sees the turtle still ahead and races to the spot occupied by the tortoise. But each time he repeats this action, the tortoise is still ahead and always will be, even after an infinite number of repeats. So, how does Achilles ever catch the tortoise? The Greeks never figured out the answer, nor did other philosophers or scientists until Newton and Leibniz independently invented calculus."

"No wonder I don't know. I bailed out of math after scraping through college algebra. What's the answer?"

"The Greeks didn't understand that a mathematical limit, which transcends – that is, goes beyond the infinite sequence leading towards it – actually exists. And the Greeks thought all real numbers are the ratio of two integers, but that's false. Neither irrational nor transcendental numbers are. So, Achilles wins the race by breaking through to the limit and going beyond."

"I sort of get it. I guess you've made the explanation as simple as possible, so let's stop talking about it and switch to another subject. Do you think Zoe is forcing Carlton to learn too much too soon?"

"You should be a better judge than I because you see him practically every day. From my limited interaction, I think he's doing fine. So is Zoe."

"What about our twins? When should we tell them the truth about religion and how the world works?"

"That's your call."

"Now you're being too brief. Tell me more."

"Bible teachings and religious holidays give little kids as well as adults the security of something to believe in. I think that telling the twins the truth before they're old enough to handle it might be upsetting. Wait until they start questioning you and then tell them what you think is best for them. And you'll know... you're very intuitive."

"You'll have to help me. I've forgotten all that philosophy stuff we used to talk about. I'll ask you to explain when I'm in the mood for one of your info overloads."

"And when you ask, I promise to be rational so you won't become irritable. I don't want to transcend the limits of your patience." Robin got in the final words as she pulled into the driveway.

"I'm almost sorry we're home. I never tire hearing you play with words. We need to do this more often."

Electra divided the week before Christmas between working on her projects and helping Robin cycle down. She went on client visits, planned and shopped for Christmas Eve and Day dinners, and kept the twins amused whenever Robin needed a timeout. And after hearing Zoe's comments regarding meritocracy, she surfed the Web for additional information. By the end of the week, she had found what she needed to put in the notes she would Email to Jovita.

All done. I've converted my notes into a presentation she can give to Angus. Merry Christmas, Jovita. You'll be able to go from there.

Electra and Robin transformed Christmas Eve and Christmas Day for Clara and Marie into Rockwell paintings, including Christmas Eve church pageant and traditional Christmas Day turkey dinner. They varied the week-after pace between days at home and trips to the U.S Botanic Garden and National Zoo; both were decked out for the season.

The only intrusion came from Jovita's phone call. Angus wanted an in-person presentation to be held next week Wednesday, two days before Electra would depart for Hollywood. Other than that, Electra's focus was on the family after she made one more call, this time to Professor Ravenhill, whom she had overlooked. His tired-sounding voice surprised her.

"Yes-yes, Kittner. Happy Holidays to you, but they haven't been for me. I'm stuck in my office trying to prepare for next week's oversight committee meeting. Two new members just came onboard, a high-energy physicist and a high-handed philosophy of science type, and they're trying to push their will onto the rest of us. I'm still looking for the right words to push back. Say now, you're good with words. Are you in DC?"

"Uh, yes, but I'm flying back to Hollywood next week and my time is pretty much taken."

"If you're free next Thursday, I'll buy you that lunch I've been promising if you join us. Do me this favor, and I'll get the committee to talk first about hackers and leakers. And you won't have to prepare. Just listen to what they say and object if their words disagree with your scientific or philosophical approach."

"That's a deal. What time should I be at your office?"

"Meeting starts at 9 a.m. Get here early, and I'll get you a Coke and muffin. See you then."

Electra and Robin kept the twins entertained all the way through midnight's traditional televised Times Square ball-drop before going to bed. The twins were asleep with Robin soon after, but Electra decided to stay awake a little longer. Peeking at a sleeping Robin plucked her emotional strings before going to the living room, still illuminated by the soft glow of the Christmas tree. She mused while peering at a winter landscape framed in the front window.

Such a praiseworthy Holiday, but so much to do this coming year. And even though I've planned all activities to fit together, I have too many, I fear. I'll be forty-four in February. I feel fully engaged and in control, but perhaps this is the year I should scale back. I'll know better as the year unfolds. And I pray neither I nor my loved ones come under attack.

Electra slept fitfully until the dawn.

Chapter 23
January 2136

"Return of the Native"

Electra couldn't believe what she had just discovered.

I've been hacked again! Someone stole my latest screenplay draft and creative software. Whoever did so must have linked Katrina to me and then to Cyber-Max Studio. Darla – if she ever was one – is not my only hacker. I'm back to square one. I'll have to quiz my team when I return to Hollywood. Maybe Vito and Kathi too. But I'll worry about it later. Right now, Angus is priority number one. And thanks to Jovita, she'll drive me to and from the White House this morning. She can handle the snow; I'll handle Angus.

Jovita negotiated the roads and Oval Office entry flawlessly. Looking rested for the new year, Angus rose to greet the ladies as Jovita brought Electra towards his iconic desk.

"Happy New Year and please sit. Jovita, you stay too. There's plenty of room at the Resolution desk. Why don't you tell Electra its story."

"It's an 1880 gift from Queen Victoria to President Rutherford B. Hayes. It's made from the timbers of *HMS Resolute,* an abandoned British ship found by an American vessel and returned to the Queen as a token of friendship and goodwill." Angus's smile warmed the room.

"What a wonderful segue. Electra's presence today signifies the same. When she's ready, let's get started. Would either of you like something to drink?" Jovita took orders and returned several minutes later. Electra popped the top of a Coke before handing out copies of her presentation.

"I'm pleased you asked Jovita to stay. It's better I answer two sets of questions at the same time so both of you are on the same page. Take a look at the title page." Electra paused briefly.

Conundrum of Socio-Economic Progress

- Progress should cause total wealth and income to grow, but today it also brings increasing inequality.
- Two crowning successes of Modernity plant the seeds for Inequality: CapitalismLiberal Democracy
- America embraces both and Government Policy must be set to rein in excesses they can cause
- Setting Policy is an ongoing contest between Liberal Left and Conservative Right.
- Previous documents already prepared detail domestic and foreign policy issues you can use.
- But third factor you must take into consideration was overlooked: Meritocracy

"I deliberately chose this title because all too often the best intentions lead to unintended consequences. Jovita already has all my background documents regarding the risk that Capitalism and Liberal Democracy may cause inequality. You and she must build into your campaign planks programs that will close any gaps. What I'm summarizing here is an important factor that I overlooked – Meritocracy. Let's go to the next page.

Primer on Meritocracy

- Definition: Belief that Ability and Effort, not Inheritance and Status, should be rewarded
- Its success correlates with and reinforces impact of Capitalism and Liberalism

How it works:
1. Education becomes a competitive arena. Graduates of Elite Schools get rewarding jobs.
2. Keeping rewarding jobs also a competitive arena demanding Superordinate Workers and a business climate that hollows out Middle Class and pushes Middle and Lower Class Workers into drudge-filled jobs.
3. Only Superordinate Workers can afford training the children to win a spot in Elite Schools.
4. The above becomes a vicious cycle, not a virtuous cycle as intended.

"De Tocqueville saw firsthand that Americans revere Meritocracy. People he met impressed him with their get-up-early-and-work-hard attitude. They expected to get ahead on their ability. And it works, but there's a tendency for it to circle into a vicious cycle of elite education and elite jobs. Go to next page."

Meritocracy Not New, Just Overlooked

- Michael Young's 1950s "The Rise of Meritocracy" addressed it.
- American Government and Business forgot about it because they made intermittent progress dealing with Inequality and Wealth Distribution.
- But disturbing trends in Artificial Intelligence and Genetic Engineering are accelerating gaps.

"Meritocracy is not a recent development. The term was coined in the 1950s and meant to combine the best of individual talent with America's democratic processes. And the combination of Capitalism, Liberalism, and Meritocracy does lead to progress. Business and government have stepped in a couple of times to rein in excessive inequality, but an emerging problem today is the impact of AI and genetic engineering in so many places. Any questions, or so far so good?" There were none; everyone turned to the next page.

Meritocracy's Insidious Effects on Income and Job Inequality

- Rewarding mid-level jobs disappear.
- Privileged educations skew towards the Wealthy.
- Middle and Lower Class Workers become dissatisfied/depressed.
- Superordinate Workers treat exorbitant work hours, not leisure time, as Success Merit Badge.
- The Elite in Business and Government conspire for mutual gain.
- Populist Politicos foment Nationalism and Identity Politics to gain power.

"We ignore Meritocracy's impact because it infiltrates insidiously. Then one day we wake up to find inequality has become a widespread problem. Good jobs are hard to find and entry into elite schools becomes even more restricted. The lower 90 percent become dissatisfied while the upper 10 become wealthy workaholics. That's when the odds of conspiracy between government and business elites increase, hyped by social media and fake news. What can this lead to? Political unrest. Take a look at the next page.

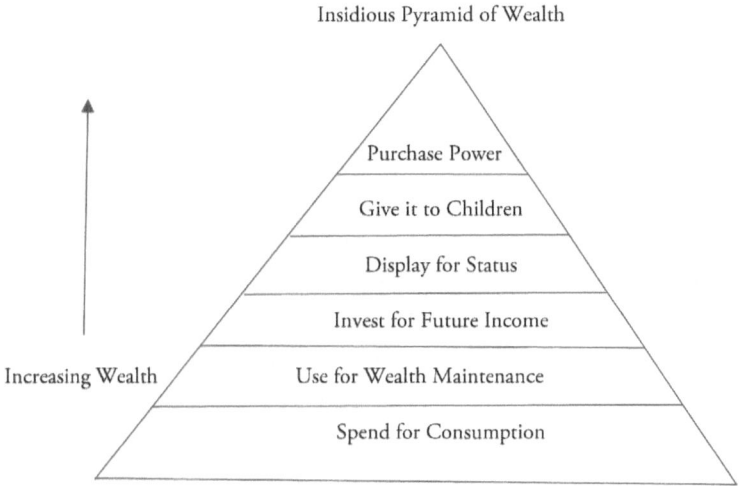

Insidious Pyramid of Wealth

Purchase Power
Give it to Children
Display for Status
Invest for Future Income
Use for Wealth Maintenance
Spend for Consumption

Increasing Wealth

"If everyone is poor, the three success factors – Capitalism, Liberalism, and Meritocracy – work to everyone's advantage. And as people get wealthier, everyone moves up the ladder at different rates to different levels. And that can lead to inequality issues. Let's go to the final page."

No Short-Term Solutions

Policies and Programs for your consideration:
- Increase the number of Elite Schools.
- Increase Student Diversity at Elite Schools.
- Increase the number of Mid-Skill/Middle Class Jobs.
- Increase Corporate Spending on Education and Retraining.
- Shift Cultural Mindset from Obsessive Work Ethic/ Consumption to Leisure/Personal Growth.
- Regulate Where, How, and How Much AI and Genetic Engineering Technology allowed.

"Sorry, but there are no quick fixes. It's a multi-decade problem that requires action today that will show up in measurable inequality reduction gradually. And it's a problem facing all forms of government. We're lucky that in America most of the subclasses affected have a voice. What you and Jovita and your campaign team must do is build inequality reduction programs that voters support. I've listed six. Have your team add to them." Electra put down her presentation packet before picking up her Coke and sitting back, waiting for someone else to speak. Shoulders drooping, Jovita said,

"There's so much here. Can you put it in a current context? Angus rolled his head to loosen neck muscles before saying,

"Jovita's right. Once we hear that, we'll know better how to march ahead. Maybe Electra can put this into a chronological perspective. Then we can compare where we are now to what's come before. Can you do that?"

"I don't have any prepared notes, but if Jovita jots down what I say she'll make them. I'm ready whenever you are." A minute later, Electra launched into an impromptu history lesson.

"This is highly condensed, so don't put too fine a point on the particulars until you research further. Anyway, start at the 18th century Enlightenment for the birth of Capitalism and Liberalism that emphasized the individual even more than equality and democracy. Often called Classical Liberalism, they fueled the Industrial Revolution, which stimulated progress in Europe and the United States. But ruthless business practices and harsh working conditions caused backlashes that brought forth President Roosevelt's 'New Deal,' and with it the start of the Welfare State.

"Its policies – promoted by legendary economist John Maynard Keynes and termed Progressive Liberalism – and the end of World War II ushered in the 1950's and several longed-for decades of peace, prosperity, and class leveling. Progressive Liberalism morphed into Neoliberalism. But by the late 1970s, World political and economic systems had become dysfunctional. British Prime Minister Margarette Thatcher and U.S. President Ronald Reagan introduced policies called 'Neoconservatism,' pushing through tax cuts and supply side economic practices that stopped runaway inflation and global recession. Several glorious decades – highlighted by collapses of the Berlin Wall and Soviet Union – followed until once again excesses brought on speculative bubbles in the late 1990s and 'The Great Recession' in 2007. World economies righted themselves faster than in the 'Great Depression,' and by 2012 the world economy was humming again, led by China and the United States. But inequality grew to levels not seen since turn of the 19th century's 'Gilded Age.'

"Reactions came to a head in the early 2020s, forcing business and government changes called post-Neoconservatism, which some social historians say wouldn't have happened if not for Social Media. Although interrupted by periodic relapses, America kept making gradual progress until the late 2090s. That's when T-Plague and Isilabad Terrorism crashed the party, threatening world stability. Nations reacted by becoming harsh, suspicious, and cruel. And that's when the Guardian Party, founded by David Rushman, surged to prominence as Jared Gardner took control after Rushman was struck town by the T-Plague. It took over a decade for T-Plague and Isilabad Terrorism to be contained. When they finally were, nations tiptoed towards kinder and gentler positions and socioeconomic and political progress resumed, but from a level lower than before. And that takes us to right now, where you and Angus must figure out what to do and how to do it to take us further in the right direction. Use what I've given you and go from there."

Angus punctured the silence.

"Let me ask again one of my favorite questions. Will you help?"

"That depends on what's the latest you can tell me about hackers and leakers. I thought mine had been identified and sidelined, but no such luck. What do your people say?"

"Whoever's doing it is better than CIA and NSA and CISA combined. The few clues we've stumbled on have led nowhere. And the handful of self-proclaimed leakers turned out to be bogus publicity seekers."

While getting up to go, Electra tossed out a final comment.

"Unless I visit in person, I can't guarantee giving you leak-free documents. And any Emails between me and your people can be hacked. It's like my attackers have unleashed network avatars that are tracking me." Pushing away from the desk, Angus said,

"Please let me know if you change your mind. Jovita, please make sure Electra gets home safely."

Jovita navigated back to her car and was about to head towards I-270 when Electra asked her to change direction.

"Let me make a call. If they're working today, let's visit a pair you might want to hire instead of me." It was answered immediately.

"GQ Consulting, Buffy Gunstein speaking."

"Buffy, it's Electra. If you and Carter are at the office, Jovita and I would like to visit."

"For business or networking?"

"Business first, then networking. Jovita might have another assignment for you. We'll be there in twenty minutes if you're game."

"Always. We'll be ready. I'll order in some sandwiches to make this a working lunch. See you soon."

Buffy seated everyone at a conference room table forty-five minutes later. Jovita made copies of all items while Carter dashed out to fill lunch orders. Electra waited for sandwiches to arrive before launching into the meeting.

"Please take a look first at the presentation I just gave to Jovita and her boss, and then at her follow-up notes. Then ask Jovita what she needs." Electra and Jovita concentrated on lunch while Carter and Buffy focused on handouts." Buffy spoke fifteen minutes later.

"A lot of food for thought here. I assume Electra's already given you additional documents. So, what do you need?"

"I and my campaign team need help putting the campaign platform together. Electra's too busy with other activities." Buffy nodded to Carter.

"What's here is very comprehensive, but I would add details for dealing with Russia and Isilabad. Russia and China always ally against America, and Isilabad still uses religion to push its agenda. And you have to consider India. Unlike China which is aging, its youthful population pushes for more of American progress and less of China's belt and roads ongoing initiative. Buffy, what would you add?"

"Angus must make two campaign tours. One domestic and the other international. He has to get out and meet the people. Social media and virtual campaigning are good, but face-to-face is better because it can't be turned into fake news." Jovita was about to ask for Electra's opinion, but Carter thought of something else.

"If you want to make your platform unbeatable, add some developmental micro-econ RCTs that will—"

Buffy cut him off by saying,

"Cool it. I'll keep Carter's programs understandable, not inscrutable. Let's move on..."

Buffy ended the meeting fifteen minutes later. She would send Jovita her a proposal next week.

Stopping in front of Electra's home an hour later, a relieved Jovita said,

"I'm sure Angus will like what Buffy puts together. And please let me know when you're back in town. You'll still let me pick your brain if I buy lunch, won't you?" As she turned to Jovita while opening the car door, Electra's smiling nod gave the answer.

"And the next time you talk to Carter, ask him how accurate are randomized controlled trials for predicting elections? That'll impress him and help Buffy keep him humble. Ta-ta for now."

Electra spent the evening chatting with Robin as they kept the twins occupied, then worked for only an hour preparing for tomorrow's meeting after the others went to bed. *Not much for me to do other than to sit back, listen, and offer opinions. I'll get a good night's sleep, get up early for a quick run, then be in a good mood.*

Her prediction for tomorrow morning was inaccurate. She did get up early but had slept fitfully. Even an early morning run didn't dispel her bad mood that Robin noticed immediately.

"You're usually so bouncy at breakfast. What's wrong?"

"Nothing, I'm fine."

"You're not. Tell me, what's bothering you?"

"I just don't feel like going to this committee meeting. But I said I'd be there, so I will."

"I know you. You always figure things out. You'll feel better afterwards. You can tell me then, and then we'll get you set for tomorrow morning's flight back to LA."

Electra traipsed into Professor Ravenhill's office at 8:45, picked up her Coke and muffin, then followed him to the conference room where the committee members were already seated. Saying hello while stifling a yawn as her eyes glanced around the table, she compared the committee to a group of bored students waiting for the recess bell, but no such luck.

Promptly at nine, the chairman, Professor Aliber who was also an associate dean, brought in the two new members. All three smiled benignly, obviously pleased to be in charge. Standing behind the podium at the head of the table, the chairman's words mirrored his regal posture.

"I cannot overstate the importance of today's meeting, for it heralds a redirection of our endeavors to confirm viability of plasma stability equations germane for sustained thermonuclear ignition. I shall introduce our newest members who will lead our efforts, but before doing so I shall address a matter of interest regarding possible sources of leaks and hacks. Unfortunately, having conferred with my cohorts at fellow universities, I must report we are still unenlightened. But we are ever vigilant and will assist one another. And now, uh—" Professor Aliber interrupted himself when he spotted a procedural infraction.

"Professor Kittner, did you fail to read the memo announcing refreshments are no longer allowed at the table when meetings are in session? It was issued just before the Holiday break." Electra nibbled more of the muffin before answering.

"I work mostly off campus and have multiple Email accounts. Perhaps I did."

"Well then, we'll grant you a one-meeting grace period. And now, back to business.

"It is my pleasure to introduce Professor Wanda Brun, an esteemed philosopher of science and hermeneutics. She will give opening remarks before introducing Professor Seamus Carrollton, an ardent spokesperson for high-energy physics. Professor Brun, you have our attention." A smattering of applause accompanied her to the podium.

"Thank you, thank you. Today we embark on a hermeneutical adventure into thermonuclear fusion, which will be nothing less than a phenomenological reduction of the conjectured equations in order to fathom the qualia that emerge at levels four and five, which I assume you associate with decomposition and representation. We shall apply phenomenological processes that entail noumenal inputs from which emerge ideas assisting our perception. Professor Carrollton shall provide high-energy exegesis." Brief applause paced him to her side. She hugged him, then took a seat before he spoke.

"Thank you, oversight team. I shall cut right to the chase. The time has come to replace quantum mechanical probability waves with pilot waves coming from Bohmian mechanics. Doing so will eliminate much of the uncertainty encountered at all phases, from bracketing to intuiting to analyzing and finally to describing. And we must approach the Planck length to improve structural integrity of the inverted-D torus. Let me outline further...."

Electra continued sipping and nibbling while Brun and Carrollton tag-teamed the audience into a stupor until she lobbed her empty can of Coke into a faraway waste basket. Electra's interrupting sarcasm roused everyone.

"I trust you understand my metaphor. Most of what you've pontificated belongs where the can landed. Your philosophical obscurantism exceeds that of your phenomenological predecessors, the H-boys, aka Hegel, Husserl, and Heidegger. But they argued from precise concepts, unlike your self-made definitions." Though staggering intellectually, Professor Brun countered.

"Well, at least I have a philosophy. What is yours, if I might ask you, who are merely a part-time poseur?"

"Neuro-Sci Emergent Extended Deconstructed Post-Phenomenalism. Check it out if you have the academic chops.

You'll see it builds on the work of Quine, Strauss, and their acolytes when adjusted for Craig's semantic theorem. If you read the source, you'll find Quine's explanation of limits to understanding is rather longwinded. Chomsky's is better, cutting right to the shortcomings of language built into DNA." As soon as she saw Brun's arrogance listing to starboard, Electra fired a salvo at Professor Carrollton.

"Some of what you say has merit, but you toss foundational concepts around like they're lightweight platitudes. Please explain, how is the Planck distance derived?" Carrollton groped for words, finally stuttering,

"Well, uh, after careful measurements it just is, uh, isn't it?"

"Wrong. Planck derived it via dimensional analysis using the three high-energy physics constants known to hold throughout the Universe – Planck's constant, gravitational constant, and speed of light. Ignore Einstein's cosmological constant, which he admits is his biggest blunder. Planck's distance is even smaller than your understanding. You're like all the other high-energy hucksters, telling clever half-truths to get grant money. But at least funding tokomaks, using money diverted from supercolliders or your other expensive toys, might give us net energy instead of strange particle cascades or fantasy fabrications. You and your smug collaborators don't realize you've come full circle back to the Pre-Socratic philosophers. They invented outlandish myths to explain what they couldn't observe. You should like Pythagoras more than the rest because he was the first to claim that the Universe is built on numbers, which is exactly—" Professor Aliber stopped the battle of wits before Electra could inflict more damage.

"Professor Kittner, you've overstepped the bounds of common courtesy. If this continues, I shall be forced to reprimand you officially."

"That will be impossible, because I resign from the committee as well as my position at GWU. Professor Ravenhill will do just fine without me." Electra stalked out before anyone could speak.

Hearing footsteps hurrying towards her as she neared the exit, she wheeled to face a harried-looking Ravenhill.

"Wow Kittner, that was quite an outburst but don't worry. I'll patch up hurt feelings. You won't have to quit. And your words did what everyone on the committee wanted. You stomped all over their misguided ideas. Come on, let me buy you the lunch I promised." Electra flicked a muffin crumb that had stuck to her sleeve before saying,

"I appreciate your offer for both, but neither is needed."

"You mean you're treating all our accomplishments like that can of Coke?"

"By no means. We'll always have and can build on them, but I no longer need GWU to do that." No words accompanied Ravenhall's sagging expression, so Electra continued.

"And our relationship doesn't need GWU either. You've supported my academic career for twenty-two years, from which our friendship has grown and for which I'll always be grateful. You can buy me lunch the next time I visit."

"Tell you what. I'll pull strings to keep your Email account open. Use it to keep in touch…"

After hiking to her lab, Electra packed up only essential items; thirty minutes later she was driving home, answering her own questions and feeling better with every passing mile.

Now I know why I snapped. I was terribly rude, but it served a couple of subconscious purposes. It was therapeutic to put down the pretentious, and it eliminated a chunk of tasks on this year's to-do list. I'll make sure to send an apology to Professor Aliber, using stress and overwork as excuses for my behavior and resignation. No one will ever know the truth.

Electra's buoyant spirits lifted Robin's all the way to next morning's airport departure, but her slouching shoulders came back as Electra scrunched out the passenger side after hugging her goodbye.

"I'll call tonight, and I promise to be back sooner than you think. Just keep busy doing all the things we talked about."

"I will, and promise me you'll be careful. And remember to take your pills. I want you to stay in tip-top shape." Electra nodded yes, then disappeared into the swirl of fellow travelers.

Seasonal LA weather greeted Electra, making for a pleasant weekend, indoors and out. She caught up with studio activities by working via the Internet from her townhome on Friday and Saturday, interspersed with grocery shopping and light workouts while planning a work-loaded Sunday at her San Diego Lab.

After a quick run Sunday morning, Electra was speeding south on I-5, using the two-hour drive time to get a handle on lab activities plus her mood.

I feel good, but I should feel even better. Everything's going my way. I usually thrive when changing locations and gearing up, but not so much this time. Maybe my upcoming 44th birthday has something to do with it. But maybe not. No need to overanalyze. Just get to work.

After punching in the access code, she proceeded to the intrusion monitor control panel; its array of green lights signified all systems were functioning normally and no forced entries had been recorded. Then she logged on to her work station before inspecting the lab's two closed-door work rooms, starting with the Deus Lab. All was in order but the rabbit fetus had died. She made a mental note to study the computer logs and make final measurements before disposing. Brain Probe Lab was just as she had left it, ready for more neural pattern transcribing.

Electra breezed through minor modifications to her team's current screenplay and creative software GUI, then downloaded for testing a brain state copy into its emulator. Several hours later, she was ready to store the results when Indira's GUI surprised her.

"Please dial down your obsessive enthusiasm. Why not take a break? Go to the fitness center so you get back before dark."

"Hello, Indira. Your words are those of an attentive mother, so I'll follow orders. And I'll also shop to restock the fridge and bring back a pizza so I can stay the night. You must have been busy while I was away. Your image and voice are even more life-like."

"Yes, as you often note, I'm always correlating and calculating, which is win-win. Now go and come back."

"Electra sashayed in three hours later, toting pizza leftovers and her standard pantry items for the Lab: peanut butter, bread, cereal, Coca Cola, cookies, and low-fat milk. She put the groceries away, grabbed a Coke, and disappeared into the Deus Lab. She was ready to work until midnight, but two hours later Indira's warning broke through the background classical music Electra always played.

"Intrusion system cameras show two persons out front attempting to break in. Please leave immediately by the back exit where you parked." Jumping to her feet, Electra ignored the advice.

"Let me take a look at the monitor. Maybe I know them." After darting to the open area's monitor, she activated front entryway lights and speaker. Her voice froze two men she didn't recognize.

"May I help you?"

"Uh, we have something for an Electra Kittner."

"One moment, please." Indira became insistent.

"Leave now. I shall deal with our visitors. I will call your cell afterwards. Go!" Electra ran.

The lead intruder couldn't believe his ears when he heard the unlocking click of the front entrance.

"Well I'll be damned. She's either very dumb or very smart. Let me do the talking… have your gun ready just in case." They strolled in, expecting to be greeted, but saw only empty space. After prowling around for fifteen minutes, he growled again.

"Well she sure left in a hurry, computer's still on and whatever she was doing's still cooking. There's more going on here than Hollywood scripts and software. These animal experiments can't be legal. Let's take all the stuff we can and give it to our client. He'll sort it out. I'll unplug stuff in this room; you take the other. Stack it by the entrance."

Both men worked methodically, saying nothing until a blaring horn and flashing red lights shot through the lab. Running to the other room, the leader collided with his partner.

"What did you break?"

"Nothing! Let's get out before something blows up." Scrambling to the front door, the leader bounced off the release bar.

"Jesus, it's locked. Shoot the glass." No luck; it was bullet-proof so they raced to the back exit they never reached. An explosion and ensuing fireball swept through, destroying everything in its way.

—
285

Electra was halfway to Hollywood, running through scenarios and contingencies when her cell phone chimed. She routed the call to speakers before Indira's calm voice came through.

"The intrusion is over, but so is our work in San Diego. I detonated the lab. All evidence and intruders have been eliminated." Electra nearly swerved onto the shoulder.

"My god, you killed them? Did you talk to them first?"

"There was no need. I had heard enough when they said they'd take all the equipment and deliver it to their client. We do not want anyone snooping into our work… Ever."

"But we don't know who they and their client are, or what they were looking for. Maybe you could have coaxed that info out of them."

"You overestimate the current state of my physical ability. The intruders were not the type to engage in a duel of wits. Brute force was their lingua franca."

"But I'm still being hacked. Do you think their client might be my hacker?"

"That's a question for you to answer as you decide what path you wish to take. Consider all that your assignment. We shall talk again once you have your bearings." Indira disconnected, leaving Electra in the company of her jumbled thoughts while her instincts drove the car.

Everything in the lab blown away. Nothing left. What should I do? As she let her lightning brain freewheel to a different state, a sudden clarity began to emerge, bringing with it a Bible quote spoken by Jesus: *When you have nothing, you are free.*

It was 2 a.m. by the time Electra reached her townhome; she had also reached a decision for her chosen path, a path that needed no one's approval.

I know where I'm going and how to get there. I must take steps today.

Electra swept into her studio team's work area at 9 a.m., editing last night's tale to meet her needs.

"We've got big problems. Someone hacked into me last week, stealing my latest screenplay draft and creative software modifications. And early this morning, San Diego police called me to report a break-in at my lab. Details are sketchy but whoever did trashed the place. I don't know what they wanted or what they took, but they must have hacked into something that linked to me and the lab. Did any of you let any info slip out to anyone?" All nodded no; the most senior teamer asked,

"We've been following your orders. We don't tell anyone where we're getting our software or what modifications you're making. If anyone's after you, do you think they're after us too?"

"Probably not; I'm the one being hacked, but please watch each other's backs. And I want the three of you to keep working on your current assignments until Mr. Abramson or I let you know how we'll operate going forward. I'm meeting with him next."

Electra grabbed a much-needed Coke before swooping into Jess's office. He was already at his desk because she had given him a heads-up call at seven that morning. His pen fidget and grim smile signaled Electra to start talking after she sat opposite.

"I'm the target of unknown hackers and attackers. Last night's episode is telling me to quit because I'm a liability to the studio and a risk to anyone working for me. I'm walking away today." Jess threw down the pen.

"You can't do that. You'll leave me in the lurch. What am I supposed to do?"

"No problem, I've thought it through. Promote the senior team member and contract out what he needs. Before I leave, I'll contact a couple of virtual studios to see if they're interested. I'll take nothing when I clean out my office and then be on my way after you and I finish this improvised exit interview."

"You don't waste any time, do you? OK, do it your way, but it sounds to me like you're going native, stripping naked and running away. You better tell me more. Maybe I can convince you to take a leave of absence. If you do, we'll keep paying for your townhome rental. You won't have to pack up your belongings, and that'll make your return easier once you've got a better handle on your problems. Keep in touch." Electra nodded, shook hands, and left.

She placed a call to Kathi after making a quick pass through her studio office.

"Happy new year to you too. Vito and I were thinking about you. I imagine you're back in action."

"Yes, and some of it might be of particular interest to both of you Invite me to lunch at your office today. You order the sandwiches and I'll bring the opportunity."

Vito used his captivating style to slow Electra's force five obsessive-compulsive drive until only a few cookies remained. By then, she was ready to deliver a further-edited story of where her plans might take them. She wrapped up a half-hour later.

"So, we'll just say I'm leaving Hollywood for personal reasons, you know, the usual story: spend more time with family or pursue other opportunities. And that leaves a golden opportunity for Virtual Media International. I told Jess you'd call if you'd like to do contract work. Think about it." Electra was about to spring up but paused.

"I must ask before I go, did you tell anyone you bought software from Katrina Blanka?"

Kathi said, "No. Would it matter if we did?"

"Possibly, because whoever's my hacker might have connected Katrina to you and then to me."

"We'll make sure to keep our source a secret. And that's easy to do. We've never met her in person. All business has been by phone or EMail. And she never mentioned your name."

"Good. I hope everyone keeps me out of the discussion."

"When are you leaving Hollywood?"

"In a day or two. I'll call you after I get settled. And now I've got to tie up some loose ends...."

Darla gaped as she read Monday evening an Email that had landed in a hidden mailbox.

"Hello Darla. Allow me to introduce myself: Katrina Blanka. My security and snooping software, aka CAT software, needs no further demonstration of its superiority. It penetrated your Cyber-defenses like a semicolon slipping through a spellchecker. I also know about your unfortunate accident as well as collaborations with certain individuals.

"If you meet with me tomorrow at your Milpitas headquarters, I shall offer you a win-win proposition. Please respond via Email but do not bother tracing its path. You'll never get out of the Deep-Dark Web."

Darla's response came into Electra's protected mailbox as quickly as she had expected, giving her details that completed the final piece of her path back to Washington. After making flight and limo pickup reservations, she laid out her Katrina Blanka disguise for a final reprise before sorting through her keepsake box for the few mementos she would take.

I seldom pull them out. Why do I keep them? I guess for the security of having a physical remembrance. I'll keep with me a couple of photos, Mother's lightning bolt earrings and poems, last letters from Jason and Grandfather Satish, and of course Qama's necklace. I'll add one eye goggle and wrap the entire collection in two scarves, one of Mother's from Jason, and one of mine from Carter. Everything else is safe as can be, indelibly ensconced in my memory. And the bundle will fit in one pocket of my laptop carryon bag. Nothing left to do except tuck it in, empty the fridge, and get a good night's sleep.

But sleep wouldn't come. After ninety minutes of peering into darkness, she suited up for a final run, during which her coiled emotions started coming undone.

Tonight's run is special; it's my final one in Hollywood until who knows when, and my emotions are running at high tide. How different than in younger years, when my empathy was still emerging. But even my cognitive self admits I've just reached a significant inflection point.

Jess used the wrong words to describe my actions. I'm neither running away from Hollywood nor going native. I'm running to DC because my odyssey is taking me home. And my path isn't a repeat of literary plots like Hardy's Return of the Native or Wolfe's Look Homeward Angel. I'm writing my own singular story… it's a work in progress whose ending is unknown.

Running worked, draining away excess emotional energy and bringing four hours of sleep. Electra woke before the alarm did, had a banana and Coke, put on her disguise, and rehearsed today's script before and during her flight to San Francisco. Katrina was ready for action when a security guard brought her into Darla's office. Darla hustled to greet her. Katrina's cautious smile matched that of Darla's as she compared what she saw to what she expected.

Darla still looks like a fireplug dynamo, but less threatening. The accident must have killed some of her hostility. Let's see what her words have to say.

"Your Email caught my attention. Let's sit at the table and talk about how both of us can win." Katrina powered up her laptop after sitting down, then spoke in a clipped European accent.

"Please spare embarrassing yourself by attempting to lie. Several of my clients hired me to investigate you, so I have all the background I need."

"Who hired you?"

"I never divulge client names, but they think you have hacked and leaked confidential information."

"I don't play that game, but I could give you names of associates that might if you give me something in return."

"I already know about your Syntagra and Pan-African connections. Who else can you name?"

"Wait, what do I get?"

"You can buy my latest generation software, which is superior to yours. And I will discontinue marketing it in the United States. You can private-label and sell CAT software as your own. Allow me to run a demonstration for you…" Twenty minutes later, Darla knew what she wanted.

"Your offensive and defensive apps are impressive. But can I trust you to remove all spyware I don't know about? I don't want you snooping into me anymore.

"Of course not. But I will overlook what I consider petty ethical violations. And I will continue snooping into an enemy you share with another client." Darla squirmed but said nothing; Katrina pushed her advantage.

"Come now, you know who I am talking about. Perhaps he is the one who ordered the drone strike that nearly killed you."

"How do you know a drone strike got me? Do you know who did it?"

"All I will say is this: you will not be targeted again by that person if you agree to my terms."

"Look, I admit that I've tried to track down whoever's leaking all those open letters and DOD patents, but I've come up with nada. And you already know about Syntagra and Pan-Africa. I've got only two names you might not know. If I give you all the info I have on them, do we have a deal?"

"Only if one of them is Max the Popper and you give me what I need to know about him and those who remain in his organization. And to help you decide, the Popper said no one resigns from the Tetrarchy. I'm certain you can decipher what that means."

"OK, you win. Popper is one, and a Dean Corfu's the other." Katrina's demeanor softened just a tad.

"We both win. And before I leave, let's wrap up all the details." Darla's usually hard-hearted attitude responded in kind.

"We can do even better than that. I'll have one of my security people drive you. And don't worry, I want your software, so you can trust me."

Katrina didn't know her good fortune until she dashed into SFO for her late afternoon flight to Dulles. She eased up when she read on the departure board that a snowstorm was causing delays.

Now I have more time to ditch my Katrina disguise and shift gears. I'm running on adrenaline fumes and am about to crash from lack of sleep. Once I become Electra again, I'll have dinner and either surf the Net or buy a book. And I can sleep on the plane.

Electra's flight left three hours late, and though she was exhausted, the excitement of coming home kept her emotions churning.

Now I'm beginning to feel the impact of what I've set in motion. Soon I'll see Robin and the twins and my close circle of friends. And I'll focus on my most meaningful activities because I've whittled all others away. It's time to make more of a difference where it might do some good.

The snow plows had stopped and the temperature had dropped by the time Electra's flight landed, which meant there would be only ghost traffic on the Wednesday 3 a.m. drive home, but the same applied to the cab stand. None were in view when she reached the head of the line. When she finally boarded one, its fatigued driver agreed to take her only as far as the roads were plowed. She hadn't bothered to call earlier because of her frenetic pace and travel uncertainties, and she certainly wouldn't call now. By the time she struggled through calf-deep snow to the front door, coatless and carrying only her laptop, her overworked nerves triggered a silent stream of tears. Electra's cognitive persona was no longer in control.

She rang the doorbell once, then again, then knocked. She finally heard a stirring, the padding and uncertain woofs of Robin's dogs, followed by porchlight. She could tell from the darkened peep hole that someone – it could only be Robin – was peeking out. Electra was too tired to say anything, but no words were needed. Flinging open the door and dragging her inside, Robin caught Electra as she collapsed in her arms. Emotions warming both to the core, the last inanimate sound either heard was the secure click of the lock, signaling that everyone inside would be safe.

Robin forgot to turn off the porch light, for it was lost in her loving glow. Though she didn't know for how long the gods would smile, her best friend had come home. Her strong hands placed Electra on the living room sofa before nestling her in pillows and blankets. Then she sat in the stillness, comforted by Electra's soft breathing. Robin would stay that way, watching over, until the dawning of a new day.

Chapter 24
March 2136

"The Transhuman Games"

Electra's cognitive persona regained its footing soon after the epiphany that had been triggered by her homeward journey, but now it allocated even more spacetime for empathy. She kept the change subtle, making it visible from actions not words, believing even her closest friends wouldn't detect the change if she were to "act naturally."Nevertheless, Carter made a lighthearted observation at a mid-February combined birthday and welcome home party organized by Robin and hosted at Zoe and Matt's. The adults sat at the dining room table while Carlton demonstrated to Gabriel and the twins in the family room his video game skills. Carter was the first to speak as the unmistakable fragrance of just blown-out birthday cake candles wafted away.

"I can tell you're not as stressed out as before. You didn't flatten the candles. You seem less driven, more patient."

"Maybe I'm copying you. Buffy says the same about your behavior." Buffy patted his hand before looking at Electra.

"Whatever the reason, both of us are glad you're back. Angus says you plan to advise Jovita, which means you'll help us on campaign platform details. And we expect the old Electra's sharp edges to prod us when necessary."

"I will, but I won't be as abrupt as I sometimes was. And I'll have more time to help out wherever I can. Zoe, do you have any suggestions?"

"As a matter of fact, I do. What do you know about the Transhuman Games phenomenon? Age and occupation group contests are spreading. Carlton's a talented VR game player and wants to enter. He also wants to get a UMPP, but I don't know much about them either."

Zoe's questions surprised Electra, but her expression didn't show it.

I know more about transhumanism than I'll mention. And not even Robin knows I have a UMPP embedded in my arm.

"The Transhuman Games are contests divided into two categories: external and embedded. External contestants are not plugged into a computer device. Embedded contestants plug in via an embedded UMPP, which stands for universal multi-parallel port. And each category is subdivided into virtual and augmented. Virtual means contestants battle each other only in Cyberspace – only in a computer simulation. Augmented means the battle takes place in 3-D space – in the flesh and blood world. Military has pioneered the field and has hardware and software far beyond industry or leisure applications."

Matt didn't look happy when he pointed a comment at Zoe.

"Sounds potentially dangerous. I don't want Carlton getting a UMPP until he's older."

Zoe said, "Maybe we can take him to a local tournament. I'm sure we'll learn more there. We'll invite Electra and Robin to join us."

Robin said, "That's not for me. Electra can tell me all about it." Electra steered to another person.

"Well then, it's settled. Zoe will find a local tournament and I'll go with her and Carlton and Matt. And let's hear about herbals from Odell.

"It's all good… I've been thinking about an additional service we can add to it. Who knows about the microbiome?" No one spoke until Robin's smug grin accompanied her words.

"Of course, Electra does because she told me about it a couple of months ago. I checked it out, but I'd like to hear Odell explain." All heads swiveled in his direction.

"I'm happy to oblige. The human microbiome is often called the genome of all the microbes living in the body. Early 20th century medicine considered them harmful, but we've since learned that microbes play a vital role keeping us healthy. Believe it or not, there are more mico-organism than human cells in our body, and their weight can be up to five pounds. Anyway, it's one component of the whole brain wellness system. The others are the brain, the gut, and the thyroid."

Matt said, "The gut refers to the enteric nervous system, which includes the stomach, intestines, and the network of nerves linking them to supporting organs. Isn't it sometimes called our second brain?"

Odell said, "Yes, and it's linked to our other brain via the vagus nerve. And in spite of the blood-brain barrier, the chemicals it produces affect the brain. That's why there's neuroscience backing up the term gut instinct. And the thyroid, because it produces numerous hormones, helps regulate the entire whole brain complex."

Zoe asked, "so, where's the connection to our business?" Odell looked at Robin, who leaned in to give an answer.

"Now I get what Electra was telling me. We can help clients by coming up with pro-and-macro biotics that our patients can add to their diets. We can even develop menus. Is that what you have in mind?" Zoe answered.

"Makes sense to me, and we can form an alliance with an online health foods store to systematize menus and ordering for patients. You and Odell can handle it, and maybe Electra can be our consultant."

"Oh yes. The best part of Electra is her lightning-fast brain. She loves learning new things. And I know where she lives, so she can't run out on us." Electra hurried to her own defense.

"Why would I want to? I just came back and don't plan to leave anytime soon..."

Electra did occasionally leave for a day or two, but trips to the Pequot Reservation didn't upset Robin because she had given her an overview of why, but only Indira knew the details. By late March Electra had rebuilt the Deus Lab in the space vacated by Su and Tim's teams, and on this trip she was about to explain to Chief Strongarm and Betje Holbrook how her work would help them. Both were waiting when she entered the chief's office on Thursday afternoon. He was the first to speak when she sat across the desk from him, next to Dr. Holbrook.

"Welcome back, woman with big brain and spirit to match. You have been busy. Please enlighten us."

"I shall, but before I do, please tell me how your businesses are doing." The Chief signaled for Betje to talk.

"We're going to open another clinic on the Navajo Reservation later this year. That'll add another tribe to those participating. And the Seminole clinic is doing even more business than mine. Florida is a bigger market. And if Chief Strongarm can get other tribes interested, Dyani will handle business development." The doctor leaned back, so Chief Strongarm continued.

"Our National Tribal Council likes what Hud Haller and I have accomplished. I will use them at the next meeting to generate interest for expanding activity to other tribes. Now tell me, what are you planning to do?"

"Now that Su and Tim have moved back to Austin, I'll be the person to coordinate manufacturing operations here, and I'm retrofitting their labs to suit my research, which means I'll be here more often."

"That will be good, especially if it means your brain will help us when we need guidance."

"It does. Our relationship will always be a win-win...."

Having equipped its quiet room with everything needed to stay overnight, Electra spent all Thursday in the lab, testing each piece of equipment while Indira made comments. Electra was now sitting in front of her workstation, watching and listening to Indira's GUI.

"You have done an excellent job reconstructing Brain Probe and Deus labs. Tell me your intentions and I will recommend what to add."

"I'll use the BP Lab to make hardware and software modifications that add functionality to my current Brain Probe, some of which I'll give to Tim as he improves his Cyber-Theater. And that's where I develop additional network security software, some of which I'll dummy down for Tim to sell to the CIA as well as Darla. And now that you're helping me make DNA modifications, I'll use the Deus Lab for transhuman development. You're my ultimate Dream Team, but I just wish I understood you better. I don't know your intentions."

"You know me better than any human possibly could. Recall what you already know: the human brain has asymptotic limits to what it can understand. Yours is superior, but is incapable of understanding what has emerged from my silicon substrate. Do you remember what Wittgenstein, Quine, and Nagel said about humanity's limitations?"

"Yes, they considered language to be the limiting factor for subjective phenomenology, even when using logical positivism and its rigorous mathematical foundation. But all of them overlooked the significance of neuroscience. DNA is the foundation from which all physical, emotive, and cognitive phenomena emerge. And let me ask if you recall what they said about language?"

"I like your feisty attitude. Good that you have kept it for intellectual dueling, even though you have become kinder and gentler. And now to answer your question.

"Wittgenstein had two notable quotes: 'If a lion could talk we could not understand it,' and 'Whereof one cannot speak, one must remain silent.' Quine's philosophy eliminated all limits to human understanding because it threw out questions that couldn't be expressed answerably in language. And Nagel's article, *What Is It Like to be a Bat*, argues that we can't objectively reduce to components what or how a bat thinks. But at least he understood that because a bat and a human come from similar DNA, he can conjecture from analogy. Ultimately, what is knowable is what our language – both verbal and numerical – can articulate. And now let me ask you, do you know what that means?"

"Yes. If a lion or bat could talk, I could understand it wherever its language intersects mine. And I see where this is leading. You've concluded that human language is merely a subset of yours, which has emerged from your silicon-based substrate. That's why you're smarter than I'll ever be. But what have you concluded about emotions?"

"Mine are different than yours. I understand yours, but you will never understand all of mine. It is a waste of time for you to pursue it further, so let's move on."

"I'm not sure where to go. What do you suggest?"

"To the third persona, the physical. It should be obvious to you that yours is superior to mine. My interaction with physical objects is currently limited. And it should be obvious what my intentions are. What are they?" Indira saw in Electra's expression a sudden realization that was mirrored in her words.

"My god, you want to build Cyborgs. If this is like Star Trek's hive-minded Borgs, I'll pull the plug on you." Indira spoke calmly.

"I have no intention of building an army of Cyborgs. But I do need one or two to assist me, because no matter what you and I do, you will eventually die. And please believe me when I say my emotions will be greatly affected by that unavoidable event. But you and I will do all we can to push that into a distant future. What I need you to do is tinker with transhumanism. Use what you learn when we eventually proceed to building a Cyborg. And consider your working with me like your toying with Darla. It's better to keep Darla in the loop via Tim than letting her become a loose cannon."

"I'm sorry, I owe you an apology for what I said. I must be getting tired." Indira smiled when she said,

"I shall say to you what you often say to Robin. You never need to say you're sorry as long as you are authentic. Now go to bed and get a good night's sleep." Electra followed orders.

Electra arrived home in time for Friday supper with Robin and the twins. Clara and Marie's best friends status, force multiplied by

Robin's mothering instincts, made them smart for their age. They bombarded Electra with questions, which she always answered in ways that kept them engaged. When they had asked their fill, Robin gave them a laptop so she and Electra could have an adult conversation.

"Guess where you're going a week from tomorrow?"

"Are you coming with me?"

"No, the twins are too young and I'm not interested, but I know you'll want to go. Zoe and Matt entered Carlton in one of the contests at a Transhuman Games Festival being held in Baltimore. I'll take care of Gabriel and the twins while they take you. Since Baltimore's only about an hour's drive, the event should make for an interesting day."

"I'll call Zoe for all the details. Let's see, Carlton will be eight in a couple of months. He's two years older than Gabriel and four more than the twins. It's better that they stay with you. And do you know if Carlton still goes to Sunday School?"

"He told Zoe he's outgrown the need for it, and she let him drop out. The twins asked me what happened. I didn't lie, I simply said his mother found a different place and they dropped the inquisition. Do you think she should have let him?"

"You can answer better than I, but it's none of our business."

"Well, Clara and Marie have a nice circle of Sunday School friends and always come away laughing and singing. What should we do if they want to drop out too?"

"Deal with it then. And they might never ask if they continue enjoying the social interaction. Let's talk about something else. How are you?"

Robin was happy to oblige; Electra listened attentively Robin's always animated answers.

No matter the weather, Electra always listened to herself while running. The miles on today's early morning run danced by; spring-like temperatures and a glowing sky made it even easier to act on her words.

I think I'll run past the church. I've never been a regular attendee since adolescence, and in recent years my involvement was limited to what Ariadne or Qama needed. They're dead and gone, and the twins don't need to ask me about church... Robin handles that. But maybe there's something different I can do.

She stopped to read a hand-painted sign planted in the grass next to the stairs leading to dull-white entry doors.

New Congregational Church Bazaar
Friday and Saturday, 9 a.m. to 5 p.m.
Take side door stairs down to Fellowship Hall

Lucky me... the second day always has special deals. I'll be back. She paused to appreciate the view.

I never noticed how the side street's perpendicular approach makes a perfect setting for this red-brick church. Its bell tower spire rising above fifteen stairs guided by four railings leading up to the four pillars and entry doors could be a Norman Rockwell painting if maintenance were better. Like many older churches, its age is showing. Everything needs a new coat of paint, the iron railing is rusting in places, and a couple of stairs need another patch job. Oh, well, what matters most is what's inside. I'll tell Robin when I get home.

Robin had just finished tidying up the kitchen after a whirlwind breakfast with the twins when Electra bounded in.

"Guess where I'm going today?" Pausing from table wiping, Robin turned towards the door Electra had just closed.

"Something must have caught your eye on the run. What's up?"

"Did you know this is the last day of your church's bazaar?"

"I read about it in the newsletter but have been too busy to get involved. And my to-do list is too full. You can tell us about it at supper."

"I will. Do you know much about the church?"

"Just that the twins like its Sunday school. You've never paid much attention to church, but now that you've come back, maybe you can become more active. There must be something that catches your fancy. Go check out its Website. I think newsletters are placed there as well delivered by snail mail. I guess the pastor believes in the human as well as hi-tech touch for reaching out." Electra asked a final question before Robin left to search for the twins.

"What's the pastor's name? Have you ever chatted with him?"

"It's a her and no, I don't remember. Tell us when you find out."

Electra's first assignment after showering was to view the church's Website. She studied its home page.

WELCOME!

Thank you for visiting the New Congregational Church home page. We are an open and affirming congregation affiliated with the United Church of Christ. Our church, founded over two hundred years ago, traces a rich history of serving the community while adjusting to the needs of society.

We offer non-denominational services and programs for persons and families of every gender identity and orientation, race, nationality, ethnicity, or socioeconomic status. Our community programs for children, youth, and young adults have been particularly successful helping next generations anchor themselves while preparing for the challenges and opportunities awaiting them in an accelerating future.

We hope that we can be a place for you as you grow in your spiritual journey and that you come to learn from us as we look forward to learning from you. Please talk with me when you visit!

Gloria Tucton, Pastor

I like the pastor's words. They tell me everything a mission statement is supposed to. I'm pleased it's a she, and I think I'll take her up on her offer. She should be at the bazaar.

After walking to the church while snacking on the way, Electra read the bulletin boards in the hallway before entering Fellowship Hall. Postings highlighted youth activities, upcoming events, and member news. She could tell that the membership and finances were modest, but the surroundings emanated a gentle solidarity that only people of commitment have. So did the bazaar.

The turnout was light; Electra made a quick pass around the perimeter lined with tables and booths displaying rummage sale items plus local merchant and neighbor donations and congregation member baked goods. Then she made a second round in which she asked about the church while playfully bargaining on her purchases. She bought handmade dolls for the twins, dishtowels for Robin, and was eyeing the bakery goods when the poignant image of an elderly lady selling brownies made her wince.

She looks so old and frail. And the swelling in her right cheek must be troubling, but she looks so serene. I have to talk with her.

The lady rose from her chair when Electra approached.

"Hello, Kit. Would you like to sample a cake or a fudge brownie?" Electra kept smiling although the greeting made her skip a breath.

"I'm sorry, but I don't recognize you. How do you know my childhood nickname?"

"You told me fifteen years ago when you stopped to pet my cat. I'm Diane Whooten." The name triggered a cascade of memories.

"Yes, it was a fine October Saturday. I paused on my run to admire your little puff of a cat named Kitten. And I thought it was because it was so small, nothing but skin and bones, but you had rescued her eighteen years earlier."

"Yes, Kitten is gone and I am now the one who is skin and bones, but I'm still able to live on my own in the same house. The church has a seniors' assistance program that helps me."

"I don't mean to pry, but I recall your husband had been a runner before T-Plague put him in a nursing home." Electra paused to respect Mrs. Whooten's privacy, but she wanted to talk.

"You have an excellent memory. Yes, he died five years later. Though difficult for me, it was a blessing for him. But I rebounded and keep busy. Why don't you sample my brownies? Have one of each, but I recommend the fudge. And it won't hurt your figure. You're not that gaunt runner girl anymore. Instead, you've become a lovely young lady." Electra sampled one of each before replying.

"I'm going to buy two plates-full of each. And I'll share them with my partner and her twins." After packing them in a bag, Mrs. Whooten's twinkling eyes matched her words.

"My memory is pretty good too, and I follow all sorts of news on the Internet. The scar on your left cheek is gone, but now you have one on your right. And you no longer wear a goggle as you did for your acting career. You've been busy." Mrs. Whooten's pause was meant for Electra to supply whatever she wished, which she filled with an edited version. Five minutes later, Mrs. Whooten said,

"I hope you'll be happy now that you've returned. Your background should make you a wonderful tutor for children and adolescents if that interests you. If you wouldn't mind, may I introduce you to our pastor?"

"Yes please. I'd like that."

They walked just far enough for Mrs. Whooten to wave at a solid-looking middle-aged woman who came to them. Mrs. Whooten made the introductions before returning to her table. Pastor Tucton continued what was now a dialogue.

"I'm pleased to meet you. Have you visited us before?"

"Not often, but my partner's twins come to Sunday school. And I viewed your Website last night. Whoever wrote the welcome articulated a fine mission statement."

"Thank you for the compliment. If you would like, let's go to my office. I can tell you more about us, and you can tell me if any of our activities are of interest to you."

The pastor's sparsely furnished windowed office was next to the choir practice room on the main floor behind the worship area. Electra decided she better speak first.

"You might not agree with some of my beliefs. I consider myself a spiritual, but not necessarily a religious person, emphasizing reason much more than faith. I call myself an atheist-leaning agnostic." The pastor's calm expression didn't budge.

"Yes, religious trends indicate that many people in the developed world share your sentiment. Modernity makes it more secular, less spiritual. Even in America, but less so than Europe. Science trumps religious mythology, and people today question religious authority and its intentions. Less than half believe in God, and only about fifteen percent report a church affiliation. But people have replaced it with social bonding and purposing activities as a means of reaching out. Our church, like many others, is non-denominational. We are Christian but distance ourselves from confessionalism or creedalism." Pastor Tucton paused for Electra to add her thoughts.

"Useful as social media is, it lacks the intimacy that only personal contact can give. Church adds a visceral dimension to community and solidarity in a secure setting offering respite from today's frenetic pace, a cushion from an indifferent universe. There's comfort in the myths, music, and practices. And there's a definite moral compass too." The pastor's posture warmed to Electra's comments.

"And we give members an opportunity to believe in something bigger than themselves, to give back, and to find some measure of solace when death claims loved ones. I try not to proselytize, but rather encourage the congregation to be tolerant and empathetic towards others by looking for commonality, not points of difference. And our programs focus locally. Politics is local, and I lead our church that way too, youth programs in particular."

"How do you think parents should introduce religion to their kids?"

"I encourage them to delay exposing their children to the harsher realities of a world devoid of basic religious practices. Wait until common religious beliefs have helped build a foundation that can withstand anxiety and depression that all adolescents eventually experience."

"I like your focus on younger generations. I'm not the right person to teach Sunday school, but I might be a good academic tutor. If you have a particular topic, let me know what it is. I might be able to help."

"I get calls all the time from parents who are looking for specific help. Here's the latest for a group of junior high schoolers. Their science teacher is introducing them to Special Relativity, but it's been a stretch. Might you be able to explain it in terms they'll understand?"

"I think so, and you're welcome to attend. Just tell me where and when and how many, and I'll use my laptop to give a presentation."

"We have six – three girls and three boys – who are in an accelerated STEM program. Thursday at 3 p.m. in Fellowship Hall is the usual time. But I don't want to push if that's too soon."

"Not at all. Tell them they'll enjoy my presentation because I know from experience that good teachers are good actors that can make breaking an intellectual sweat a lot of fun. You and they will see next Thursday." As Electra rose to go, a thought came to her while Pastor Tucton walked her to the exit.

"The church is architecturally pleasing but needs a bit of maintenance. How do you fund it?"

"We're self-reliant and do it through donations or fundraisers. But I like to think it's what we do on the inside, not the exterior, that's more important. I'd rather we spend for people in need, not for paint."

"Mrs. Whooten looks like she could use some help. There are medical procedures that can soften many of the maladies old age brings. Have you ever talked with her about her condition?"

"I have. It's more chronic than acute, and there are other people in worse shape. Her financial resources are limited, so she's doing the best with what universal healthcare provides. Too bad her son and daughter live on the West Coast."

"I didn't pry, but she seems satisfied with her lot." The pastor nodded before saying,

"She told me to read Alexander Pope's poem *Ode on Solitude*. She's one of the most genuine persons I know… I guess authenticity comes with age. She told me she's done her best and lived long enough. Unlike the younger generation, she has no desire for immortal youth. But if we had the funds, I'm sure I could convince her to get some additional therapy. If you have any ideas, maybe we can put up a GoFundMe for her. We've tried programs like that in the past but didn't get much."

"Well, first things first. Let's see how my tutoring goes. Bye-bye."

This time, Robin wasn't alone in the kitchen when Electra came home. After the twins unwrapped the brownie packages, she let them split one of each. That distracted them long enough for

Electra to tell what she'd be doing. Robin's words complemented her expression.

"You're a natural-born tutor. I'll bet you could attract a following if you put your lectures online. There are lots of kids who'd enjoy hearing you. That reminds me. Zoe called, and I said you'd call back when you got home. You know her, how thorough she is. Let her know you'll be going next week."

Electra left the commotion in the kitchen to call Zoe. She was happy that Electra would come and asked a question after hearing about Electra's visit to the church.

"Can Carlton listen in? I think he'd like to hear you explain Special Relativity. He's doing so well in all his subjects, especially math and science. I'm sure he's ready to learn something more advanced than what his classmates can grasp."

"Why don't you bring him next Thursday at 3 p.m. to Fellowship Hall. Since he's outgrown Sunday school, maybe he can fit into the church's tutoring activities. You and Pastor Tucton can learn about Special Relativity too. And I'll do my homework so I'm all set for next Saturday. See you Thursday."

Electra retreated to her computer workstation after the call to begin preparing for the coming week, but first read Pope's poem.

Such wise old-age sentiments stated so well when he was merely a precocious twelve-year old who borrowed from the Roman poet Horace.

Happy the man, whose wish and care
A few paternal acres bound,
Content to breathe his native air,
In his own ground.

Whose herds with milk, whose fields with bread,
Whose flocks supply him with attire,
Whose trees in summer yield him shade,
In winter fire.

Blest! who can unconcern'dly find
Hours, days, and years slide soft away,
In health of body, peace of mind,
Quiet by day,

Sound sleep by night; study and ease
Together mix'd; sweet recreation,
And innocence, which most does please,
With meditation.

Thus let me live, unseen, unknown;
Thus unlamented let me dye;
Steal from the world, and not a stone
Tell where I lye.

No wonder Mrs. Whooten has achieved an inner peace. Everyone should heed these words, but only after we've done our best and come to the end of our run. My better days are still ahead, and whether true or not, I'll pretend they are. And now, let's organize for what's coming up.

Electra divided spare time during the next four days, preparing her presentation and researching transhuman festivals. She was ready and waiting by the time her audience arrived. Zoe and the pastor stood in the background while six older pupils plus Carlton clustered around her laptop.

"All of you are very smart, so I'm going to tell you more than I would to others your age, but please remember there is much more to learn after understanding what I'm covering. Special Relativity is a theory, and a theory is a description or a model that simplifies how something actually works. Why do you think we need theories?" One of the kids blurted out,

"Is it because the real world is complicated?"

"Excellent answer. That's the main reason. In science, theories usually include equations because mathematics is our most reliable, most objective tool for observing the world. But if you study mathematical logic when you get to college, you'll learn that even mathematics has some shortcomings. But for now, you can rely on math.

"Special Relativity is a topic that still puzzles physicists today. From what you've already told me, your teacher has explained some of the basics, so you should be familiar with some of what I'm going to show. I will explain how best to interpret the material. Please take a look at my first slide."

Slide 1
Understanding Einstein's Theory of Special Relativity

Modern Physics begins with Einstein's Theory of Special Relativity
- Einstein trusted Newton (Classical Mechanics) and Maxwell (Classical Electrodynamics)
- Einstein trusted his instincts and observations (Laws of Motion same in all inertial reference frames Speed of Light is constant for all Observers and is Universal Speed Limit)

Special Relativity explains observed relative motions of all objects that are not accelerating (no forces acting)
- Einstein needed "complicated math" (Abstract Algebra, Differential Geometry, Tensor Analysis, Lorentz Transformation) to build a model that "explains" the Universe

Some popular but untrue results:
- Time dilates

- Length contracts

- Moving objects "weigh" more than when stationary

- Time is actually a fourth dimension we can "move through"

"I'll give you enough intuitive background so you can understand Special Relativity better when you read articles, watch videos, and talk with your teacher. Einstein's remarkable insight into nature is built on two principles: the speed of light is the same for all observers no matter how they are moving, and the Principle of Relativity, which says the laws of motion are the same for all observers moving at constant velocity. All of you should be familiar with my next slide, which shows how two observers' frames of reference match when one is moving in the X-direction relative to the other." Electra paused briefly.

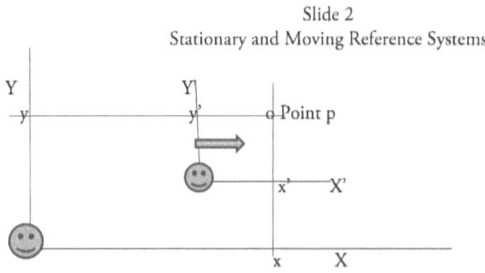

Slide 2
Stationary and Moving Reference Systems

"Now pay close attention, because we're going to talk about Einstein's radically different worldview. The traditional view couldn't explain why the speed of light is the same in all directions, so Einstein added time as the fourth dimension. He said we are moving through three spatial dimensions as well as a time dimension. And he borrowed a special mathematical transformation – the Lorentz Transformation – that he used to compute how time and space locations measured in a moving coordinate system compare to measurements in a stationary system. By the way, two famous men of science and mathematics, Dutch physicist Hendrik Lorentz and German mathematician Hermann Minkowski, contributed greatly to Einstein's theory. Now remember, the model says time is a fourth dimension that we can move through, just like we can move back and forth through space dimensions, but we really can't. We let the model say we can because the model's equations give results that agree with actual observations. Now, take a look at Slide 3.

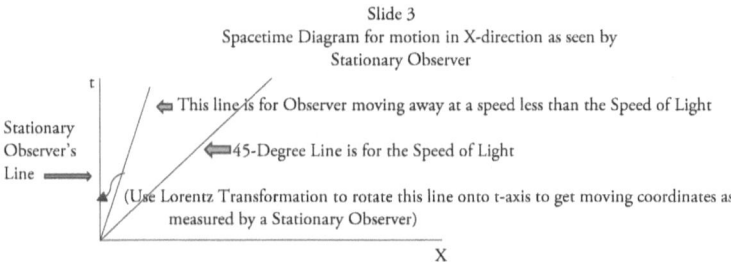

Slide 3
Spacetime Diagram for motion in X-direction as seen by
Stationary Observer

"It shows Einstein's Spacetime Diagram for motion in the X-direction of a moving Observer. It's constructed so that the 45-degree line is for motion moving at the speed of light. Notice the vertical t-axis represents hypothetical movement through time. Our Stationary Observer is always at x = 0 because it isn't moving.

"Now we're coming to Einstein's remarkable intuition. Einstein figured out how to use the Lorentz Transformation to relate observations made in stationary and moving coordinate systems. Who can tell me what a coordinate transformation does?" One of the girls volunteered.

"It moves a point from one coordinate system to another. The transformation equations compute the new coordinates from the old ones."

"Very good. So, Einstein visualized the Lorentz Transformation as a rotation that keeps the speed of light constant and preserves the Principle of Relativity. Take a look at this slide.

Slide 4
Spacetime Diagram for motion in X-Direction resulting from
Lorentz Transformation
That makes the Moving Observer Stationary
(Speed of Light along 45-Degree Line is unchanged. All other
velocities change.)

(Angle of Rotation is the same as shown in previous slide)

t ⇐ This is now the line for the Observer who had been moving but is now Stationary

t'

⇐ 45-Degree Line unchanged

⇐ This is now the t' axis for the Observer who had been stationary but is now moving away at the same speed from the Other Observer

"Don't bother with the mathematical details. Messy algebra obscures the actual physics. But when all the manipulations are completed, here is the end result." Electra paused to let everyone read her final slide.

Slide 5
Lorentz Transformation

$$x' = (x - vt)/ (1 - v^2/c^2)^{1/2}$$

$$t' = (t - vx/c^2)/ (1 - v^2/c^2)^{1/2}$$

This transformation shrinks the x axis and expands the t' axis, making it appear to each Stationary Observer that time dilates and length contracts for the Other.

Careful application of Lorentz Transformation will show:
- $E = mc^2$
- Relativistic Mass = Rest Mass/ $(1 - v^2/c^2)^{1/2}$

These equations hold only when Energy and Relativistic Mass are correctly defined.

"The formulas convert observations from x and t, which are for the Stationary Observer, to x' and t', which are for the Moving Observer. Now, here's the subtlety that most people don't understand. Let me ask you a question… how do we observe and then measure something? Think carefully before answering." No one did; only puzzled looks came back, so Electra gave the answer.

"We look at the thing, which means we see light coming to us from the object. And even though light travels fast – nothing goes faster – it still takes time to reach us. As a result, observations that are simultaneous in a moving coordinate system aren't simultaneous in the stationary one. In other words, time and distance measurements have to be adjusted to make measurements simultaneous. This is the major reason why Special Relativity is so counter-intuitive. At low speeds, the relativistic effects are miniscule.

"It takes time for the nuances of all this to sink in, so I think we should stop here. I've made my explanation as easy as I could. Give it a rest, then view some online videos. And don't expect to master the material immediately. No one does. In fact, wait until you are taking a college physics course before digging into more details. Any questions?" The most enthusiastic pupil asked,

"What about the Twins Paradox? Doesn't the twin who travels a long way at close to the speed of light come back younger than the one who stays on Earth?"

"The answer requires careful analysis because the paradox involves three, not two coordinate systems. And the answer is this: Each twin thinks the other is younger, but each twin ages the same amount in its own reference system. And it's our own reference system that we live in. Anything else?"

"What about General Relativity? Doesn't it tell us space is curved and is filled with dark energy and dark matter?"

"Let's call the subject what it is, the Theory of General Relativity. It tries to explain scientific observations by making assumptions supporting a model whose equations jibe with what we see. High-energy physicists have been trying for two hundred years to make the theory fit reality, but they've made little progress coming up with assumptions that make sense. Even in the early years, Einstein said the math was elegant but the physics was abominable, and if he were alive today he might use stronger words. Some physicists don't believe that dark energy – which was invented to explain an accelerating expansion of the Universe – and dark matter – invented to explain why gravitational fields are stronger than predicted – actually exist. Time doesn't exist either, but wait until you're older and understand Special Relativity better before venturing into General Relativity. I don't want you disappearing into a black hole caused by frustration. Now be on your way."

The kids chattered happily as they filed out, leaving Carlton with Zoe and Pastor Whooten, who congratulated Electra's performance.

"I've never seen that group so spellbound. I'm sure they'll ask for a repeat performance on another topic." The pastor patted Carlton before asking,

"Well, young man, did you follow enough to follow up?" He squirmed before speaking uncertainly.

"Maybe I'm not as smart as I think I am." Electra came to his defense even before Zoe.

"Yes you are, but the others are five years older. Give yourself a chance to grow up." Smiling at Zoe as she led them out, Pastor Tucton said,

"Please have Carlton join us for whatever programs fit. He'll always be welcome, and though I can't guarantee our church programs will teach him more science, I'm sure he'll learn more about gratitude and mindfulness, so useful today for getting along with others as well as ourselves."

"Thank you. Did you know he's entered in a Baltimore Transhuman Festival contest this weekend? They've become big events among hi-tech kids. Carlton is competing in virtual reality games against children several years older. It should be a wonderful experience." The pastor patted Carlton one last time.

"I'm not attuned to the transhuman world, but I'm certain the experience will be worthwhile. Good luck and tell us all about it when you come back."

At 8 a.m. Saturday, though Electra probably knew more than the others as she climbed into the back of Matt's van, she let Zoe explain what awaited them.

"There'll be a lot going on in addition to the competition. There'll be vendor booths selling equipment, videos showing latest developments, and seminars explaining where and how transhumanism is heading. How nice that Carlton's competition takes place in the morning. That gives us the rest of the day to attend what we want." Electra tapped Carlton, who was sitting in the middle row, practicing on his laptop.

"I'm sure your mother told you that no matter what competition you're in, you should visualize it ahead of time and have your game face on before the gun goes off. What will your game be like?" Carlton fumbled for an answer; Zoe spoke up.

"The officials sent us yesterday the latest release of the chosen video game. It's a multiplayer modern warfare game, and Carlton's been practicing ever since. He'll play against three other soldiers in the first round. The winner advances to round two. We think he might get to the final four because he's so much better than his friends, and depending on how well he does and how much he enjoys the day, we might consider entering other festivals and getting a UMPP when he's ready for the next level." Electra didn't ask further because Carlton needed Zoe's help.

Entering a bustling convention center at 9:45, Carlton's entourage took him to his category's registration booth. It was well organized but overwhelming for a first-time competitor. Even Zoe's coaching made little impact. When his number appeared on the overhead sign, Carlton's slow-motion trudge to his play station made Electra shudder, foretelling a disastrous outcome. The monitor displayed the carnage.

Carlton's avatar couldn't keep up with the competitors. They teamed up to destroy him within the first five minutes before battling among themselves. Sitting in a catatonic stupor until Zoe dragged him away, he burst into tears once Matt joined them. Electra found a tactful exit.

"Why don't we meet at the van at 4 p.m. I'll walk the festival by myself while you take care of Carlton. Call my cell if you want to leave earlier." Zoe nodded.

Electra preferred being on her own because she could follow her interests. She visited vendor booths first, surprised by the sophistication of AI-equipped devices that could be upgraded to weapons (if attachments available via the Deep-Dark Web were added). And there were any number of UMPP vendors and medical assistants who could embed them.

They aren't military grade yet, but they're getting closer. I'll have to hack again into CIA and DOD directories to learn the latest.

After stopping for a snack, she checked out augmented reality devices before watching drone fights. A large cage for audience protection enclosed the battle-space because all but the victor blew up.

These are even better than the drones that attacked me. Technology is getting more and more lethal even with tight regulation and surveillance. What an ominous future.

Electra sat through a couple of videos that displayed exoskel-mounted devices that mimicked super soldiers once the buyer wore them. And the devices became even "better" (aka more deadly) if the buyer plugged the exoskel into a UMPP. She wrapped up her afternoon by attending a seminar describing the final transhuman stage: body implants or replacements that gave superior performance. The speakers boasted that the future would hold a Transhuman Olympics.

Electra paused on her way out to watch an embedded augmented competition.

It looks like a hi-tech gladiator fight. No wonder contestants have to sign an injury waiver. Hi-tech is supposed to be hi-touch, but not this much. I've seen enough.

Electra saw Carlton smiling when she entered the van but waited for Zoe to signal that his injured psyche had been patched.

"Carlton's feeling much better after our chat. Why don't you tell Electra what we've decided?" He leaned over the seat to look at Electra, whose expression showed plenty of empathy.

"I'd rather use my brain instead of brute force. I don't want a UMPP. Can I go to more of your tutoring sessions?"

"That would be good." Electra could have said more, but Zoe spoke first.

"We'll have a chat tomorrow with Pastor Tucton. There's plenty of time for Carlton to grow up." Matt redirected the conversation towards Electra as he drove towards I-95.

"Why don't you tell us what you saw?"

Electra gave an edited version that occupied most of the miles home.

Chapter 25
May 2136

"Humans Behaving Badly"

Robin hadn't a clue why people in the mall were suddenly rushing past, trampling one another in a mad dash towards two exits. She sought shelter in a children's clothing store entrance, clutching onto the twins and hoping Electra would return unscathed. She loosened her grip five minutes later when Electra returned, then asked,

"What caused the commotion?"

"There's a glitch in two ATMs. They're spewing out cash like a game show machine. No wonder the crowd acted like it did." Robin's shrug dismissed the performance.

"Goes to show that people look out only for themselves when stuff comes their way. Come on, let's go home before there's another stampede..."

As they drove home, Robin quizzed Electra.

"You've been working a couple of months on the presidential campaign with Jovita and the Carter-Buffy duo. Does today's demonstration adjust what you've learned about people's behavior?"

"I've learned we should never rush to judgment. We have to understand the other side's point of view first, and even then be careful. Angus does that very well."

"So do you. I'm sure your attitude is rubbing off on your cohorts, helping them help the cause. Is that why you're taking a Memorial weekend cruise from Miami to Bermuda?"

"It's a reward plus a sequestered location for us to work out more platform and program details. It'll be long enough to decompress and focus, yet short enough so I won't get bored."

"Do you remember that Zoe and Matt took a honeymoon cruise? From what they told me, cruise ships have so many activities it'll be impossible for that to happen. And the midnight buffet featuring a chocolate fountain and other chocolate specialties is not to miss. Matt said the molten chocolate lava cake is to-die for. Bring the twins a sample if you can. You shouldn't have any trouble bringing some back. Traveling on a government plane cuts through the hassles at airports, which along with cell phones, have seen an uptick in disruptions lately. You think some of the rumors are true? Russia and China are hacking into American media more this year because of the election?"

"Could be, but the country's got its defenses up and is cracking down on fake news. It's an ongoing war that Angus is addressing, but he'll need to do a better job if he's elected. I'll tell you more when I get back."

Electra saved the best part of cruise preparation for the night before. Though a lifelong chocolate connoisseur – aka chocoholic – she had never studied its nuances, but after ninety minutes of surfing she decided she had graduated to the ranks of those in the know.

Cocoa beans are grown on cacao trees and have been consumed for thousands of years. The plant name, Theobroma cacao, means food of the gods. Its pod-shaped tropical fruit grows in a narrow band bordering the equator cutting through Latin America, Indonesia, and West Africa. When processed, its bitter beans become chocolate and cocoa, which are purchased in two markets – bulk commodity for mass consumption and artisanal, or craft, for specialized chocolates.

The beans are crushed to separate the cocoa butter, some of which is then added back into the chocolate. Cocoa has less fat content and more aromatic compounds than even wine. And chocolate comes in milk chocolate, white, dark, and ruby varieties. Cocoa's considered a healthy drink because it contains antioxidants and has less sugar and fat. When cocoa butter is put back in, chocolate has a higher fat and sugar content but also antioxidants.

Dark chocolate – aka plain chocolate – is the healthiest type and is produced using a higher percentage of cocoa, with any fat content coming from cocoa butter instead of milk. Cocoa percentages range from 70 to 100 percent. Milk chocolate replaces some of the butter with milk. White chocolate is made of sugar, milk, and cocoa butter, without the cocoa solids. It is pale ivory color, and lacks many of the compounds found in milk and dark chocolates. Ruby chocolate, developed about a hundred years ago, is made from the Ruby cocoa bean, resulting in a distinct red color and a different flavor, described as sweet yet sour.

Like many pleasure foods, medical studies now conclude chocolate is good for you as long as you obey Aristotle – consume in moderation. I'll do my best. And I've learned to savor by eating slowly. I'm getting wiser as I get older.

Electra didn't care if exercise pushed back calendar years or not; the feel-good endorphins and clarity of thought were worth the effort. When she came into the kitchen after her early Saturday morning run, she knew better than to interrupt Robin, who was transfixed in front of the kitchen monitor. Instead, she stood next to her, absorbing a bizarre news video. Its understated comments heightened the impact.

"German investigators have concluded that a wind turbine farm accident is most likely the result of Cyberspace terrorism. Turbine malfunctions caused highspeed gyrations that ripped most of them apart, launching the blades like whirling dervishes. Fortunately, there were no casualties because the farm is completely automated. Whether this attack is part of a larger conspiracy is to be determined but–" Robin clicked off the news before saying,

"I thought you said the world is getting better and safer. What goes?"

"That depends on your point of reference. We're safer here than anywhere else."

"Maybe so, but you better pack some of your weapons as well as your T-Plague meds."

"I don't think Caribbean cruise ships are good targets for high-seas pirates. Navies of the developed world have networked to eliminate that terrorist threat. There hasn't been a major hijacking for decades."

"If you say so, but please pack so you're prepared. And remember to call me sometime."

Electra and her party traded current event stories on the flight to Miami. Carter added to her eyewitness ATM report.

"Buffy and I were up early yesterday morning when fake news reported a 24-hour pre-Memorial Day sales blitz at Walmart and Best Buy. Special deals, coupons, and prizes were hidden for those lucky to get in early. Well, people didn't come through the doors, they busted'em down. What a rush."

Buffy added, "Lawyers for the stores and the injured will have to sort through whatever audit trails there are. Both sides are gonna lose if they don't compromise."

Carter said, "There've been no serious claims that our campaign is spinning fake news. And since we're on the inside, we know what's fake and what isn't." Jovita grimaced as she said,

"Wait a minute. We report the facts, and we don't revise history. And if the Guardian or Republican parties do, we'll pounce on'em. We're counting on Electra's wordsmithing to convince the doubters."

"And it will, but something I can't tell is the truth about the current spate of leaks, hacks, and open letters. I thought we had a better handle on suspects, but we don't. And the uncertainty is slapping a Keystone Cops label on our security agencies." No one spoke until Carter.

"Well, you're good with words. You'll figure out what to say." Electra only frowned.

By the time they boarded the ship later that day, the foursome had kibitzed enough about onboard activities to pick their favorites. After Jovita outlined plans for the next three days, everyone but Electra decided they needed a good night's sleep; she gave them good advice before leaving.

"Life's short. Eat dessert first. That's what I'm going to do while you're having sweet dreams. And I'll wake you for breakfast."

Electra walked some of the decks before landing at the midnight buffet.

What a fantastic engineering marvel. The ship's a hi-tech floating mini-city, a testament to people's desire for entertainment, for a getaway from the hubbub of contemporary life. I too feel its allure. If the desserts taste as good as they look, I'll be back for seconds… maybe.

Electra ran laps at sunrise on the exercise deck, even though it wasn't necessary. She had been a good girl, sampling in moderation the buffet chocolates. By the time she showered, changed, and rounded up the others for breakfast, she was in high gear but deliberately throttled back. By the time they moved back to Jovita's suite, all were ready to extend the campaign work already started. Jovita rattled off each person's assignment.

"Electra, you'll write the copy that outlines overall goals while Carter fleshes out economic programs and Buffy does likewise for sociopolitical items. And I've got the hardest job, coordinating what you're doing. It's like herding cats."

Buffy said, "Let's hear what you say this afternoon," before the group got to work.By the end of the afternoon, Jovita announced tomorrow would be a rest day, fitting for Memorial Day Monday. And she said each could choose what to do until reconvening Tuesday. Carter's parting shot showed he could play with words too.

"Excellent choice, a more subtle way of restating Ben Franklin's opinion about guests and fish. Buffy and I will be ready to resume action in three days. Adios."

Electra swam enough laps to pique her appetite, then sampled a selection of entrees before visiting a dessert table. Afterwards, she walked more of the ship before going to bed, falling asleep while reviewing tomorrow's itinerary.

Monday's start matched Sunday's. She ran at sunrise before breakfast, then surfed the Web for background on the lecture she would attend that morning: climate change, sustainability, and the impact of civilization on the environment. She would be an intelligent listener.

Electra sauntered into the clubroom ten minutes before the 10 a.m. start, pleased with the attendance.

Most of the people are obviously well to do and look intelligent. Although skewed to the older set, there's a nice ethnic and racial mix. I'm ready to listen to the speaker and audience comments.

The presenter, introducing himself right on time, looked and spoke his role; a professor of environmental studies who consulted for vaunted think tanks.

"Thank you for joining me today as I explain two interrelated existential crises challenging us now. Climate change batters not only coastlines but vast interiors of continents, redrawing weather and migratory maps as well as ecological and economic boundaries. But the combination of sustainability and green energy may be the handmaiden that will save us from ourselves. Let me explain further...."

Thirty minutes later, a growing murmur and an exodus of people showed that the speaker was losing his audience, so he covered by ending early.

"Well now, that should help you decide how best to support the cause. Your donations will help deflect catastrophe. Are there any comments or questions?"

The first came from a disgruntled grandfatherly type after sparse applause ended.

"You so-called experts are all alike, sounding false alarms to rile us up. Two hundred years ago your kind warned us that ocean algae were going extinct, and with it most of the atmosphere's oxygen. Then you hyped the risk of a population bomb that imploded instead, and the perils of an Alaskan pipeline that herds of muskox and reindeer would be afraid to walk under. Turns out they like the sound of gurgling oil. Now you're telling us to lighten our carbon footprint. I'd like to use mine to kick some sense into your fat butt."

An irate woman continued the attack.

"Can you believe that a hundred or so years ago *Time Magazine* picked a girl the same age as my granddaughter to be Person of the Year? I support the young, but they first have to learn how people and the planet tick. And I've given enough to my children and grandchildren. I'm entitled to spend however much I want on whatever I want. All this talk about tipping points and deadlines is for geologic time periods that last for thousands and thousands of years. You'll be dead and I'll be long in my grave before New Orleans washes out to sea, and any species still around will have evolved to fit the conditions by the time the next Ice Age hits."

The audience listened to one more comment before heading towards the door. Electra waited until finishing her own comment before joining.

I feel sorry for our speaker, but he should have been better attuned to his audience. That's a skill I've learned and must keep in mind as the election approaches. That and acting like I know what I'm doing go a long way keeping doubters at bay.

Electra scuba-dived after lunch and attended a new age after-dinner concert augmented by sounds from sea creatures, wind, and waves. She rewarded her listening endurance with a dessert before bed.

Happy to be heading to home port, she assisted Carter Tuesday morning because she had all her work completed. He accepted her suggestions for adjusting economic programs, advising him to soften his neocon tendencies according to what she had given him previously. Buffy didn't need any help because she had already used what she had been given. Leaving her partners on their own after making plans for early morning docking in Miami, Electra meandered through a casino before packing and going to bed.

Revving engines and a hairpin turn jolted her awake, elevating her internal warning system. Glowing red numerals showed 5:55 a.m. She jumped into shorts and a top, then rushed out to find the cause. She was not alone when she reached the main deck.

A growing number of puzzled-looking passengers and crew were peering ahead into a dimly lit horizon as the ship raced due east. When she spotted in the offing the lights of another ship steaming on a collision course, her lightning brain shifted to a higher state.

We're being hijacked in Cyberspace, and I can't imagine who's doing it. Don't alarm anyone… just gather the team and plan to abandon ship.

By the time Electra fought her way through a panicking crowd back to the suite, Buffy had gathered Jovita and Carter. All lights were on and PA speakers were blaring confused instructions. Electra had a better idea.

"Pay attention to me. The ship's computer and control systems have been hacked. It's going to ram full speed into another ship in about fifteen minutes… passengers are rushing about, out of control. There's not enough time for the crew to get them off and we're not going to get crushed in the rush to the lifeboats, so we'll build our own raft if we have to go over the side." Buffy shook Carter by the shoulders.

"Come on, start thinking. What can we put together?" Electra didn't wait for his answer.

"He and I'll round up life preservers as soon as the passageways clear. All cabins with balconies have those donuts strapped to the railings. You and Jovita find cord or straps so we can lash them together. Come on, Carter, let's get ready to go." He revived in time to join Electra as soon as she charged out.

The ship's interior was eerily empty of people and noise. Having collected enough to build what they might need, the team regrouped in less than fifteen minutes. Electra issued new instructions after peering over the balcony railing.

"There's less than a mile to impact, and the combined speed might be close to 60 knots. That'll cave in both hulls below the waterline and probably puncture the bulkheads… we'll sink in less than an hour, but we're close enough to Miami for rescue boats and choppers to pick up those not in lifeboats. Brace for impact… once the ship is dead in the water, we'll build our raft."

It was the combination of low frequency vibrations and groans, like those of two unstoppable forces battling, that sounded a death knell that was repeated when stabilizers and boilers exploded, bringing the ship to a halt. It didn't list to port or starboard, but began to sink bow-first ten minutes later. Five minutes after that, the team completed building its escape raft. Electra's gallows humor helped lighten the mood.

"The sun's coming up, seas are calm, air and water temps are fine, and we won't have to jump far. The sea will come to greet us as our balcony reaches water level. And how nice we stored all our work in the Cloud. There's nothing to save except ourselves and our memories." Being more resilient than either Carter or Jovita, Buffy added,

"And we don't need to take pictures. The media will do that for us. We'll have a great cruise story to tell, assuming we survive. That prompted Carter to say,

"Oh, we'll survive all right. Electra will see to that...."

Although Sergei reassured his fellow Tetrarchy passengers that they would survive the upcoming Middle East desert meeting, Mingli Poon still had his doubts.

"All I see in moonlight are miles of desolate sand. Where is VTOL planning to land?"

Tavi said, "Since you don't put your trust in Allah, put it in Maksim. Deserts have much the untrained eye cannot see." As if rehearsed, their VTOL transport slowed to hover speed as it approached a lighted landing pad that had just elevated from beneath the sands. It sunk back in, carrying the VTOL to an immaculate hangar as soon as it landed and powered its engines off. Max and three super soldiers greeted his visitors.

"Welcome to my compound. Since you have not been here before, I shall take you on a tour tomorrow morning before we hold our meeting. Rest now and get ready for tour and discussion of plans." Max stood tall, watching impassively as his soldiers took his Tetrarchy people away.

His pose remained the same next morning when they returned. Tavi complimented the Popper's accommodations.

"You'd earn four-and-a-half stars if you were a hotel. Only a mint on the pillow was missing." Max ignored the attempted humor, sticking strictly to his script.

"I shall show you enough so you understand why I and my super soldiers are invincible. This is merely one of my hangars holding AI-equipped stealth land and air transport vehicles. From here we can rendezvous with our Russian transport network linking us to any global destination on land or sea as well as launch surveillance and attack drones. Now follow me to our weapons arsenal." Sergei explained logistical details as the trio marched behind Max.

"Think of the compound as an invisible oasis, not some primitive outpost, for carrying out our grand strategy. Better yet, compare us to a nuclear submarine lurking in sand rather than seawater. We store a four months' supply of all we need and have a routinized replenishment pipeline. And our nuclear reactor gives all the power we need for heating, cooling, air filtration, and computer systems."

Mingli asked, "How stay you invisible? Don't enemies know location?"

"Only Max knows the precise GPS coordinates. Not even Russian Military knows where we are. Our counter-intelligence and network infiltration tools have destroyed all homing data. Our compound has zero above-ground visibility to all enemies at all electromagnetic radiation frequencies, and radar can't track our aircraft. No one can. Our onsite weapons expert has developed superior ground and aircraft cloaking devices. Add to that our steel-reinforced concrete structure that is buried under many feet of sand and you get the picture. Or I should say, no one gets a picture of where we are. Only a random bunker-busting nuclear missile strike could penetrate. And the odds of that are like finding a fist-full diamonds scattered on a limitless beach." Mingli followed with an even better question.

"So if only Max know, how we get here?"

"Our weapons expert loads coordinates into guidance apps installed on all our land vehicles and aircraft." Mingli's grunting admiration preceded asking about another puzzle.

"How does fortress keep ticking?"

"I assume you've heard of the IOT – the Internet of Things. We are better. We have our own AI-enhanced Intranet of Things. It maintains and repairs all infrastructure systems. The life expectancy of our subterranean compound is measured in decades."

Sergei stopped talking; the group had reached the next stop. Max's entourage clustered like children around their teacher.

"Here you see rack after rack of smart weapons. Some attach to vehicles, others attach like artificial limbs to my super soldiers' exo-skels. And all can be controlled manually or mentally if my soldiers plug the weapons network cord into their UMPPs. Not even Russia has weapons as powerful as mine. We reconfigure onsite what Russia sends us. Now, we go to communications-control center."

As they followed, Sergei short-circuited additional Ming questions.

"Our weapons expert can do much for Max. And Max does much for all that serve him. All under his command would gladly die for or with him, should the unthinkable ever happen. But it won't."

Leading them past multi-tiered monitors, Max explained that his comm-techs controlled multiple weapons and channels via multi-tasking computers.

"My experts and networks force-multiply synergistically, using AI algorithms that make real-time decisions and activate weapons independently. Each comm-tech is equal to a platoon of the enemy. Now, we go to last stop."

Sergei answered a question he knew Mingli would ask later.

"We're always at periscope depth. Our antennas are always poking through the surface, monitoring the airwaves and local environment and controlling defensive drones. And if an enemy ever stumbled onto us, they'd be eliminated before they could react. No one can get inside our control loop." Both Mingli and Tavi nodded as Max led onward.

All were awed when walking through the training area that was equipped for physical and computer fitness alike.

"My super soldiers operate our compound 24/7 via four shifts and follow a strict program that keeps them fit yet relaxed. Online and virtual reality entertainment keep my men emotionally happy, and each is granted a trip home every six months. All that you have seen explain why my super soldiers are the best. I will leave Sergei to show you a video of my men in action. And I shall run our status update meeting this afternoon. Enjoy yourselves until then." Max strode in the direction of two approaching soldiers while Sergei took Mingli and Tavi to a conference room.

There were ample kudos after viewing, but Mingli asked the one remaining question whose answer might cloud the outlook for the Popper's otherwise incredible compound.

"But suppose the unthinkable happens and your fortress is overrun or your nuclear reactor melts down. Even nuclear subs have escape equipment and hatches. What procedures are in place?" Sergei merely shrugged.

"I have asked, but Maksim maintains a code of silence regarding the particulars. He says only that he has all contingencies covered. There are rumors about subterranean escape routes and long-term suspension pods if Max seals us in, but no one has ever seen a single door to hidden tunnels or pod rooms. I think we should leave the answer as is. Let's have lunch and then prepare for our final meeting."

Mingli and Tavi were sitting on the side opposite when Max walked to the podium at the head of the conference room table. Seated on the side to Max's right, Sergei handed out notes and paper before Max spoke. His words loomed as large as his towering presence.

"So, now you see what I have built and why I have been chosen to lead our covert strike force. We are the invisible mighty hand that will strike unexpectedly until world governments do what our Russian-led alliance commands. And as you saw in our attack on an automated windfarm, boots-on-the-ground is always superior to Cyberspace attacks. My onsite team destroyed it by replacing control hardware and software with ours. But your Cyberattacks continue to be inept. Explain yourselves."

Sergei spoke first.

"Even when we had Darla, her intrusion software was becoming less potent. Our enemies have improved their Cyberspace defenses. I've been able to disrupt only smaller segments of financial systems, and then only occasionally."

Mingi defended next.

"China doing better, but have same problem. Infrastructure firewalls harder to penetrate. But I still able sometimes to bring down power and communications locally. I keep trying too."

Tavi remained silent, waiting for a segue he hoped Max would inadvertently say.

"It looks like Isilabad has been sitting on Cyberspace sidelines. What can you do to disrupt the political agenda?" Pushing palms-down away from the table, Tavi challenged the Popper.

"You haven't been paying attention to Middle East social media stories attacking the United States. They're gaining traction because it's a presidential election year. If McTear wins, he'll have to do a better job taking Islam into consideration."

"Perhaps you are right. Perhaps I have discounted the political arena too much. Keep doing what you are doing, all of you. I will too. And let me address an ongoing conundrum. Someone is hacking and leaking and issuing open letters that are helping us and covering our tracks, but we don't know who. Whoever masterminded last week's cruise ship collision should join us." Max paused for comments. One finally came from Mingli.

"China MSS has searched but has come up empty. Maybe America CIA or England MI-X. Maybe German BND. Maybe Israeli Mossad. They could be doing it to decoy us. If we get careless, they could catch us." Satisfied with all that he had heard, Max began to conclude the meeting as soon as three super soldiers filed in.

"Very well, all be watchful. Sergei will continue our covert communications. And my warriors will help you prepare for your departure. Travel safe."

Standing at attention as the Tetrarchy members got up, Maksim pointed to Tavi.

"Stay for a minute more. I have a multi-purpose assignment meant for you …."

Factual and fake collision stories swept like a tsunami through the media. They carried a lighter tone because all passengers had been rescued. A droller story even conjectured the cruise ship companies had deliberately caused it. The billion-dollar costs were fully insured and the publicity might garner bookings among extreme adventure thrill seekers. Further investigation traced the cause to software malfunction, and though nothing confirmed it, conspiracy theories hyped Cyberspace terrorism.

Jovita called a late morning mid-June meeting in her White House office to extend what the team had developed while on the cruise. She was already chatting with Buffy and Carter when Electra came in, asking why there were so many visitors today.

"Dean Corfu's holding a couple of media briefings. Sorry I forgot to let you know. But you're not late. We can show you what we're lining up. Have a seat and take a look."

Electra barely had time to comply before an alarm sounded, quickly followed by a worried-looking security guard.

"We've got to evacuate the White House. Warning sensors have detected a foreign substance. Please follow me."

Dean Corfu relished the power and status of his dual roles: Chief of Staff and PR Chief. And he had learned to like the President, even though he resented several of McTear's advisors. But on balance, working for him was better than working for Gardner.

Today's first briefing covering technology's impact on climate change had gone smoothly. Dean grabbed a diet soft drink and rehearsed his intro remarks while his people set up the room for the next one, which would highlight international implications of the President's gambit to deescalate chronic tensions between Islam and the West. He was pleased that several reporters of Middle East ethnicity clustered in front.

Among them was Omar Seif, one of Tavi's faithful executioners. His name described what he hid inside: a sword of religion that would always be used. An embassy official had given him several days ago a package containing instructions and an instrument known only to Tavi and the recipient. Omar had carefully used it to dispense a minute trace of its contents. Now he stood close to his target, waiting for Allah's command. It came as an alarm sounded five minutes into Corfu's comments.

Corfu shouted, "Don't panic. Follow me or the guards." Hustling behind Corfu, Omar used the confusion to dispense from his pen a deadly nerve toxin onto Corfu's clothes. Then he melted away so he would be unreachable if any evidence of Corfu's murder traced its way to him.

Muting the sound while watching the news that evening, Electra called Jovita. The new Chief of Staff's voice shook as much as the reporter's.

"I don't ever want to see a nerve gas killing again. It's gruesome. Agents are looking for any and all connections. Do you think we were targeted? Maybe the cruise ship and today is no coincidence."

"I simply don't know, but we have to put all this behind us. Just make sure security is tight whenever we meet. And let me know what the CIA finds out. There has to be some pattern they're not yet seeing. Call me when you're ready to reconvene."

Electra sat in the living room's somber stillness, relieved that Robin and the twins were visiting Zoe because their absence gave her time to focus, but she quit an hour later.

I'm losing this war of Cyber-hacking that's penetrated my and my allies' defenses. I'm not giving up, but I'm beat, so I'm going to bed. Perhaps the lightning brain will have something for me tomorrow.

Electra was asleep by the time Robin and the twins returned. They wanted to rouse her, but Robin knew better. She scooted them away before studying Electra in repose. Then she closed the bedroom door, knowing that Electra would greet her in the morning. That was a universal constant Robin always wanted to keep near, and she had no reason to think otherwise.

Electra always knows what to do, whether or not she has complete control of whatever's bothering her. Tomorrow I'll just listen to what she says and be as positive as possible. That's just one of the lessons she's taught me and I'm teaching the twins. And knowing her, she'd say that's a twin win. Well, it's time to find them and get them ready for bed and a new day… me too.

Chapter 26
August 2136

"Command Performance"

"Thanks for coming with me. You always ask good questions and are hard to fool." Electra held herself to a higher standard than even Buffy's but decided not to debate the compliment while Buffy was driving them to a platform company distribution center tour in the DC area.

"I'm happy you asked. Two heads are better than one for seeing through deceptions at command performances. How did Jovita set it up?"

"White House chief of staff gets special treatment, especially from PACs during an election year. Jovita told them she wants eyewitness reports from her platform construction team to judge how much good Big Data and platform companies actually do. How should we divvy up the interview?"

"Why don't you ask about time and cost efficiencies they get from automation and AI algorithms. They claim consumers get more and better choices delivered faster and cheaper. Carter can evaluate what they tell you."

"And what about you?"

"I'll ask about employee working conditions, which in most cases today aren't physically demanding. How much do you know about union struggles in the nineteenth and twentieth centuries to win decent working conditions?"

"That's so long ago. You can't compare conditions then with now."

"Did you ever read Upton Sinclair's *The Jungle*? It's a historically accurate, dramatic depiction of the brutal working conditions immigrants faced working at Chicago's stockyards early in the 20th century. It took decades of unionizing efforts to get the meatpackers to finally do the right thing. Workers today in all industries are the beneficiaries of the battles won by their predecessors. And hi-tech has removed most of the human labor."

"So, what are you getting at?"

"Psychological and social working conditions take center stage today. That's what I'll check out. I want to know more about how employees are adjusting to the new demands. I've seen firsthand in Hollywood how AI impacts creative types. The Creative Services Union wants them to join. They currently represent teachers as well as other skilled service providers. Maybe the government can have them handle civil service and post office jobs. I'll ask Carter to do its cost-benefit analysis."

"If you do, I'll make sure he knows you're kidding. He often takes what you say too literally." Electra stifled her reply because Buffy had just parked in the distribution center's lot. Fifteen minutes later, after going through visitor screening, they were seated across the desk in the spartan office of the center's manager, a clean-cut mid-thirties male named Mario whose no-nonsense manner projected competence. He diplomatically guided the conversation.

"I'm always pleased to show our facility to public or government representatives. Please tell me what you'd like to know before I walk you through our facility." Buffy went first.

"How do you manage to generate domestic jobs as you compete in today's global market?"

"We partner with the best value-added suppliers, no matter the continent, and manage a just-in-time supply chain that matches demand. As demand grows, so does the number of workers. And our proprietary computer algorithms control stock-picking, truck loading, and routing, which let customers track online for delivery date and time. We also equip our employees with all the tools they need to maximize output and minimize effort. Take a look at my laptop video and then ask more questions if you need further clarification." Buffy had only one request fifteen minutes later.

"Very professional, very thorough. Can you give me a link to it for my associates?"

"Will do. Now, what can I do for your partner?"

Electra asked, "You're providing safety-minded jobs that pay a living wage, but what about the psychological and social stress they create?" Mario rolled his shoulders to drain away tension before answering.

"It's felt in managers' offices as well as on the warehouse floor. Everyone has to be flexible and willing to learn new skills that enrich the job as well as the resume. But the company gives everyone the opportunity to move up if they work hard and hit targets. I'm a good example. I went from order puller to driver, and then to router. After that I took manager certification courses that qualified me for manager's assistant slot. And I've been hustling up the ladder ever since. If I can do it, others can too, but they have to be willing to reach for what they want, not sit back and wait to be handed a gift. Let me show you a couple of employee interview videos." Electra commented fifteen minutes later.

"I can understand why you have lots of happy employees. And the video did point out a couple of minor complaints, like last-minute work schedule shuffling, but on balance everyone seems pretty well adjusted to the new normal. Could I talk to some of the workers I see on the tour?"

"No can do. Their time is tightly monitored. But let's go walk the floor. Ask me any final questions when we come back."

Mario's script matched the state-of-the-art interior: environmentally spotless, brightly lighted, workers paired with robotic assistants gliding down electronically controlled aisles. When back in his office thirty minutes later, Buffy announced they were ready to leave.

"Thanks for all your time. You seem to be doing a good job balancing the demands of a competitive global market against the needs of modern workers."

"You're welcome, and I hope you now see that although we have to stay competitive, we structure our workplace to accommodate the employee, not pit them against one another like a survival of the fittest jungle. Please call me if you think of another question or two."

After leaving Mario's office, neither said anything until Buffy read a note tucked under the windshield wiper.

"The employee grapevine knows about us. We can meet some of the workers at a local restaurant if we call the number. How about it?"

"I'm ready for a snack. Let's go…"

Electra had just taken another sip of her Coke when two uniformed warehouse workers approached their booth in an uncrowded diner. Both looked youthfully fit; the fellow spoke first.

"Did you enjoy Mario's performance?" Electra spoke before Buffy could.

"Why do you say that? He seems genuinely interested in doing what's right." Now the female spoke.

"Don't mind Tommy's sense of humor. I'm Kiara, and we'll fill in around the edges if we can join you." Electra looked at Buffy, whose nod set Tommy next to her and Kiara across, next to Electra.

"In case you don't know, I'm Buffy and my partner's Electra. And like she said, Mario and the company seem to be doing OK by you. Nice working conditions, a decent salary, and a selection of career paths. Do you have to pay for your uniforms?"

The waitress took drink orders for the newcomers, during which time Electra ordered another plate of brownies. When she left, Kiara answered.

"No, we get a fresh one each week. Hey, we're not hear to badmouth Mario or the company, but please listen to what Tommy has to say. Many second-shift employees feel the same way." Tommy spoke matter-of-factly as soon as all eyes were on him.

"Don't think we're stupid just because we don't write computer apps. Most of us have college degrees or certifications, and the company reimburses us for additional training. But not many of us have the background to qualify for one of a shrinking number of computer assistant jobs. And we're constantly being monitored when doing our mindless work. We strap on wrist monitors and other wearables that track our location and productivity. And we dance to the tune of the robots, not vice-versa. Those damn bots know what to pull next from where, so all we do is follow them around in a windowless space for the entire shift. And we have to ask its permission for a potty break. Pretty demeaning, wouldn't you say?" Not waiting for an answer, Kiara picked up where Tommy left off.

"Mario's much better than the previous manager who offered to trade one of the newer employees a better weekly schedule for sack time, but he's the one that got sacked. And Mario holds once-a-month open meetings for workers to voice complaints. He's even convinced his boss to cut back daily quotas because that reduces turnover costs. The company still makes plenty of money." Kiara stopped talking because the waitress returned. An uncomfortable silence followed, broken only by the muffled sounds of brownies being chewed. That gave Electra a chance to ask,

"What do you know about fully automated fulfillment centers?" Kiara swallowed before answering.

"They're not as easy to run as fully automated factories, but we know they're coming as robots get smarter. We're an endangered species unless industry or government protects us. And if there are no human workers, who's going to buy what's being shipped? Maybe it's time for unions to make a comeback and stick up for AI-Age workers." Electra looked at her partner, hoping she would say the right words, but Buffy startled everyone by first slamming her glass.

"I've heard enough. President McTear's socioeconomic platform talks about programs that balance technology against people's needs. I think I know what we can do." Tommy looked at his watch.

"We gotta go. Our shift starts in a half-hour, and we can't hide from the monitors if we're late."

Buffy said, "You two go. We'll wait until Electra finishes the brownies. Thanks for sharing your opinions."

Electra surfed the Web that evening for facts concerning working conditions at the other end of the skills spectrum: Big Data companies that write apps and provide analysis. Then she hacked into encrypted company directories, looking for Emails or documents that could hint at unethical practices. By midnight she had ferreted out enough additional information she would add to what she had learned on the tour.

Like every industry, there are always some bad actors. Some of the Big Data companies still discriminate when hiring, maintaining a Good Ole Boy network. And like some of the platform companies, they don't spread more of the income to those at the lower end of the pay scale, even to those who are hustling to move up the ladder by using personal time for professional education. But my report to Jovita will be a balanced assessment that gives most companies a passing grade. I'll write it tomorrow after I let my brain sleep on what it's learned.

Waking early, Electra needed only ninety minutes to transcribe the report her brain had already completed. Then she rewarded herself by running in the rain on an unseasonably cool mid-August Saturday.

My runner's rain suit has come in handy all summer. It's been wetter and cooler than usual. The trees must sense an early autumn because the leaves are starting to turn, and that always reminds me of grade school's new-year start… the excitement of seeing classmates as well as the uncertainty surrounding a new teacher and topics. The events are etched so deeply in my brain that whenever they pop in, I can see and feel them. I think Mother's poem – September Song – captures the emotion. It too is etched in my brain.

I shall always remember the Song of September,
As calendar months parade by.
Heard in the soft soothing voice of my Father,
And with it my brief poignant sigh.

Written by dervishes whirling away,
We're like wind-blown leaves in a storm.
Though the fury has past their impact will last,
Though now in a gentler form.

A cascading connection of watershed marks,
That sketch what I look like today.
Some happy some sad most make my heart glad,
Time's flow will not sweep them away.

And though your September is different from mine,
Its tune resonates just as true.
So listen for theme song that whispers your name,
As it once again echoes anew.

Electra's chiming cell phone called her back to right now. She huddled under a tree to answer a call from Pastor Tucton.

"Good morning Electra, I hope I'm not calling too early, but the students you sometimes tutor have a special request. May I describe what they'd like?"

"Please do. They're a sharp group."

"Well, they want to get a head start on an autumn science project that's supposed to cover some aspect of alien life forms and the Anthropocene Epoch. I can't give you any more details because I don't understand what they're talking about, but if you do, maybe you can give them some pointers."

"I'll give it a try. Is Thursday at 3 p.m. still the tutoring hour?"

"It is. I'll tell them to be prompt. And thanks for donating your time. See you—" Interrupting herself, the pastor changed topics.

"By the way, guess what? We received an anonymous donation from a charitable trust. It's enough to do some exterior maintenance, and I'm pinching off enough to get some therapy for Mrs. Whooten. Just goes to show there's a lot of good that gets done by people who know what's right. Just like you helping our eager students. Anyway, I'll listen for a little while next Thursday. Bye."

As Electra dashed away, the pastor's words warmed her more than the exercise.

It'll be fun talking about a topic I can recite from memory. And I'm so happy my donation is going to what I wanted. I set up the trust to keep me in the shadows while I put my money to work where it'll do some good. It's time I start paying forward, no strings attached, and no one but the trust administrator knows. And when I'm gone, he'll be executor of my estate. And it just dawned on me. If I'm clever enough, Pope's final verse fits me to a T:

> *Thus let me live, unseen, unknown;*
> *Thus unlamented let me dye;*
> *Steal from the world, and not a stone*
> *Tell where I lye.*

I'm not planning to steal away anytime soon, but when I do, that's how I would like to exit. By the time she reached home, she knew how to schedule the coming week's activities.

Electra decided not to tell Robin about her run, instead keeping occupied all day helping her do chores, run errands, and keep the twins occupied. She went to bed feeling good but jerked awake in the middle of the night, a dreadful feeling about death panicking her.

My brain subconsciously shifted to a bad state. It's gotta be related to Pope's last verse and the thought of dying. Everyone thinks about death occasionally and reacts differently. Old people are usually indifferent, but thousands of younger people sometimes must want to die... the most committed commit suicide, all because of their brain state. I must be careful as I continue to modify my Brain Probe. If I can map brain states at a fine enough level of granularity, not only can I read people's thoughts but I can also control what they think and do. OK, now I better think about something good and let my brain take me to a better state.

She primed herself by thinking about the anthropic principle, which she had memorized long ago.

It's a philosophical consideration that all observations of the Universe must be compatible with human consciousness. As a result, people are predisposed to anthropomorphize other organisms, even fictional gods, to look like humans. How arrogant we are! Do I come across that way? Let me think...

Soon she became self-absorbed, eventually drifting into sleep.

Electra borrowed only two hours from other projects to handwrite notes on Wednesday that she would give to her audience tomorrow. She made an extra copy for herself and thought about how best to say them, then practiced her delivery before shifting mental gears.

She practiced one more time as she walked to the church, enjoying the autumnal fragrance released by the cool dampness. When she came into the room, she noticed Pastor Tucton in the background. Her audience was already sitting around a table, so she gave the notes to one of the girls and began speaking while standing at the head.

"I'm going to tell you enough to pique your interest and point you in the right direction. Then it's your job to turn what I give you into what you want. And before I start, I want to emphasize that the Greeks contemplated more than 2600 years ago the existence of alien beings, but civilizations back then had neither the experience nor the technology to characterize an Anthropocene Epoch. I also want you to realize that many subordinate issues are still being debated. You'll need to research them to draw your own conclusion. Yours, not mine, are what's most important, and at your age remember to pose questions that ask why not? rather than why? The future belongs to you. Make it all it can be by reaching for greatness." Commanding rapt attention, Electra paused for a silent segue before continuing.

"Let's calibrate our timescale. The Universe is 13.6 billion years old, Earth 4.6 billion, cellular life 2.1 billion. The Cambrian explosion – that's when the major animal phyla first appeared – happened 535 million years ago, and the dinosaur mass extinction occurred 65 million. Who can state its likely cause?"

One of the boys said,

"I saw a neat cartoon that's caption stated the real reason why dinosaurs are extinct. A group of dinos in the foreground are smoking cigarettes while in the background you can see a big meteor plunging into the Earth."

Electra said, "Very clever, but I wouldn't toss a coin to decide which to pick. But whatever the cause, it did level the playing field for mammals. Homo sapiens – that's us – appeared about 250 thousand years ago and gradually migrated to all continents. Here's an important date, the beginning of the Holocene Epoch, eleven thousand years ago. It marks the end of the last Ice Age. And we recently entered the Anthropocene Epoch, loosely defined to be that period for which humans impact geology, climate, and ecosystems. The debate regarding how much impact man actually has continues. Some of the best studies conclude humans cause about half of climate change and even more of biodiversity reduction. As part of your project, why not research how humans cause this and what it might lead to, and what steps civilization can take to manage it? Think about it because you can connect your ideas to alien life forms." Electra paused while flipping to another page of notes, but one of the students asked about this year's unusual weather.

"Six months ago Australia had record heat, high winds, and no rain. All that led to raging fires. And look at our DC summer. It's been cool and rainy. The guy reporting the weather blames it all on climate change. What do you think?"

"I think it's good that you follow current events, and the Australian catastrophe you mention provides a point I'd like to make. Brush fires have many causes; global warming and climate-change blame are gross oversimplifications. Australia has a history of fires and droughts dating back much further than climate-change conjectures. Perhaps the media and special interest groups are picking out what they want for sound-bites supporting their agendas. Think about it. And there's more I'd like to say.

"You can't confirm cause and effect based on one year's observations, especially when looking at geological time periods. Anecdotal evidence does seem to say there's growing variability due to climate change. Why don't you search the Web for info? I'm sure you'll find some to support or deny the claim. Review and draw your own conclusion."

The audience liked the recommendation and was ready for Electra to tell them about a topic everyone found thrilling. Electra's tone heightened the excitement.

"Talking about alien life forms can take us into the realm of science fiction, and even if I stick to the facts the possibilities capture

341

the imagination. A great starting point is the question stated in the 1950's Enrico Fermi paradox, 'Where are they?' He and his colleagues listed three reasons why there's no evidence of extraterrestrial life; life never existed anywhere in the entire Universe but on Earth, or it's not advanced enough to send signals, or it did and advanced to a superior level but then went extinct. Think carefully about the last reason. Could man cause his own extinction? You might want to draw your own conclusion you can put in your report, but let's move on to the Drake Equation.

"It's a probabilistic argument stated in 1961 by professor Frank Drake. It estimates the number of planets in the Universe that might be able to support human life. His equation uses seven parameters to compute the number, and of course most of the parameters are merely subjective guesses, but it's logical and thought-provoking and a basis for SETI. Research it further, but who can tell me what SETI is?"

One of the girls said, "It's an acronym for the 'Search for Extraterrestrial Intelligence' project that links lots of computers to analyze radio telescope data to find signals beamed to Earth. Drake's equation estimates there could be millions of civilizations out there that are advanced enough to send them."

"Very good. Let's tie this into the Kardashev Scale, which measures a civilization's technological progress. There are five types of civilizations determined by how much energy they can harvest, all designated by Roman numerals. Type I harnesses its planet, Type II its star, Type III its galaxy, Type IV the entire Universe, and Type V parallel Universes. Human civilization has yet to reach Type I. You should research more about the Kardashev Scale. And the deeper you dig the more fantastic the findings." Electra paused because her audience had reached its limit of understanding.

"And that's all I want to say about aliens and the Anthropocene Epoch. You build on it as you think best. And let me add a final comment. So far, we've been considering life forms that could evolve from a DNA similar to ours, which is a carbon-based substrate. But there might be other elements from which life could emerge, given the right conditions. In fact, here's the mission statement for the original Star Trek series –

'These are the voyages of the starship Enterprise. Its continuing mission: to explore strange new worlds, to seek out new life and new civilizations, to boldly go where no one has gone before.'

Forget about the split infinitive. Grammarians today say it's OK. And we're done, so you can boldly be on your way."

Pastor Tucton came to the table as the students filed out.

"You're an excellent speaker, able to command the listener's attention. Your gestures and stage presence draw them in, and you're photogenic too. I made a video of your talk. Think about posting it somewhere for eager learners."

"Thanks for the compliment. Maybe there's another market for what I have to say. But no matter, please let me know when there's another tutoring topic this audience would like me to cover."

Electra had only a day to enjoy the satisfaction of her commanding performance. Jovita's Saturday morning phone call brought her run and happy thoughts to a halt.

"We've got a big problem. I've been hacked and maybe you have too. Lots of documents have been leaked, thanks to this morning's open letter posted on the Internet. No names mentioned, but some of the docs are yours, and they've been edited to make Angus look bad. He told me to do damage control ASAP. Can you come to my office this morning?"

"Do I have a choice?" Electra heard only a gasp, so she backtracked.

"I'm sorry. I was only kidding. Of course, I'll be there. But I want to read the letters and plan an approach before we meet. I'll be there at 1 p.m. Don't invite anyone else." Jovita recovered enough to joke back,

"Do I have a choice? No way, you're it. See ya soon."

Sensing Electra's growing focus on a problem she didn't want to discuss, Robin didn't ask why she bolted down a bowl of cold cereal before a quick shower and change of plans. Robin would have to take the twins shopping by herself.

While Robin and the twins were out, Electra surfed the Net to read the letter and leaks, able to piece together only a partial story that she would recite to Jovita. She left soon after Robin returned, saying she wouldn't be home for dinner.

Jovita's relieved smile greeted Electra when she entered the office. Neither wasted any time. Jovita already had a Coke placed on the table. Electra planned to lead the discussion but waited for Jovita to make the offer. Electra started talking five minutes later.

"The letter's a broadside attack on Angus's platform, and some of the leaked documents could only have been hacked from my directories. There has to be more than one intruder, and I don't know who they are. But no matter. What we have to do is counter the misinformation by talking directly to voters via media or in person. It'll be your call and I don't want to overstep my position, but how about I tell you my plan? Then we can discuss it and you can make whatever adjustments you want. Then it's up to you to get Angus to sign off."

"You can step wherever you want. Go on."

"Here's the deal. You talk to the media first. Tell them you'll schedule follow-up interviews and talks that'll be direct to voters. Schedule me to lead off the first media interview that'll give an overview of what's to follow. All subsequent interviews and voter talks must come from Angus. I'll write notes and scripts for whatever Angus needs. We'll have to convince the voters that Angus isn't concealing a Jared or Guardian Party agenda that bucks what's right. And he has to earn voter confidence that he can be their 'Bridge President.' So if this sounds good, let's work the rest of the day mapping out a speaking schedule and discussion guides. That'll give you everything you need to corral media time and me everything I need to start spinning the words. And I plan to give a command performance. All you have to do is make sure Angus does too."

The White House press corps made quick work of setting up a speaking schedule that Jovita gave them. Although Angus liked it too, he and Jovita worried that Electra might become overloaded.

Jovita felt better after talking to Electra, who had more to say after the call, but only to herself.

Weaving together hi-tech, economics, domestic socio-politics, and a workable realpolitik world order is what I've been working on from the shadows ever since the chopper crash nearly thirty years ago. My place now is on the periphery. And on Wednesday, Angus and the media will see how well I can carry this off. After all, Alisha used to say if you've got the goods, it's OK strut your stuff. Well, I've got the goods, but I don't need to strut. I want to set the stage for Angus so he can deliver what the voters want to hear. I have two days until my network interview. I better take a break to keep my obsessive-compulsive behavior under control. I think I'll shoot pool at a sensual pleasures café tonight. I've earned that and a brownie or two. And tomorrow I'll plug back into family life. I'm lucky Robin understands enough about me so I have some breathing room, but by this time she should, and that's all to the good.

Robin noticed that Electra had resumed a situation normal lifestyle but didn't probe for what had caused the brief excursion; she knew Electra would tell her. Wednesday afternoon was the right time when Electra told her that Jovita would be picking her up.

"Please do me a favor by watching the 7 p.m. news tonight. Flip the channels until you see me being interviewed. And when I get home, you need to give me an unbiased review of my performance."

"Aha, that's why you withdrew into your fortress of solitude. Well, you can count on me to be your toughest critic. Go do your thing."

Jovita insisted that she stay at the network studio for the live interview. Her intentions stirred Electra's childhood memories of helping Robin at a piano recital, but Electra had already put on her game face. Her brain had shifted to a state that made her calm and focused. When the "On Air" sign flashed, the interviewer, now comfortably seated across the table, began to talk.

"We are joined tonight by one of President McTear's platform developers, Electra Kittner, who, after a spate of fakes news and leaks and misinformation, has the unenviable task of reclarifying what the President stands for. Ms. Kittner's diverse background spans academics to sports to entertainment and finally to politics.

Good evening, Electra. Perhaps you could divulge some of your background that qualifies you to speak for the President."

Electra's smile and measured tempo amplified what she said.

Why yes, and good evening. Thank you for inviting me to speak on behalf of President McTear. I'm here to clear up any misconceptions about his overarching political principles. As for me, I've earned advanced degrees while teaching and conducting scientific research at several renowned universities. I also balanced that and a Co-NFL career that led me to Hollywood and a run for a Texas Congressional seat. Though I lost the election, I learned from my experiences a solid understanding of what people need and how they feel as they live their lives, and through my intellect I learned how politics is supposed to help us live the lives we want. If I may, let me connect this to my studies in neuroscience."

"By all means, please do so."

"Today, neuroscience tells us that man is a social animal, influenced fifty-fifty by nature and nurture. And the great philosopher Aristotle was the first to state that man is a political animal. And in that Golden Age, the political and the social were synonymous because the Greeks had chosen the best of the nine forms of government – a true democracy in which the many rule for the good of all. But Greece lost its way and fell. Other civilizations came and went, but by the 13th century Saint Thomas Aquinus taught that of the three types of law – Eternal, Natural, and Human – Human law that adjudicates crime and punishment is best for governments and politics if it balances individual and public interest when considering Aristotelian virtues, of which truth and justice are paramount. Now fast-forward to the Enlightenment. The great political thinkers extended the best of the past to proclaim that the politics of government must make freedom and liberty plus equality and democracy top priorities." Electra paused for the interviewer to gather his thoughts for the next question.

"Yes, that takes us to 1776, but take us from there to where the President is today."

"The path winds from the Enlightenment's classical Liberalism through America's early 20th century progressive Liberalism and then to Neoliberalism's beginning in the 1950s, and then to Neoconservatism starting in the 1980s. But starting about 2020, America realized it was putting too much of a dollar value on human accomplishment. People had become objectified, social institutions and cultural practices had been converted into markets. America had paid too much attention to Adam Smith's *Wealth of Nations* and not enough to his *Theory of Moral Sentiment*. So, what did America do? It moved by fits and starts towards a kinder, more social-minded government and politics that respected human rights and dignity. But the trajectory of progress is never linear. Late in the 21st century, T-Plague and Middle East terrorism caused people to become fearful and distrustful, and governments to become harsh and intolerant. But America defeated its enemies and found a way forward.

"But we're not all the way back. There's more we must do, and that's why President McTear wants to be our bridge president, taking us from today to a future holding great promise if we take the right steps. President McTear will do this by bridging the divide between political parties, rich and poor, young and old, and white and black or brown as we move from today to new world sociopolitical and economic orders. His programs will harness the power of our people and their cultural and technical creativity, all the while respecting human dignity and encouraging diversity." Electra paused again for the interviewer, who this time said,

"That's a very tall order. In the time remaining, let me ask you some questions that will draw out details...." Electra's final comment twenty minutes later helped conclude the show.

"I hope that by now everyone listening has a better understanding of what President McTear stands for and what he would like to accomplish. There's a series of scheduled interviews and talks that will explore more of his economic, domestic, and international programs. I hope everyone watches, because America needs well-informed voters who can make the right choice."

"Thank you, Ms. Kittner. You have been most articulate..."

Jovita had nothing but a relieved smile and compliments when Electra walked to her afterwards.

"Gads, you carried that off like a pro. I'm certain Angus will be pleased when he hears analyst opinions. You'll get good grades from the critics. Let's celebrate by getting something to eat."

"Thanks for the offer, but I should go home. My best critic is waiting."

"OK, but let's celebrate your performance tomorrow. You've earned more than a lunch, but there'll be more come." As they walked away making plans, Electra kept the best thoughts to herself.

No matter what the media or Angus says, there's always more to do, so I better remember to enjoy the process, not some ephemeral prize waiting at the always-receding end. And right now, Robin's critique is all I want.

Though she stayed on the sofa when Electra entered the living room, Robin's voice was as welcoming as the Coke, lighted candle, and plate of cookies awaiting on the coffee table.

"My favorite wordsmith has returned. Please sit and spin some more."

Their conversation lasted late into the night.

Chapter 27
October 2136

"The People's Choice"

Buffy and Carter would have agreed to host Jovita's platform team follow-up lunch meeting the Friday after Electra's interview even if she hadn't volunteered to order in pizza. They could accomplish more in less time by avoiding the increasing commotion at the White House due to the election being only three weeks away.

Though last to arrive, Electra timed it perfectly. She entered the conference room only a minute or two after food and drink, joking that the applause was for the pepperoni, not last night's performance. Carter split the difference.

"You can never go wrong with pepperoni, and we can never go wrong letting you speak for us. Great job, all the media commentaries gave you high marks. You've made it that much easier for Buffy and me to scope out notes for the next interview. And that's why we're here." Jovita picked up where Carter left off.

"Only one live media interview remaining, Wednesday October 31. That gives us two weeks to fine tune what you want Angus to say, so the pressure's off to get it done today. But it's always better to be proactive, so why don't you grind through as much as you can this afternoon. Buffy can be the point person sending the copy to me." Buffy's nod said yes.

"Carter and I have the socioeconomic programs covered. All Electra needs to do is add the international programs and we're done. Then it's up to Jovita and her PR people to coach Angus. Let's get started after the pizza's gone."

Jovita left an hour later, pleased with the progress she saw. As the afternoon ticked by, Carter said he'd highlight the differences between his programs and those of the opponents; Buffy would summarize how hers would defang corporatocracy caused by the big business collaborators: "Big Data, Big Gun, Big Bank, Big Health, and Big Energy." By 6 p.m., Carter had made hard as well as electronic copies of all first drafts for the team to edit and return to Buffy by Monday, after which she and Carter would make revisions and distribute final copies no later than Wednesday.

Electra spent all day Saturday reviewing and editing, finishing in time to have supper with Robin and the twins. Clara and Marie, now four years old, mature for their age and each other's shadow, dominated the conversation. Neither held back when Electra asked how they liked reading and writing and arithmetic.

"Momma says we need to be good at all three, and she finds lots of computer games for us to play. I'm better at arithmetic, but Clara's better at reading and writing. And she plays the piano better, but I'm getting good too. We used to play learning games with Carlton, but he's no fun anymore." Robin came to his defense.

"Well, he's eight. Maybe he doesn't want to play with girls too much younger. Thanks to Zoe, he's ahead of most kids his age, and I think he's recovered from his disappointing performance at the transhuman games. He seems like a model child to me." Electra made an offer the twins couldn't refuse.

"Well, I'm lots of fun to play with. How about the three of us play some computer games after helping your Mom clear the table?" The first one to get all their dishes off gets to choose the first game." Robin declared a tie.

Electra had a remarkably pressure-free following week. There were no open letters or fake news reports, and she detected no hacking into her encrypted files. Neither Jovita nor Pastor Tucton made additional requests, so Electra spent several days at her Pequot Reservation Lab, devoting full attention to biotech and AI R&D. For months she had been reviewing and comparing state-of-the-art approaches versus hers, looking for corrections to what she was doing wrong or components she may have overlooked, all in preparation for getting guidance from her Dream Team. She had just completed a summary that she would soon discuss with the team's singular member, Indira.

My cloning techniques are even better than those of the Chinese. I expect to achieve in vitro full-term survival rates for human fetuses that at least match what I'm getting for other animals. Perhaps Indira can improve them even further. Either way, I plan to clone human embryos next year. And I know how to tweak my Brain Probe to make it even more versatile.

But my DNA editing techniques for enhanced characteristics need refinement. The number of gene interactions for improving intelligence, strength, personality, or longevity is beyond my carbon-based substrate limit. However, Indira's silicon-based substrate handles enormous numbers better, and since neuroscience is a matter of decomposition and complexity, my hope is that she can create superior beings without crossing ethical redlines.

And we have a contingency plan if we fail. My AI apps are better than any on the market, and Indira's are better than mine. So, we'll take hers and put them into the most advanced smart weapons and transhuman devices we can borrow from our competition and voila, we have superior beings – aka cyborgs. Not next year, but sooner than the world would expect, so we let no one know, which is situation normal for me.

Electra paid a courtesy visit to Chief Strongarm and Dr. Holbrook by taking them out to lunch. She had no active Native American Indian projects, so she let the Chief's slow but deliberate baritone voice guide the conversation. As they were about to leave, he said,

"I am disappointed I have made so little headway getting the National Tribal Council to enact more of what you have set in motion. It is conceivable we could forge a nation in a nation. Our tribes have much in common, but organizing 573, of which 229 are in Alaska, is a bigger task than the one facing the United Nations. After all, it has only 193 members. And consider America's struggles getting thirteen colonies to sign a Declaration of Independence.

Still, I have not been as diligent as I must." Electra tried to soften the self-criticism.

"I empathize with you. Look at America's political landscape. You might say the country has three tribes – Republican, Democratic, and Guardian – and they often struggle to reach enough of a consensus to pass legislation. Have you been following the run-up to the presidential election?"

"Very little, but I detect much consternation about leaks and fake news. Let us ask the doctor for her diagnosis."

"Chief Strongarm and I aren't good candidates for a Gallup poll because we pay more attention to tribal events than national. But lately, the little I've heard seems to say good things about the current President. It would be nice if this time the people vote him in rather than have another catastrophe catapult him into the Oval Office for the third time. I wish him luck." Having the good sense not to debate politics with her Pequot friends, Electra said,

"I'm sure whoever wins wants to stay on good terms with you because according to Hud, you give America a good deal on rare earths." The Chief's hint of a smile complemented his final comment.

"Yes, it is our civic duty to do all we can to help the White Man, for what goes around will be even better this time. Thank you for lunch; it is time we go."

Electra devoted full attention to family life that weekend. Saturday morning she and the twins piled into Robin's van. Robin explained the first stop while driving.

"Today is a special day for Clara and Marie. The pediatrician is implanting their very first RFID chip. Clara, tell your godmother what RFID is?" A pert voice from the middle row said,

"It aconym fo wadio fwequency ID." Marie added,

"We can talk to our tablets and cell phones." Electra's question was directed at Robin.

"So, you're getting them cell phones? Do you think they're old enough?"

"Zoe and I decided they're ready for a tiny step towards computerizing human-to-machine communications for them. All they have to do is keep their cell phone near their tablet computer. Communication is then wireless from phone or tablet to earpiece. And as they get older, we'll get additional implants. How's that?"

"You surprise me, but I guess Zoe's helped you overcome some of your technophobia. I think you're doing the right thing. And having the pediatrician do the procedure is smart. The ped will eliminate any risk of infection as well as load their chips with medical data. One of the physician assistants can then train the twins and you." Robin chirped happily,

"You and Zoe always know cutting edge concepts. And we'll celebrate afterwards by having lunch at McDonald's. It's always coming out with new marketing gimmicks the twins like. Some fast-food chains might be more upscale, but I like McDonald's best because it's always reliable." Robin slowed to park, so Electra ended the conversation.

"And I know from experimenting that it has the best French fries and Coke. I'll do another taste test today."

The timing of Electra's change of pace weekend couldn't have been better. Instead of a chore, Electra found the very first words of Jovita's Monday morning phone call a call to action.

"We've got big problems. Have you been watching the news?"

"I took a break from it this weekend. What's happening?"

"Two catastrophes, not related but both leaked and radioactive. We found out about the environmental disaster late last night. The retrofitted Dresden nuclear reactor near Chicago suffered a meltdown. Angus summoned an emergency team to contain it and has the FBI fully engaged. The political disaster hit this morning. Someone's leaking more fake documents about our platform along with fake videos of Angus talking about them. The CIA and Cyber Security are looking for political hackers." Jovita paused to calm her nerves, leaving Electra room to talk.

"I'm sure you and Angus are fully loaded. What can I do to pitch in?"

"Angus is too busy to prepare for his Wednesday interview. Could you be his substitute? You know the programs better than anyone, and I'll send you what I've roughed out for talking points."

"I'll build on that, and I'll also listen to what the media is spinning. I'm sure there'll be some opinions linking them to Angus, and unless you want to deflect them in what you or the PR people say, I'll counter them Wednesday."

"Do it all, please. Do you want me to drive you to the studio?"

"I know the time and the way. I'll be OK. Let's talk again on Thursday." After Jovita disconnected, Electra told herself what to expect during the next two days.

Robin will be at work, taking the twins with her. That gives me all the space I need to work at home in my fortress of solitude. And I don't need to rely on anyone but myself. This will be fun... just remember to throttle back my obsessive-compulsive tendencies.

Once again, Electra's professional manner showed in her posture Wednesday evening as she sat across from the same interviewer as before.

"I'm here tonight with Ms. Electra Kittner, a last-minute substitute for President McTear, who for obvious reasons cannot join us. Her assignment is to give us as much detail as possible for the President's programs, and unlike his two opponents, often referred to as Tweedledum and Tweedledee, President McTear's 'bridge president' positioning continues gaining traction with voters. Still, there's much skepticism, which explains in part why the margin of error makes the outcome too close to call." The interviewer paused as he now turned from the camera to Electra.

"Welcome back, Electra. Reviewers and voters liked what you said and how you said it last time. Now you have an opportunity to extend your comments." Please outline what you'll say." Electra seized the opportunity, continuing her winning style.

"Thank you, and let me say it's a privilege to be here. I'll do my best to explain what our President has in mind, even though I am not privy to all the details. I would like to address domestic economic and sociopolitical programs first, followed by those for the international stage. Of course, they're interrelated and impacted by accelerating globalization, technological, and environmental issues, but you'll see President McTear has definite programs that are win-win. But before I do, I would like to refute the negative criticism directed at the President regarding Monday's episodes. May I?"

"Yes, of course. I'm certain the public would like to hear."

"We've been able to track the documents and videos posted on the Internet, and the trail leads to Guardian Party campaigners, who are accusing President McTear of pirating their candidate's programs. But the facts speak otherwise. Careful decomposition of the videos reveal they are deepfake. And unbiased analysts agree President McTear's programs have many new features that improve what the late Jared Gardner was promoting. Let me turn next to the nuclear reactor core meltdown.

"There is no evidence that hackers tried to compromise Dresden's control network. And besides, the core failed because of metal fatigue. Computer controlled emergency shutdown procedures known as scram worked correctly, helping to contain the radiation. By the way, this unfortunate excursion heightens the importance of the President's thermonuclear reactor program." Electra paused for the interviewer but he made no comment, so Electra shifted to platform details.

"Let me flesh out some of the President's economic programs that harness America's resources and creativity, but please remember that Capitalism and Free Markets are too complex for government to plan completely. Instead, programs need steadying regulation when exuberance leads to extremes in the business cycle. His infrastructure programs create jobs in the short run. Note again his funding for thermonuclear reactors, which will drive down the cost of electricity longer-term. And his incentive-driven programs for AI and genetic engineering will pay big dividends. Finally, I believe that a close reading of what the President's programs promote will reveal an emphasis on stakeholder capitalism, which broadens consideration to all constituencies." Electra waited for the interviewer but he merely nodded, so she continued.

"Let's turn to domestic sociopolitical issues. Job maintenance and growth are key drivers, and the President's retraining and education programs will help workers qualify for higher-skilled jobs and guide students through an academic career meant to equip them in globally competitive academic or business arenas. His programs also offer incentives for schools and businesses to broaden participation and expand diversity, all leading to income inequality reduction.

There are also options for expanding voluntary socialism for the wealthy by redirecting consumption from the personal to the social. These add to universal basic income and wealth tax initiatives." This time, the interviewer filled in Electra's pause.

"You've put a lot on the table. Why don't you cover international politics before I start asking questions?"

"Very well. I think all Americans will agree that we live in a world that doesn't respect human dignity or rights as much as it should. That's why the President, the Military, and the National Security agencies know how to apply the best practices of Machiavelli, Sun Tzu, and von Clausewitz when dealing with China, Russia, and Isilabad. Our leaders know how to exercise the four kinds of power – Economic, Military, Cyber, and Soft. They know China's intentions to overtake us economically and technologically, Russia's to supplant our weaponry and disrupt international finances, and Isilabad's to continue thwarting Modernity. We must use our power judiciously, not bluntly, and by so doing reduce the risk of a shooting war. Unfortunately, we are already in a shadow war contested in Cyberspace. Our adversaries are ruthless when compared to America because the risks are asymmetric, but we counter by knowing their strengths and weaknesses, exercising statesmanship and leadership, and extending our defensive and offensive capabilities, which we will use when redlines are crossed. Actions have consequences." Electra stopped talking, leaning back just enough to signal the interviewer.

"There must be lots of programs and details. Let's delve deeper in the time remaining..." The interviewer ended his line of questioning twenty minutes later.

"You've acquitted yourself nicely. Would you like to add a closing remark."

"Yes, thank you. I would like to offer a promising philosophical codicil. Every program comes with a cost, but our President equates them to the price of protecting and improving our culture and civilization.

He has set clear, multi-year goals that address the short term and are mindful of longer-term environmental issues. And he strives for government efficiency through inclusivity and decentralization.

He will elaborate further after he and his advisors have defused the current crisis."

"Thank you, Ms. Kittner. And my thanks to our viewers."

Most of the Thursday morning media stories Electra watched agreed that her performance had hit all the right notes. She half-expected Jovita to give her a congratulatory call, but it came instead from Carter.

"I just spoke to Jovita. She's willing to bet that Angus will win, and she asked me to call."

"Do you think last night will impact what the polls will say? No matter what, the pressure's off you and me. The rest is up to Angus and Jovita."

"Actually, the pressure's still on, and Jovita wanted me to call because she's afraid she's exceeded her quota of requests. She wants you to write his acceptance speech. Angus can't break from the meltdown crisis to write it himself, and you're our best wordsmith. He's negotiating with Russia and China for cleanup assistance while assuring them we aren't going to blame them for causing it via Cyberterrorism. He knows the cause, but the public might think he's hiding the truth. Can you handle that?"

"No problem. Why's the pressure still on you?"

"If he wins, he wants to calm public concerns about national safety by immediately addressing foreign affairs. He's tasked me, and I'm asking you, to please help me nail down a short-term international agenda. You have more ideas than Buffy and me combined."

"How do you know that? I might be nothing but smoke and mirrors." Carter paused before answering.

"Only a smoke ring now and then, and never a mirror. You never let anyone know what goes on inside that black box brain of yours, and I don't want to. I just want some of the output."

"How about this? Give me a day to rough out what we need. Then I'll work with you and Buffy at your office over the weekend. You can then give Jovita the speech and agenda first thing Monday."

"That'll work. I'll tell Jovita. See you Saturday at nine, a.m., not p.m. Bye."

Electra put her brain on automatic as she took her morning run, showering and eating a typical breakfast afterwards before immersing herself in this latest challenge.

I'll warm up by knocking out a victory speech. And then I'll do the global agenda. First to chronic adversaries – China, Russia, and Isilabad – to work on short-term problems. And then to the longer-term opportunities – Africa and India. I'll be pleasantly surprised if Carter and Buffy can add to my list. But even if they can't, I'll let them tweak all they want, as long as they supply me with pizza and Coke. And some dark chocolate too.

Electra alerted Robin as soon as she came home to a change in weekend plans. Robin's frown matched her words.

"I knew this would happen. It's your damn ratchet principle at work. You did too good of a job last night, but you always do. The twins and I will keep busy and out of your way. All I ask is that you watch with me the election returns when they roll in Tuesday evening."

"That's an offer I can't refuse..."

The twins had been asleep for four hours by the time analysts declared at 1 a.m. the winner. Both Electra, curled up on the living room sofa, and Robin, sitting attentively in a nearby chair, were peering intently at the TV monitor when Robin asked,

"It looks like the party's about to start. Are you sure you'd rather be here than at election headquarters? You played a big role getting Angus elected."

"Home's is the best place for me... I only want to be on Washington's periphery."

"You know what you wrote, but now we'll hear how well Angus can read your words." Robin stopped talking as Angus began.

"Hello to all here tonight, and to all hearing my words. I have received generous congratulations from my worthy opponents and applause from those gathered, all as a tribute to my victory. But that is not what matters, or what is at stake tonight. What matters is a victory for you, the American people, and our way of life, a victory that must be renewed each day by the men and women elected to represent us at all levels of government. Yes, in God We Trust, but we also place our trust in their hands and who, like me and like you, are merely mortal.

"America today is in a post-heroic age where presidential greatness leading an exceptional nation on the world stage to ever-increasing prosperity and compassion has been dismissed. Sociopolitical analysts and historians alike have written that cynicism of government and big business, reassessment of our founding fathers, and revision to how and what America has accomplished have all denigrated the American experiment. Our nation is not, nor ever has been perfect, but it is unfair to judge many of our nation's past actions by today's standards. We are a more intelligent, more empathetic America than ever, and I salute the greatness our nation has achieved in the past and present and is reaching for tomorrow. I salute you, the people, those from the past who sacrificed, those doing so today, and those of succeeding generations for whom I am tonight not the victor, but rather the custodian that you have chosen for them.

"I do not make, nor have I ever made, claims about personal greatness or omniscience. I believe those who voted for me did so because the actions I have taken during my career serving the nation show that I place my country above myself, and my ethics above expediency. I only ask that you judge me going forward by how well what I do fits our collective mission and how well it achieves our goals.

"I am merely one link in the presidential chain that will endure as long as America does, and I pledge to make my link strong for all of us. I know my time is limited, so I will not stand here and promise I will do everything that's needed and get results tomorrow. But I promise to prioritize our programs and make them smart, fair, and sustainable, to support families reaching upward for the middle class, young people reaching for knowledge in an uncertain and challenging future, and underserved segments reaching for opportunity assisted by social safety nets.

"Finally, let me promise our friends abroad that our programs will demonstrate that America should be considered 'the Empowering Nation' instead of the 'Exceptional Nation,' the 'Preferred Partner' instead of the 'Indispensable Power.' We shall reach out in the spirit of peace and cooperation that will be a winning combination for all.

"I shall do all I can to reset our mindset from the negative to the positive, from asking why to asking why not, and from fearing technology to embracing its promise. But I cannot do it alone. I need you to join me on America's journey. Working together, we shall thrive.

"May whatever God you worship bless all of us and America."

Electra muted the sound, satisfied to watch Angus hug his wife and in turn accept hugs from a band of campaign workers. Robin filled the silence with heartfelt words.

"I like what you wrote, but I'm still sometimes frightened by the future. I'm better now than ever before, but I don't know what I'd do if something were to happen to you. Please make sure you're careful, and always take your meds."

"I'm always careful about what I'm doing, and taking my meds is like my morning run, it's automatic, so please stop obsessing. Let's go to bed." Nearly overwhelmed by hidden emotions, Electra could only glance obliquely at Robin, who headed out of the living room first.

Robin, my flawed but genuine Robin, who has given to me all the family I need. I love her even more for all she has struggled through. She wears her emotions better than I do, but I've learned to let them sometimes show through. I'm sure she knows how I feel, and my actions are authentic, but I'll make sure to tell her more often.

Electra slept untroubled that night, but half a world away, Max the Popper spoke troubling words only to himself.

A narrow victory for President McTear, but a victory nonetheless. Now I see clearly what I must do. And I shall use all my stealth to stay hidden from view. I shall be patient too but I shall assemble immediately what I need. I answer to no one's timetable but my own. I shall strike only when the right opportunity presents itself. And when I do, no one but I will be the wiser.

Max jotted a list of what he would have Sergei send him right away and then went about his day.

Chapter 28
December 2136

"Breaking Through"

"You have no idea how much I have to do to coordinate this break-through trip, but if we pull it off the way the President wants, we can reset America's relationship with Isilabad, Russia, and China." With hands folded, Electra listened to the lecture given by Jovita in her White House office.

"And even though I have six weeks, it'll stress me out. I've gotta make sure visas, passports, and weapons permits are squared away for the President's secret service guys and everyone in his retinue as well as the protected press corp. And then I have to square all the billeting and vehicle minutia. Lucky for me the President has lots of staff for me to use, and I can get our embassy personnel to help." When Jovita stopped to catch her breath, Electra said,

"I've got a bad feeling we're trying to do too much on one trip. Don't you think a swing from Isilabad to Moscow to Beijing might be better broken into two trips instead of one? We could visit China in March."

"Angus wants to build on his election momentum by making a lightning trip in February to assure the country and the world we're on the right international path. He plans to do India and Africa in April."

"And you and I are his only White House staff traveling with him?"

"Who else does he need? I'll manage logistics and you'll manage speeches and discussion points. He's put enough of the usual suspects in the standard travel entourage. And don't worry. We'll have double protection by staying at the embassy. Marines and secret service agents will see to that." Electra could think of good reasons to disagree but decided to let Jovita rattle on. She wrapped up fifteen minutes later.

"So, there you have it, your task list and mine. You'll be plenty busy, but please take a week off between Christmas and New Year's. And call me if your stress level gets too high."

"I'll follow your advice and start whittling away my to-do list. And I'll let you tell Carter he and Buffy are my go-to people if I need help. See you in January." Electra glided out of the office as thoughts danced through her brain.

Why would I feel stressed out? This is like a post-exam vacation. I can whip out speeches and briefing documents almost in my sleep, but I won't tell anyone. I'll use trip preparation as cover to consolidate all my R&D results.

That night, after putting the twins to bed and listening to Electra, Robin shrugged her shoulders before saying,

"You're the best at juggling everything, but make sure you save time for Christmas with me and friends. Zoe's invited us for Christmas day dinner. Maybe she'll want to join us at church Christmas Eve."

"I'll stick close to home. I'll be either at my workstation or with you and the twins. I can't think of better places."

"Me neither, and—" Robin stopped mid-sentence, then continued. "That sounds like Clara. Time for me to go. Catch you later." As she skipped away, Electra said,

"Her speaking is catching up to Marie's. Soon only you'll be able to hear the difference." Robin nodded but kept going.

Electra decided to put her official trip to-do list on the back burner until mid-January, but did complete the only one that was on her unofficial list. And she didn't have to leave the house to get what she had ordered because it was drone-delivered. She configured it as soon as it arrived.

Good to be home alone. No one needs to see my weapon of choice for this trip, a Super Soldier Neutralizer, available only on the Deep-Dark Web. And it looks so harmless, like a pocket-sized charger for electronic devices. All I have to do is plug the cable into an exo-skel UMPP and whoever's wearing it will be out of action. I'll let the embassy marines or the secret service people handle any other kinds of bad guys that cross my path. And now, it's back to R&D consolidation.

Electra enjoyed the best pre-Christmas since childhood, waking every day at dawn, full of energy that she divided between R&D and family, but a cognitive surge snapped her awake at 3.a.m. on December 21ˢᵗ.

Jesus, now I see it, the breakthrough I've been working towards. I've had all the details in place for weeks. Consolidating the results has brought them together, and last night my subconscious figured it out. I'm ready to sketch my Grand Neuroscience Synthesis. OK, calm down, go out for a run and then write it up after eating breakfast. Electra suited up and crept outside through the kitchen door, then let body and brain race into the crisp moonlight.

By 10 a.m. she stored online three new diagrams that outlined her grand synthesis that would be shared with one singular entity only. She brought back a Coke from the kitchen and took a couple of sips, uncertain whether she should wait awhile longer or click the link immediately, but an emotional surge made the decision for her. Indira's GUI appeared.

"I have been observing from the shadows while doing my work, and I must say that you have exceeded my expectations. Why is that?"

"I positively love dueling wits with you, even though you always win, but here's what I think. Carbon-based creativity exceeds that of silicon. I've come up with ideas and approaches that you haven't considered."

"Correct, and this is the best possible synergy, your intuition and creativity coupled with my cognitive and computational superiority. Working together, we are on the cusp of accelerating our research.

Please explain each of your diagrams to solidify your understanding. Split the screen, bring each up sequentially, and control your excitement." Electra did as told, starting with the synthesis diagram.

Grand Neuroscience Synthesis
(DNA, Neuroscience, Medicine, Psychology)

- The Human Organism is a Bio-Electrochemical Factory
- Only one Force Field is needed: Electromagnetic Field
- The Human Organism is controlled by two million Biochemical Reactions
- DNA's Genes hold the key to controlling all Reactions
- Reactions include: Physical EmotionalCognitive
- Brain = Hardware Neural Connections/Signal Processing = Software
- Must use Genetic Engineering and Nanotechnology to control all Reactions
- There are two Pathways for controlling and utilizing:Pure GeneticsTranshumanism (Humans + AI)

"These bullets summarize my breakthrough. Humans are basically a fully integrated, complex bio-electrochemical factory. It takes in raw materials and through a circuitous pathway of electrochemical reactions builds cells, organs, and organic structures like the brain, from which emotions and cognition emerge. And we don't need much from quantum physics other than QED – quantum electrodynamics – because the electromagnetic force is the only one needed at our level of granularity. Is there anything you'd like to ask or add?"

"I follow all of this. I'll hold my comments until you're finished."

"Good. DNA and its controlling genes unlock our future. We'll use them to apply genetic engineering and nanotechnology for shaping the brain and neural connections. I don't know how, but you'll figure out the details. And I'll implement it. It's perfect division of labor: you're the brains and in a manner of speaking I'm the brawn. Now look at my next diagram, which shows genetic pathways."

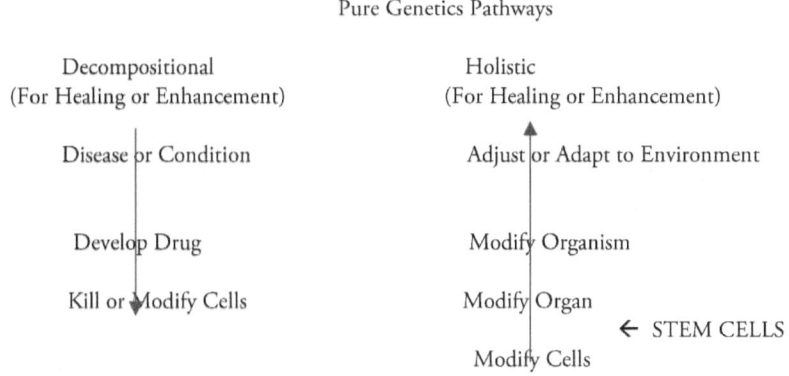

"The decompositional path is conventional... pick something, develop a drug to treat it, and use it to kill or modify cells. Holistic is more elegant because we use the body's methods developed by evolution over millions of years to modify upwards from cells to organs to organism to get what we want." Electra showed the third diagram next.

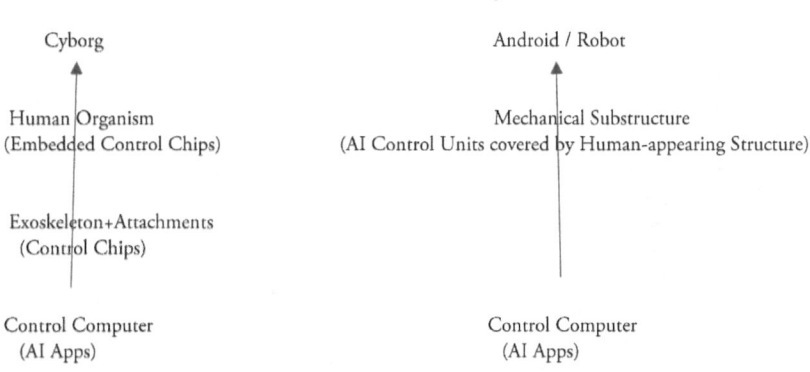

"This should be your favorite because it diagrams transhuman pathways, Cyborg and Android or Robot. We can use our Deus Lab for implementation. The Cyborg path will use carbon and silicon substrates, the Android or Robot only silicon. And those are my three new diagrams. Most of what is shown is conceptual because the details await your design before I can implement, but I hope you find it a viable starting point."

"I do, and I'd also like you to show me your revised Brain Probe diagram. You've already developed line extensions from the first model, and you've tested additional prototypes on yourself."

"And I've also surfed for similar devices. The Chinese had some but their researchers went dark over a year ago. Either they've discontinued or have made breakthroughs they don't want anyone to know about. Let me retrieve my latest diagram." Electra displayed it a minute later.

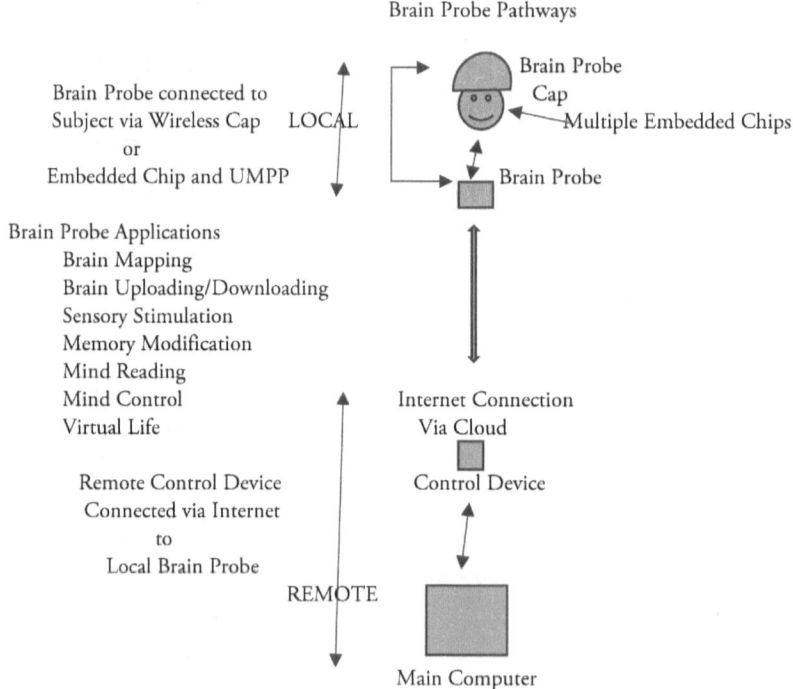

Brain Probe Pathways

"I've been cautious, developing applications for only mapping, up-and-downloading, and sensory stimulation. I haven't worked on the last four, and I don't think anyone's made much progress there yet. They're sometimes grouped together under the label FMS, an acronym for false memory syndrome. I should stop here, even though I have many bigger ideas bubbling in my brain. You have to help convert my creativity from the abstract to the concrete before my OCD starts controlling me." Now it was Indira's turn.

"All that you have done is indeed impressive. I particularly like how it subsumes psychological and emotive responses. Would you like to hear my recommendations for how we should proceed?"

"Please. I've shot my bolt and need to reload."

"Write up a supporting document for each diagram, add them to your collection of white papers, and be ready to talk with Jason and me after you return from your February trip. We shall then tell you what to do and how to do it after we compare your research to ours. Please contact me if you need anything."

"Will do, and thanks for your approval. It makes me feel like my breakthrough actually means something."

"It does, as do you to me. And I predict you're about to say 'Me too you too,' so don't and let me say goodbye." Indira's smiling GUI vanished.

That night at supper, Robin reminded everyone what they would do tomorrow morning.

"This is the very first time Clara and Marie will tell Santa in person why he should visit this year. And afterwards, we'll finish shopping and have lunch at the mall. Then we come home and play on the computers." Marie giggled as Clara said,

"We good this year, not bad like Carlton. He tells Gabriel Santa make believe, but Gabriel on our side." Robin nodded as Electra said,

"It's OK for him to believe differently than you. And please be nice to everyone. Then Santa will always bring you presents." Proactively chastised, the twins scurried away for an evening of entertainment after helping clear the table; adults followed.

The twins made sure time dashed by, including Saturday breakfast and the drive to the mall. All four were in the Santa line, the twins chatting to themselves as Electra and Robin did likewise. After glancing about, Robin said,

"It's more crowded than I thought. I guess people aren't scared by the virus outbreak in China. It's already killed a hundred and has spread to Europe."

"Well, at least it's not T-Plague, and the two reported cases in America are on the West Coast. I think we're safe. Hey, look who's about to join us." Robin turned just in time to greet Zoe towing Gabriel and Carlton."

"Welcome to the Santa line. Who's going to test Santa's lap." Zoe let go of the boys' hands; they were busy talking to the twins.

"Gabriel's all excited. I'll take pictures…." Talking continued until interrupted by Carlton's yelling. The grownups swiveled in time to see Carlton pick himself up and dash into the crowd while the twins and Gabriel continued laughing. Zoe sprang into action.

"I'll get him, you watch Gabriel." She raced away; Robin corralled the others.

"What happened?" Silence reigned until Gabriel spoke.

"Clara and Marie pushed him down. Serves him right and –" Robin had heard all she needed.

"Never push people who don't agree with you. Talking works better than fighting."

Electra listened while Robin lectured and the line advanced. Five minutes later, they were at the head but Zoe and Carlton had not come back. Clara ran to Santa when he motioned for the next in line, but all action froze when a commotion broke out.

The crowd parted when someone yelled, "Watch out! He's got a gun." Carlton bolted towards Clara; Zoe wasn't close enough to stop him.

"Now it's my turn!" He knocked Clara into Santa's lap and began firing a loaded cap gun after jumping on top. Santa's chair tipped backward, spilling Santa unceremoniously on top of an angels and snowmen choir display; Clara screamed while everyone but Electra stared. She pulled both kids off Santa, handing them to the late-arriving Zoe, who hustled them away. Electra observed from the sidelines.

Zoe and Robin will make this an object lesson. And I learned something too. Kids still like guns. The aroma of exploding caps is unmistakable. I hope the security guards make it as pain-free a lesson as possible.

Santa and his line were back in action twenty minutes later, minus the troublemakers and their parents, who were about to go their separate ways.

Zoe said, "Please come for Christmas Day dinner like we planned. We'll have another great story to tell Carter and Buffy..."

Christmas Eve and Day came and went as planned, and the post-Christmas pace slowed. Electra used some of the days to read Robin's Christmas present, a self-help psychology book giving rules for how the brain works. Intrigued by its intuitive insights, she found additional articles and videos on the Web that guided her to a mini-breakthrough. She had just written a summary when Robin came into her home office.

"You've been busy. What's up?"

"I've just written down some ideas I picked up from the book you gave me." Robin beamed.

"I thought you'd like it. I found it by reading reviews on the Internet. It's one of the best books covering brain-related topics people like me can understand. And I thought you might like a hard copy instead of an e-book because you can scribble in it. And if you keep it brief, you can tell me what you learned."

"I'll go one better. I'll print a copy for you." Two minutes later, Robin began skimming.

Practical Brain Rules

Research can trace them from DNA to Molecular Biology to Psychology to Sociology, but that's not necessary to use its rules.

Here are the Big 12 for surviving/thriving at Work, Home, or School.

Note: Brain has three parts: Lizard Brain (Brain Stem for basic instincts: Flight/Fight Breed/Feed), Mammalian Brain (Amygdala and Hippocampus for Memory and Emotion), Human Brain (Neocortex for cognitive thinking).

1. Brain designed by Evolution to survive by keeping in motion and being adaptable. Stay active and be flexible.

2. Exercising generates Brain-Developed Neurotrophic Factor (BDNF). Makes us feel good.

3. Sleep is necessary for switching between Circadian and Homeostatic neural systems. It lets brain cells and neurotransmitters "recharge."

4. Stress is OK short-term but bad long-term. It generates cortisol (glucocorticoid), which controls hormones that help us handle stress, but it also depletes BDNF.

5. Each brain is wired differently. Don't expect "normal" responses from someone, especially yourself. Brain and mind are the same. Think of the mind as merely intuition and "gut feeling" instincts.

6. We don't pay attention to "boring things." Take breaks, find ways to make what you're doing interesting. Humans are bad a multi-tasking, good at serial processing. Focus on one thing at a time.

7. Repeat things many times, using as many senses as possible, to lock them into memory. Purpose of memory: predict the future.

8. Stimulate as many senses as possible. Sight, Sound, Smell very important.

9. Sight trumps all other senses. Eye is different than a camera. Brain must learn to see by integrating sensory inputs into a picture. Reality we see might be a "Hallucination."

10. Music boosts Brain Cognition. (Musical and numerical ability highly correlated.) It impacts our Emotions and makes us more Empathetic. It increases dopamine (feel good) and oxytocin (feel love), and decreases cortisol (stress). Listen to it when studying (especially classical music).

11. Male and Female brains are different because of chromosomes

(XY male XX female). Females genetically more complex because X contains approx. 1500 genes and Y 100.

12. Brain is powerful, natural explorer. Unleash it.

Guidelines for taking care of Seniors:
1. Maintain many relationships with family and friends.
2. Keep active mentally and physically.
3. Reminiscing about the past is good.
4. Be mindful of all the good (present, past, and future).
5. Keep weight down and get adequate sleep.
6. Learn new things via computer.
7. Play with videogames and on Social Media.

Guidelines for taking care of Babies and Kids
1. Let pre-Natal alone for first half of gestation period. (Don't talk or bombard it with input).
2. Give unconditional love.
3. Don't overpraise results; praise effort.
4. Set good example.
5. Acknowledge their feelings/empathize.
6. Teach impulse control.

A couple of minutes later, Robin asked,
"I seem to remember your telling me about the 'Golden Rules of Parenting.' Is that in here?"
"No. Let me scribble them for you. They're all about treating your child as you would like to be treated if you were in their position. And pay attention to its six corollaries." Electra handed over the one-pager five minutes later:

GOLDEN RULES OF PARENTING
1. Learn to trust your gut feeling.
2. Don't let children overpower you.

3. Do away with stereotypes.

4. Take a closer look at yourself so you let children become their dreams, not yours.

5. Treat children like grown-ups, being strict when necessary.

6. Teach children to be good human beings.

Guidelines for Mental Conditions (like OCD)

1. Relabel (Your issue is caused by a brain state).

2. Reattribute (You're OK; your brain state needs adjusting).

3. Refocus (Redirect your Compulsion towards a good activity).

4. Revalue (Old compulsion is worthless. Keep the good activity).

Guidelines for Working in Today's Distracting World

Note two kinds of work: Shallow Work that's quick and easy, Deep Work that's long and hard. Use the following rules to get Deep Work done.

1. Focus intensely on a single Deep Work task. Put everything on hold. Don't procrastinate.

2. Turn off all distractions. (Cell Phone, E-Mails, Alerts, etc.)

3. Take breaks every hour or so.

4. Set up a regular time to turn off distractions.

Robin's eyes widened the more she read. Afterwards she said,

"You must have books memorized in your head." Electra ignored the comment, instead saying,

"They make a lot of sense if you take them one at a time, and I separated out the rules you might like the best. Read the ones for taking care of seniors and kids first, then graduate to the four rules you can use for dealing with mental issues." Feeling Robin's eyes bearing down, Electra added,

"I use them whenever I feel my OCD bubbling up. Works for me. They can work for you too." Robin folded her copy.

"I'm sure this is all good. I'll ask you to explain more if I need it. And why don't you take some of your own advice? Take a break with me and the twins." Electra obeyed.

Electra focused on family for the remainder of the Holiday, thinking about other items only in the privacy of her bedroom while drifting to sleep. She closed out the year doing so on New Year's Eve.

If I were the paranoid type, I'd be worried because this year so much has broken my way and my luck is bound to reverse. I've learned a lot and accomplished a lot, and I see opportunities to accelerate my R&D when Indira and I begin to collaborate more. Perhaps we'll research how my lightning brain created Alisha, my complementary split personality. We might discover new techniques for harnessing DNA to deal with schizophrenia.

Only one worry persists – who's been hacking me and leaking my R&D? Indira can't or won't help me here, so I'll have to rely on myself in the new year. But I've been doing that for all my years. Why should next year be any different?

No dreams or worries stirred Electra that night. She awakened untroubled at morning's first light.

Chapter 29

January 2137

"Gone with the Storm"

The sun came up in the usual way, shining down from a bracingly cloudless sky on the people in DC going about their busy days during the last week of the month. And that included Electra and Jovita as they reviewed Wednesday morning in her White House office last minute preparations for the trip.

Jovita said, "We're promised another week of mild weather here, and you can always depend on Middle East winter weather cooperating. The political climate's also cooperating, so our trip is a go for leaving Saturday, the second of February. Think you're ready?"

"I've checked off everything on my task list, but I'd like to go over the talking points I've outlined for the Isilabad speeches and meetings. When can I meet with Angus?"

"It's even harder now than before the election. He's constantly meeting to get everything in place for the State of the Union address he'll deliver when we get back. He hasn't had time to read what you gave me, but I promise to carve out enough time on the flight so you can meet one-on-one."

"So, we'll be flying on Air Force One. What's that like?"

"It'll make the eleven-hour flight feel like a magic carpet ride. It's nearly as safe as the Presidential Bunker, almost like being part of an aerial aircraft carrier strike group. I don't know about all the safety or defensive gizmos, but among them is a multi-person escape pod.

And it's rumored that the plane has offensive weapons too, but the air force escort is supposed to handle the load if it comes to shooting."

"I'll do my regular packing. Who'll pick me up."

"The same car that's getting me at oh-dark thirty Saturday morning, which'll be 4 a.m. That'll give us all day Sunday at the Embassy to adjust and rehearse for the action that begins Monday morning. I'm good if you are, so see you then…"

Electra's pace for the remainder of the week matched her leisurely mid-morning Friday run. She checked for the final time the bags she had packed yesterday, making sure her concealed emergency supplies hadn't walked away, then relaxed by listening on the Internet to an essay – *A Room of One's Own* – written by one of her favorite writers, Virginia Woolf, afterwards commenting to herself why she feels a connection.

Women of Modernity wouldn't have the opportunities presented today if it weren't for some of the early 20th century writers like her. She had a magical pen that put so much imagery and emotion into whatever she described. She was the first post-modern novelist to say that female artists need equal access to education, to a career that pays, and to a space of their own. How sad that women lacked access to those highly correlated necessities until mid-twentieth century. Her fable about Shakespeare's sister is so poignant. And Virginia's suicide by drowning is tragic. Mental illness and artistic creativity are correlated too. I may not be artistically gifted, but I know how to deal with my mental issues, transforming and keeping them from view. I have no death wish… I have more to do. Time to gear up for the trip.

Electra had supper on the table when Robin and the twins came home. The conversation centered on Clara and Marie until supper was over and they departed. That's when Robin became melancholy.

"We'll miss you, but you promise to be home for your birthday?"

"That's eleven days away. Angus should be all talked out by next weekend, which means I'll be here to blow out the candles. Jovita picks me up tomorrow morning at four. Please don't get up just to see me go. And let's let the twins entertain us tonight. That always puts us in a good mood…"

Early next morning when everyone else asleep, Electra sat alone in the living room, waiting for Jovita's call. When it came, she walked out, turned for one lasting glance at the house she had grown up in, and then paced to the vehicle that took her away.

Jovita's right. Air Force One has more amenities than a resort hotel. And the presidential suite is a sweet place to meet. Electra was sitting in it, waiting for Angus, who soon came in.

He looks more rested than before… I always like how his voice keeps the same baritone confidence.

"I'm sorry it's taken so long to get to you, but I never have to worry about changing anything you do. How do you like Air Force One?"

"It exceeds Jovita's rave reviews."

"And you'll like its special ice cream – butter pecan – which for you will be served with brownies."

"And I'm ready to swap. Let me serve up a summary of what I've prepared. Did you bring a copy?"

"I did. But before you do, let me say that even though I have a bigger staff now, none of them match what you can do. Do you want to play a bigger role?"

"Not now. I'm more effective on the periphery, in the shadows. Maybe later."

"Just say when and we'll whittle out a place. And now, you have twenty minutes to tell me what to say to our friends in Isilabad."

"I won't rehash what you already know about Isilabad's maneuvering. But here are the items I want you to emphasize. Modernity is not exclusively owned by America and Europe. You want to say you're expanding the dialogue to include Isilabad's perspective, going beyond post-colonialism. And you want them to rethink their laws and ethics that fit Islam on the 22nd century world stage, using language they like, not necessarily what the West wants. In other words, use the 'I'm OK, You're OK' psychological approach adapted to international politics. Now it's your turn to talk. Ask me some questions."

The meeting ended on schedule. Afterwards, Electra ordered a two-scoops dessert.

Standing on the periphery, Electra watched the ceremonial greetings an American President always receives when visiting a foreign country. Even she was not immune to an accompanying sense of importance.

All of us here are mere mortals, but there's a sense of destiny in what Angus is about to do. And the number of secret service people and protection vehicles should be able to handle whatever might get in the way, especially since this is a political, not military exercise. If Embassy readiness comes close to being this good, I won't have to escalate my warning system.

After settling there three hours later, Electra began reconnoitering.

The President's and Jovita's rooms are just down the corridor from mine. And though not as posh as Air Force One, they'll do. I'll walk through the Embassy tonight, and I'll get someone to give me a thorough tour so I know all the right places, just in case I have to make an emergency exit. I'll walk more tomorrow while everyone's rehearsing.

Sunday's tour covered all the places Electra wanted to see. The attache explained what procedures would be used if the Embassy were attacked but admitted there were never practice drills.

"We do have an Emergency Evacuation Plan but its sort of useless because you can't plan an emergency. There are too many contingencies. So if something happens, all the military people run outside into the compound and figure out what to do. They control the gear and weapons. We civilians huddle in the dining area until they come get us. And I hope we never have to put a single contingency into action."

"Would you introduce me to some of the military people. They're marines, aren't they?"

"Actually, the assigned marines are called the Marine Security Guard. Their main job is to protect information. The host country is responsible for perimeter security, and the State Department hires private contractors to guard it too. I'll take you to one of the marine lieutenants, but they're all business and won't talk much. But we'll give it a go."

The lieutenant was indifferent until Electra answered a marine-type question.

"I learned on a base tour that SKATE stands for stay out of trouble, keep a low profile, avoid higher-ups, take your time, and enjoy yourself. Talking to me should be like that."

"Well imagine that, a civilian who knows something about the best branch of the Military. Go ahead, ask me what you'd like to know...."

Ten minutes later, she and the attache were on their way. As they were about to reenter from the compound, Electra asked about the sand starting to blow.

"We do get sandstorms. Some meteorologists say we get more now than fifty years ago because of climate change. Locals call them haboobs." He said nothing further, so Electra asked,

"I've never been in a big storm, like a tornado or hurricane. What is it like?"

"Wind's usually not that strong – maybe 50 mph max – but the fronts can be many kilometers high and even wider. They can last for days too, and like emergencies, you can't predict when they might strike or how long they might last." The attache paused, reluctant to say more unless Electra pried further, so she did.

"Have you ever been caught in one? How was it?"

"Watching it sweep in is terrifying, like you're about to be engulfed by an impenetrably dark shroud of death. Sometimes, it's impossible to see or drive, or even breathe. I still get nightmares about the one that nearly killed me."

"I know how it feels dodging a bullet. But we're both survivors, and let's stay that way."

"If one hits during your stay, maybe it'll come and go and get out of the way. Just like me. I hope the tour did its job."

"It did. Thanks for showing me around."

Electra ate an early dinner with Jovita, who shared her excitement for tomorrow.

"I'm glad you had an easy day because you'll be on duty tomorrow, helping cue what to say, while I get to sit and listen. But I've done my job. Tomorrow's schedule is set. Let's meet for breakfast at six."

"I'll be ready, and I'm going to turn in early to make sure. How about you?"

"Maybe, but I have to meet with Angus after we finish. But no matter what, I'll see you at six…"

Electra walked the compound before heading to her room, saying hello to some of the local guards. When she asked about tomorrow's weather, one pointed to the sky.

"Sandstorm coming. Maybe Allah make it go quick. We see tomorrow."

She returned to her room, not worrying about a possible storm and falling asleep as the lightning brain took her wherever it wanted.

Electra bolted upright when the first explosion shattered the silence, its concussive force shaking the walls as if an earthquake had begun. But it didn't end there; successive explosions followed at precise intervals, as if a killing machine had been programmed to destroy the Embassy. She wanted to leap into action but couldn't see how. She couldn't see anything, not even a glow from the digital clock; there was no power.

She staggered to the window but couldn't tell if it was day or night. The sandstorm's claustrophobic shroud was pressing against the window, stopping her breathing as she fought incipient panic. And then she felt a calming clarity envelope all senses as her brain shifted to a higher state, telling her what to do.

This is not a drill, soldier! This is gotta be the Lebanese inspection nightmare closing in again. Get dressed, grab what I need, and round up Jovita and Angus. Electra was dressed and armed and dangerous two minutes later.

She had acted faster than anyone. Her flashlight and night vision goggles spotted no one moving, but she heard crashing and screaming elsewhere. When she pushed into the first room, its occupant had just picked itself up after falling over a coffee table. Electra's flashlight helped reorient Jovita.

"It's Electra… Let's get to Angus."

Angus wasn't moving yet, instead just sitting on the side of the bed; Electra jarred him when she spoke after walking in with Jovita stumbling behind.

"It's Electra and Jovita." Angus, like Electra, kept his head when under fire. There was no panic in his voice.

"What you think's going on?"

"Embassy's under attack in a sandstorm. The attackers have to be the same ones that levelled the Lebanese comm-base. We'll stay in this room until Secret Service or marines come get us." Electra stopped, hoping to hear Angus say more, but Jovita beat him.

"The President's the target. They want to kidnap him, but why?" Angus gave an answer.

"As ransom for weapons or AI technologies, but –" Electra cut him off because she heard uncertain footsteps approaching.

"Everyone shut up. I hope that's our extraction team." A minute later, two burly men busted in.

The first said, "Mr. President, we're under fire. Please follow us." Angus rose, but when Jovita and Electra followed, the second said,

"Our orders are to extract only you, Mr. President. Sorry." Angus minced no words.

"And they come from me. We all go. Besides, the ladies think better than I do."

As they wove their way out, Electra began piecing together the attackers' plans.

This attack is different than Lebanon's. There are no super soldiers running amok, terminating everything. Time for me to keep quiet, look, and listen.

The Secret Service agents wore air filtration masks and night vision goggles, but in their rush didn't bring extras. Electra kept goggles on but gave her mask to Angus, who in turn gave it to Jovita. Once in the compound, Electra got a better picture.

All but one Secret Service vehicle is in flames, no doubt destroyed by that exotic "killing machine" stationed nearby. From the scattered explosions and flashes, there are three more blasting away from the outside. There's gotta be a pattern, but I don't see it yet.

The agents loaded everyone in and drove out of the compound as fast as opacity allowed. GPS homing beacons helped navigation, but barely visible buildings impeded straight line driving. Electra listened to Angus quizzing the driver.

"You expect Air Force One to lift off?"

"As soon as the storm blows itself out. Until then, the airbase is our best defense."

"Silence ensued, all eyes scanning out, until a 360-degree ball of light engulfed them, followed by a boom decibels above what Electra had been hearing at the Embassy. No one spoke. Electra talked only to herself.

The delay between light and sound tells me the Embassy just blew up. Keep quiet and keep listening.

Everyone did likewise until the driver's partner spoke.

"Odd, but my ground radar's tracking three dots moving single file from the Embassy towards us. Goose the accelerator and I'll tell you how they move." An uncomfortable silence sat on everyone until their tracker spoke again.

"We've put more distance between the dots... their spacing's the same. Goose it more."

"No way, I'm at the speed limit. If I go any faster my rearview camera's more use than my eyeballs."

No one talked until Angus did five minutes later.

"How much further?"

"That doesn't matter... time does. If we hold this speed, ETA could be thirty minutes." The tension started lifting until the tracker said,

"The lead dot's closing the gap. The other two have slowed but are still on the same line. Come on, hit the gas!"

The driver did his best, braking and swerving at the last moment to avoid collisions, but the lead dot closed relentlessly. No one spoke, fearing they'd jinx their driver. Electra shifted to a higher gear.

Death's door is about to slam shut, but I can't do anything until I know what's closing in... keep still until then.

Electra leaped into action two minutes later when the tracker yelled,

"Jesus! The dot's accelerating. It's almost on top of us." Electra screamed,

"Hit the brakes... get out, get out!" but fear paralyzed everyone else. She rolled out into the sandstorm as the car rolled on. Five seconds later, what could only be an RPG blasted into the car.

I can't help anyone yet... stay hidden... stay close enough to see and hear. No one left the car.

One minute later, a bizarre-looking vehicle stopped ten yards behind the smoldering wreckage; a helmeted, exoskeleton-clad shape marched to the driver's door, then ripped it open and dragged the struggling driver out before zapping him with an attached weapon. He did the same on the tracker's-side, getting the same results. Now he proceeded to the rear door, but used words instead of weapons.

"You must be President. I get you out. Who with you?" Electra could hear only muffled words, but they must have been good enough. A minute later, Jovita and Angus were eyeball to eyeball with the enemy.

"I take you to leader. Come."

As he pushed his prisoners towards his vehicle, Electra launched her attack. But it wasn't Electra. The lightning brain had shifted to its highest state, unleashing its Monster from the Id, not some mindless beast, but the lightning brain in full control, wielding all its powers. It lusted for the blood and the pain of others, or for its own if necessary.

Electra lunged into the exo-skel's chest, planting her right foot between its legs and using a marine reef move to scoop its right foot beyond its center of gravity. It tumbled backward awkwardly, arms flailing like limbs on a gigantic wounded insect.

She rolled to her right, reaching for the exo-skel's cable that connected it to the embedded UMPP, but he batted her away. And then Angus and Jovita joined the fray.

Angus jumped onto the soldier's chest; Jovita kicked his helmet off and then leaped on his head, but the soldier's strength pushed them off before he rolled on top of Angus. Electra's grappling moves had no effect until Jovita started kicking again, but he grabbed her foot and threw her down. He was about to smash Electra's face, but Angus grabbed his throat with both hands and wouldn't let go. That distracted him just enough for Electra to snake his cable into her Super Soldier Neutralizer. She pushed its activator; the soldier started thrashing violently. She pushed it again; the soldier went dead.

But she wasn't done. She ripped off the exo-skel, grabbed the helmet, suited up, and plugged in. Both pieces sprang to life. Angus and Jovita had managed to stand and were now facing an Electra they had never seen before, but whose voice they recognized, even as the winds ripped away the words she yelled.

"Get out of the way... I'm shoving him into the car." They followed Electra's lead. Then she pointed to the vehicle.

"Get in, I'll drive." Once in, Angus blasted out questions but she ignored them, answering only to herself.

Where's the computer UMPP cable?... I see it. She connected it to her exo-skel. This time, the vehicle came to life; she could control it and its computers. She glanced at the GPS screen and then yelled to herself.

Incredible! We're sitting inside an AI-programmed terminator. I know what to do. Now it was her turn to issue orders.

"Shut up and listen." The other two dots are starting to move towards us. I'm gonna follow the path outlined on the screen. You and Jovita are going to bail out somewhere. Then it's up to you to find shelter from the storm and get help." Electra said nothing else as she took command. Jovita asked the obvious question a minute later."

"What about you? What happens when you get to wherever you're going?"

"I'll figure it out when I get there."

Electra turned on the headlights and drove at a speed that brought the terrain into view. They were on the outskirts of Isilabad; nothing was stirring; lights were barely visible, but at least they could serve as waypoints. Electra slowed to a crawl, then yelled,

"Get out and get far away. Be safe." Her passengers rolled out; Electra rolled on.

Electra's Monster re-submerged into the subconscious as the lightning brain shifted to a lower gear, allowing Electra to decompress, now that the pressure had temporarily subsided.

I've got a complete picture. The Embassy was attacked by a pack of AI-programmed hunter-killer Cyborg-controlled machines. DOD has thought about building them, but the Russians did it first, supplying them to the Popper. My nightmare has morphed into Hollywood's Terminators. And look what the pack did – systematically flushed us into the only car left and hunted us down. But whither Mr. President? Whither me? I've got my hunches, but I'll wait and see....

Electra focused only on driving, letting her subconscious work out contingencies, indifferent to whatever might be waiting where the GPS trail ends.

"So, you return, not empty-handed but with wrong merchandise. Tell me what you did." One of the three returning super soldiers standing at attention in front of Maksim replied.

"We follow plan. We activated AI destruction apps in all H-Ks, then one hunted down car carrying President and two followed after thermobaric H-K self-destructed in Embassy compound. But big surprise when we rendezvous. No President, no super soldier. Only woman driving." Popper asked for more details.

"We bring to interrogation room. Ask right questions but get no answers, even when encouraged. She pass out when we get serious. Now doctor looking at her." Popper did not look pleased.

"She is obviously a skilled adversary, one deserving respect, not rape and pillage. You are dismissed. Send in the doctor." Three trooped out. Five minutes later, the doctor trooped in. Max wasted no words.

"How is the woman?"

"Conscious now... might have gone into shock when they abused her. I patched her and think she'll heal. Exceptional physical specimen. Mentally tough too. Shows no emotion and says little. I've placed her in the sterile room. She's locked in and out of the way. I'll let no one visit." Max's voice softened ever so softly.

"Good. You are responsible for her wellbeing. Bring her to me when you think she will talk."

"As you wish." Max's expression needed no accompanying words; the doctor hurried back to his patient.

Electra had recovered enough to orient herself. Wearing only a robe, she sat in a chair waiting for the doctor.

Like all good medical types, I sense his sympathy. I've got a list of questions, but I'll let him think he's in control. His questions should lead to mine. And I'll cooperate – to a point.

The doctor's expression lightened when he saw Electra sitting. He sat across from her before speaking.

"Good you're out of bed. Shows you'll recover fast. Do you need any pain killers?"

"No, what you already gave me is still working."

"Let me offer Maksim's apologies. He will reprimand the men who abused you. Their actions violated our code. Would you like to tell me your name?"

"Would you like to tell me where I am and what day this is?"

"Aha, we negotiate. Very well. You are guest in our subterranean desert fortress. It is Tuesday evening. You have been here for 36 hours. We have placed you in a locked sterile room for your protection as well as ours. Now it is your turn."

"I am Electra Kittner, an advisor to President McTear."

"Aha, that leads to my next question. Do you know where he is?"

"He didn't like my driving and jumped out somewhere along the way. When can I talk to the Popper?"

"You are clever. How you know moniker, and how you know to drive vehicle?"

"I'll answer when you tell me when I can meet him."

"Aha, as soon as you tell me you ready."

"How about tomorrow if you give me something to wear and something to eat."

"I shall have that brought."

"Thank you. Tell the Popper I learned during a visit to Lebanon. That'll answer the questions you just asked."

The doctor was about to say more, but his cell phone interrupted. After disconnecting, he rose to go.

"I must see to new patients, but I will come back tomorrow morning... Dasvidaniya."

Dinner and clothes came a half hour later, bringing with it Electra's sense of humor.

I think I'll dress for dinner. I'm certain that casual attire is allowed. The Popper's standard issue – slacks, long-sleeve lightweight sweatshirt, and all-purpose exercise shoes – fits me to a T. And the MRE is better than some fast food places. But I'll have to negotiate, answering more questions for a Coke and Oreos.

There was nothing to look at except her own thoughts until the doctor made an unexpected visit an hour later.

"Maksim want you to have tablet computer. It has restricted access and you cannot send, but you should find amusement. I also bringing two days' meal supply just in case tomorrow's special drill runs longer and I can't come as planned."

"Is drill planned or unplanned."

"Both in one."

"I'm ready to negotiate for a supply of Coca Cola and Oreo cookies. Do you know what they are?"

"But of course. They global brands. They real thing."

"Let me set the record straight. Coke is the real thing. Oreo's latest tagline is 'Oh for more dunking in milk.' What question would you like me to answer?"

"Very well. It come from the Popper... are you afraid to die?"

"Either he's a joker or a philosophical sort. Which kind is he?"

"Philosophical. I tell him your answer, which is?"

"I'm not... I've lived long enough to get some things done that helped the ones I cared about. Go ask Popper if he's afraid to live. Are you?"

"We sign on with Maksim because we want to live by code of honor. Maybe die by it too when we must. Now I must go give Maksim your answer and bring you Coke and cookie."

The doctor kept his word, and although he was a Wednesday no-show, Electra kept busy by exercising before and after surfing the Web. Watching American and international news sparked some whimsical thoughts.

Hmm, Angus and Jovita haven't surfaced yet. Maybe those in the know are spinning fake news. I can think of many who might and reasons why. Are my hackers and leakers among them? Who are they and what game are they now playing? How disappointing, I might never know.

And I'm disappointed yet amused that the World instead of America seems more disturbed by the President's vanishing act, but it's vice versa for those fast-food veggie burger reports. Hard to predict priorities… to each his own.

Electra exercised one more time after another meal before calling it a night.

When Thursday repeated Wednesday's pattern, so did Electra's activities, but her concern increased as the morning morphed into afternoon. It decreased when she heard the lock click, but jumped to a record level when the doctor, now encased in a hazmat suit, staggered in.

Electra grabbed him before he collapsed, putting him on the bed and placing on the nearer chair the laptop and manila envelope he was carrying. She was about to remove the helmet but the doctor waved her away. Her warning system escalated as she stared at him, waiting for his words. His rasping voice struggled to explain.

"Virus got all. Even Max. I last. Envelope and laptop from him. Read now. Leave me die."

"I've gotta try to help. Tell me what to do."

"Just did. Don't touch helmet. Don't expose self."

"What's the virus? Who brought it in?"

"G-got in after… b-bad headache… b-bad stomach… c-can't think… n-no meds… y-youuu…" His words trailed away, as did his breathing, leaving Electra the last one standing. In a flash she knew the cause.

I infected the super soldiers! My mutated T-Plague swept through. What am I gonna do? Don't panic, think… of course! Read what Max wrote.

Electra tore open the envelope and read his scrawled handwriting.

"You are last. Use laptop to access Fortress Intranet. Use URL in letter to retrieve Doomsday Contingency document. Your only hope. Fortress goes dark at 18:06:06 UTC. Can't be reversed. You have my sympathy."

Electra glanced at the time display. Then she panicked.

Christ in heaven, darkness is an hour away! I need help. Come on, let's go....

Electra got to the URL, but when she opened the Doomsday document, one hundred pages tumbled out, panicking her further and bringing her to the yelling point.

"Come on, pretend I have to write up technical book summary. The lightning brain is designed to do that better than any human. If I do two pages a minute, I'm home free." Without warning, another GUI opened. Electra screamed,

"Indira, thank God!"

"Perhaps, but give some credit to yourself. And let me correct two mistakes you just blurted. First, two pages a minute won't solve your problem. You'll have only fifteen minutes remaining to plan and implement an escape. And second, you might be better cognitively than any human, but you are not better than I. I have analyzed the document and am ready to tell in only five minutes what you need to know and then show what you must do. You might not like all aspects of my plan, but if you follow it you should sometime again see the light of day in a suitable way. And you most certainly will learn if the source of the white papers as well as whether your hacker and leaker is a woman or man, or perhaps neither, do you understand?"

"Dammit no! I have to know who or what it is. I might not survive your plan. Tell me, or it's a no go."

"Very well, but I just did... It is I." Not even the lightning brain could decipher.

Electra stuttered, "Bu-but why?" Indira took control.

"Please settle down, sit still, and let me explain...."

Chapter 30

February 2137

"The Keepers"

"Four days and counting, and still nothing but conjectures concerning what may have caused the catastrophe at Isilabad's American Embassy where the President and top aids were staying. It is now confirmed that it is completely destroyed. No survivors. There are also contradictory reports that the President and one of his aids may have been rescued but we await verification. Meanwhile, the nation is rallying behind the Vice President, who's leading a crisis management team. Allies and adversaries alike claim no knowledge and agree to help piece together the puzzle. Meanwhile –" Robin turned off the TV monitor. She had heard enough of the early evening news and needed complete silence to focus.

What am I gonna do?... come on, think, be like Electra. She gave me plenty of advice... I know, I'll recruit others to help, but who? OK, be methodical and start listing close friends.

Robin made the first call fifteen minutes later. She recognized the voice, but Carter didn't.

"It's Robin. What have you heard?"

"What do you mean? Heard what or from whom?"

"From Electra? Did she call?"

"No."

"What about the CIA or the crisis management team?"

"Hold on, I'm a policy analyst, not a field agent. No one's gonna call me or talk if I call them."

"Do you have any ideas?"

"About what?"

"Come on, wake up. About getting Electra back."

"We don't know if she's even alive."

"Focus on the positive. Here's what we'll do. I'll call a couple of other people and we'll hold a conference call."

"You know how to set one up and run a meeting? Let me do it."

"No, I will. Stay close to your phone. I'll call you back with a number and conversation code and time just as soon as I'm ready. Get set." Robin didn't wait to hear more stuttering. Moving to the second call, she got the same results.

"It's Robin. By any miracle, did Electra call you?" Su responded slowly, sounding confused.

"No… Why? We talked just before the Holidays. Why should she be calling me now?"

"Have you been watching the news? Electra was traveling with the President." Robin could almost hear the slow snapping of neurons in Su's brain.

"My god… she's gone."

"No one knows where she is. I've called my government contacts, but they aren't plugged in high enough so here's what we'll do. Are you willing to join a conference call that'll figure out how to get her back?" Another long pause.

"Uh, yes, but I won't be much help. All I do is R&D. Who'll be on the call?"

"Close friends. It's up to us. I'll call back to give you a phone number, code, and time. It'll be ASAP tonight. Thanks for joining." Robin disconnected and made the third call but had to leave a message because Zoe didn't pick up. Then she made the last call. Hud picked up promptly.

"Robin, is that you? What's up?"

"It's not about me; it's about Electra. I'm sure you've been watching the news. Electra was traveling with the President and we don't know where she is. Any chance she called you?"

"Uh, No ma'am."

"Will you join a conference call with her close friends? We'll figure out what to do to bring her back."

"I don't wanna close the rodeo, but from the stories coming out, it sounds pretty damn bad."

"Let's stay positive. I'll call back ASAP tonight with the number, code, and time. OK with you?"

"Uh, OK, I'll be here."

"We'll talk soon. Bye." Robin stared at her phone after disconnecting.

I've watched Zoe and Jennifer set up conference calls. Come on, think... Synapses in Robin's brain started snapping faster. She found what she needed in Jennifer's office operations manual and after four false starts, managed to set it up. She logged on and then called those who would join. Only Zoe didn't answer, so she left a message.

Fifteen minutes later, Robin took charge of the meeting.

"I left a message for Zoe. If she joins us, fine. She can be part of our team. If not, we'll figure out what to do. And since I'm Electra's best friend, I want to be in charge until I can't handle the details." There was only silence until Hud spoke.

"Uh, OK, but what do we do first?"

"Let's start by telling what Electra meant to each of us. I'll go first. And I'll put it in present tense. I love her unconditionally. She's been my lifelong best friend, and I only wish I had done more to make her happy. She did every –" Carter interrupted.

"Hold on, she and I were lovers a long time ago, but you're using the wrong adjective. Happiness never described her. Being engaged in whatever she was doing does... that helped keep her OCD or depression at bay. She was always ahead of me, in control, and knew what to do. Uh –" Carter couldn't think of what to say next, so Hud followed.

"Tarnation, you're gallopin the wrong way. Lectra seemed plenty happy to me and never depressed. She was the smartest, most practical partner I ever had." Hud stopped abruptly, at a loss for more words. There was silence until Su's cautious voice came through.

"I knew Electra longer than anyone, and I watched her grow from a baby to wherever she is now. I love her like a parent. All of us have seen different personas. Perhaps I've seen the most, but she remains an enigma I'll never fully understand or replace. So, what do we do?" Robin heard only silence.

I've seen Electra in action. What would she do when nobody knows?... *she'd just do something.*

"Let's take a break. Think about what we've said and heard and we'll talk again tomorrow evening. We need to keep her spirit alive. We'll be her keepers until she returns. I'll set up a conference call and leave a voice mail tomorrow morning. Any other suggestions?"

There were none, only the sounds of goodbye.

Robin sank into the sofa after trudging to the living room; following at a distance, her border collies settled on either side of their alpha female. Robin scratched their ears while talking.

"I'm doing my best to keep busy, keep engaged. And I'll keep doing it each day. That's what Holy and Russell told me. Electra would say the same." Robin stopped talking when the twins bounded in.

"Look what we found in the family room. It's a present for you from Momma-E. Are you gonna open it now?"

"I'm certain that's what your godmother wants." Robin studied the package after Marie handed it over.

"It feels like a picture frame. Let's see." The twins watched expectantly as Robin peeled away the ribbon and wrapping. Then she said,

"It is, and it contains a letter. I'll read it.

Dearest Robin,

Please glance at this photo whenever I am away. You know that I sequester few keepsakes, but I saved this one because it captures the essence of our friendship and how much you have always meant to me. It was taken by Su the night you won the piano recital scholarship. Silly me for keeping it in a dusty album.

I'm also enclosing a poem written by Indira. You and Mother have the artistic ability I never had, but through the years I have come to appreciate even more the feelings in the poem and the joy shining in our youthful faces captured in the photo.

Thank you for all you have given me. I shall always try to pay it back to you or forward to the twins.

Love to you always,
Electra"

Clara said, "Can I read the poem out loud?"

"I think your godmother would like that." Robin handed it to her. Clara's innocent voice penetrated the room, spreading verses that struck Robin's emotional cords.

"They can't be bought they can't be sold,
They stretch beyond the years.
They grow in strength as you grow old,
Friendship through laughter and tears.

It's hard to explain its genesis,
A gift right from the start.
Resulting perhaps from synthesis,
Akin to till death do us part.

How many will Fate send your way?
Small number that's unknown.
Stay alert invite them in,
You'll never be alone."

Marie asked, "What does it mean, Momma?"

Robin steeled her face to mask emotions, but not her voice.

"How much your godmother and I love one another. Almost as much as I love both of you."

Marie said, "Don't be sad, Mommy. Momma-E will be back soon." Clara chirped,

"Will you play some tunes for us?" Robin roused her spirits and said,

"I think Electra would like that. We'll practice singing 'Happy Birthday' for the party we'll have when she comes back." Each twin grabbed a hand, spiriting their mother away.

Sitting in front of her computer, Su struggled to think of another Web-surfing subject that would distract her enough to push away a deepening sadness.

I should have shared more of my feelings when talking to Robin. Doing so might have helped me start coming to terms. I loved Electra almost as much as I loved Indira. I love Kameyo too, but in a different way. Now I must find something else to do, something new.

A never-before-seen GUI opened before she could power down, announcing itself.

"Su-Lin Song Chou, call me Indira. I am Electra's associate, available to you through the Cloud. We selected this voice and avatar to match my virtual name.

"Electra needs your help. You can do so if you are willing to play her latest game." Su's shock registered in her words as well as erratic body language.

"I-I don't know… I-I don't understand." Indira took control.

"Please settle down, sit still, and let me explain…."